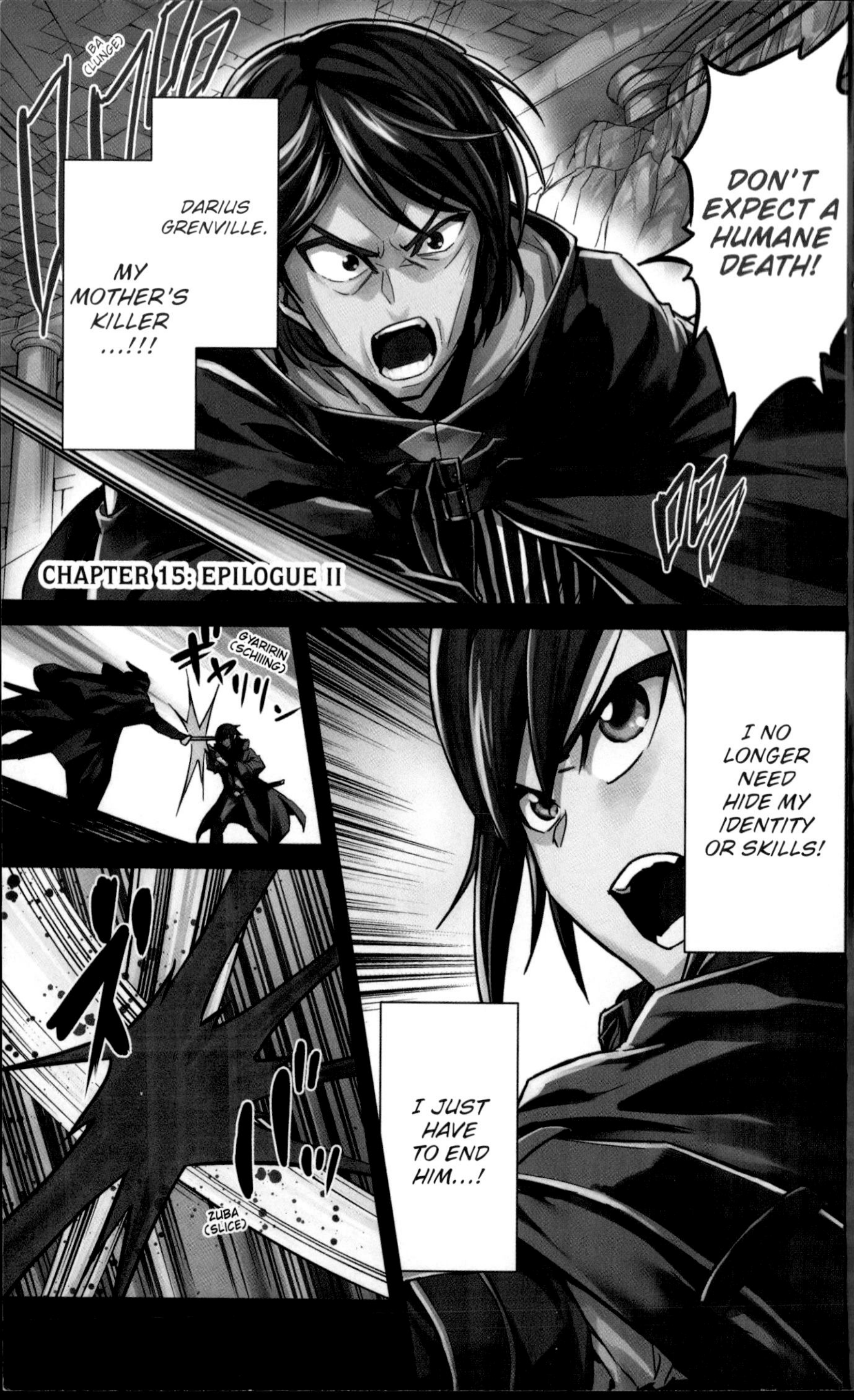
DON'T EXPECT A HUMANE DEATH!
BA (LUNGE)
DARIUS GRENVILLE.
MY MOTHER'S KILLER ...!!!
CHAPTER 15: EPILOGUE II
I NO LONGER NEED HIDE MY IDENTITY OR SKILLS!
I JUST HAVE TO END HIM...!
GYARIRIN (SCHIIING)
ZUBA (SLICE)

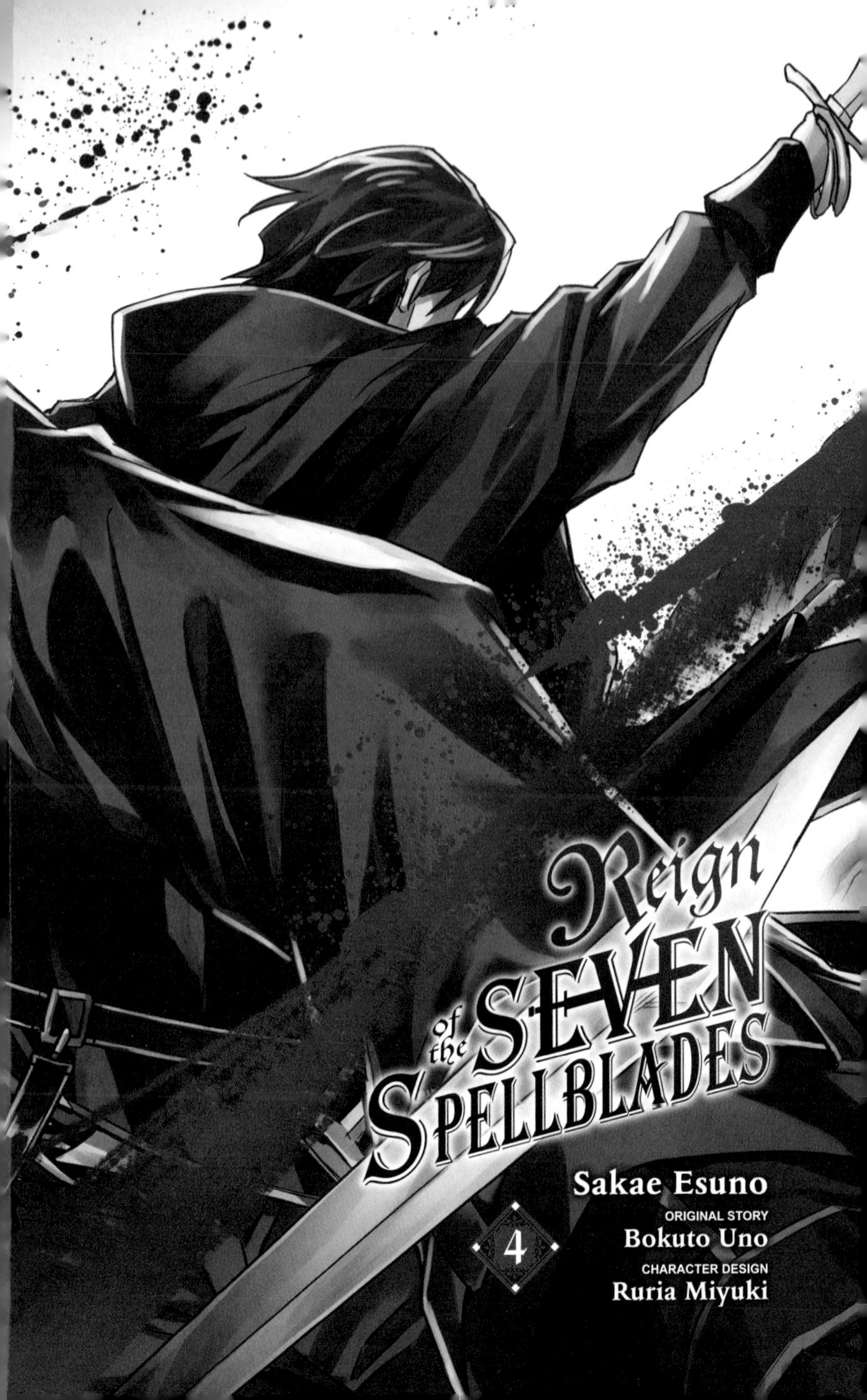
Reign of the SEVEN SPELLBLADES
4
Sakae Esuno
ORIGINAL STORY
Bokuto Uno
CHARACTER DESIGN
Ruria Miyuki

CHAPTER 15: EPILOGUE II

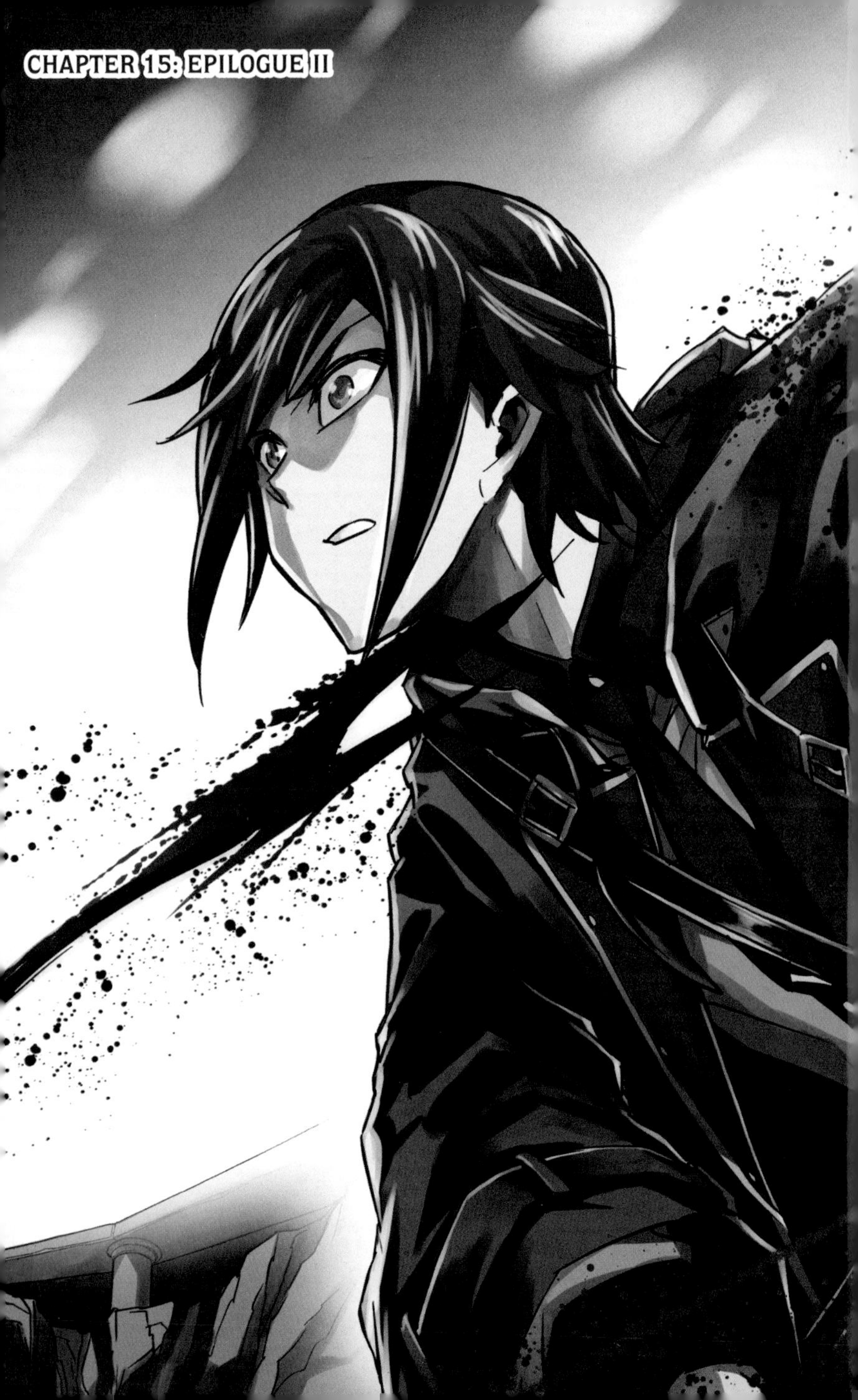

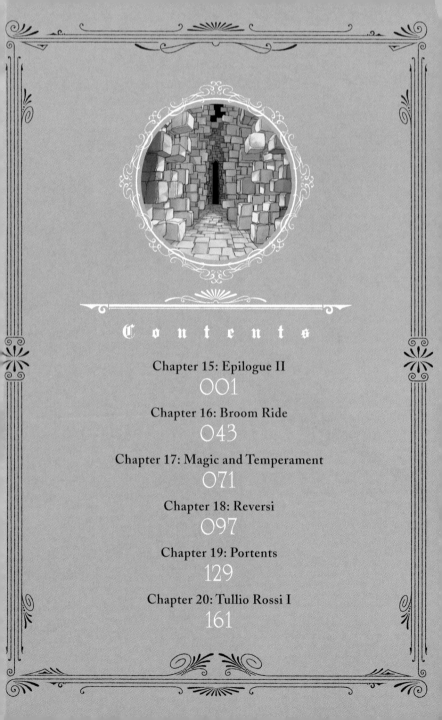

Contents

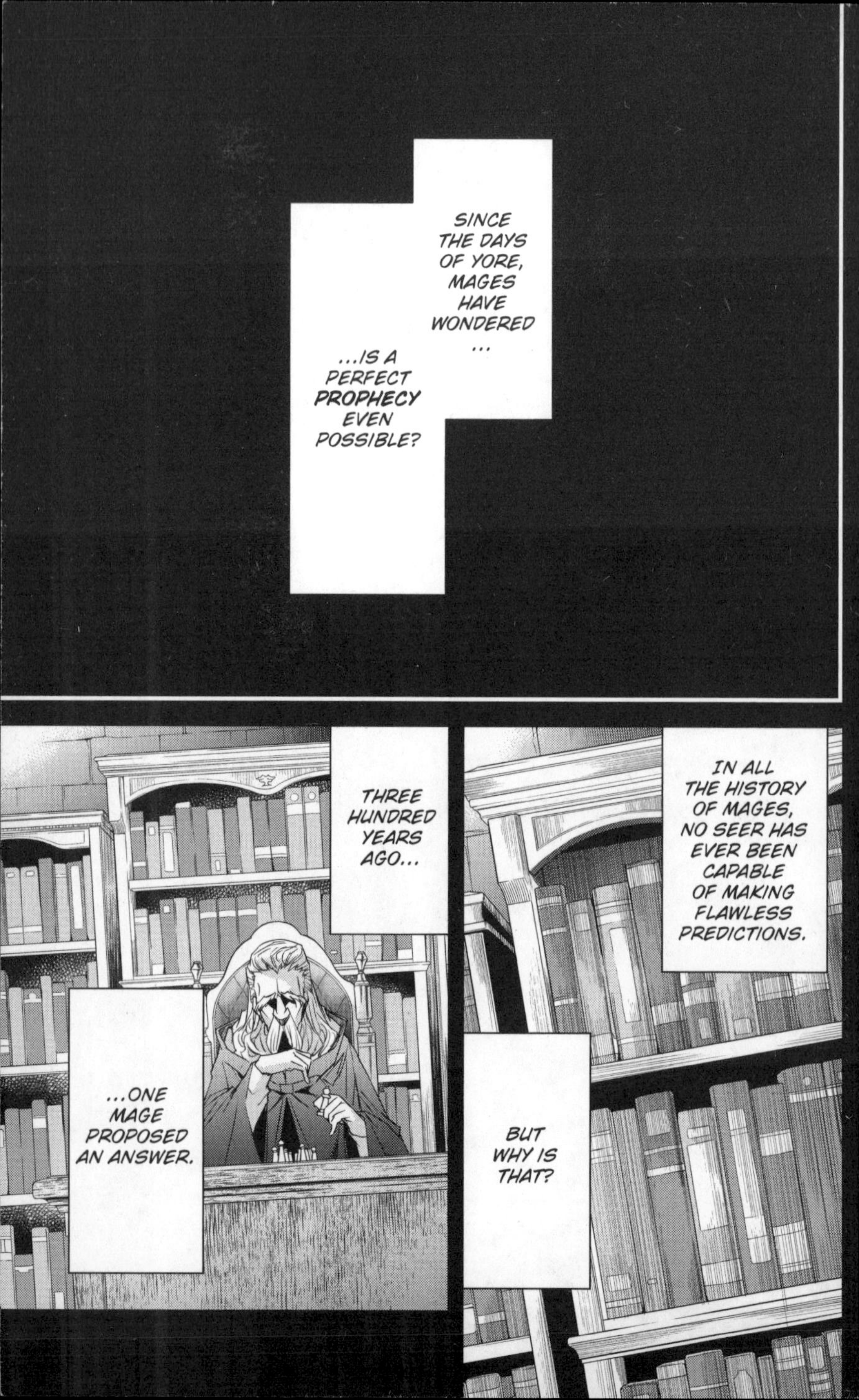
SINCE THE DAYS OF YORE, MAGES HAVE WONDERED...
...IS A PERFECT PROPHECY EVEN POSSIBLE?
IN ALL THE HISTORY OF MAGES, NO SEER HAS EVER BEEN CAPABLE OF MAKING FLAWLESS PREDICTIONS.
BUT WHY IS THAT?
THREE HUNDRED YEARS AGO...
...ONE MAGE PROPOSED AN ANSWER.

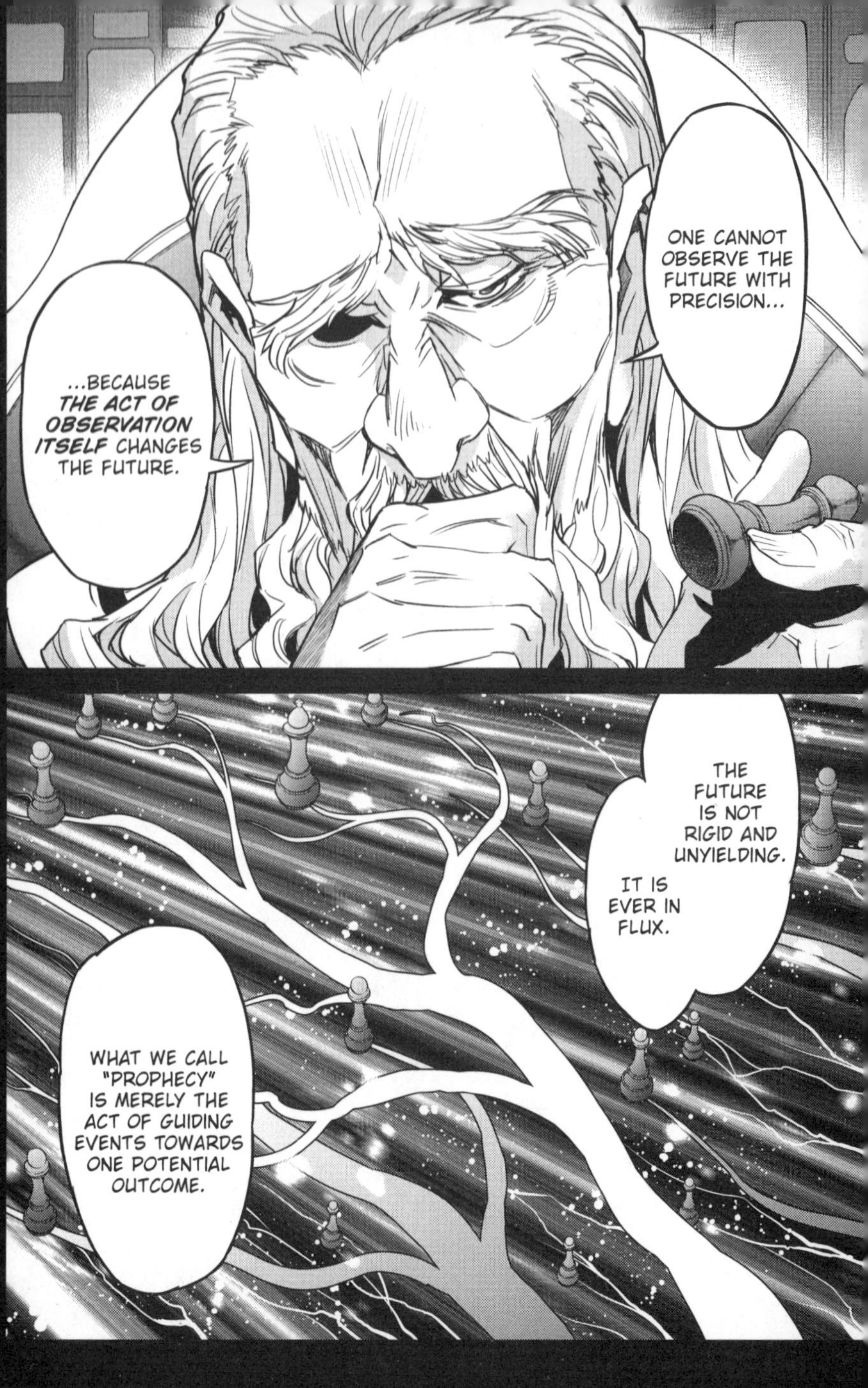
ONE CANNOT OBSERVE THE FUTURE WITH PRECISION...
...BECAUSE THE ACT OF OBSERVATION ITSELF CHANGES THE FUTURE.
THE FUTURE IS NOT RIGID AND UNYIELDING.
IT IS EVER IN FLUX.
WHAT WE CALL "PROPHECY" IS MERELY THE ACT OF GUIDING EVENTS TOWARDS ONE POTENTIAL OUTCOME.

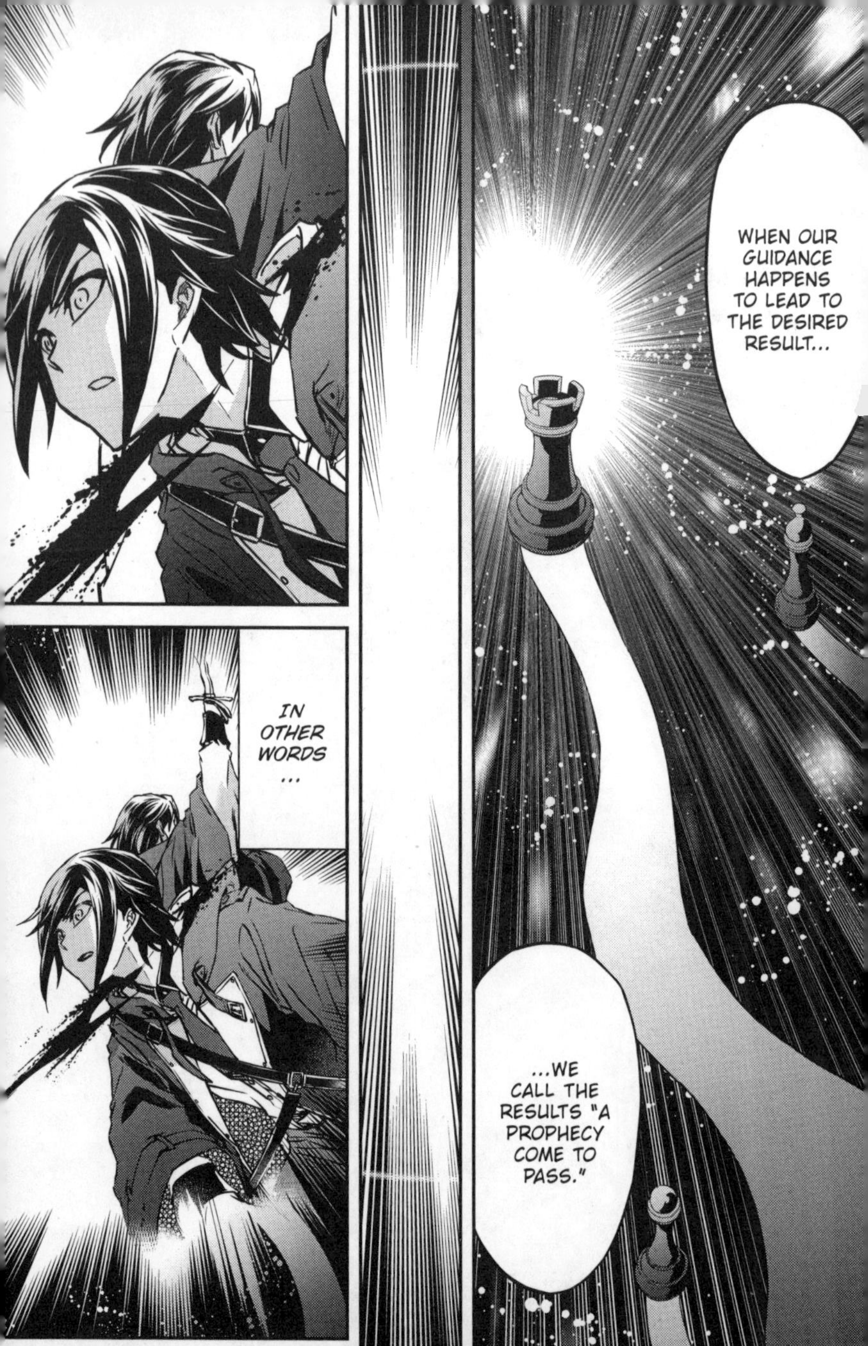
WHEN OUR GUIDANCE HAPPENS TO LEAD TO THE DESIRED RESULT...
...WE CALL THE RESULTS "A PROPHECY COME TO PASS."
IN OTHER WORDS ...

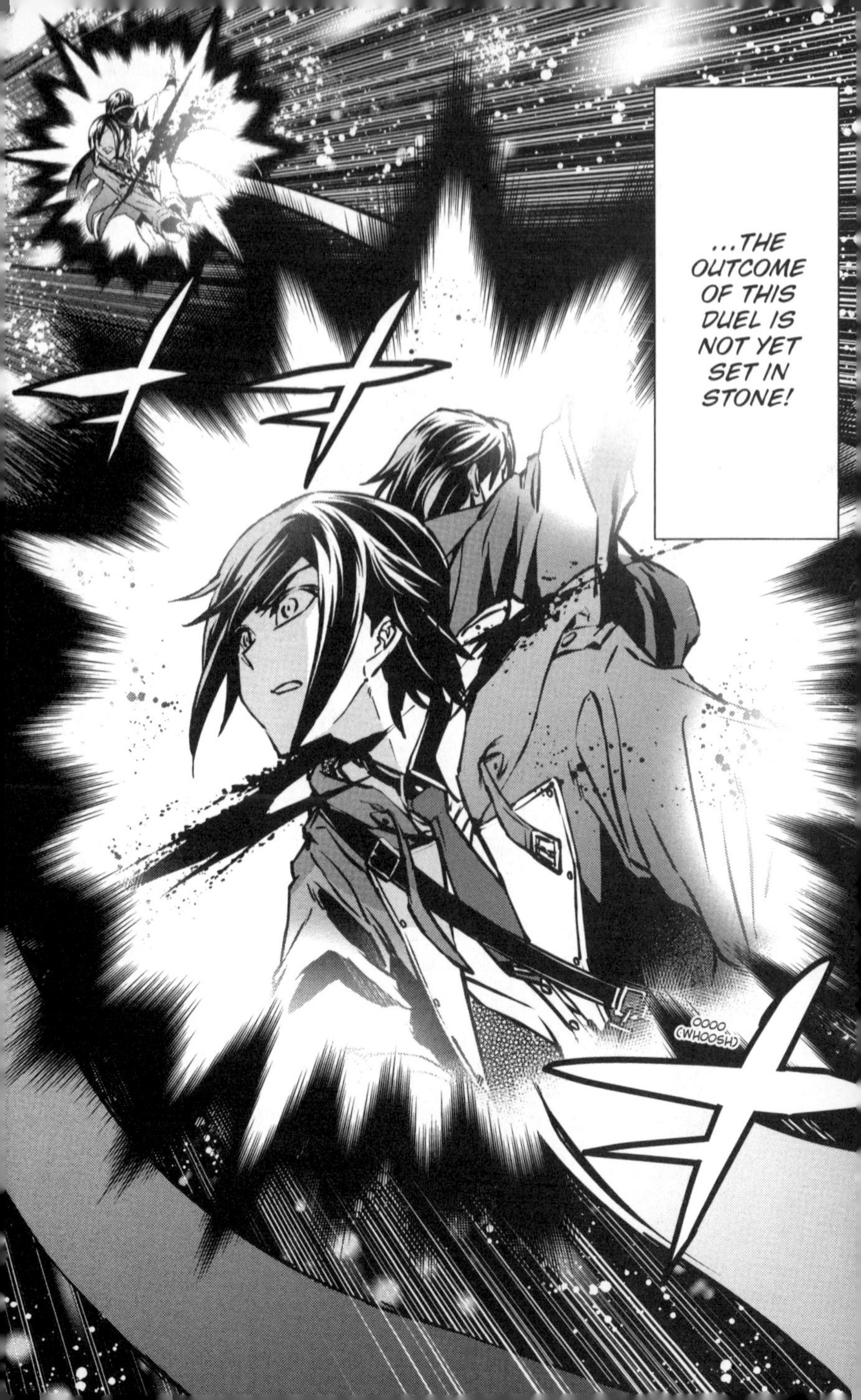
...THE OUTCOME OF THIS DUEL IS NOT YET SET IN STONE!
OOOO (WHOOSH)

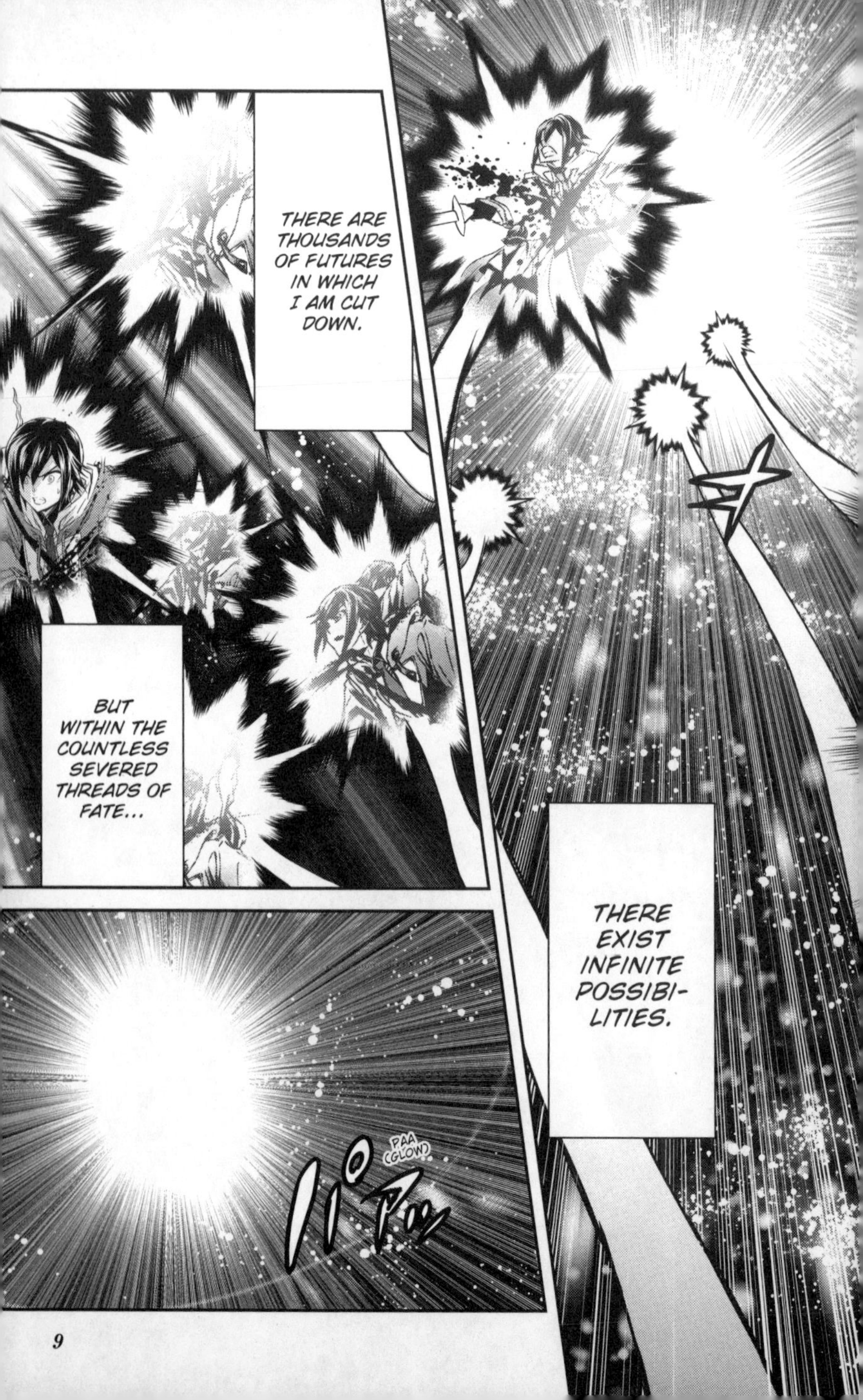
THERE ARE THOUSANDS OF FUTURES IN WHICH I AM CUT DOWN.
BUT WITHIN THE COUNTLESS SEVERED THREADS OF FATE...
THERE EXIST INFINITE POSSIBILITIES.
PAA (GLOW)

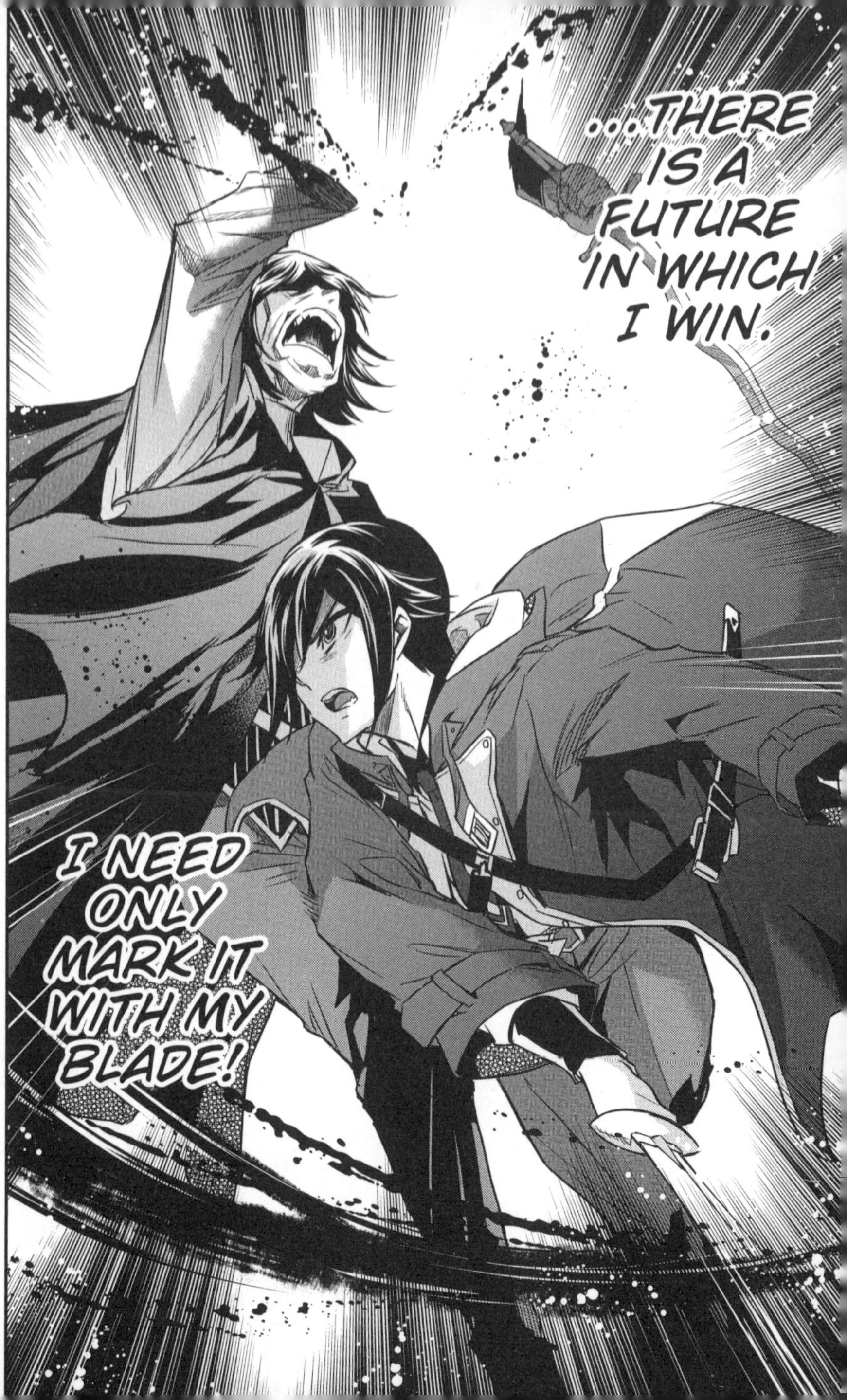
...THERE IS A FUTURE IN WHICH I WIN.
I NEED ONLY MARK IT WITH MY BLADE!

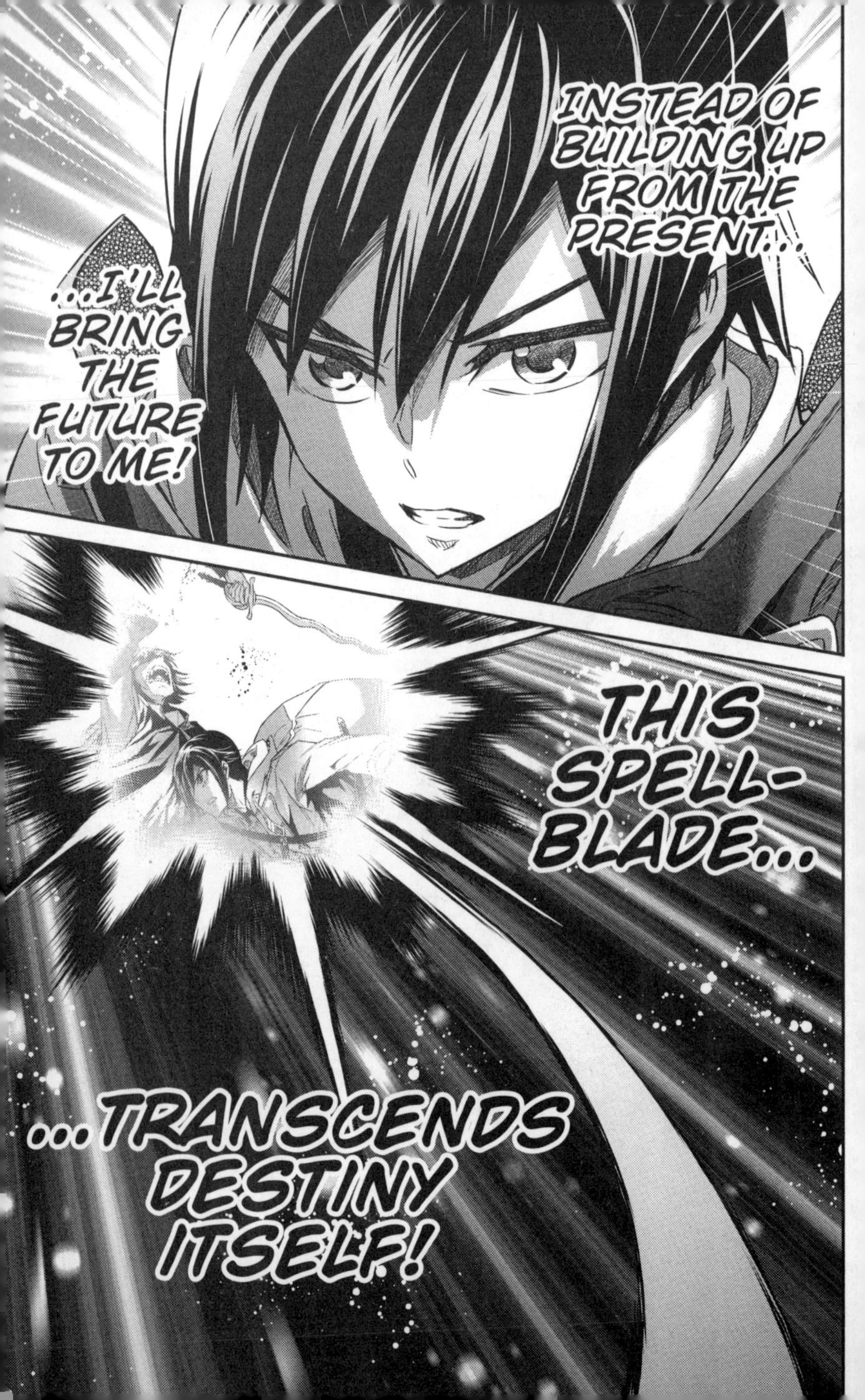
INSTEAD OF BUILDING UP FROM THE PRESENT...
...I'LL BRING THE FUTURE TO ME!
THIS SPELL-BLADE...
...TRANSCENDS DESTINY ITSELF!

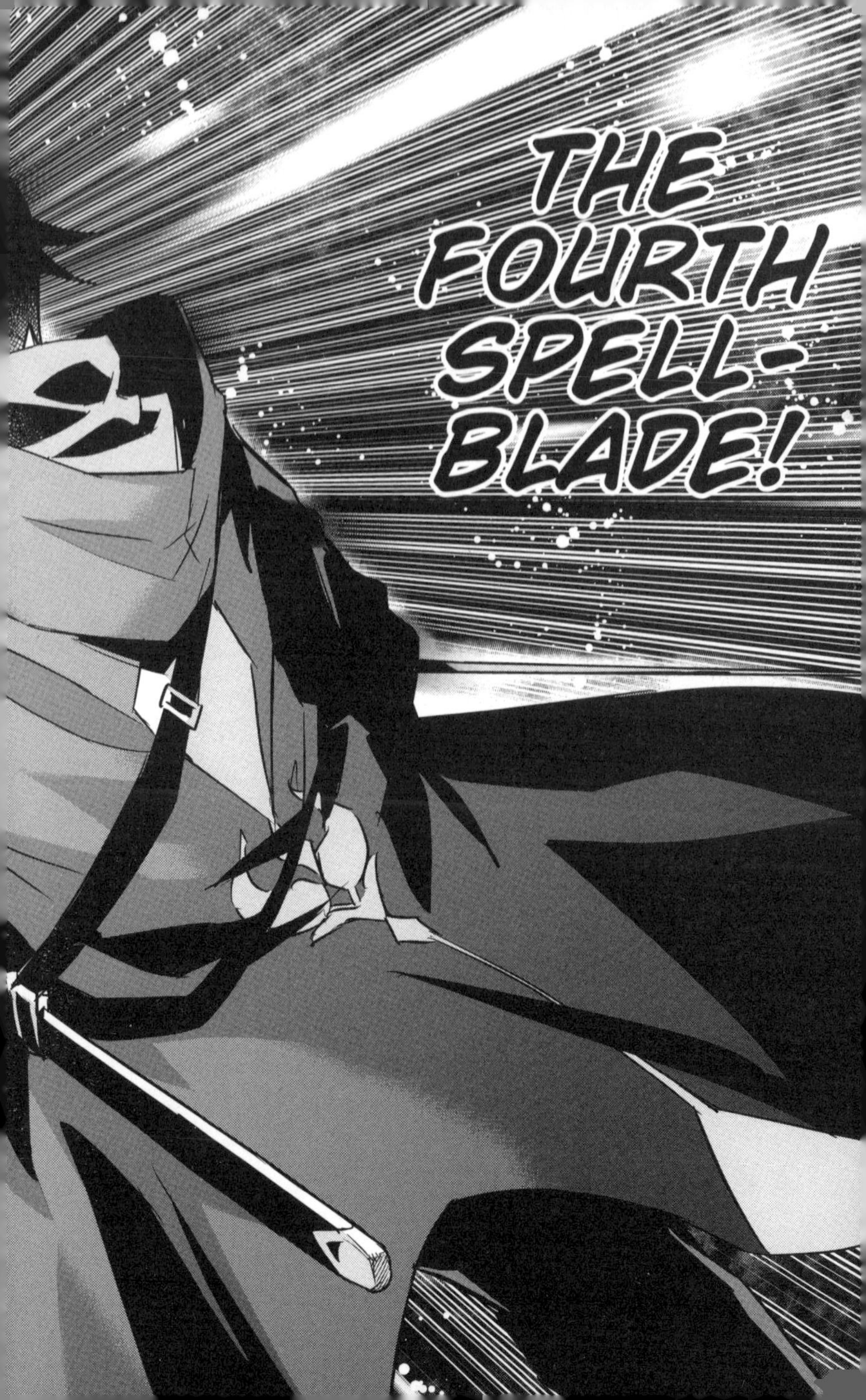
THE FOURTH SPELL-BLADE!

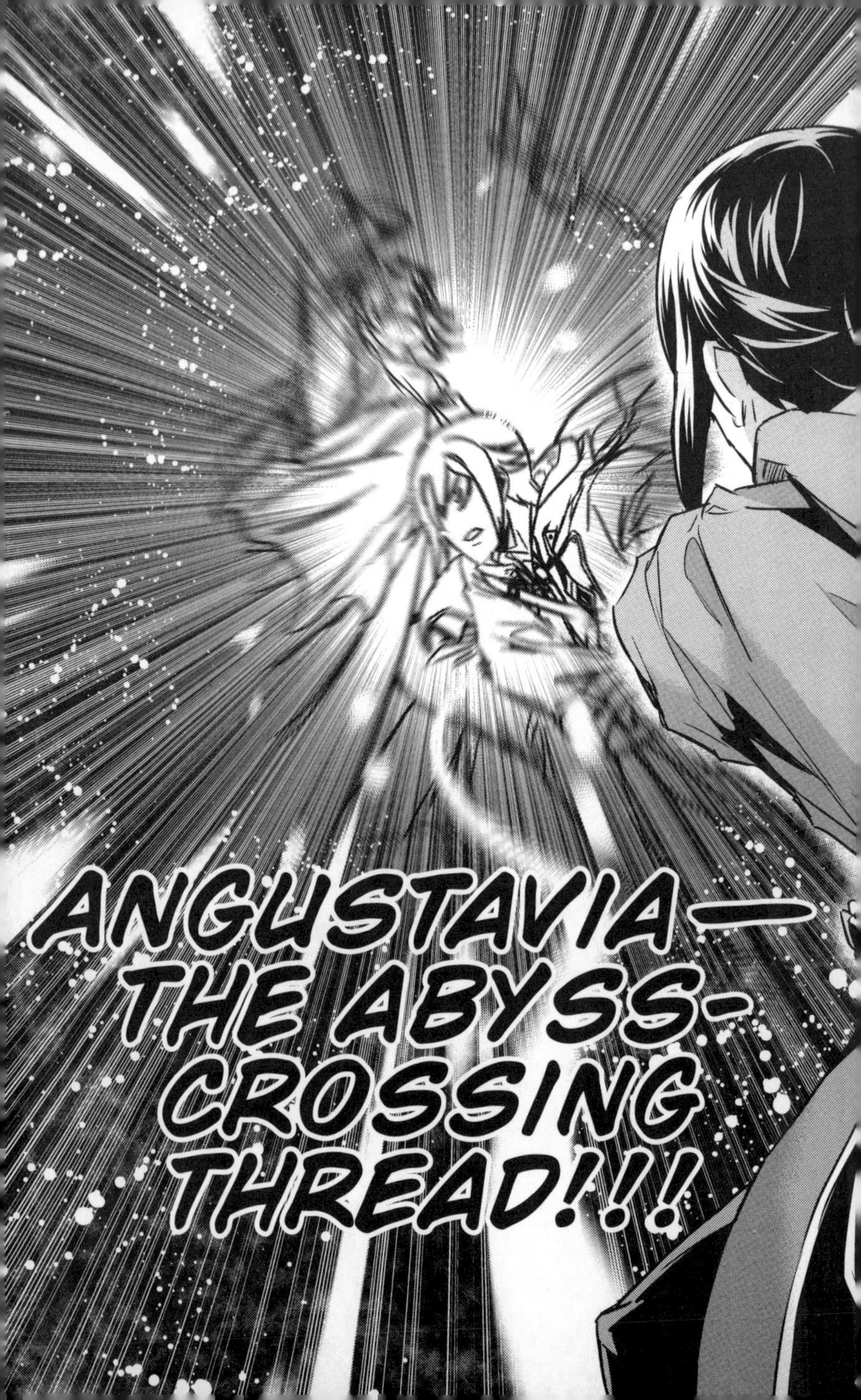
ANGUSTAVIA—THE ABYSS-CROSSING THREAD!!!

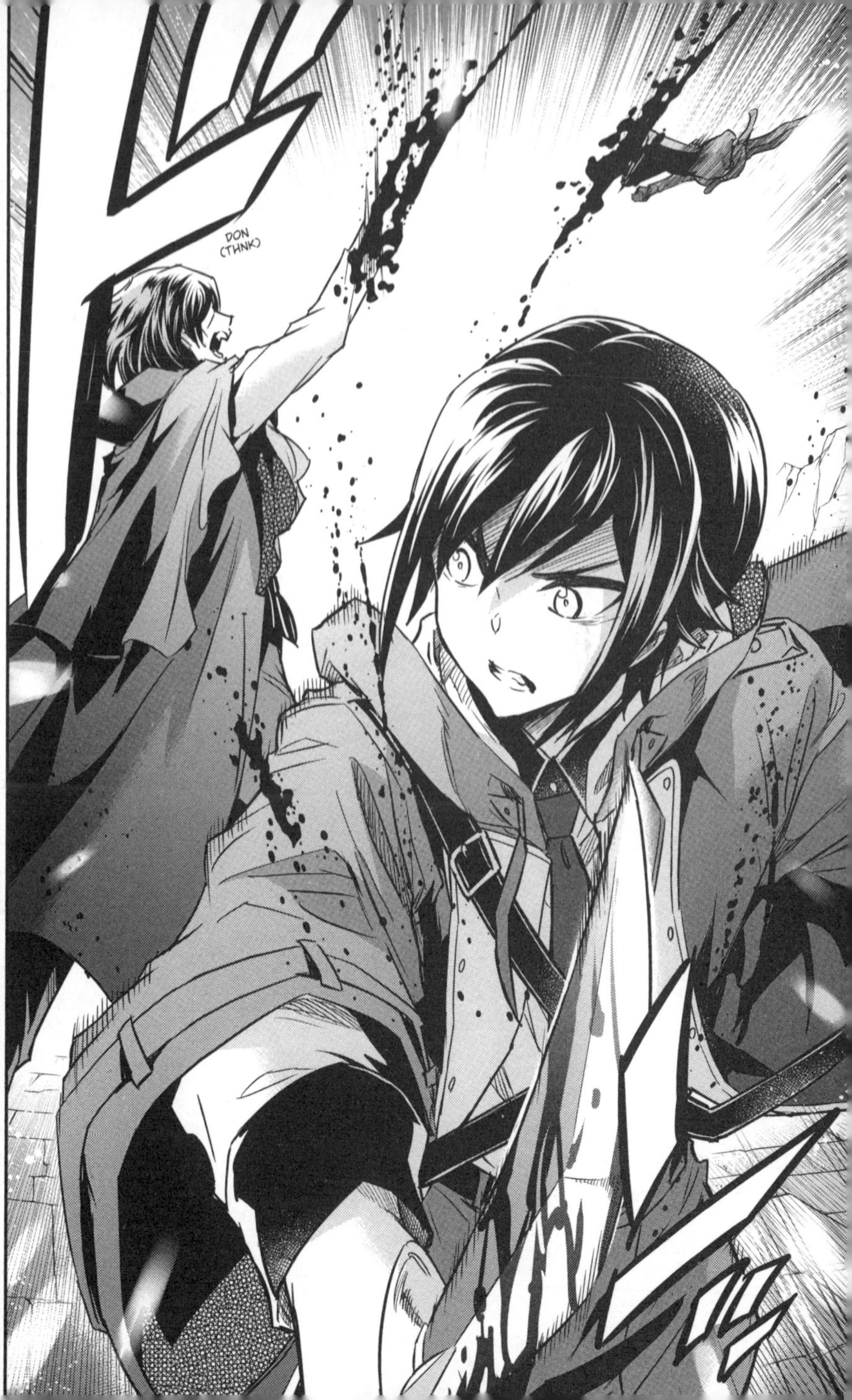
DON
(THNK)

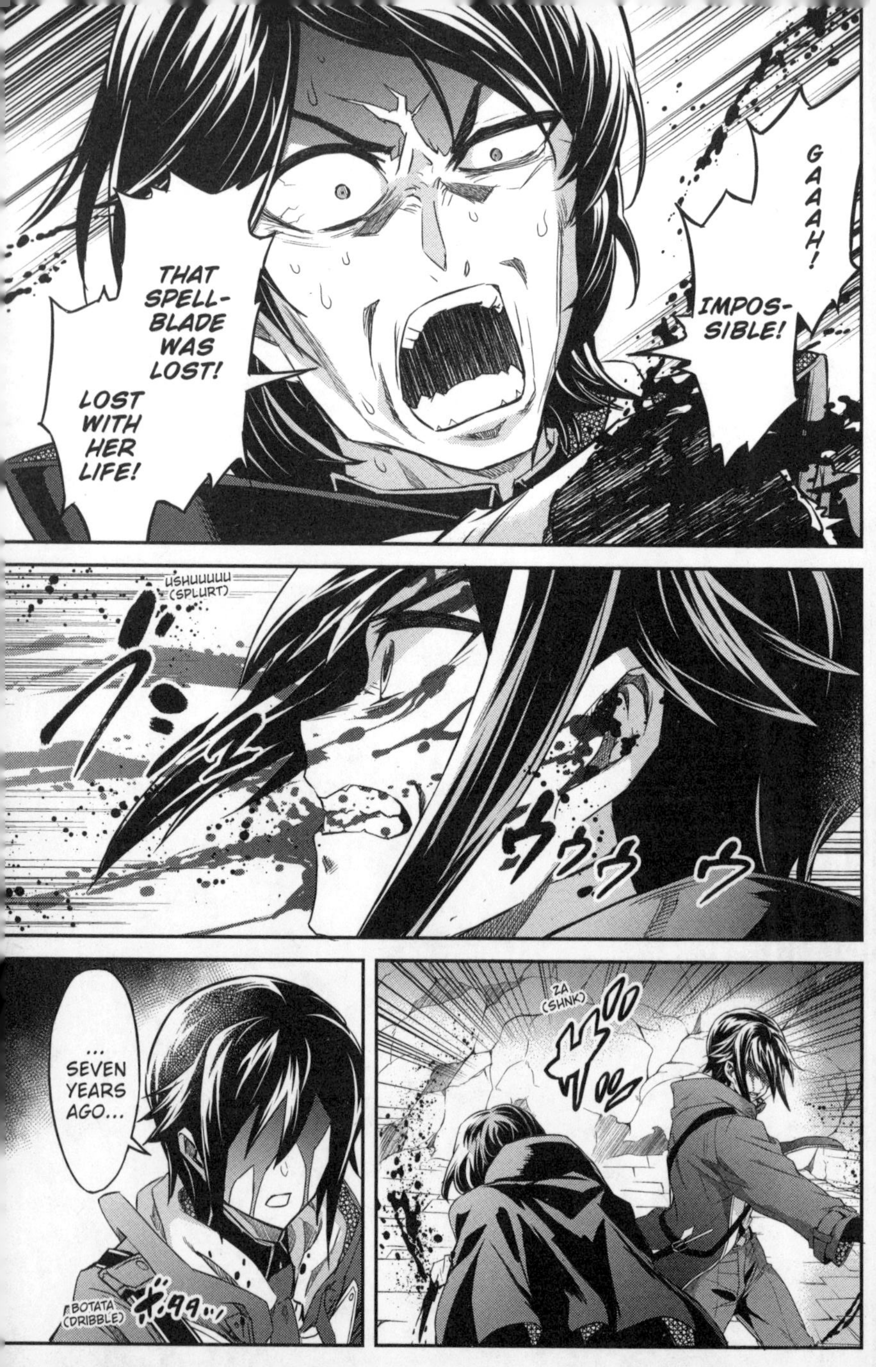
GAAAAH!
IMPOSSIBLE!
THAT SPELL-BLADE WAS LOST! LOST WITH HER LIFE!
USHUUUUU (SPLURT)
ZA (SHNK)
...SEVEN YEARS AGO...
BOTATA (DRIBBLE)

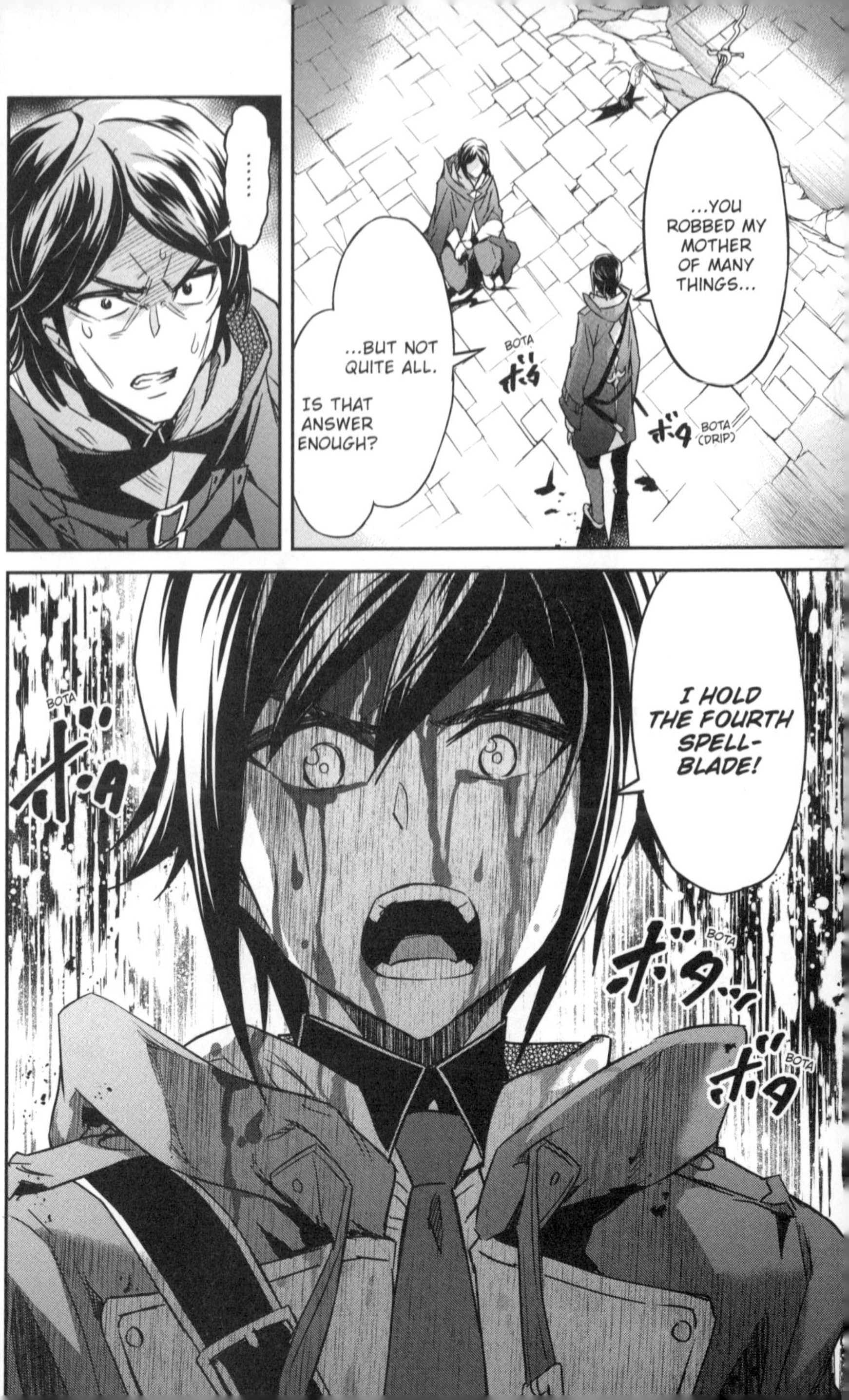
...YOU ROBBED MY MOTHER OF MANY THINGS...
BOTA (DRIP)
BOTA
...BUT NOT QUITE ALL.
IS THAT ANSWER ENOUGH?
......
I HOLD THE FOURTH SPELL-BLADE!
BOTA
BOTA
BOTA

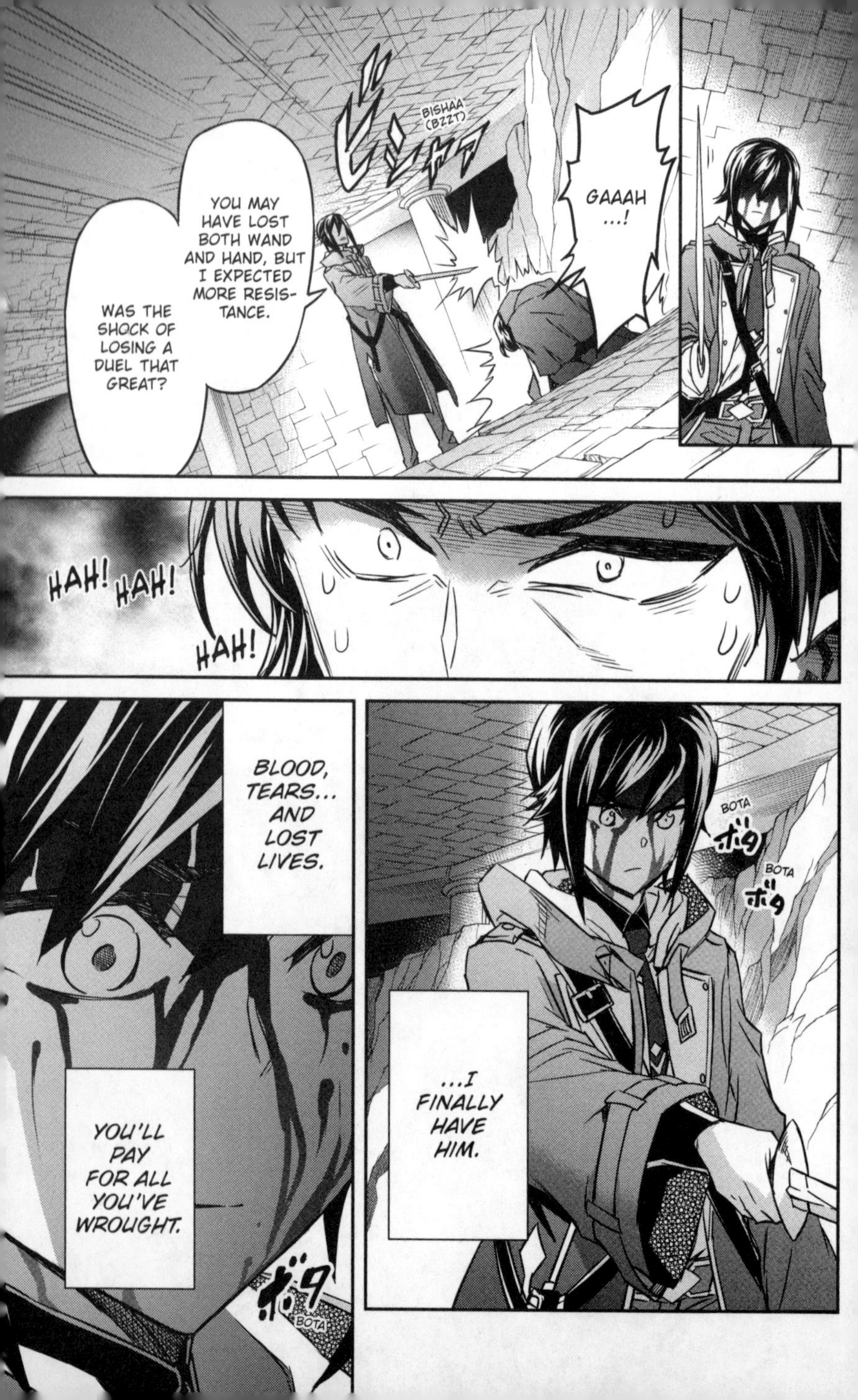
GAAAH ...!
BISHAA (BZZT)
YOU MAY HAVE LOST BOTH WAND AND HAND, BUT I EXPECTED MORE RESIS-TANCE.
WAS THE SHOCK OF LOSING A DUEL THAT GREAT?
HAH! HAH!
HAH!
BOTA
BOTA
...I FINALLY HAVE HIM.
BLOOD, TEARS... AND LOST LIVES.
YOU'LL PAY FOR ALL YOU'VE WROUGHT.
BOTA

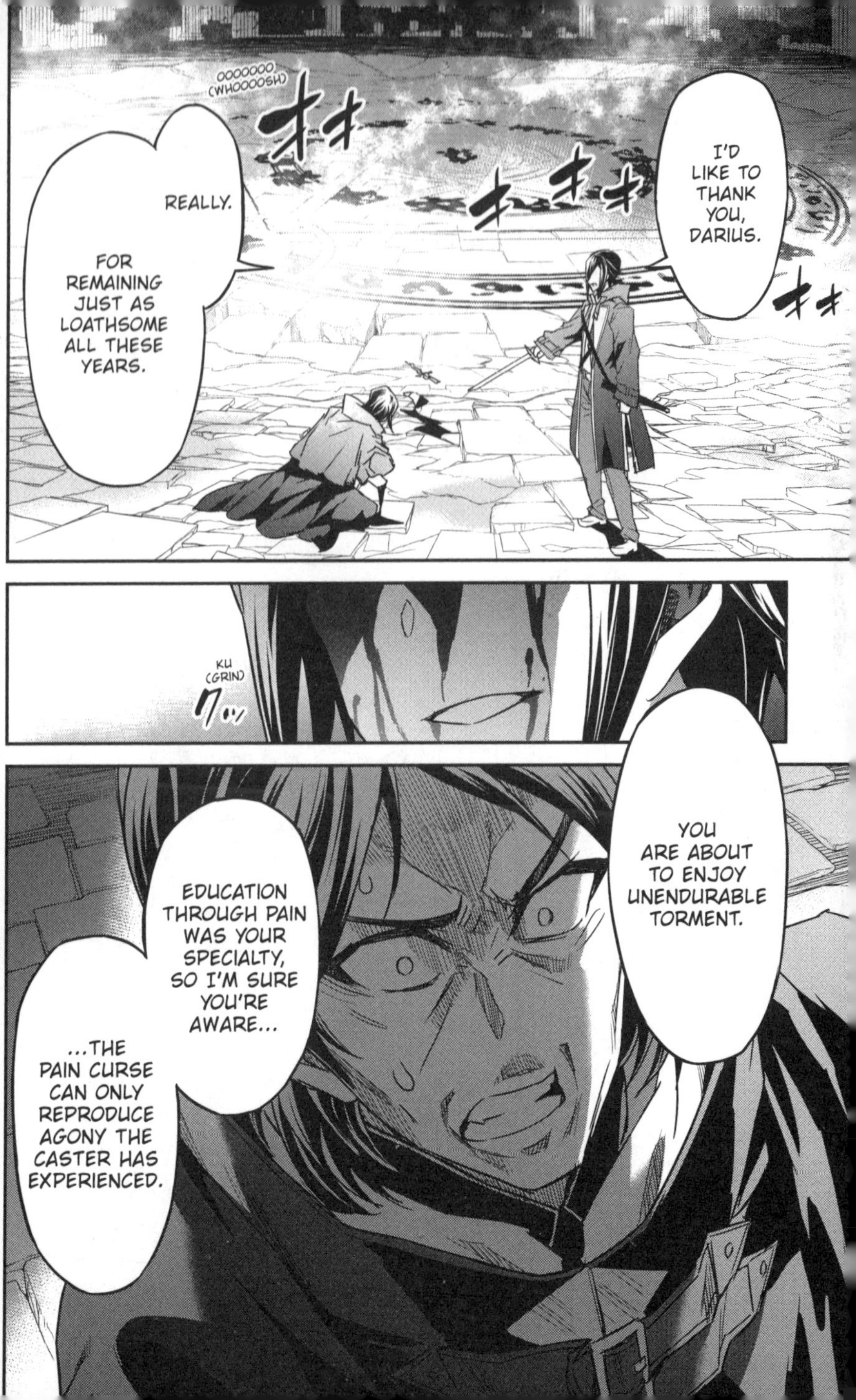
I'D LIKE TO THANK YOU, DARIUS.
OOOOOOO (WHOOOOSH)
REALLY.
FOR REMAINING JUST AS LOATHSOME ALL THESE YEARS.
KU (GRIN)
YOU ARE ABOUT TO ENJOY UNENDURABLE TORMENT.
EDUCATION THROUGH PAIN WAS YOUR SPECIALTY, SO I'M SURE YOU'RE AWARE...
...THE PAIN CURSE CAN ONLY REPRODUCE AGONY THE CASTER HAS EXPERIENCED.

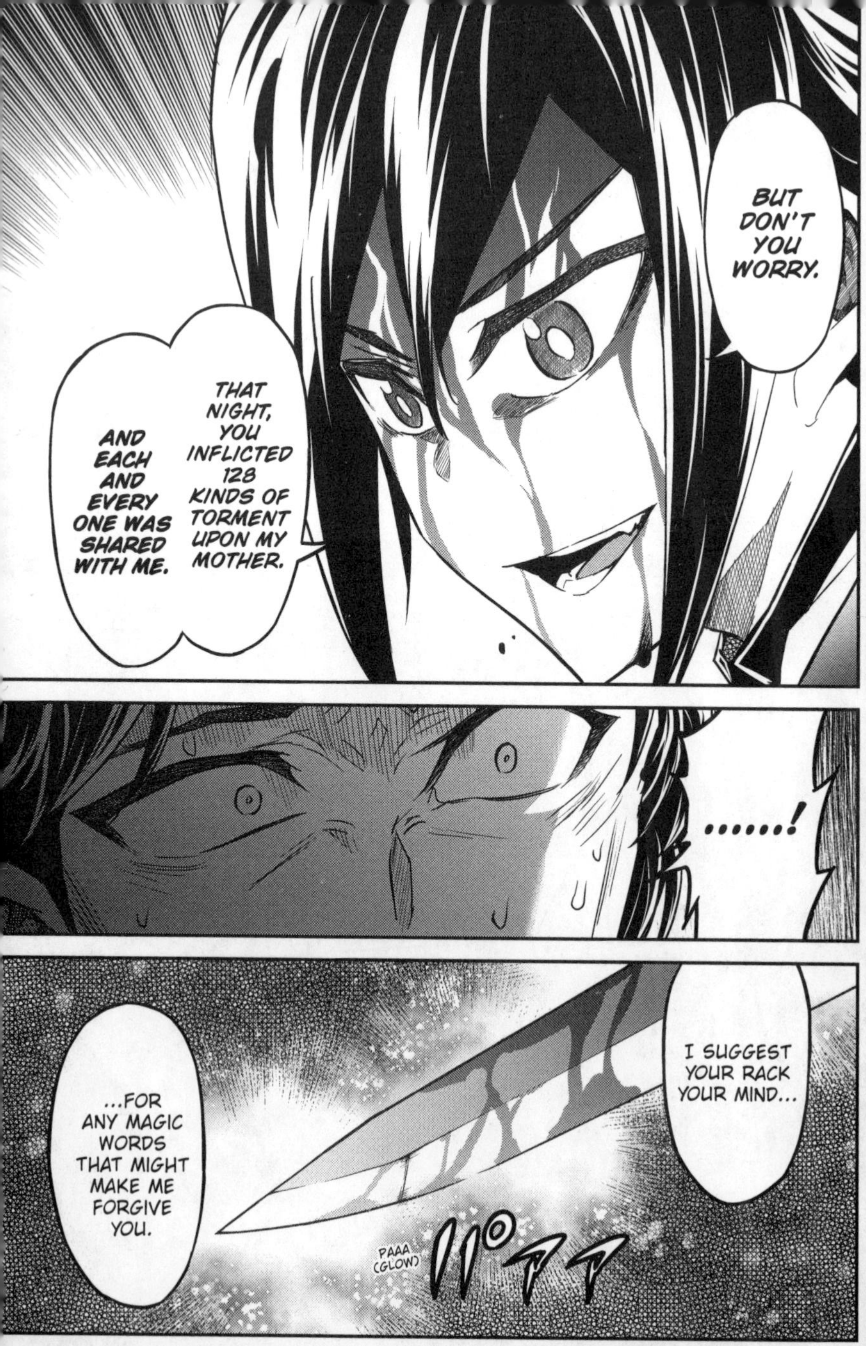
BUT DON'T YOU WORRY.
THAT NIGHT, YOU INFLICTED 128 KINDS OF TORMENT UPON MY MOTHER.
AND EACH AND EVERY ONE WAS SHARED WITH ME.
......!
I SUGGEST YOUR RACK YOUR MIND...
...FOR ANY MAGIC WORDS THAT MIGHT MAKE ME FORGIVE YOU.
PAAA (GLOW)

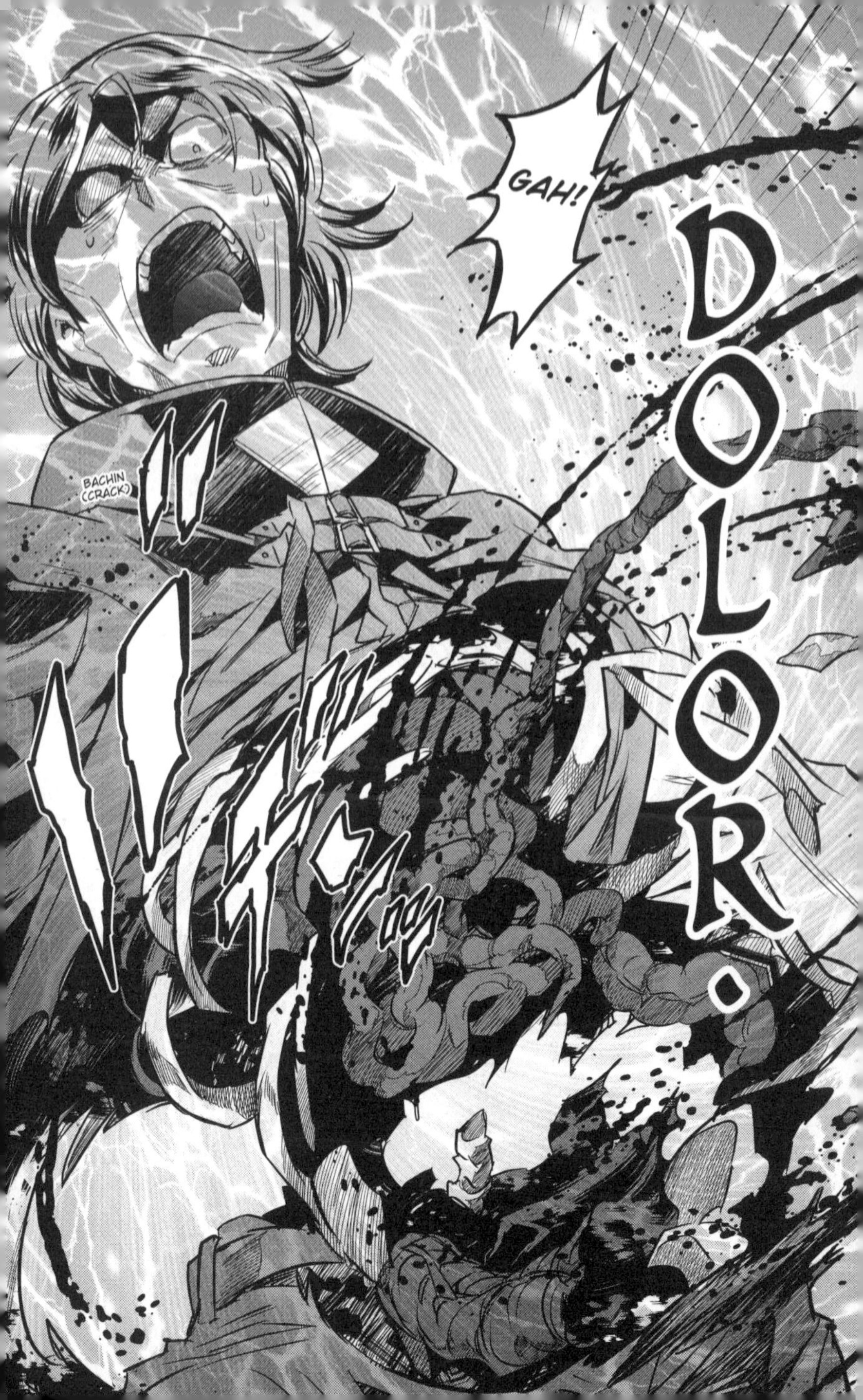
GAH!
DOLOR.
BACHIN (CRACK)

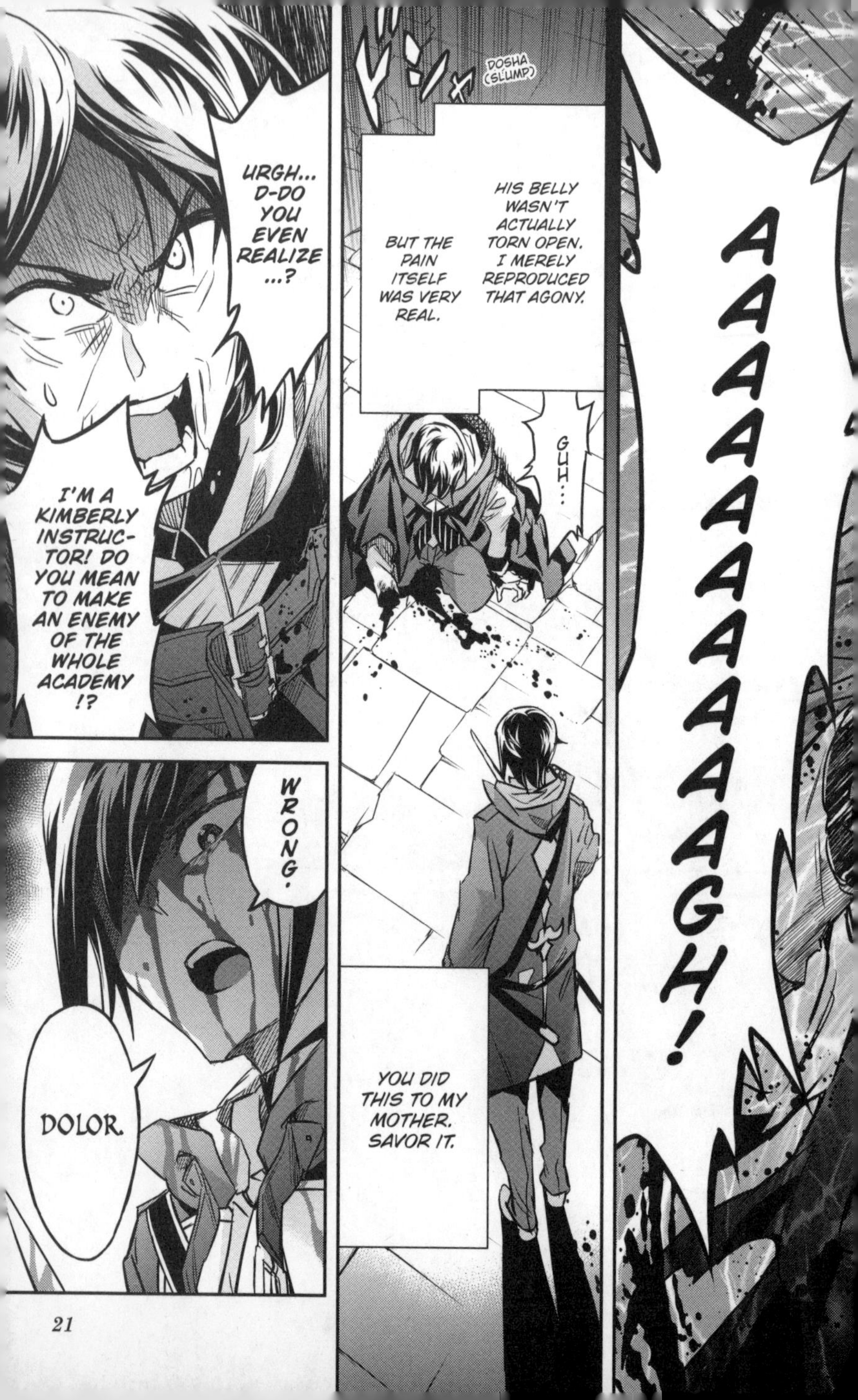
AAAAAAAAAAAAAAAAGH!
DOSHA (SLUMP)
HIS BELLY WASN'T ACTUALLY TORN OPEN. I MERELY REPRODUCED THAT AGONY.
BUT THE PAIN ITSELF WAS VERY REAL.
GUH...
YOU DID THIS TO MY MOTHER. SAVOR IT.
URGH... D-DO YOU EVEN REALIZE ...?
I'M A KIMBERLY INSTRUCTOR! DO YOU MEAN TO MAKE AN ENEMY OF THE WHOLE ACADEMY !?
WRONG.
DOLOR.

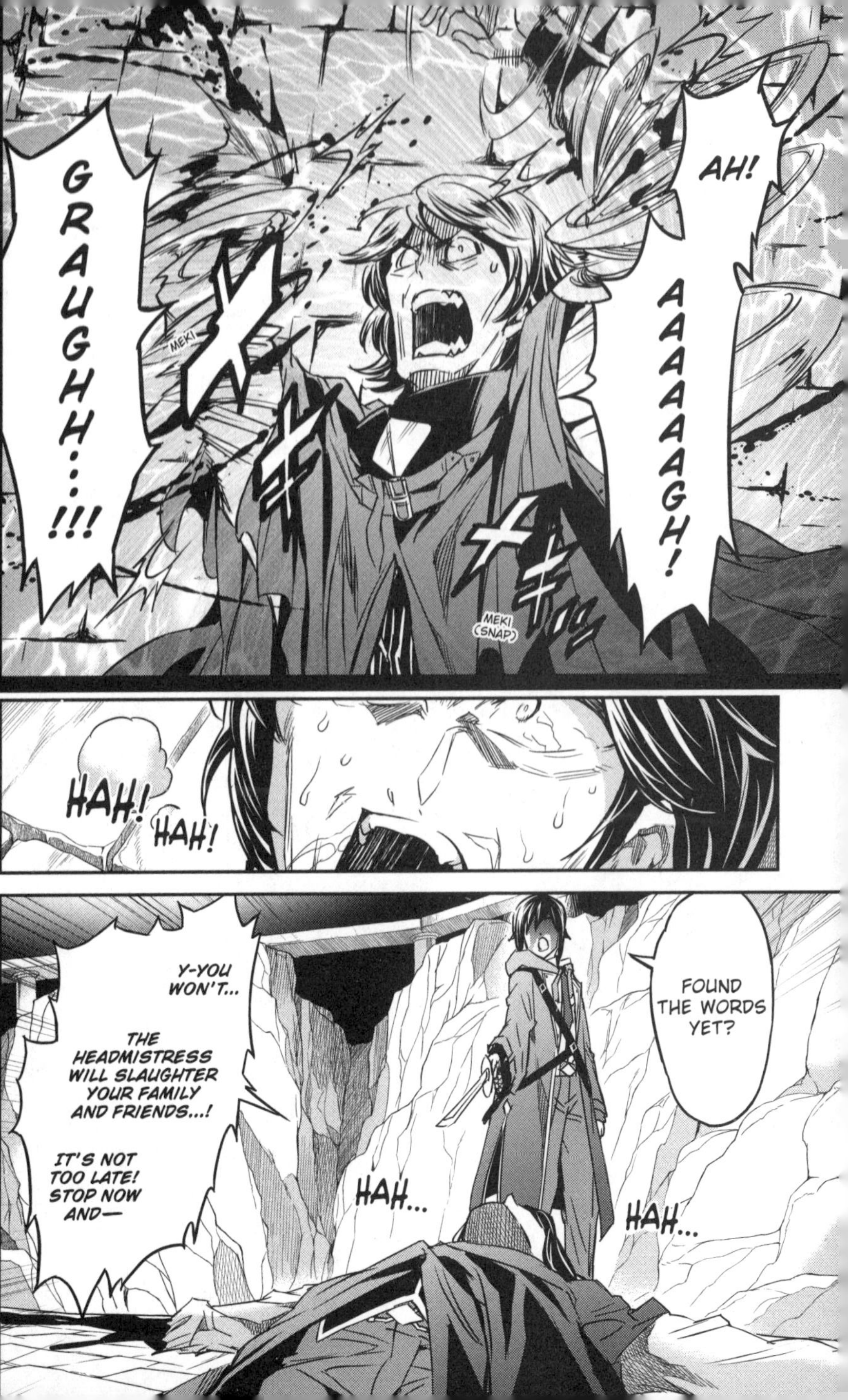
AH! AAAAAAGH!
GRAUGHH...!!!
MEKI
MEKI (SNAP)
HAH! HAH!
FOUND THE WORDS YET?
Y-YOU WON'T...
THE HEADMISTRESS WILL SLAUGHTER YOUR FAMILY AND FRIENDS...!
IT'S NOT TOO LATE! STOP NOW AND—
HAH...
HAH...

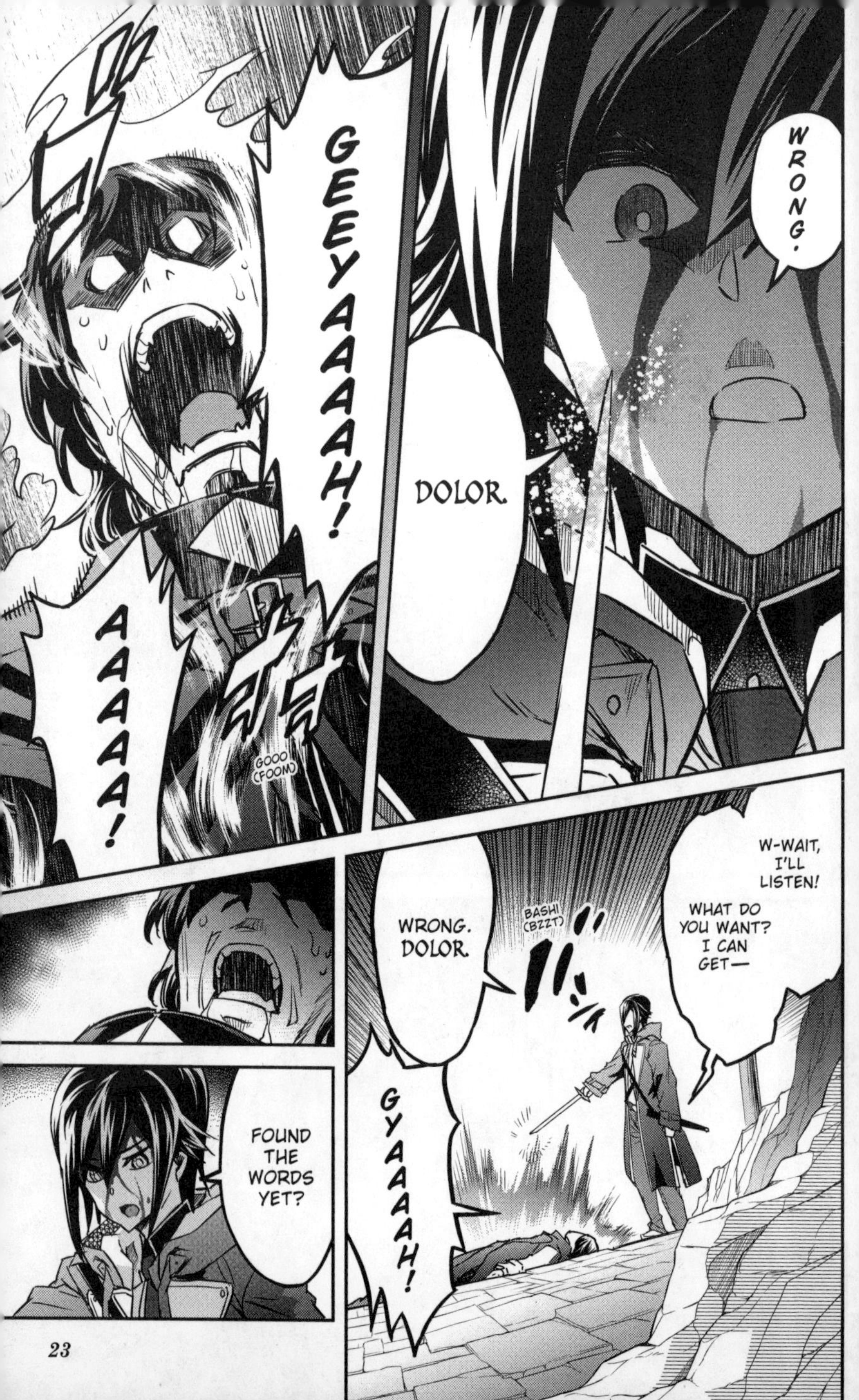
WRONG.
DOLOR.
GEEYAAAAAAH!
AAAAAA!
GOOO (FOOM)
W-WAIT, I'LL LISTEN!
WHAT DO YOU WANT? I CAN GET—
BASHI (BZZT)
WRONG. DOLOR.
GYAAAAAH!
FOUND THE WORDS YET?

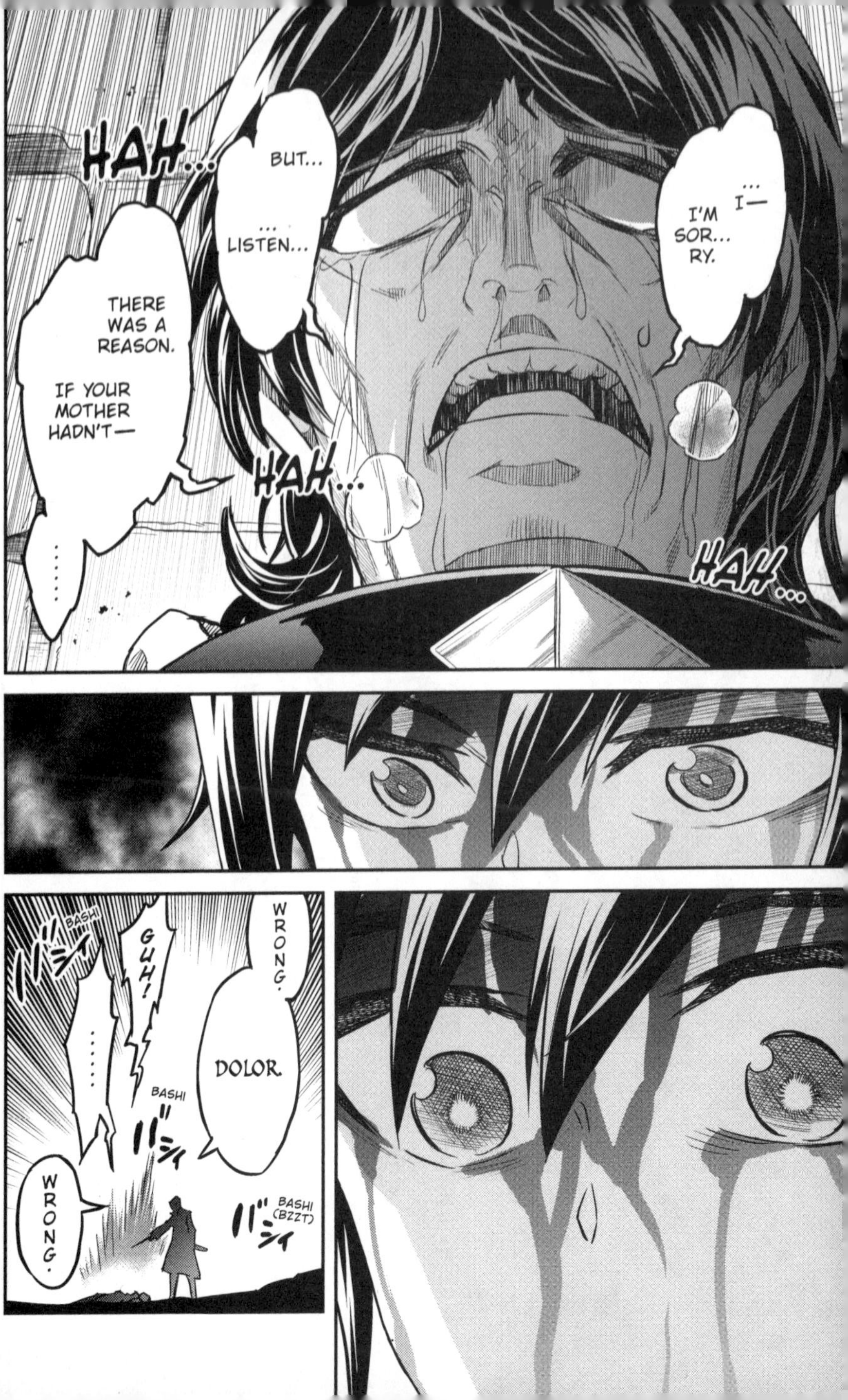

... I— I'M SOR... RY.
HAH...
BUT... ... LISTEN...
HAH...
THERE WAS A REASON. IF YOUR MOTHER HADN'T—
HAH...
......
WRONG. DOLOR.
GUH!
BASHI
BASHI
......
BASHI (BZZT)
WRONG.

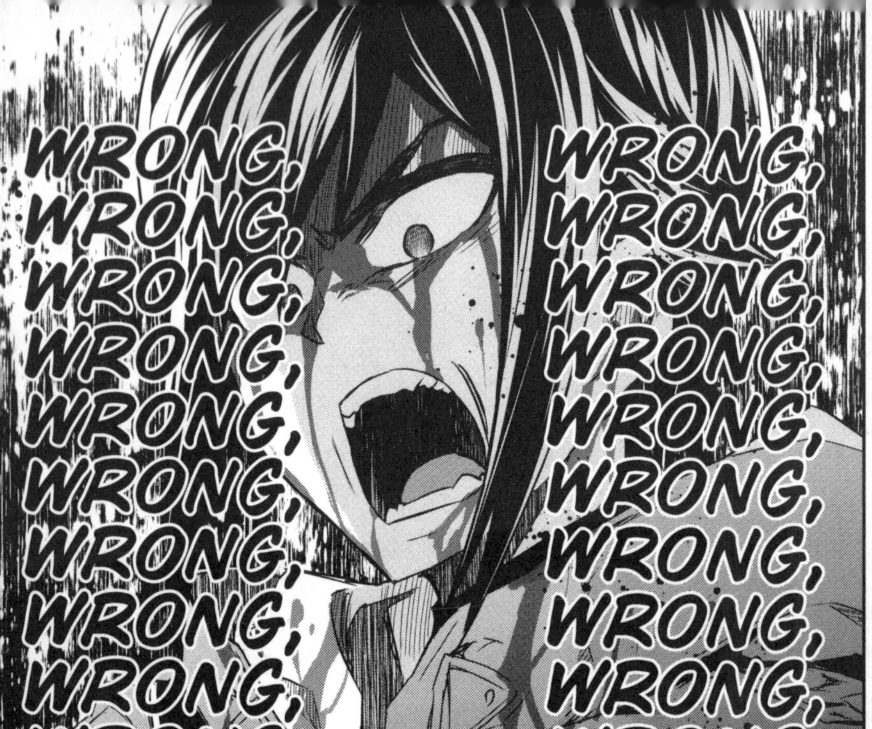
WRONG,
WRONG,
WRONG,
WRONG,
WRONG,
WRONG,
WRONG,
WRONG,
WRONG,
WRONG,
WRONG.
WRONG,
WRONG,
WRONG,
WRONG,
WRONG,
WRONG,
WRONG,
WRONG,
WRONG,
WRONG,
WRONG.

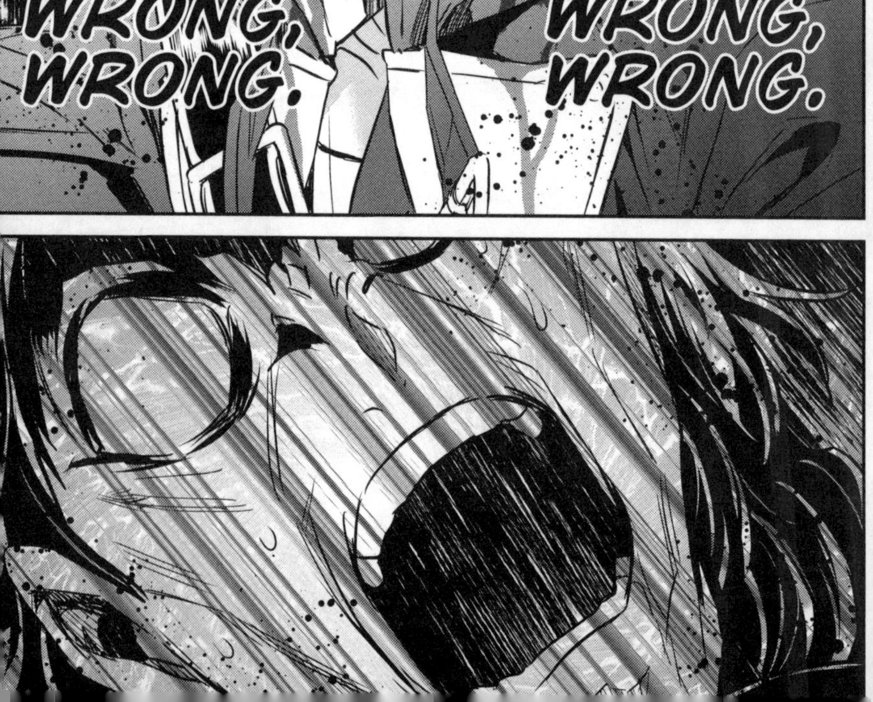

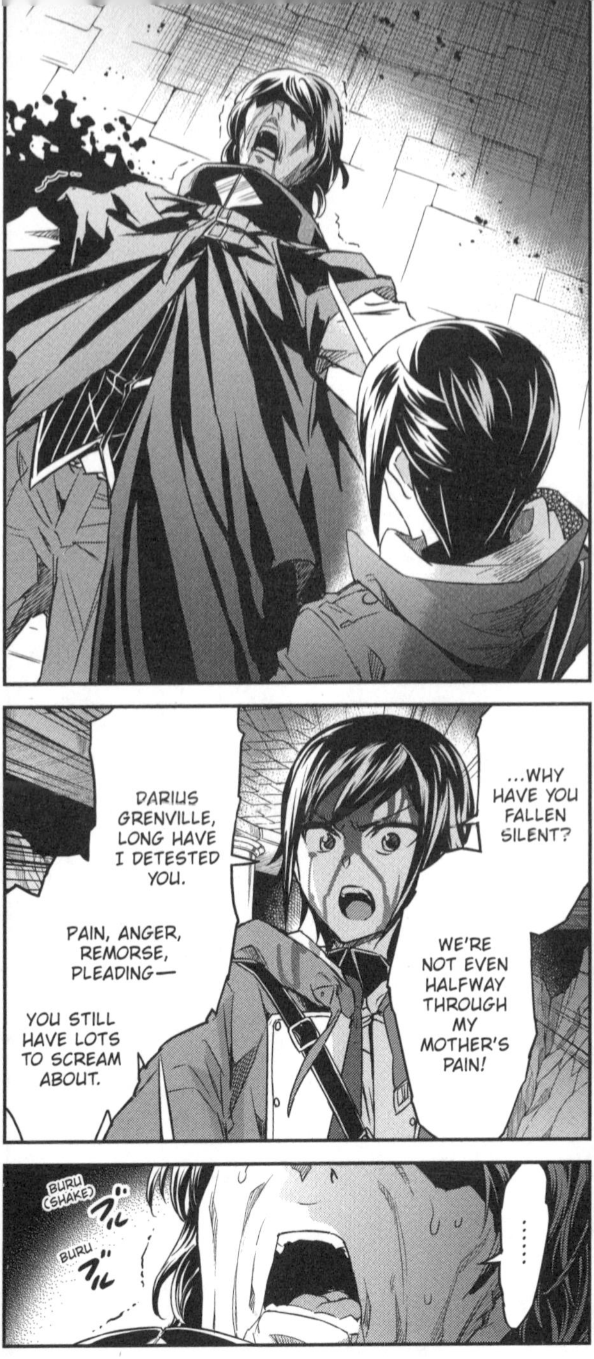
...WHY HAVE YOU FALLEN SILENT?
WE'RE NOT EVEN HALFWAY THROUGH MY MOTHER'S PAIN!
DARIUS GRENVILLE, LONG HAVE I DETESTED YOU.
PAIN, ANGER, REMORSE, PLEADING—
YOU STILL HAVE LOTS TO SCREAM ABOUT.
......
BURU (SHAKE)
ブル
BURU
ブル

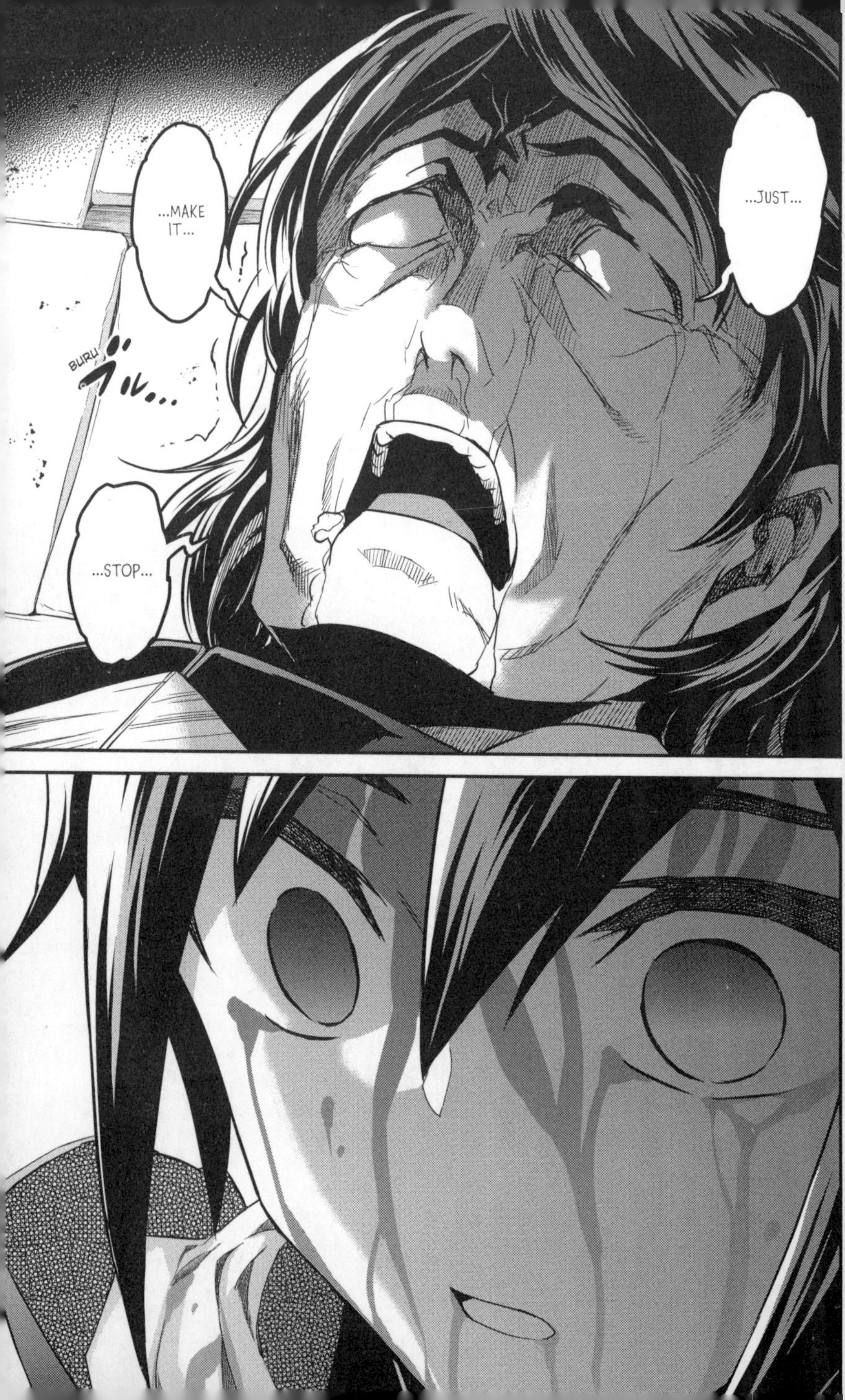
...JUST...
...MAKE IT...
BURU
...STOP...

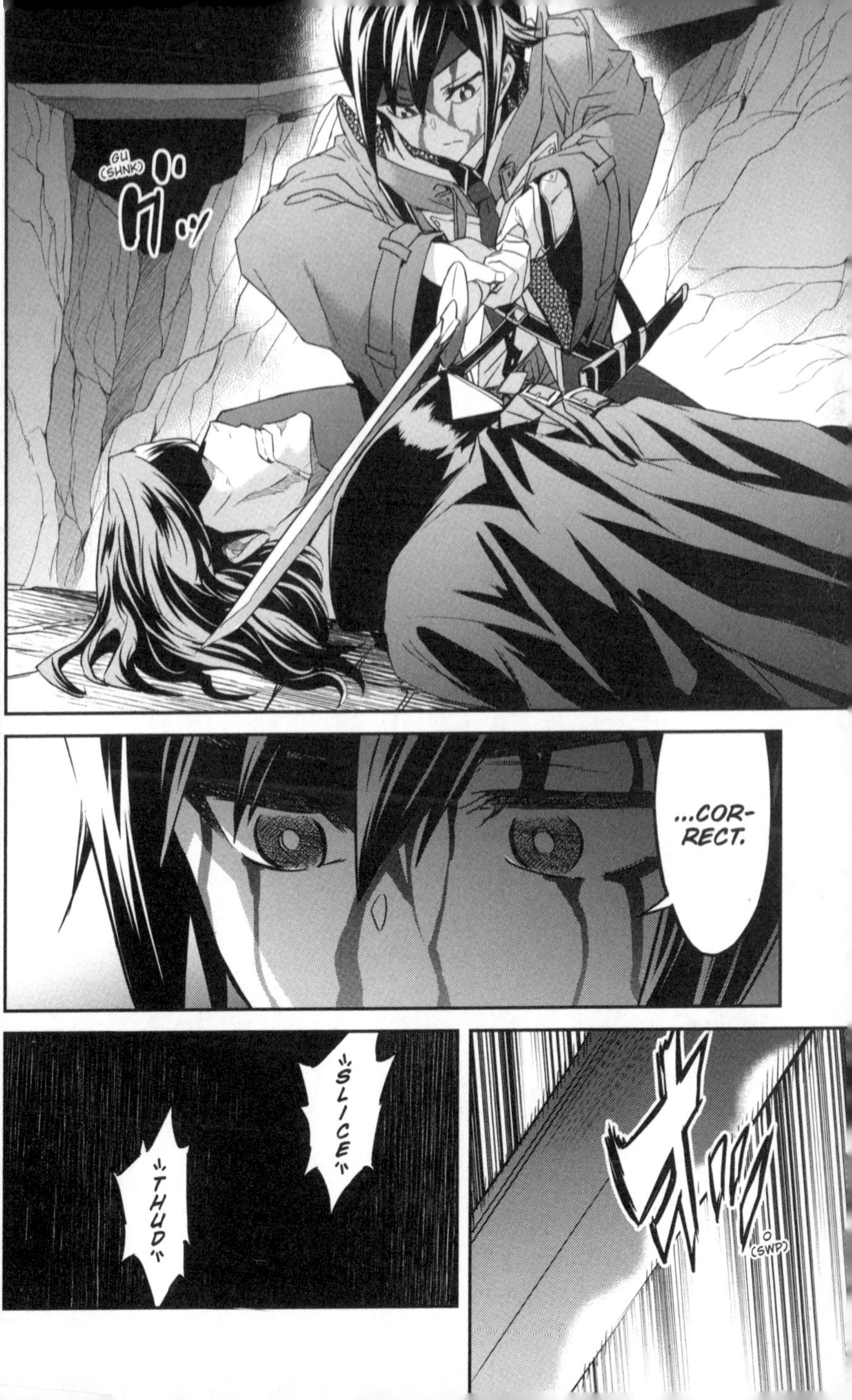
GU (SHNK)
...COR-RECT.
(SWP)
SLICE
THUD

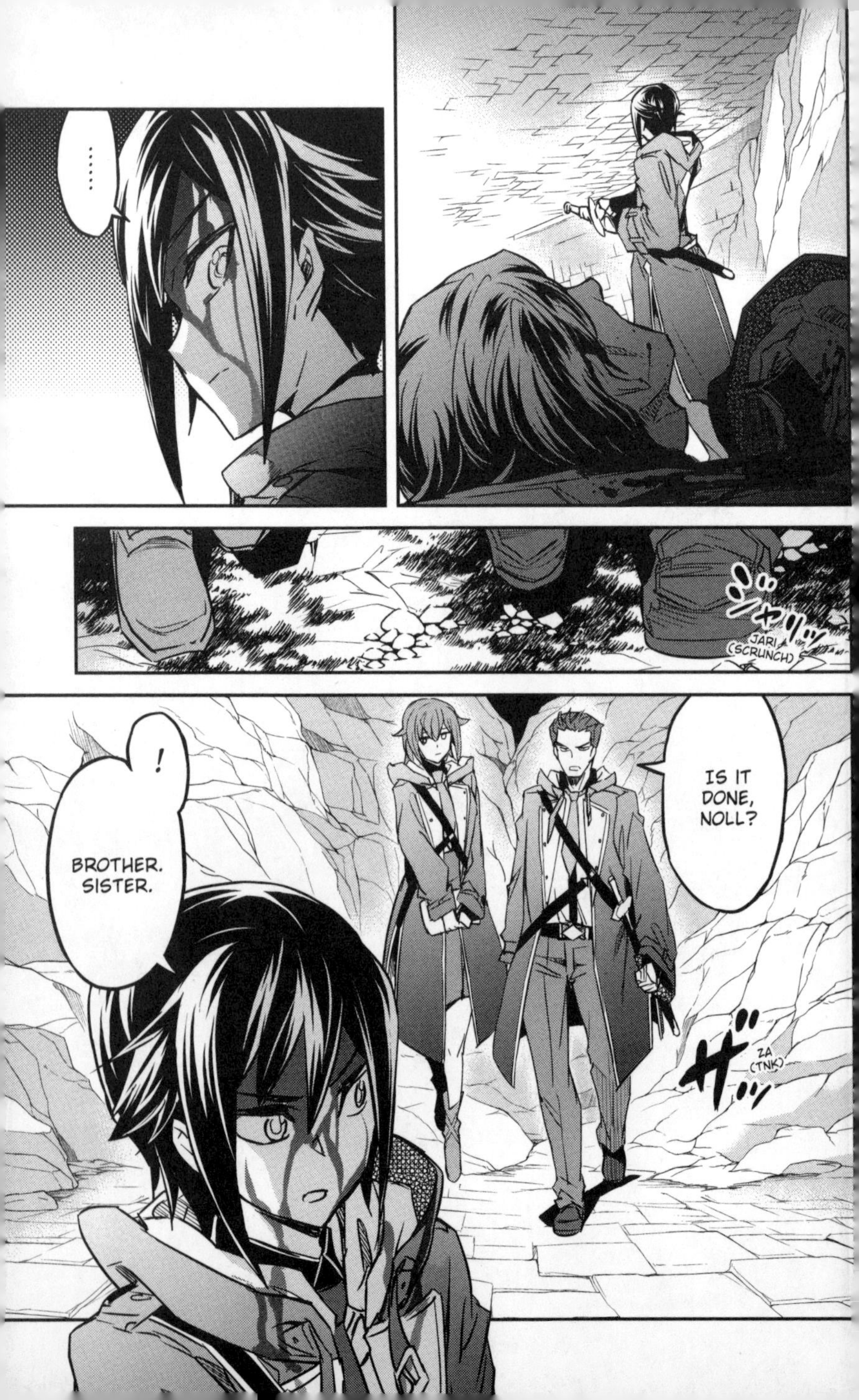
……
ジャリッ
JARI (SCRUNCH)
IS IT DONE, NOLL?
ザッ
ZA (TNK)
!
BROTHER. SISTER.

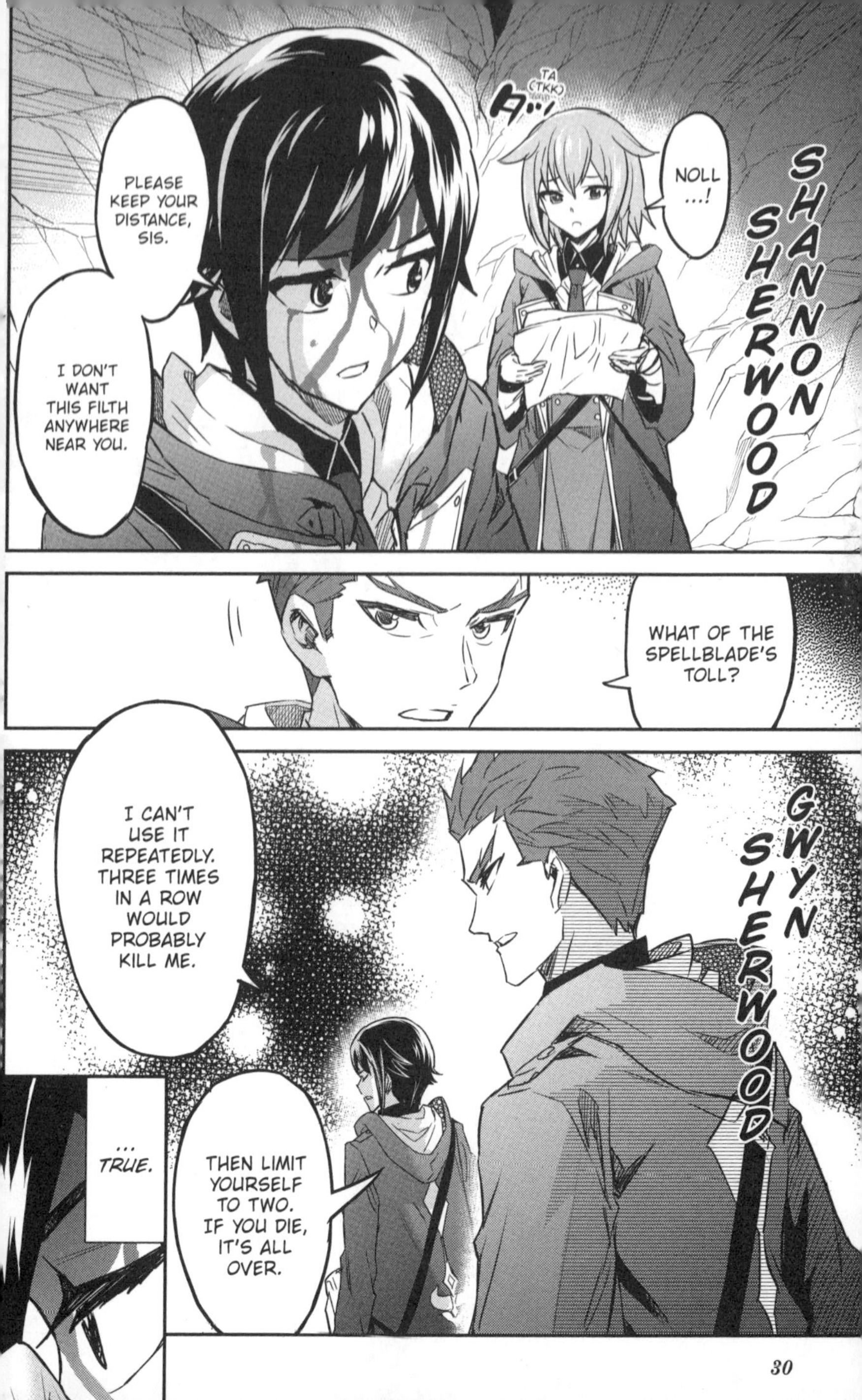
SHANNON SHERWOOD
TA (TKK)
NOLL ...!
PLEASE KEEP YOUR DISTANCE, SIS.
I DON'T WANT THIS FILTH ANYWHERE NEAR YOU.
WHAT OF THE SPELLBLADE'S TOLL?
GWYN SHERWOOD
I CAN'T USE IT REPEATEDLY. THREE TIMES IN A ROW WOULD PROBABLY KILL ME.
THEN LIMIT YOURSELF TO TWO. IF YOU DIE, IT'S ALL OVER.
... TRUE.

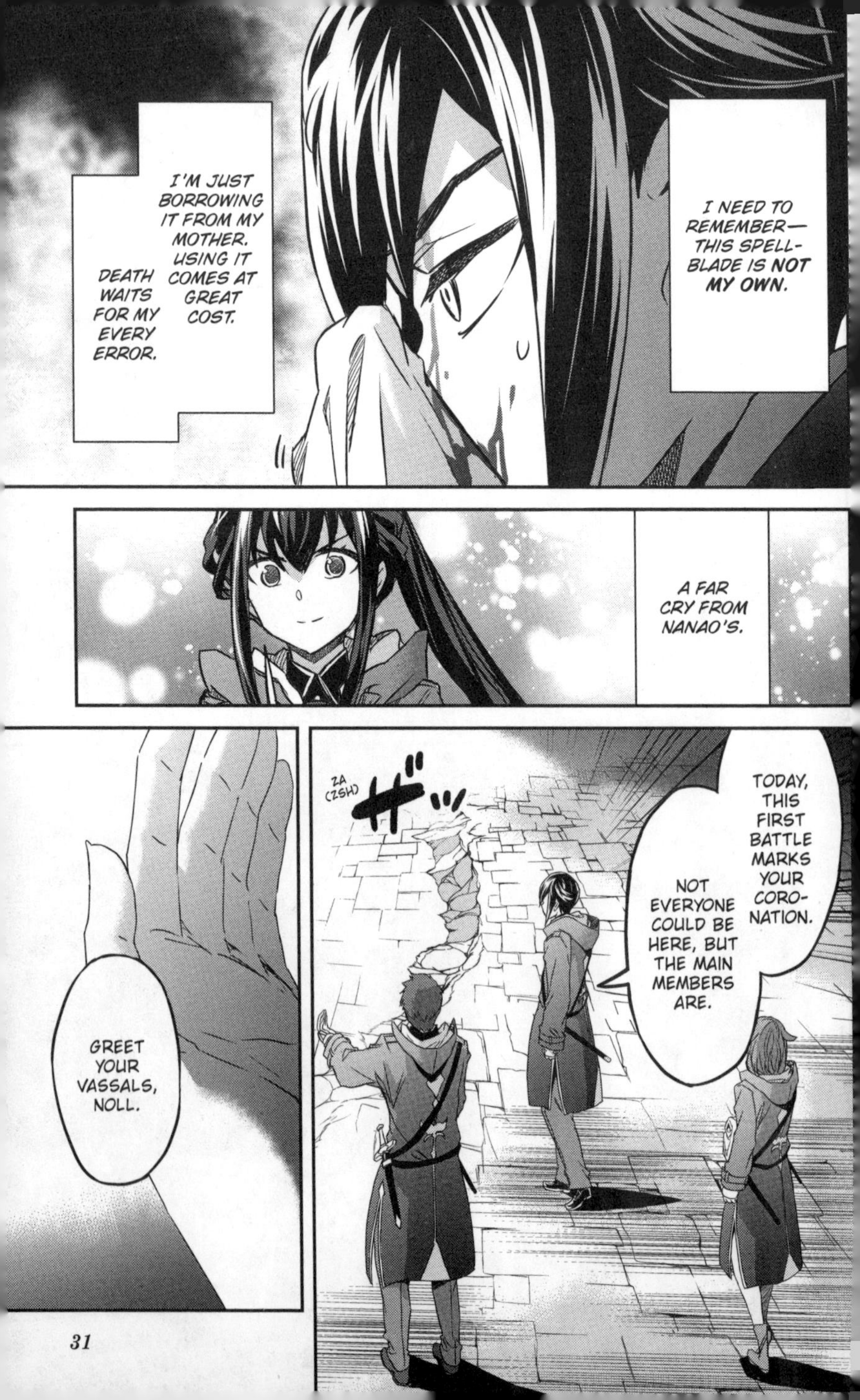
I NEED TO REMEMBER—THIS SPELL-BLADE IS **NOT MY OWN.**
I'M JUST BORROWING IT FROM MY MOTHER. USING IT COMES AT GREAT COST.
DEATH WAITS FOR MY EVERY ERROR.
A FAR CRY FROM NANAO'S.
TODAY, THIS FIRST BATTLE MARKS YOUR CORO-NATION.
NOT EVERYONE COULD BE HERE, BUT THE MAIN MEMBERS ARE.
ZA (ZSH)
GREET YOUR VASSALS, NOLL.

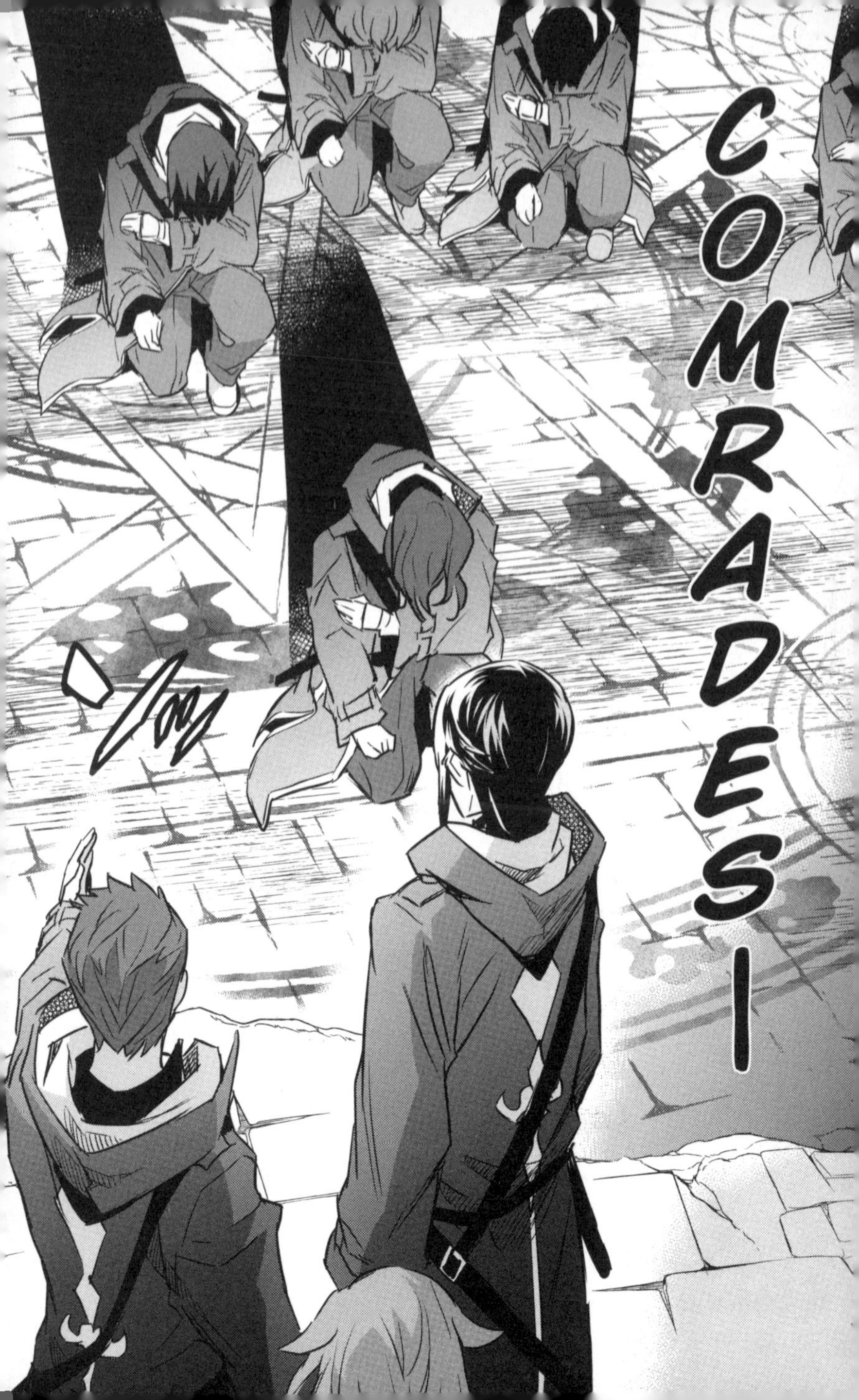
COMRADES!

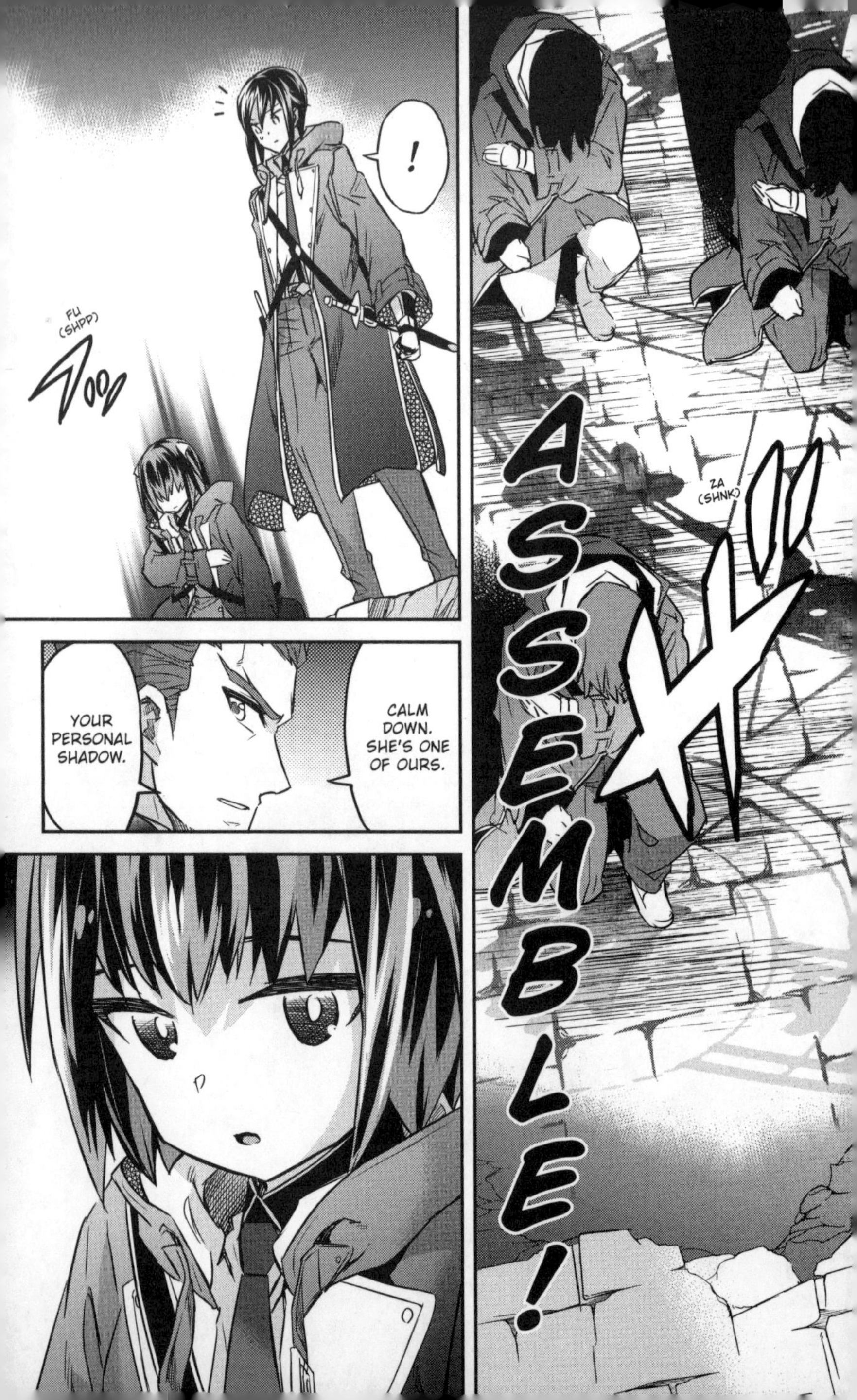
ZA (SHNK)
ASSEMBLE!
!
FU (SHPP)
CALM DOWN. SHE'S ONE OF OURS.
YOUR PERSONAL SHADOW.

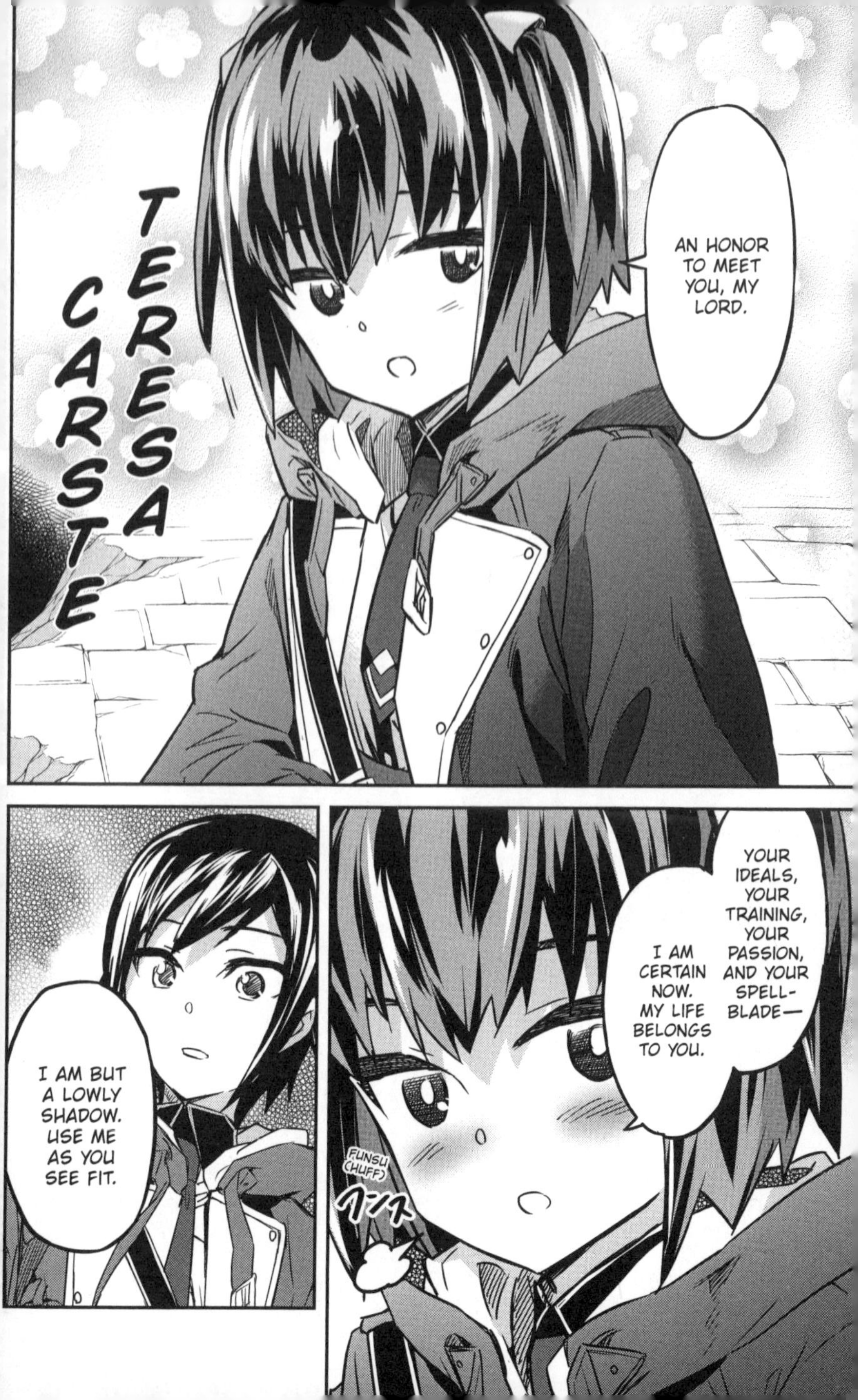
AN HONOR TO MEET YOU, MY LORD.
TERESA CARSTE
YOUR IDEALS, YOUR TRAINING, YOUR PASSION, AND YOUR SPELL-BLADE—
I AM CERTAIN NOW. MY LIFE BELONGS TO YOU.
FUNSU (HUFF)
I AM BUT A LOWLY SHADOW. USE ME AS YOU SEE FIT.

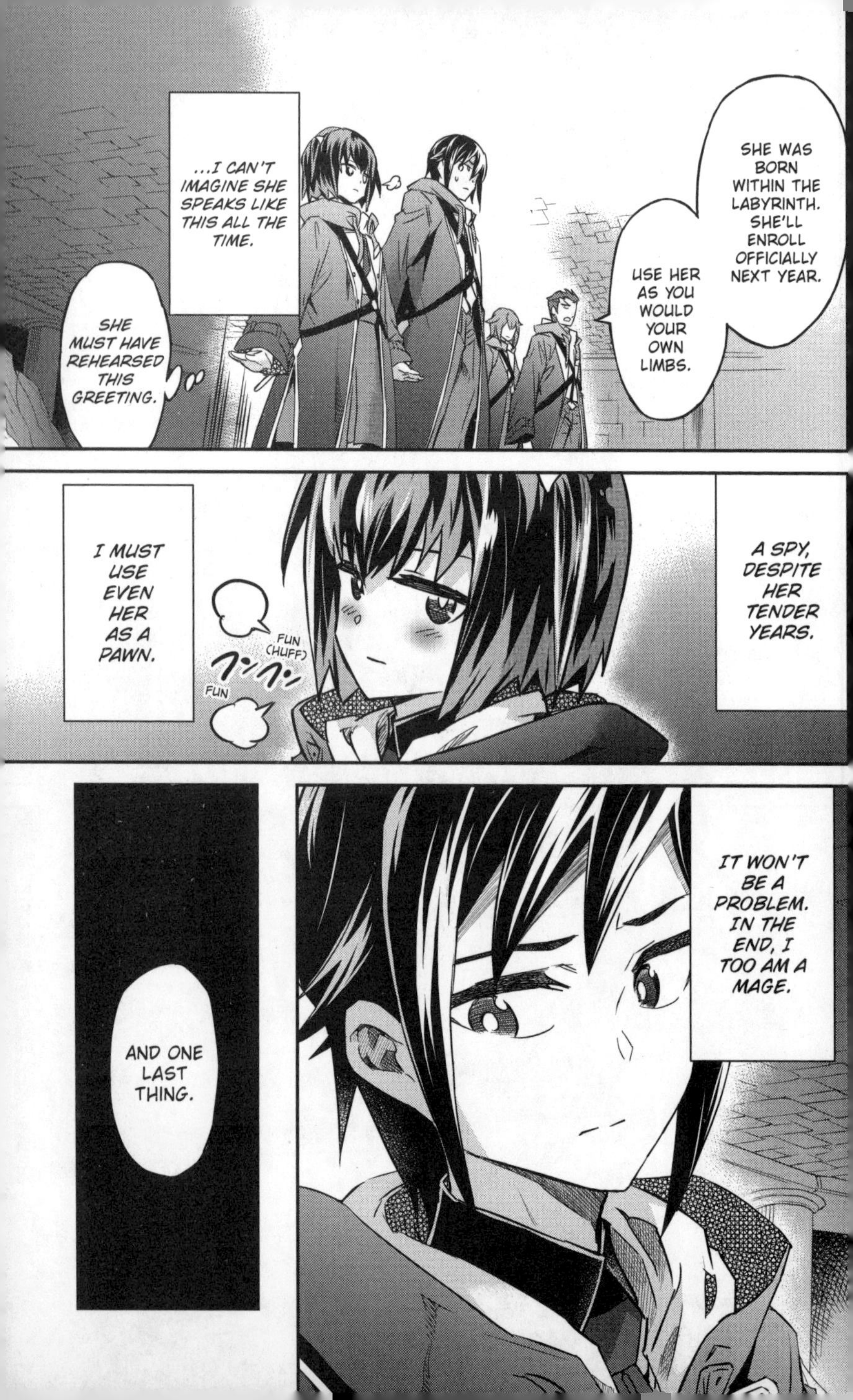
SHE WAS BORN WITHIN THE LABYRINTH. SHE'LL ENROLL OFFICIALLY NEXT YEAR.
USE HER AS YOU WOULD YOUR OWN LIMBS.
...I CAN'T IMAGINE SHE SPEAKS LIKE THIS ALL THE TIME.
SHE MUST HAVE REHEARSED THIS GREETING.
A SPY, DESPITE HER TENDER YEARS.
FUN (HUFF)
FUN
I MUST USE EVEN HER AS A PAWN.
IT WON'T BE A PROBLEM. IN THE END, I TOO AM A MAGE.
AND ONE LAST THING.

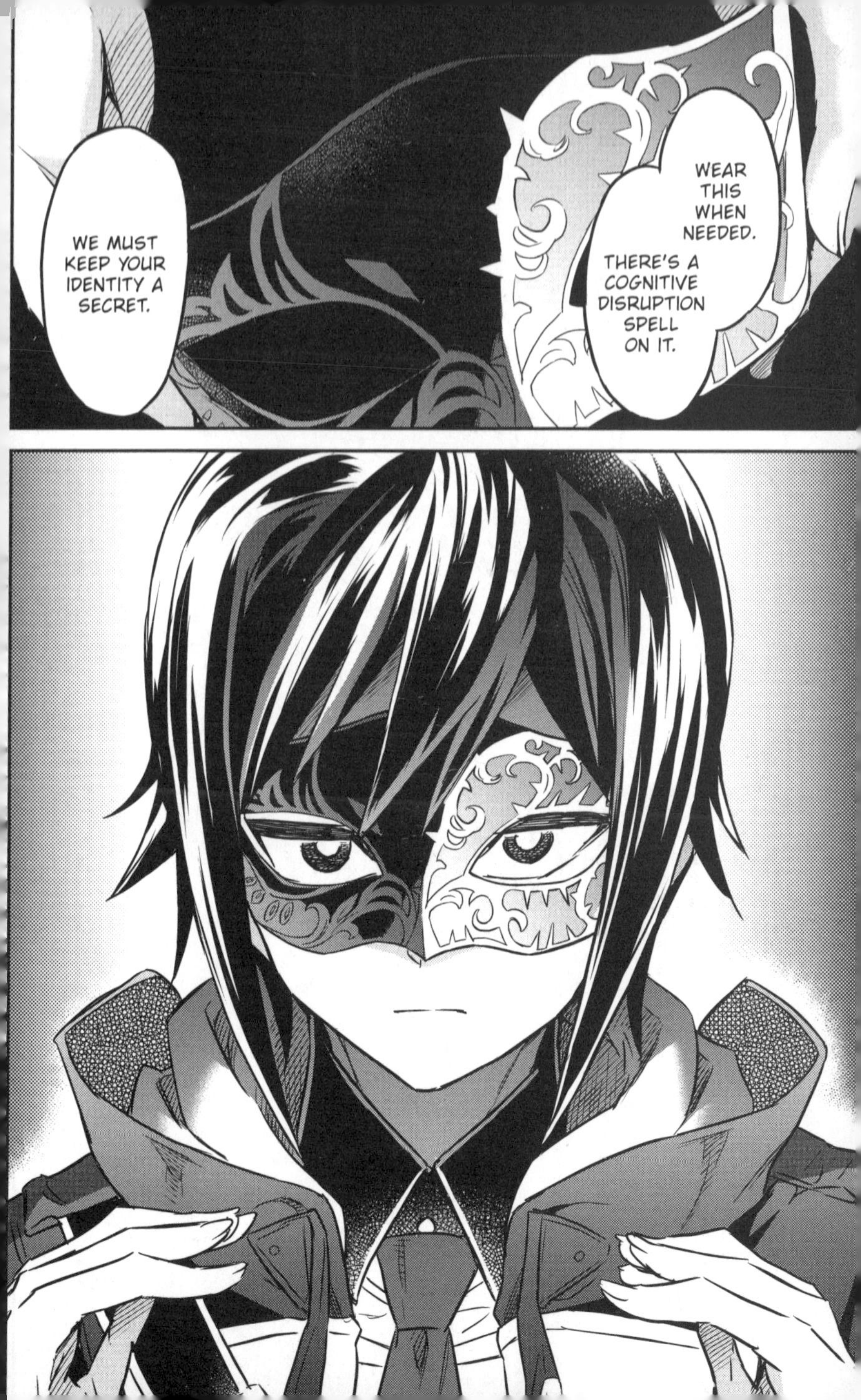
WEAR THIS WHEN NEEDED.
THERE'S A COGNITIVE DISRUPTION SPELL ON IT.
WE MUST KEEP YOUR IDENTITY A SECRET.

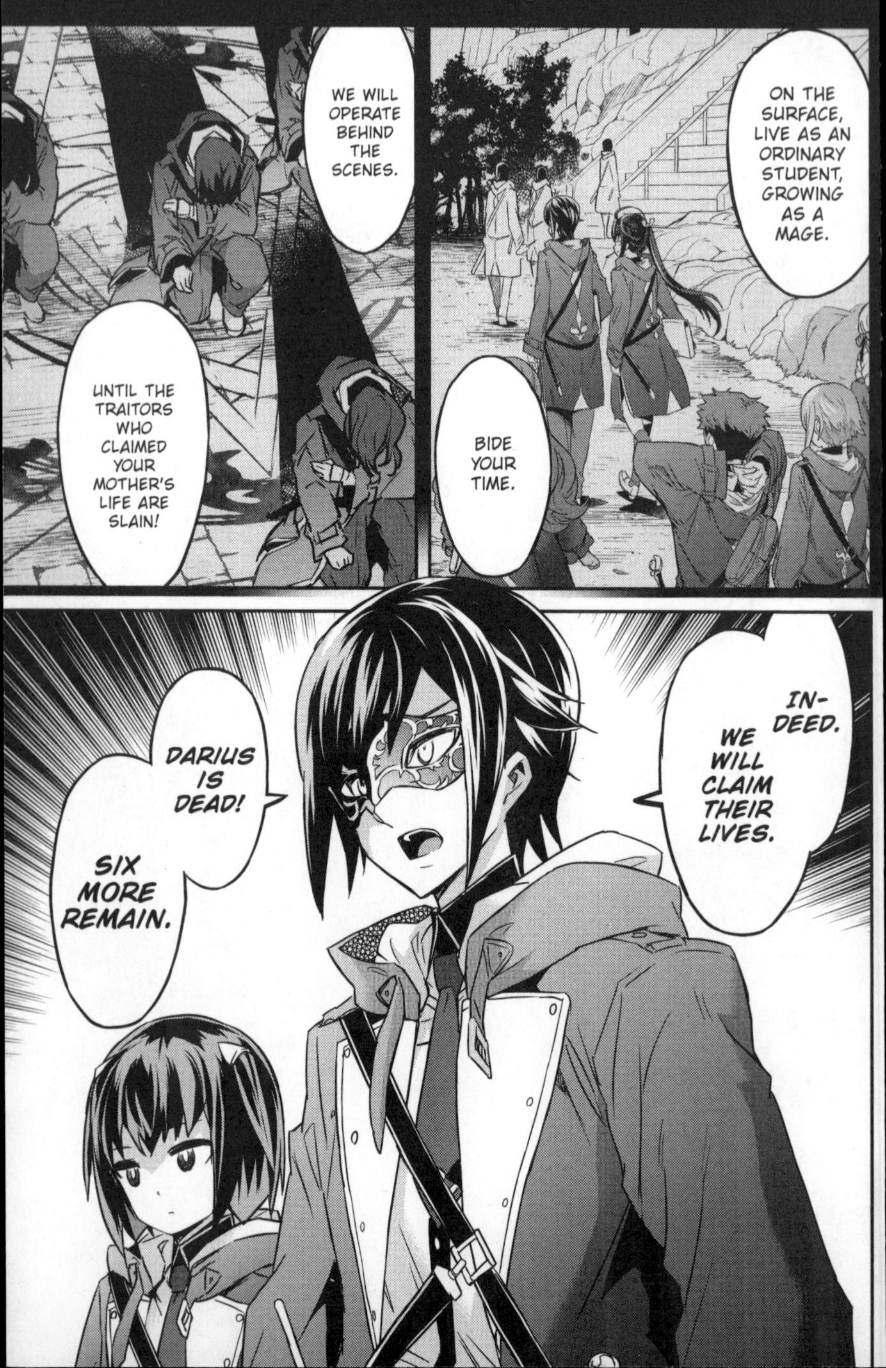
ON THE SURFACE, LIVE AS AN ORDINARY STUDENT, GROWING AS A MAGE.
BIDE YOUR TIME.
WE WILL OPERATE BEHIND THE SCENES.
UNTIL THE TRAITORS WHO CLAIMED YOUR MOTHER'S LIFE ARE SLAIN!
IN-DEED.
WE WILL CLAIM THEIR LIVES.
DARIUS IS DEAD!
SIX MORE REMAIN.

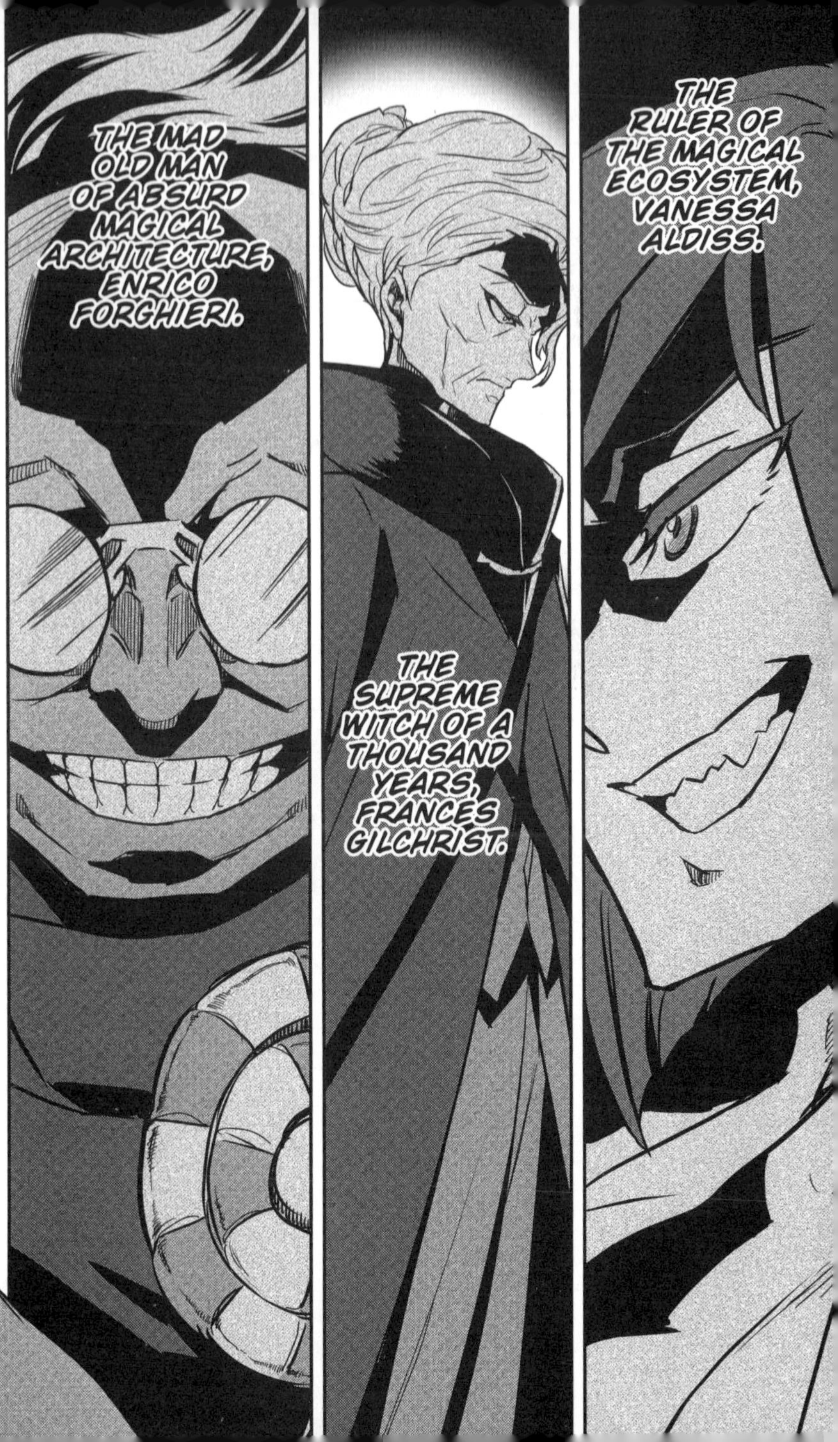
THE RULER OF THE MAGICAL ECOSYSTEM, VANESSA ALDISS.
THE SUPREME WITCH OF A THOUSAND YEARS, FRANCES GILCHRIST.
THE MAD OLD MAN OF ABSURD MAGICAL ARCHITECTURE, ENRICO FORGHIERI.

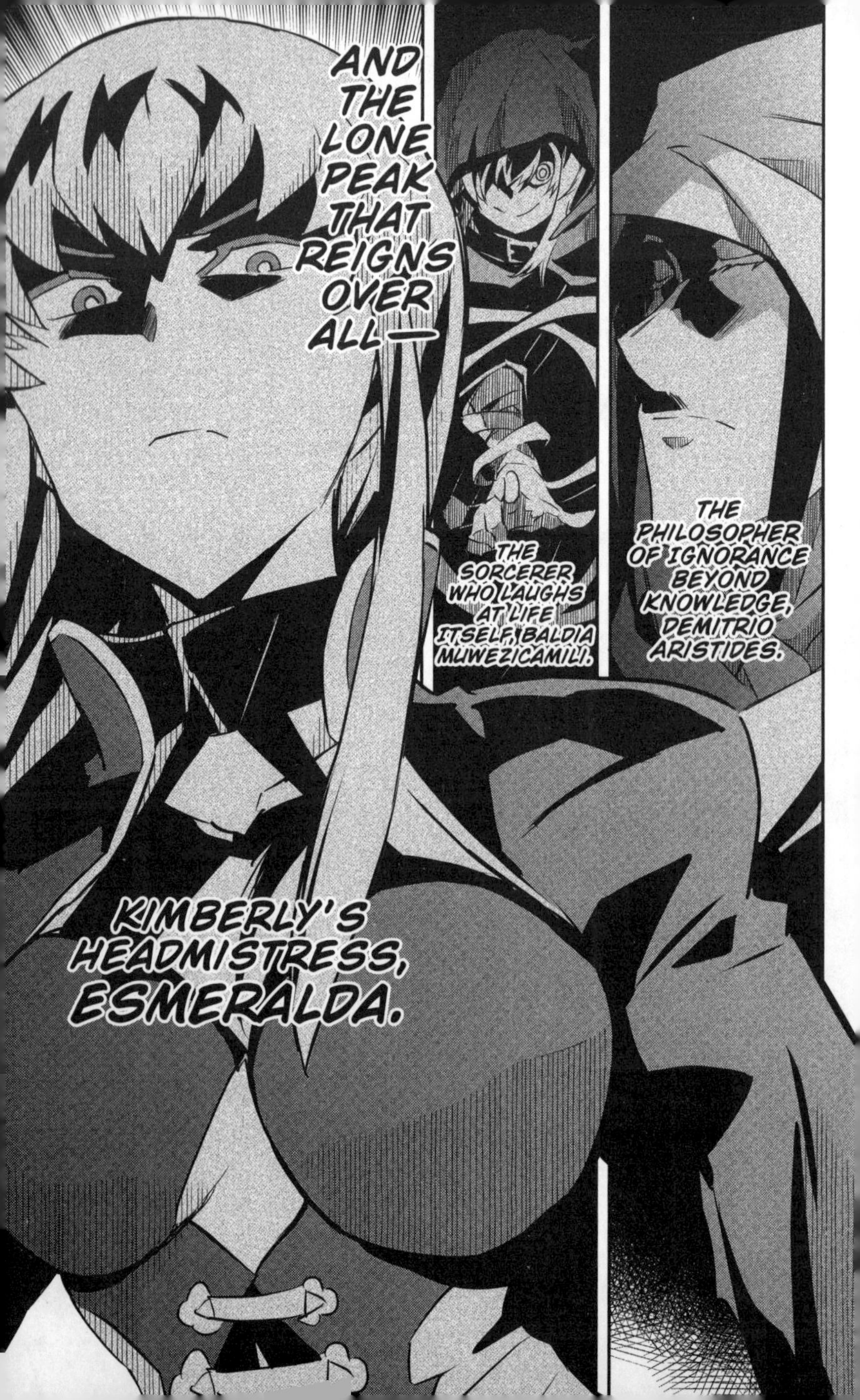
THE PHILOSOPHER OF IGNORANCE BEYOND KNOWLEDGE, DEMITRIO ARISTIDES.
THE SORCERER WHO LAUGHS AT LIFE ITSELF, BALDIA MUWEZICAMILI.
AND THE LONE PEAK THAT REIGNS OVER ALL—
KIMBERLY'S HEADMISTRESS, ESMERALDA.

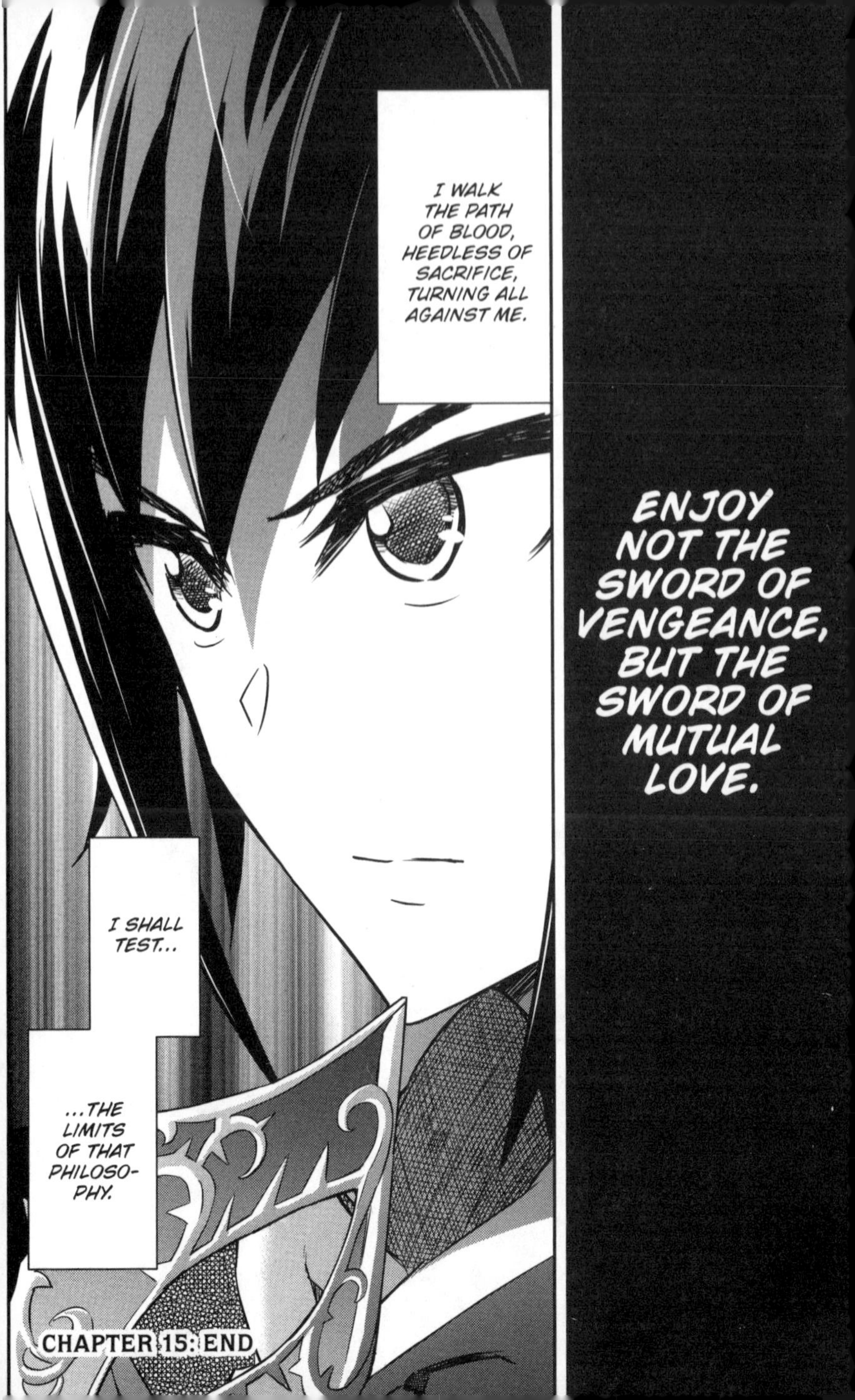
ENJOY NOT THE SWORD OF VENGEANCE, BUT THE SWORD OF MUTUAL LOVE.
I WALK THE PATH OF BLOOD, HEEDLESS OF SACRIFICE, TURNING ALL AGAINST ME.
I SHALL TEST...
...THE LIMITS OF THAT PHILOSO-PHY.
CHAPTER 15: END

Reign of the Seven Spellblades

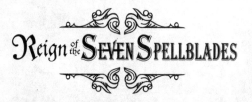

Reign of the Seven Spellblades

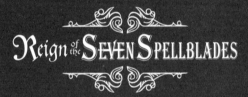

CHAPTER 16: BROOM RIDE

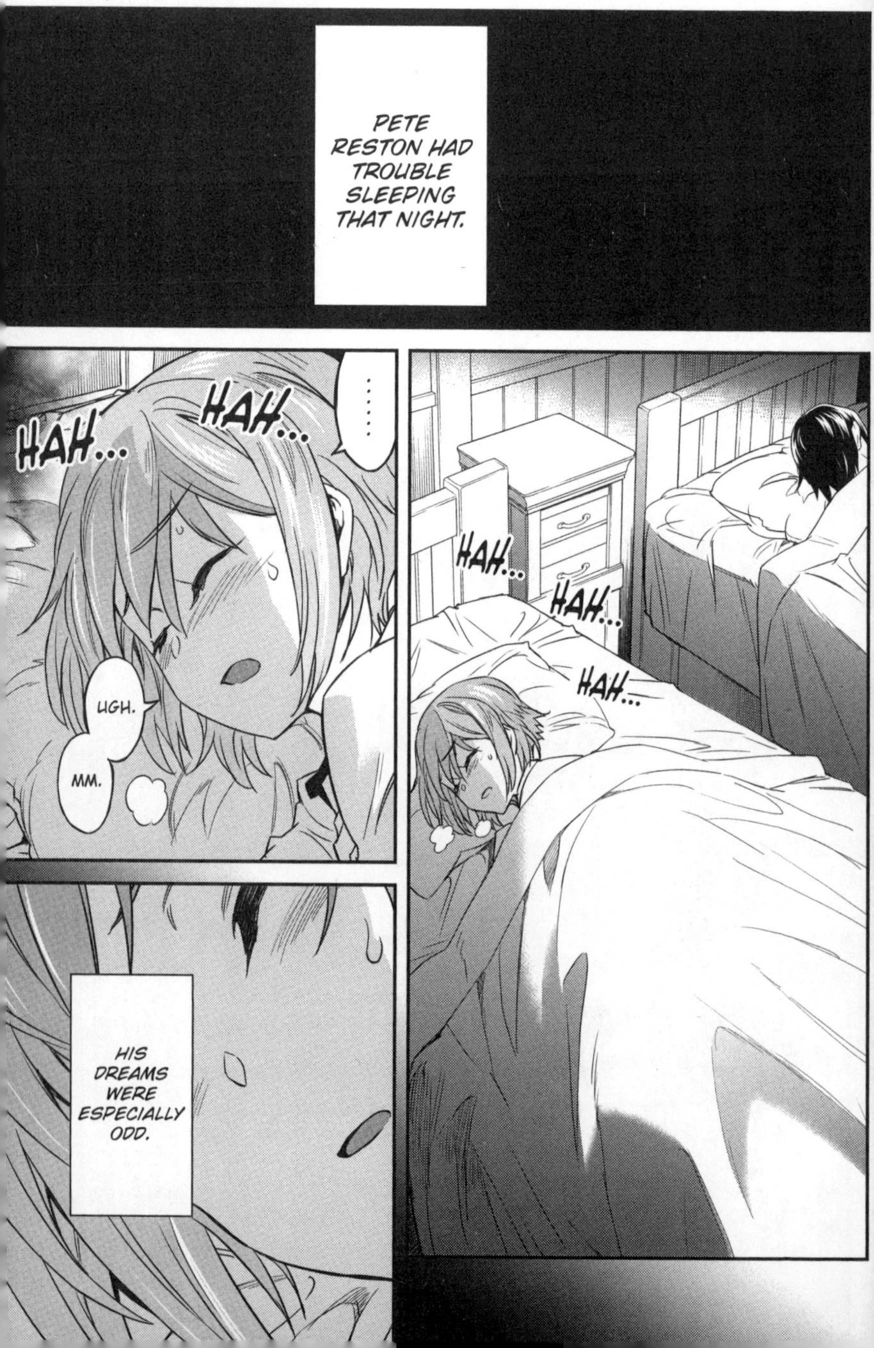
PETE RESTON HAD TROUBLE SLEEPING THAT NIGHT.
HAH...
HAH...
HAH...
......
HAH...
HAH...
UGH.
MM.
HIS DREAMS WERE ESPECIALLY ODD.

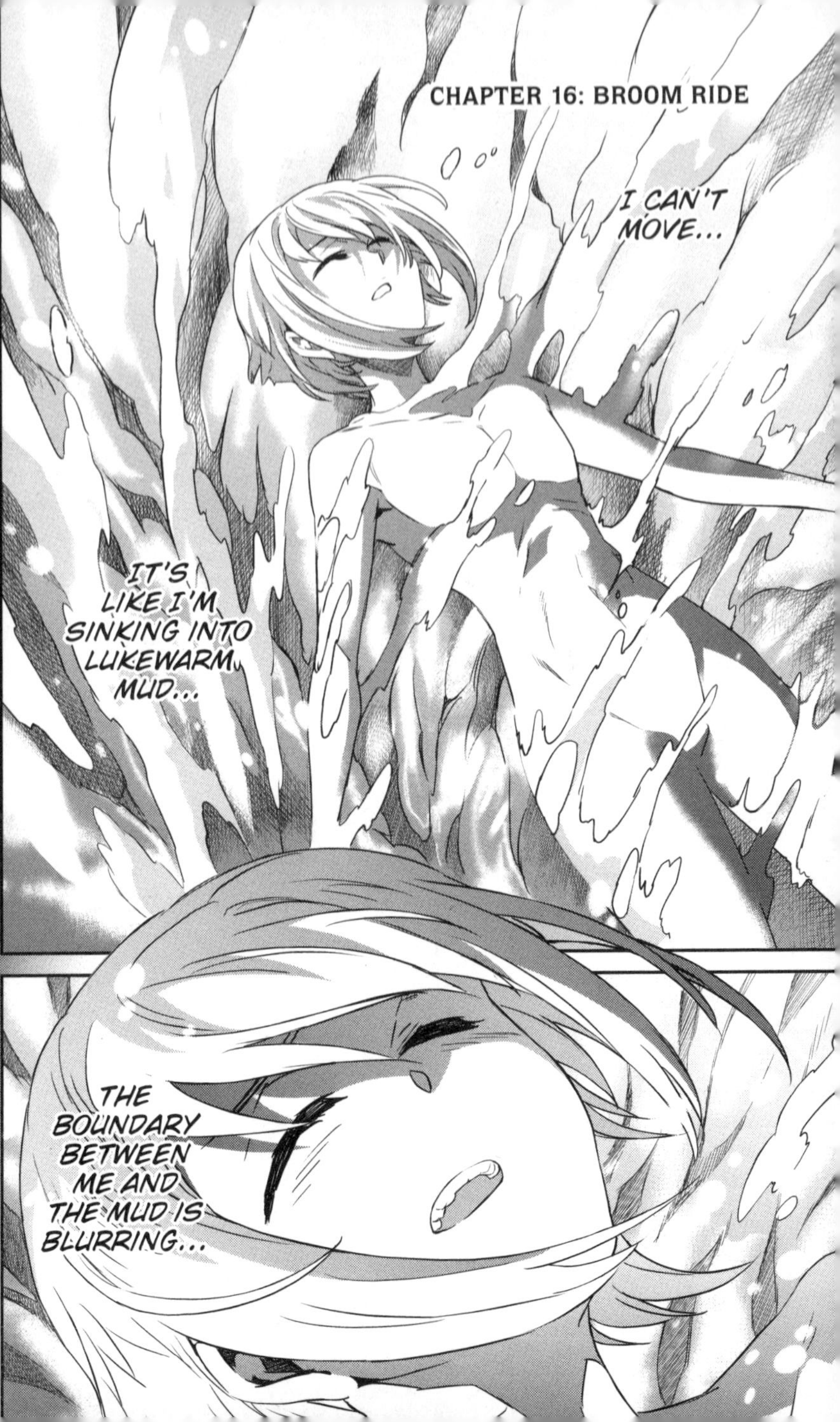
CHAPTER 16: BROOM RIDE
I CAN'T MOVE...
IT'S LIKE I'M SINKING INTO LUKEWARM MUD...
THE BOUNDARY BETWEEN ME AND THE MUD IS BLURRING...

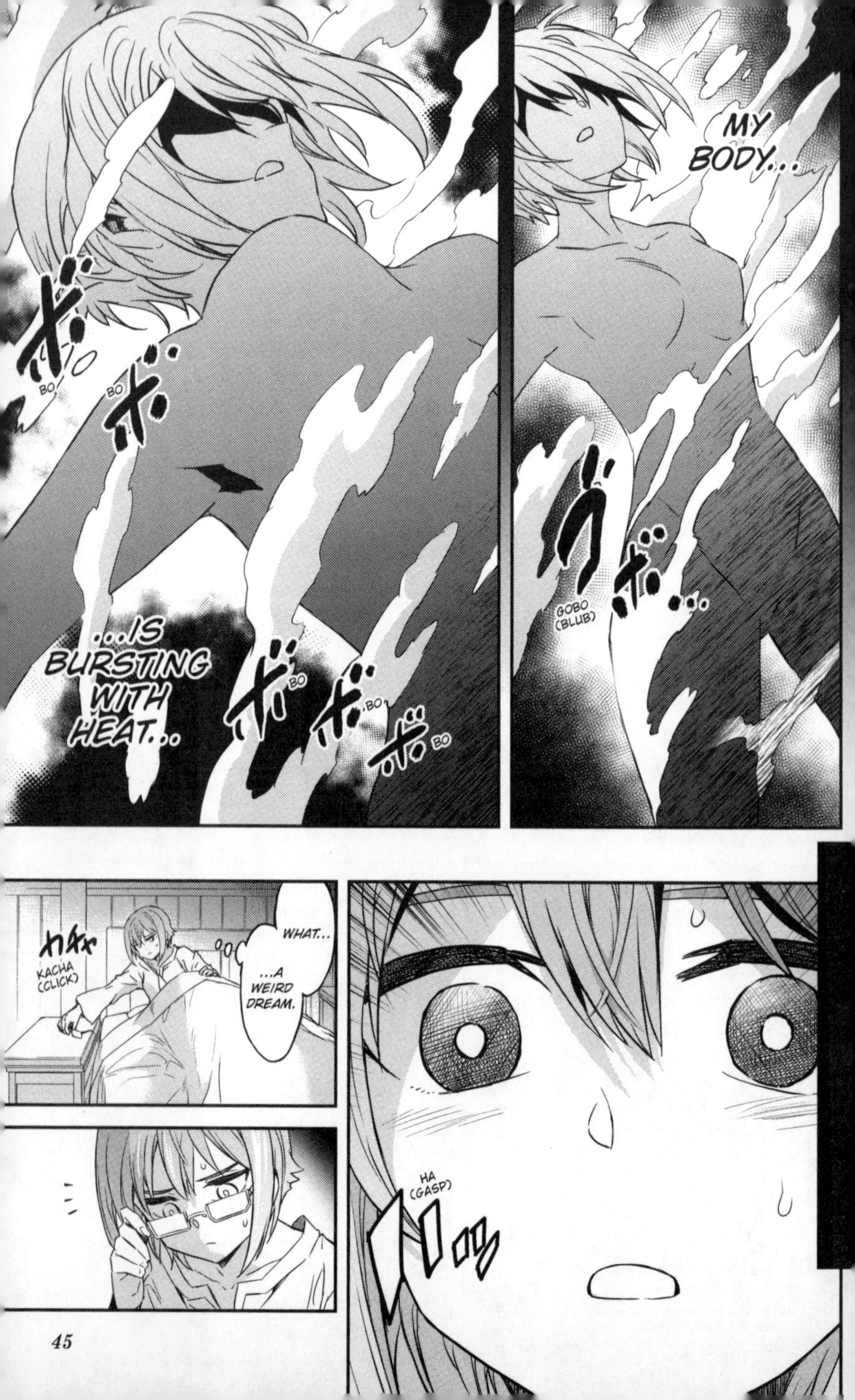

MY BODY...
GOBO (BLUB)
BO
BO
...IS BURSTING WITH HEAT...
BO
BO
BO
HA (GASP)
KACHA (CLICK)
WHAT...
...A WEIRD DREAM.

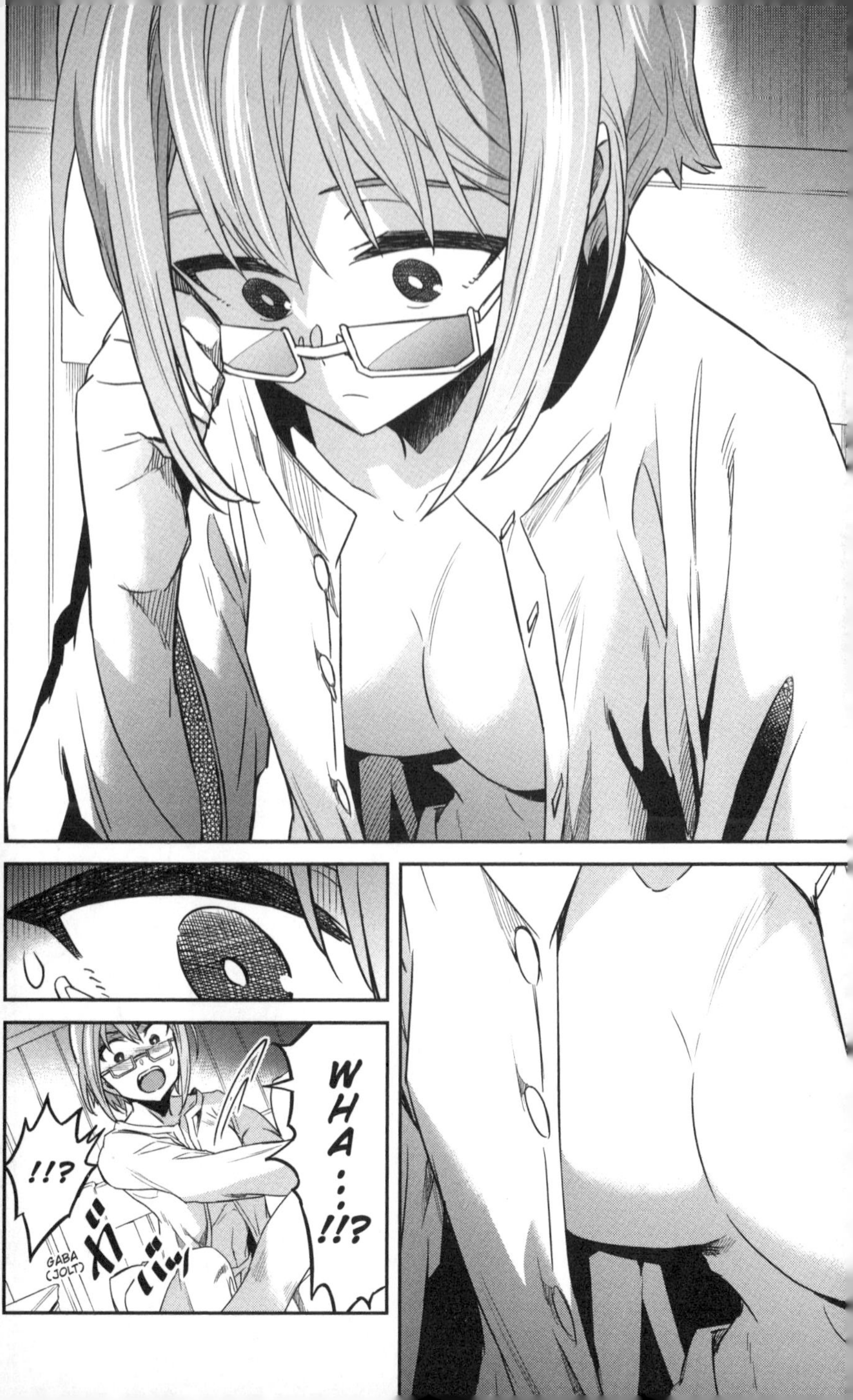
WHA...!!?
!!?
GABA
(JOLT)

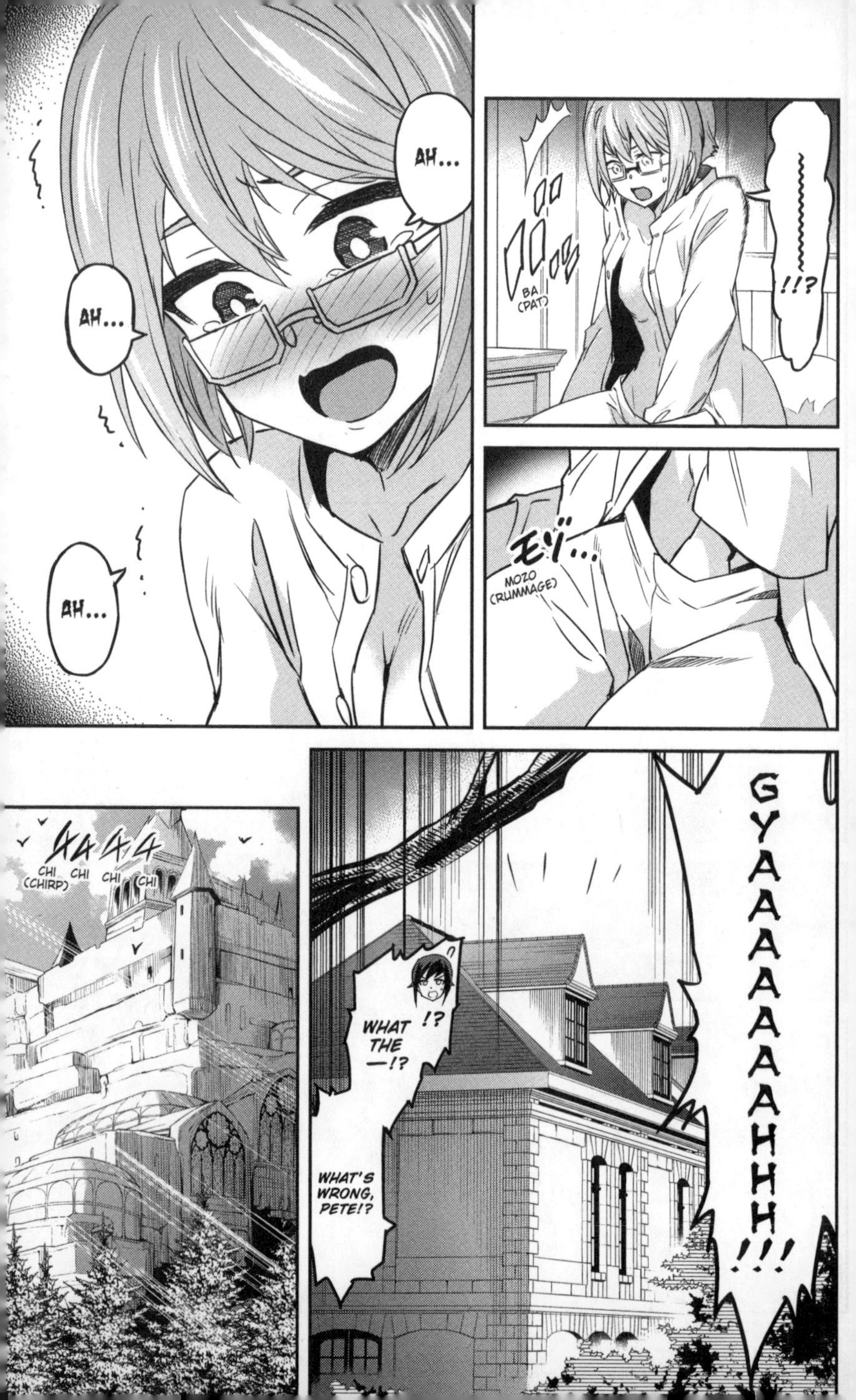

!!?
BA (PAT)
モゾ…
MOZO (RUMMAGE)
AH...
AH...
AH...
GYAAAAAAAAHHH!!!
WHAT THE—!?
!?
WHAT'S WRONG, PETE!?
CHI (CHIRP) CHI CHI CHI

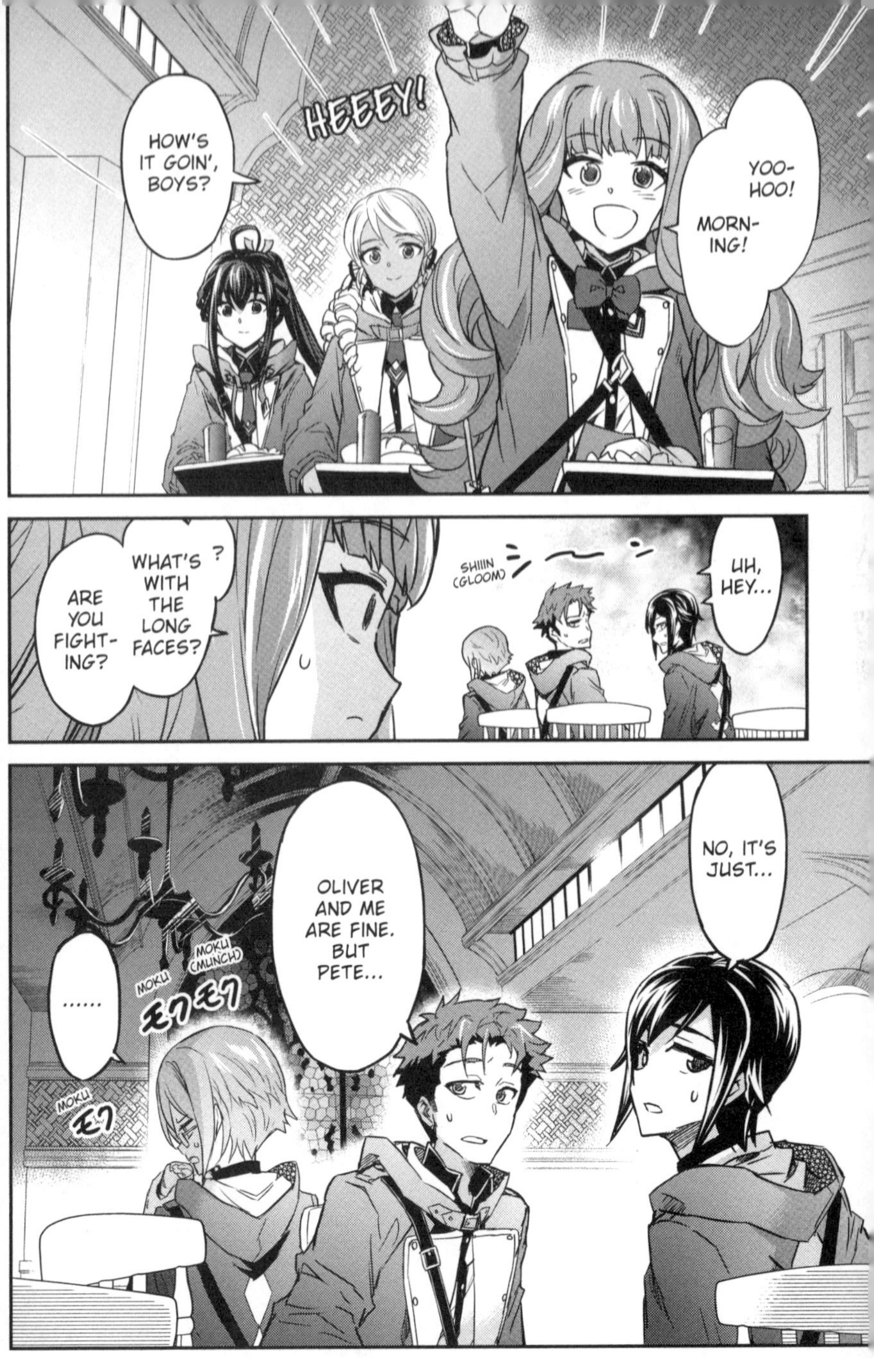
YOO-HOO! MORNING!
HEEEY!
HOW'S IT GOIN', BOYS?
UH, HEY...
SHIIIN (GLOOM)
WHAT'S WITH THE LONG FACES?
ARE YOU FIGHTING?
NO, IT'S JUST...
OLIVER AND ME ARE FINE. BUT PETE...
MOKU (MUNCH)
MOKU
......
MOKU

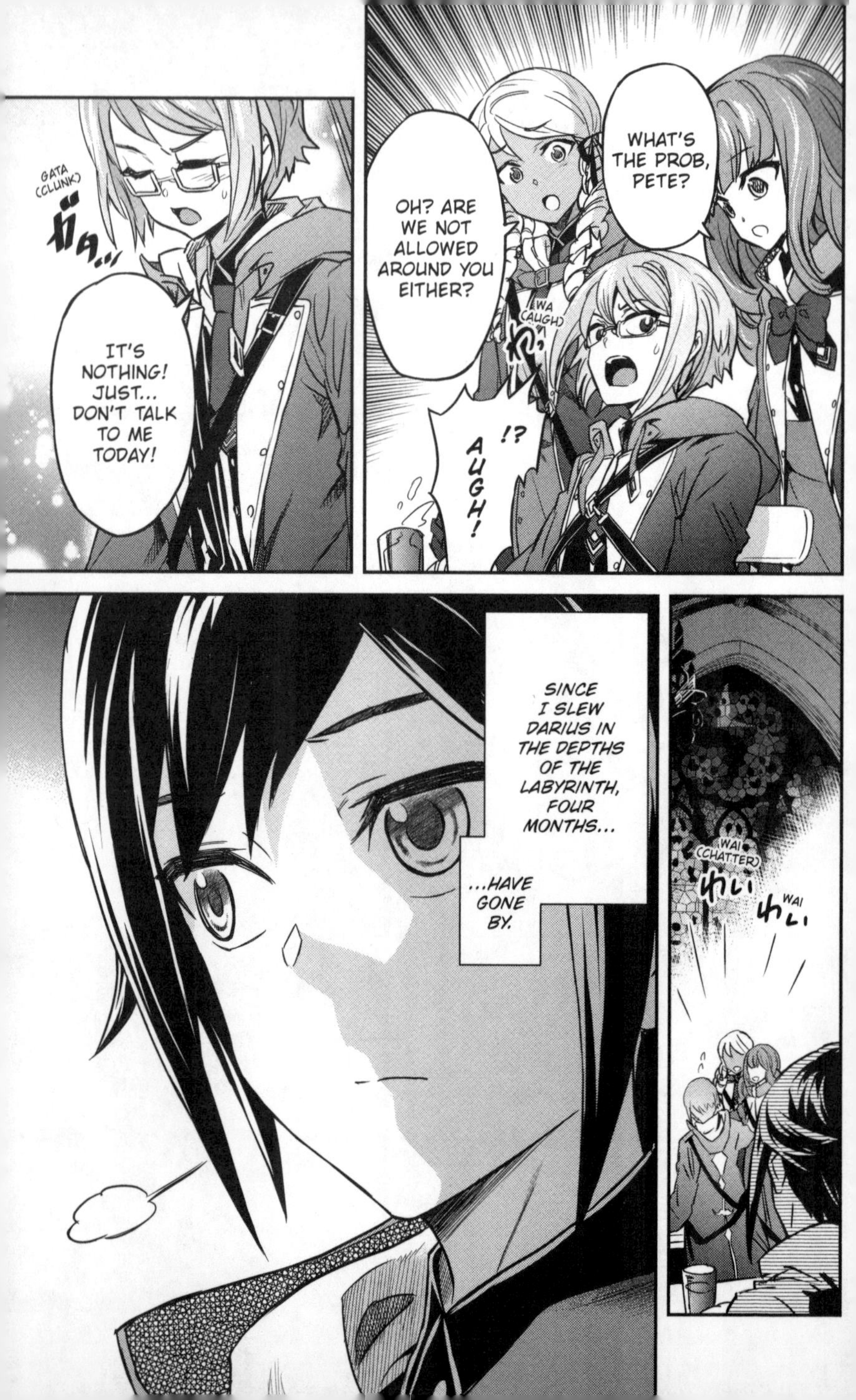
WHAT'S THE PROB, PETE?
OH? ARE WE NOT ALLOWED AROUND YOU EITHER?
WA (AUGH)
!?
AUGH!
GATA (CLUNK)
IT'S NOTHING! JUST... DON'T TALK TO ME TODAY!
WAI (CHATTER)
WAI
SINCE I SLEW DARIUS IN THE DEPTHS OF THE LABYRINTH, FOUR MONTHS...
...HAVE GONE BY.

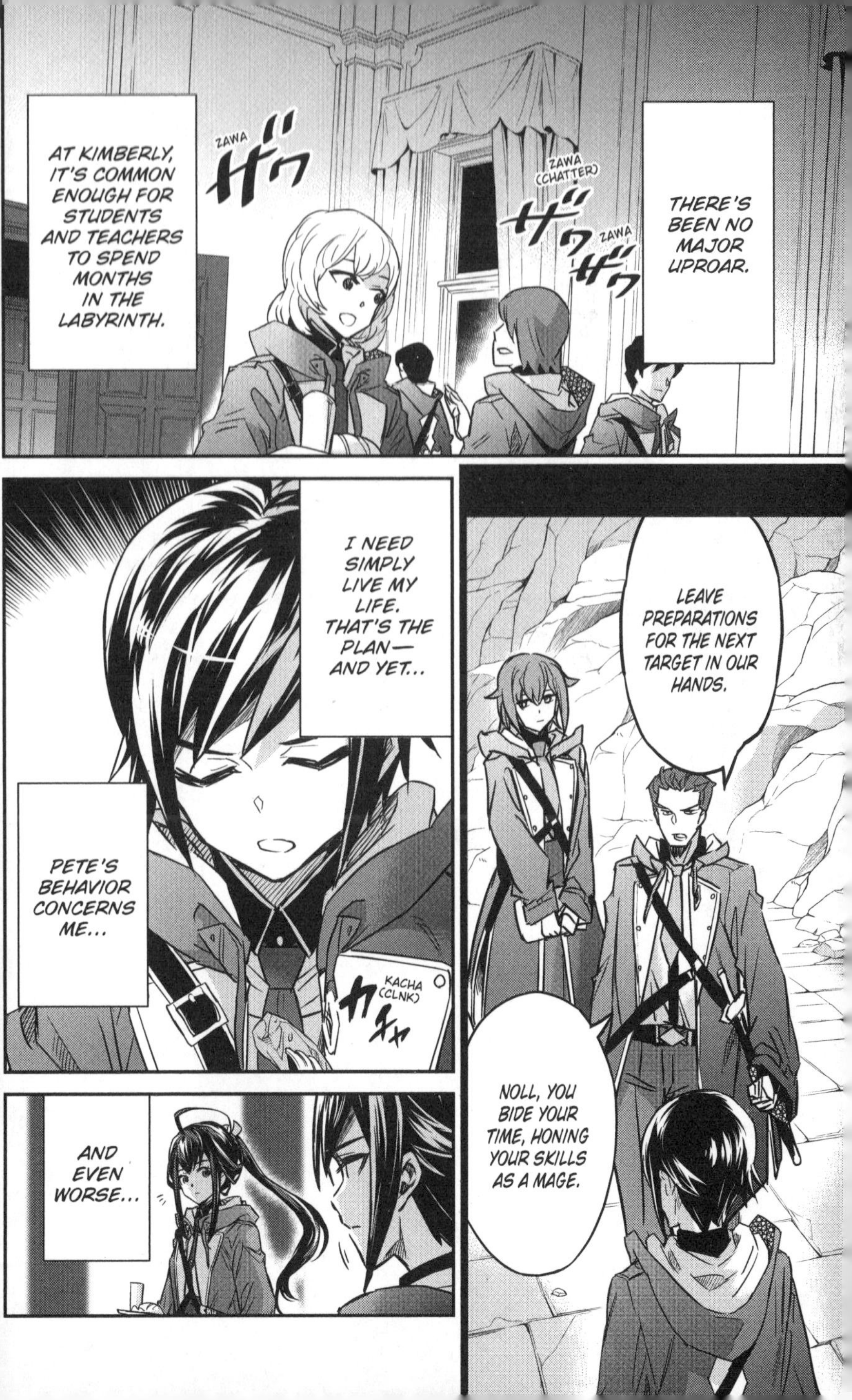

AT KIMBERLY, IT'S COMMON ENOUGH FOR STUDENTS AND TEACHERS TO SPEND MONTHS IN THE LABYRINTH.
ZAWA
ザワ
ZAWA (CHATTER)
ザワ
ZAWA
ザワ
THERE'S BEEN NO MAJOR UPROAR.
LEAVE PREPARATIONS FOR THE NEXT TARGET IN OUR HANDS.
NOLL, YOU BIDE YOUR TIME, HONING YOUR SKILLS AS A MAGE.
I NEED SIMPLY LIVE MY LIFE. THAT'S THE PLAN—AND YET...
PETE'S BEHAVIOR CONCERNS ME...
KACHA (CLNK)
カチャ
AND EVEN WORSE...

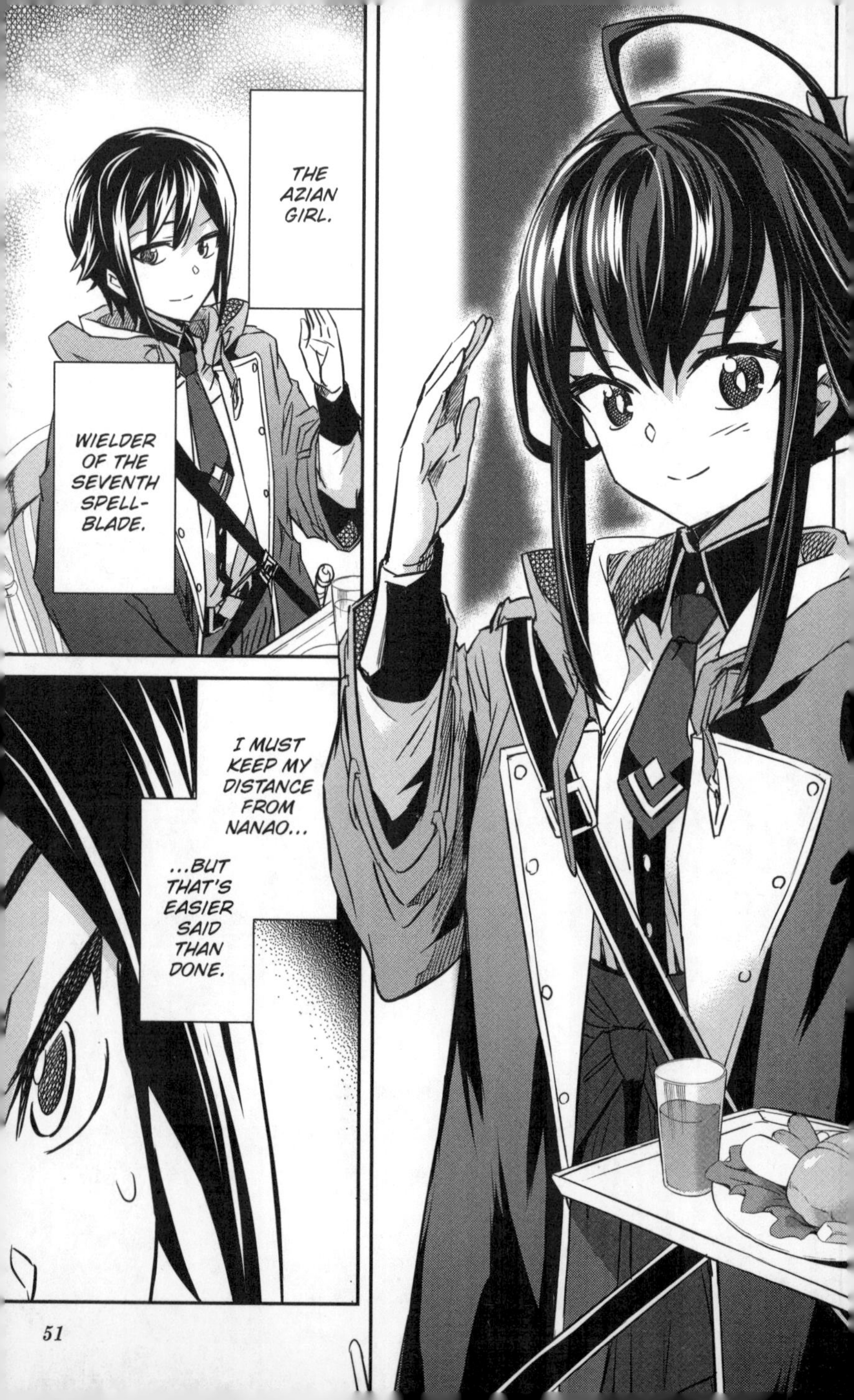
THE AZIAN GIRL.
WIELDER OF THE SEVENTH SPELL-BLADE.
I MUST KEEP MY DISTANCE FROM NANAO...
...BUT THAT'S EASIER SAID THAN DONE.

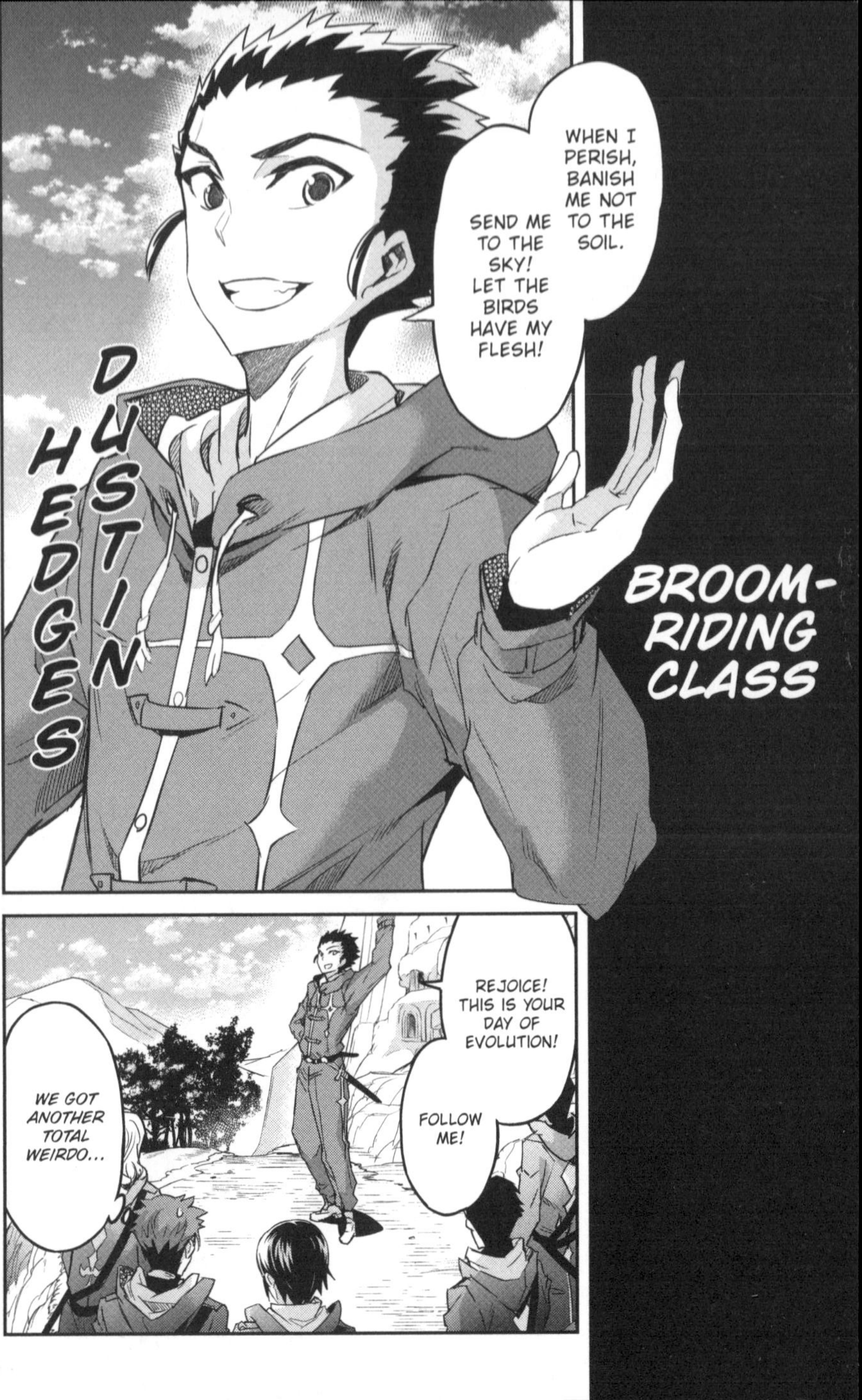
WHEN I PERISH, BANISH ME NOT TO THE SOIL.
SEND ME TO THE SKY! LET THE BIRDS HAVE MY FLESH!
BROOM-RIDING CLASS
DUSTIN HEDGES
REJOICE! THIS IS YOUR DAY OF EVOLUTION!
FOLLOW ME!
WE GOT ANOTHER TOTAL WEIRDO...

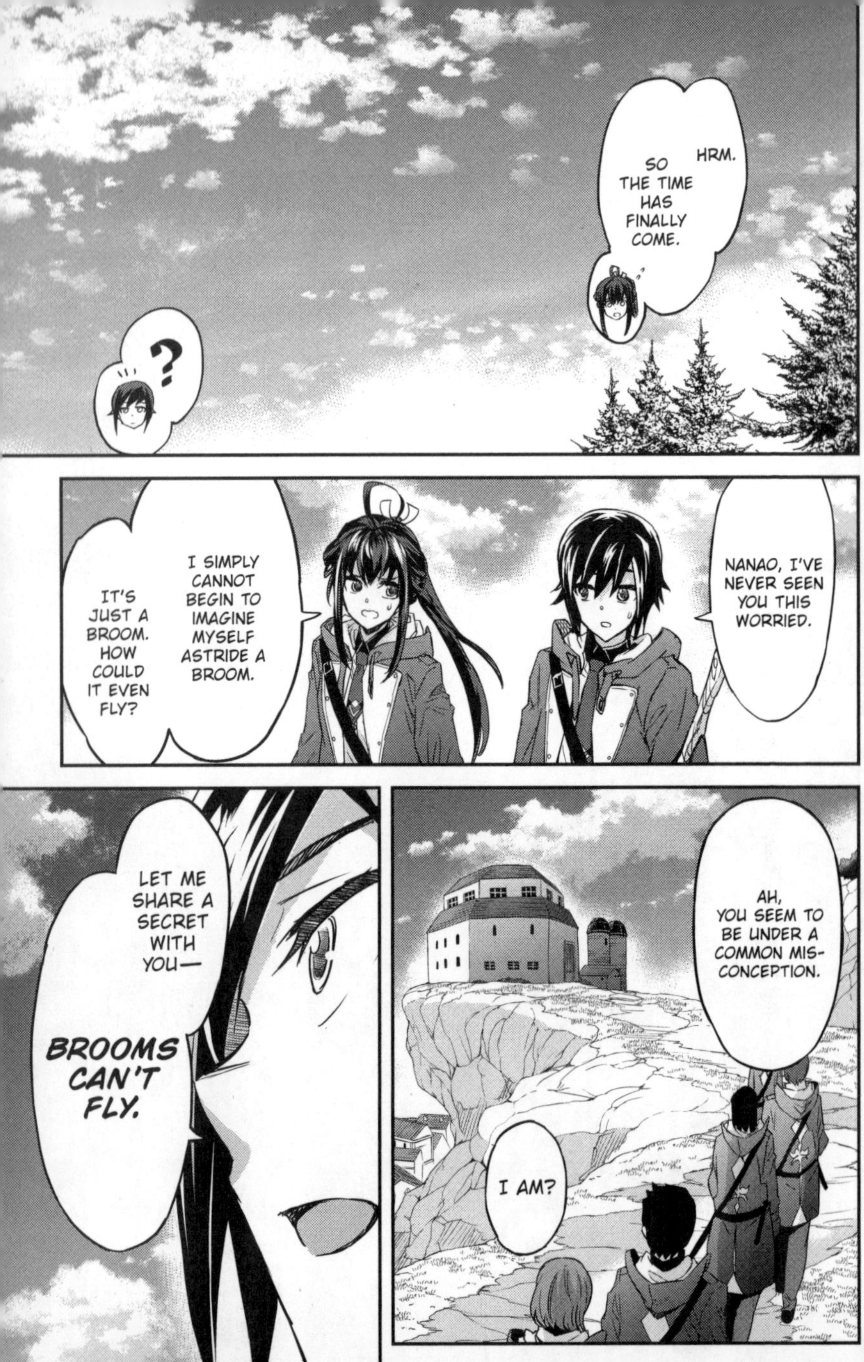
HRM.
SO THE TIME HAS FINALLY COME.
?
NANAO, I'VE NEVER SEEN YOU THIS WORRIED.
I SIMPLY CANNOT BEGIN TO IMAGINE MYSELF ASTRIDE A BROOM.
IT'S JUST A BROOM. HOW COULD IT EVEN FLY?
AH, YOU SEEM TO BE UNDER A COMMON MIS-CONCEPTION.
I AM?
LET ME SHARE A SECRET WITH YOU—
BROOMS CAN'T FLY.

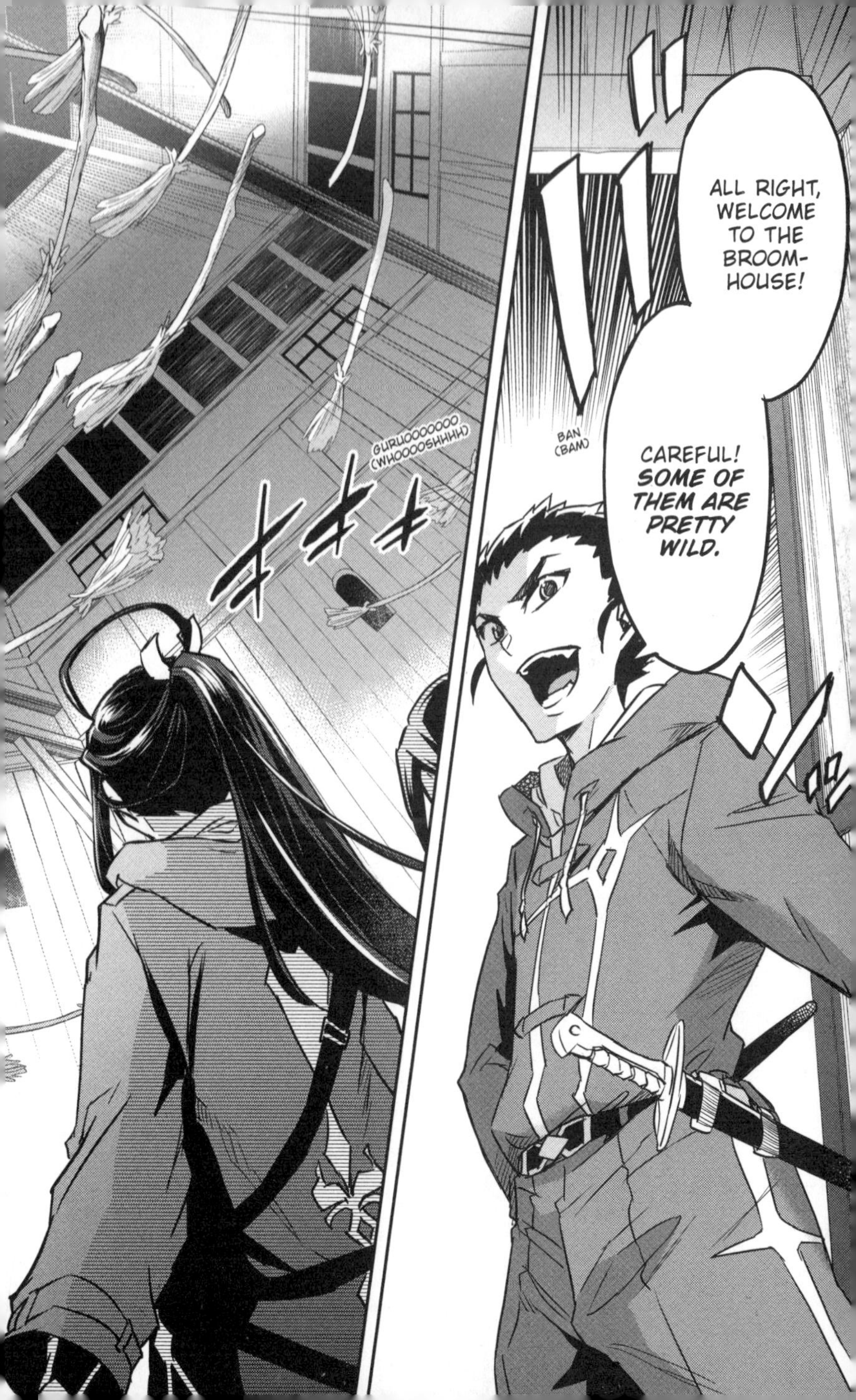
BAN
(BAM)
ALL RIGHT, WELCOME TO THE BROOM-HOUSE!
CAREFUL! SOME OF THEM ARE PRETTY WILD.
GURUOOOOOOOO
(WHOOOOSHHHH)

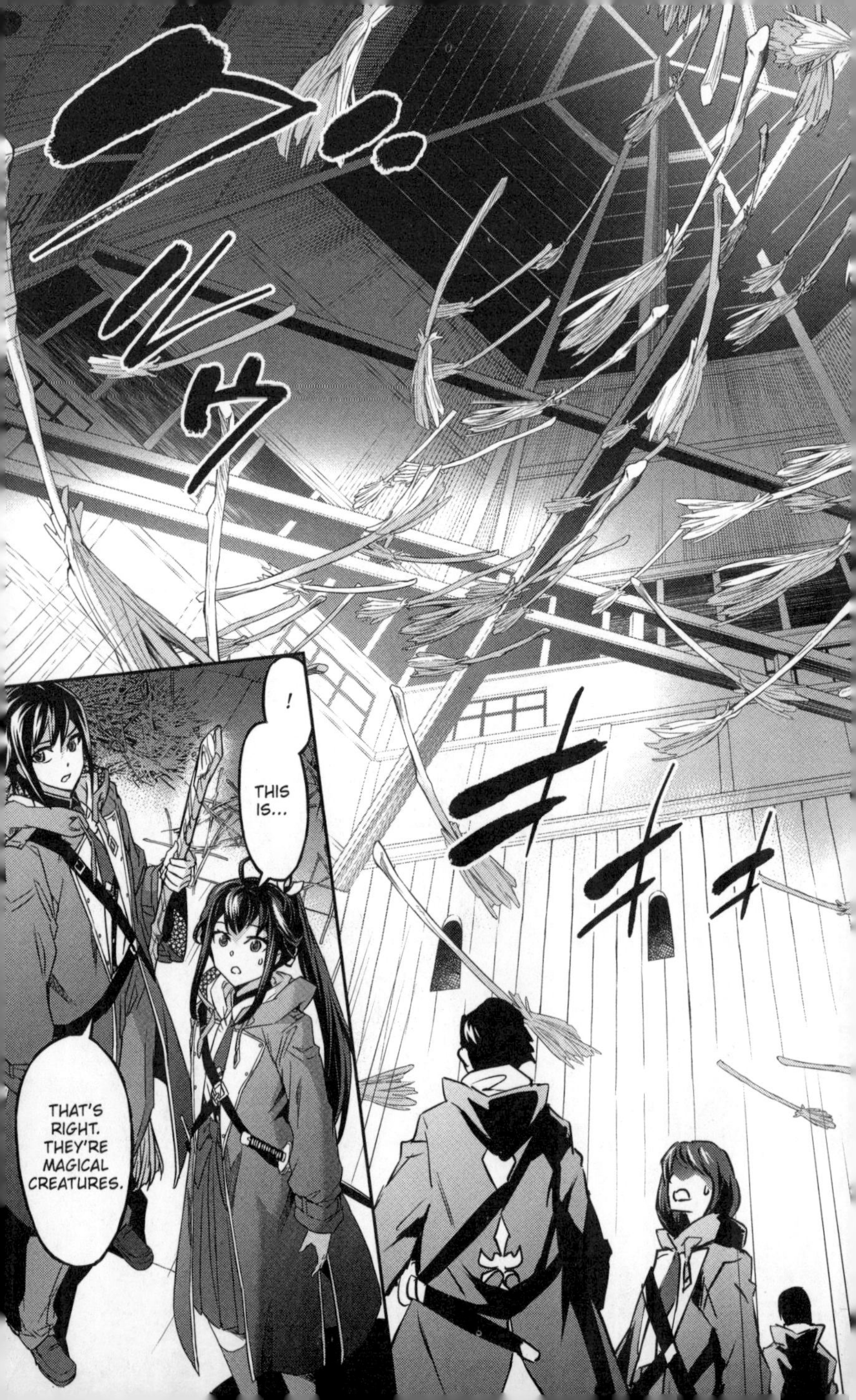
!
THIS IS...
THAT'S RIGHT. THEY'RE MAGICAL CREATURES.

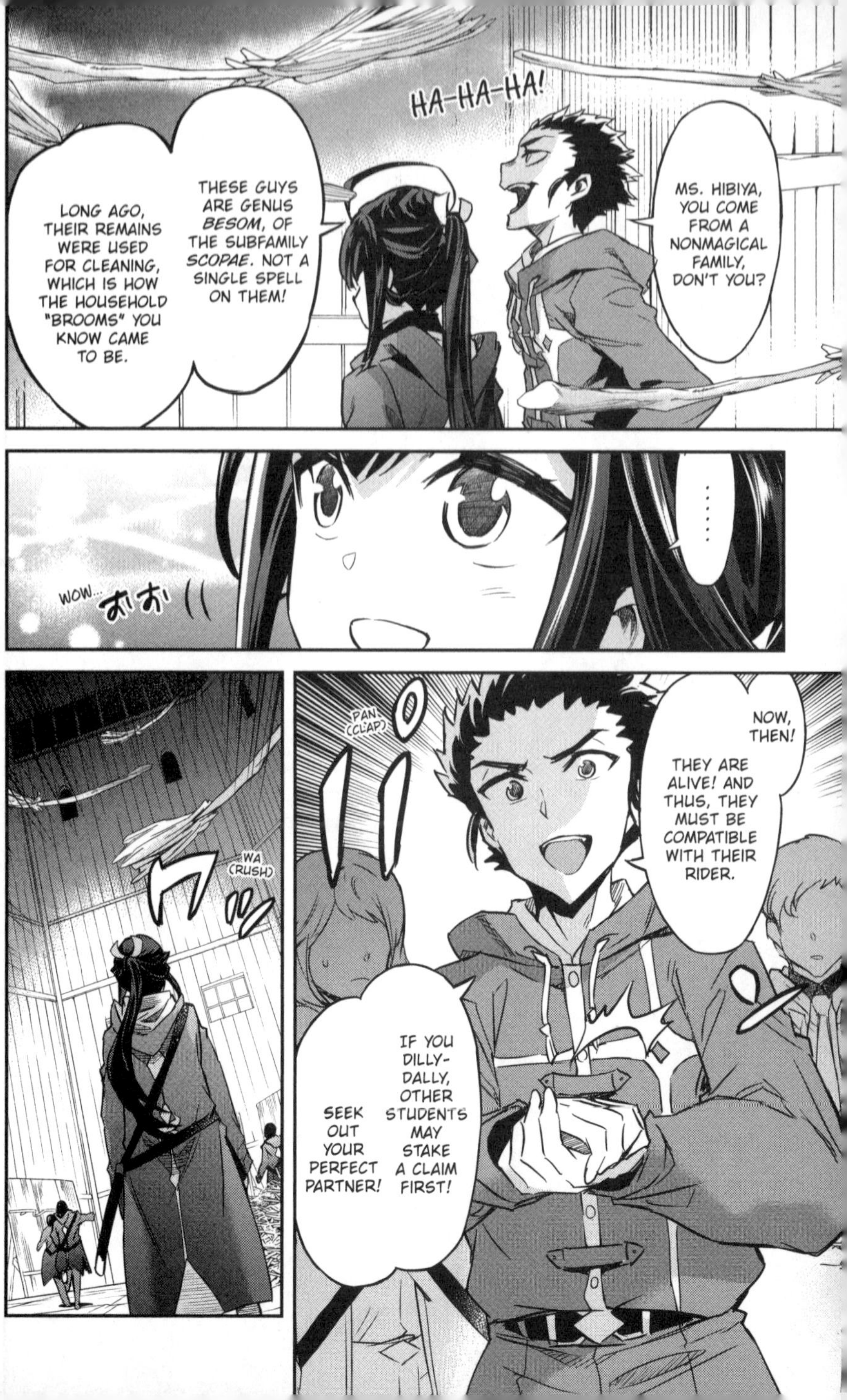
HA-HA-HA!
MS. HIBIYA, YOU COME FROM A NONMAGICAL FAMILY, DON'T YOU?
THESE GUYS ARE GENUS *BESOM*, OF THE SUBFAMILY *SCOPAE*. NOT A SINGLE SPELL ON THEM!
LONG AGO, THEIR REMAINS WERE USED FOR CLEANING, WHICH IS HOW THE HOUSEHOLD "BROOMS" YOU KNOW CAME TO BE.
......
WOW... おお
PAN (CLAP)
NOW, THEN!
THEY ARE ALIVE! AND THUS, THEY MUST BE COMPATIBLE WITH THEIR RIDER.
IF YOU DILLY-DALLY, OTHER STUDENTS MAY STAKE A CLAIM FIRST!
SEEK OUT YOUR PERFECT PARTNER!
WA (RUSH)

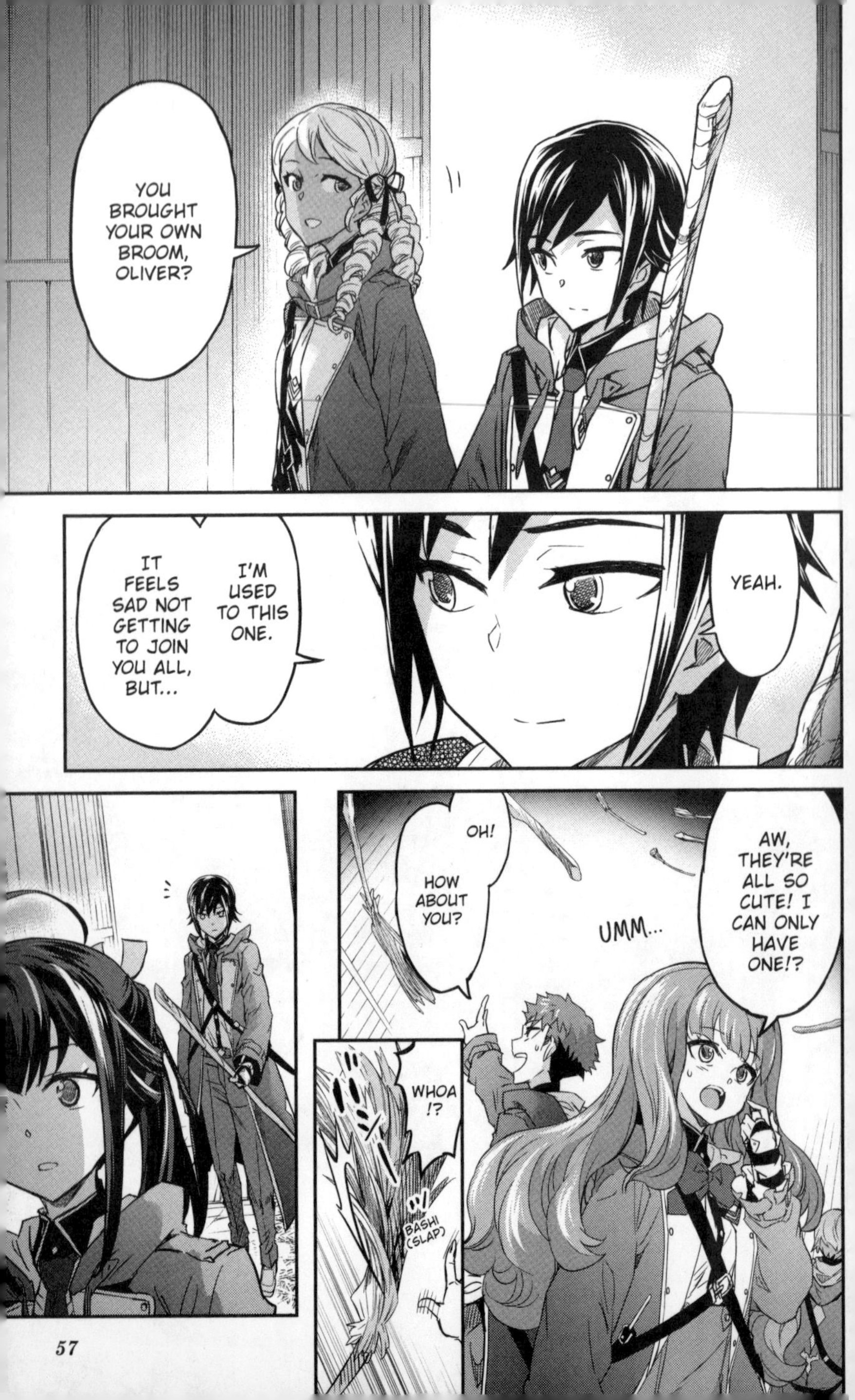
YOU BROUGHT YOUR OWN BROOM, OLIVER?
YEAH.
I'M USED TO THIS ONE.
IT FEELS SAD NOT GETTING TO JOIN YOU ALL, BUT...
AW, THEY'RE ALL SO CUTE! I CAN ONLY HAVE ONE!?
UMM...
OH!
HOW ABOUT YOU?
WHOA!?
BASHI (SLAP)

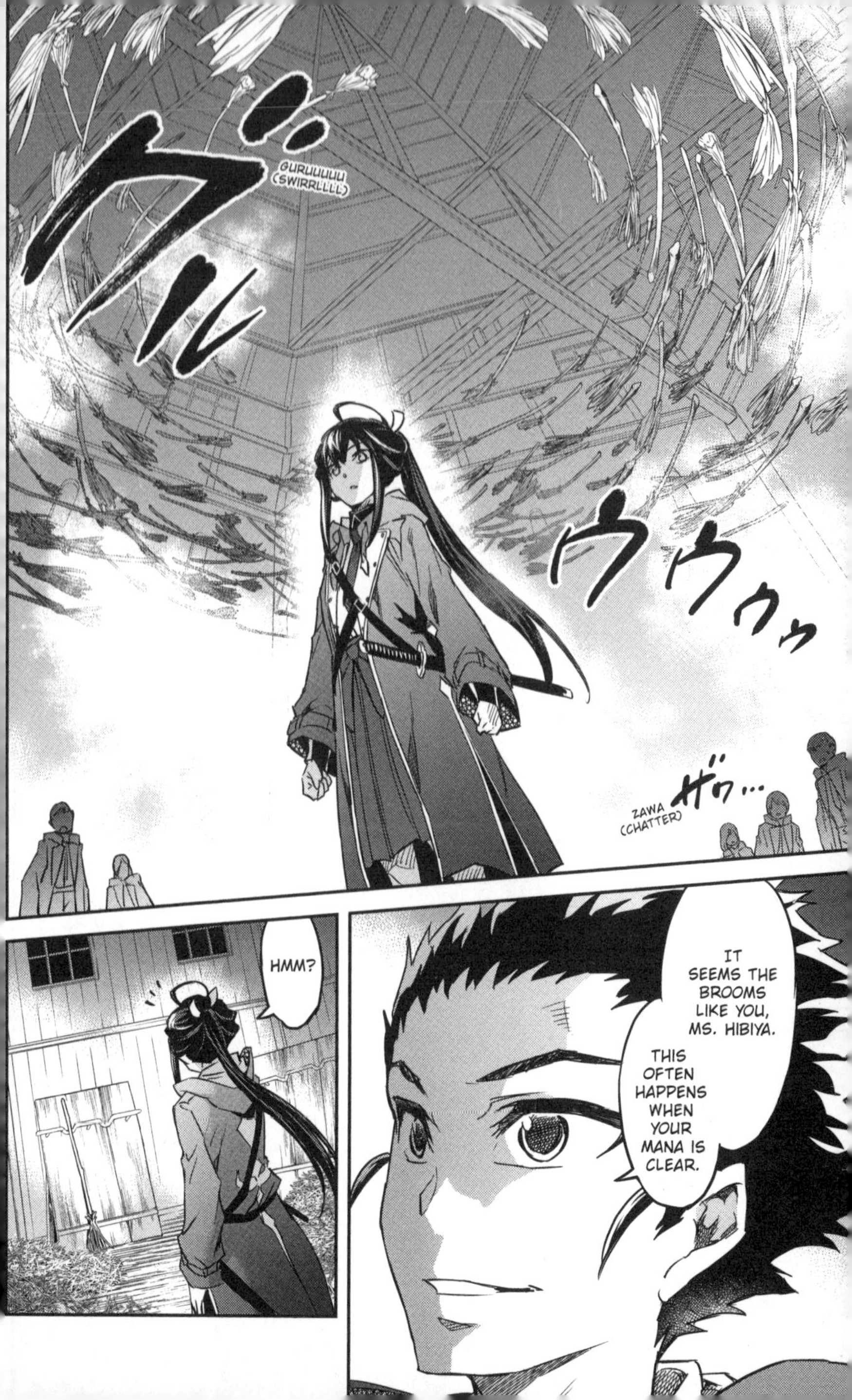
GURUUUUU
(SWIRRLLLL)
ZAWA
(CHATTER)
IT SEEMS THE BROOMS LIKE YOU, MS. HIBIYA.
THIS OFTEN HAPPENS WHEN YOUR MANA IS CLEAR.
HMM?

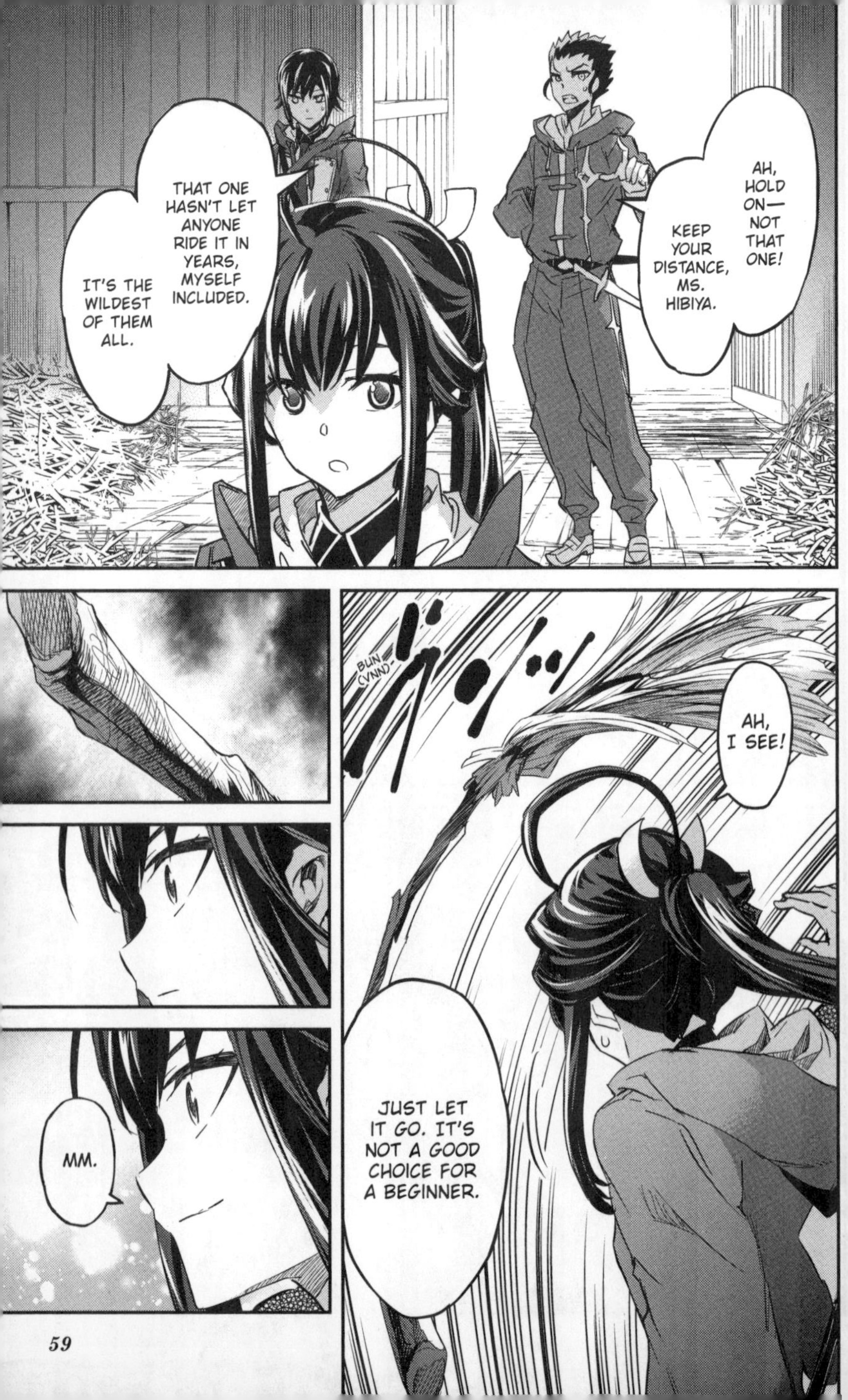
AH, HOLD ON— NOT THAT ONE!
KEEP YOUR DISTANCE, MS. HIBIYA.
THAT ONE HASN'T LET ANYONE RIDE IT IN YEARS, MYSELF INCLUDED.
IT'S THE WILDEST OF THEM ALL.
BUN (VNNN)
AH, I SEE!
JUST LET IT GO. IT'S NOT A GOOD CHOICE FOR A BEGINNER.
MM.

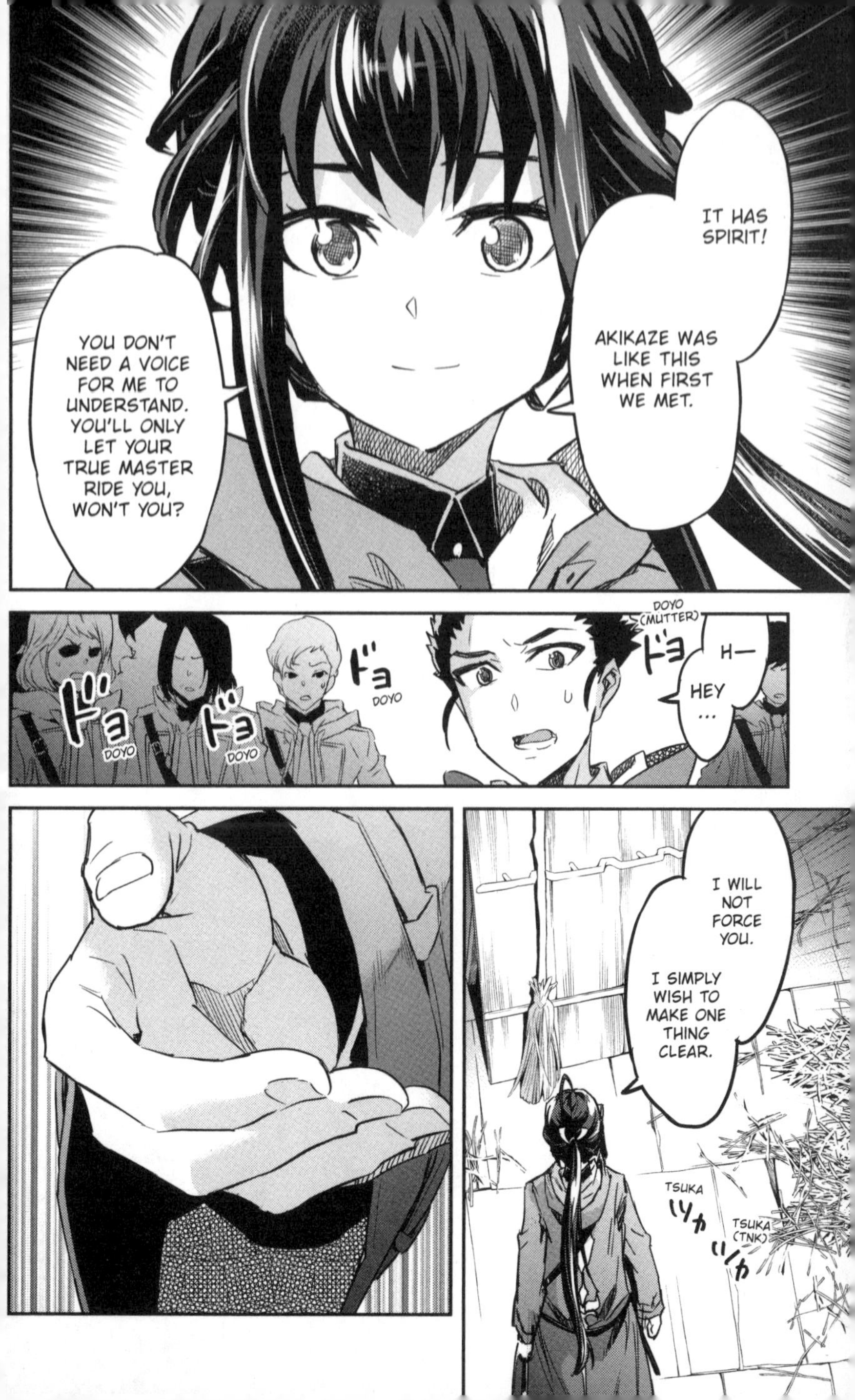
IT HAS SPIRIT!
AKIKAZE WAS LIKE THIS WHEN FIRST WE MET.
YOU DON'T NEED A VOICE FOR ME TO UNDERSTAND. YOU'LL ONLY LET YOUR TRUE MASTER RIDE YOU, WON'T YOU?
H— HEY ...
DOYO (MUTTER)
DOYO
DOYO
DOYO
I WILL NOT FORCE YOU.
I SIMPLY WISH TO MAKE ONE THING CLEAR.
TSUKA
TSUKA (TNK)

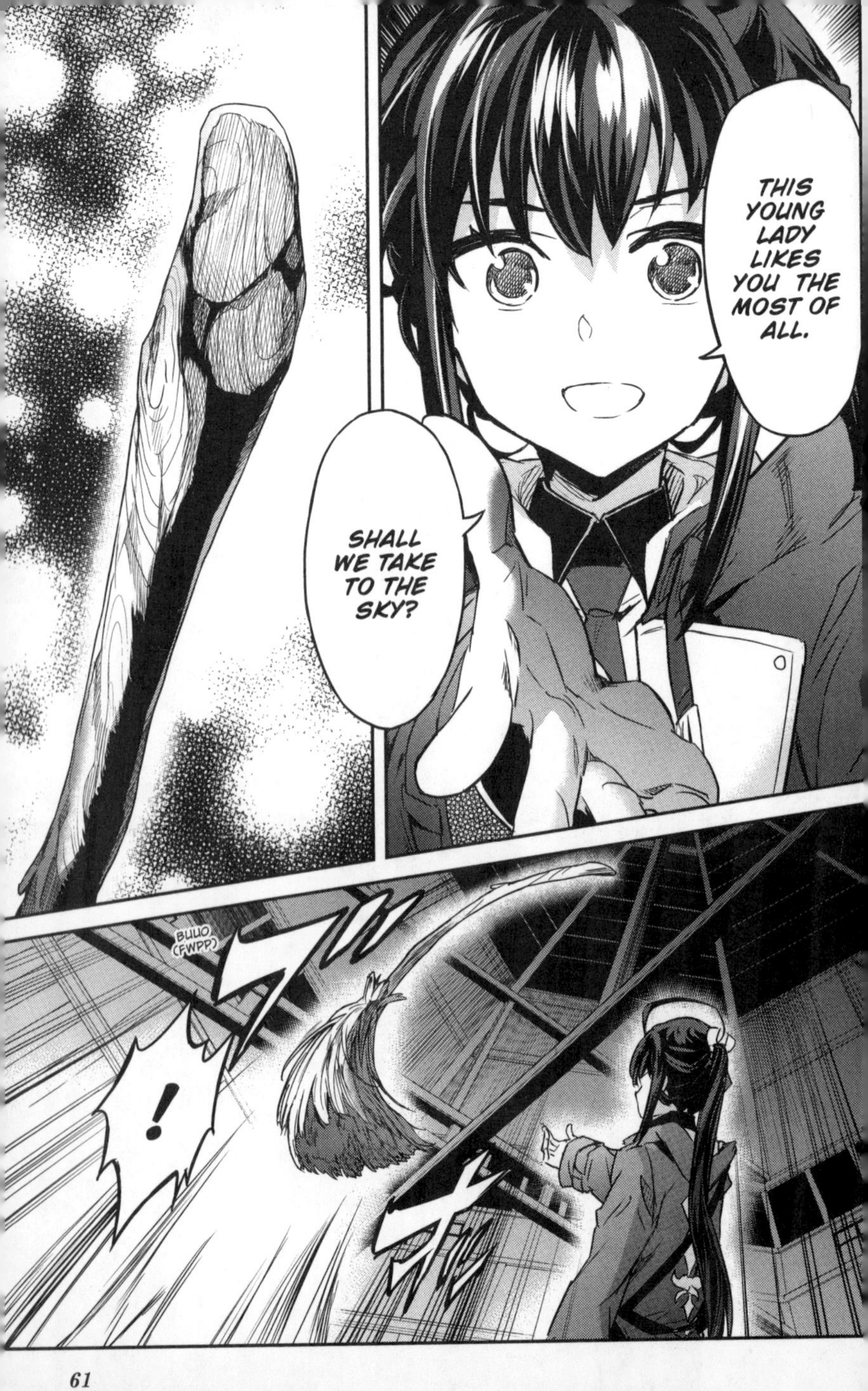
THIS YOUNG LADY LIKES YOU THE MOST OF ALL.
SHALL WE TAKE TO THE SKY?
BUUO (FWPP)
!

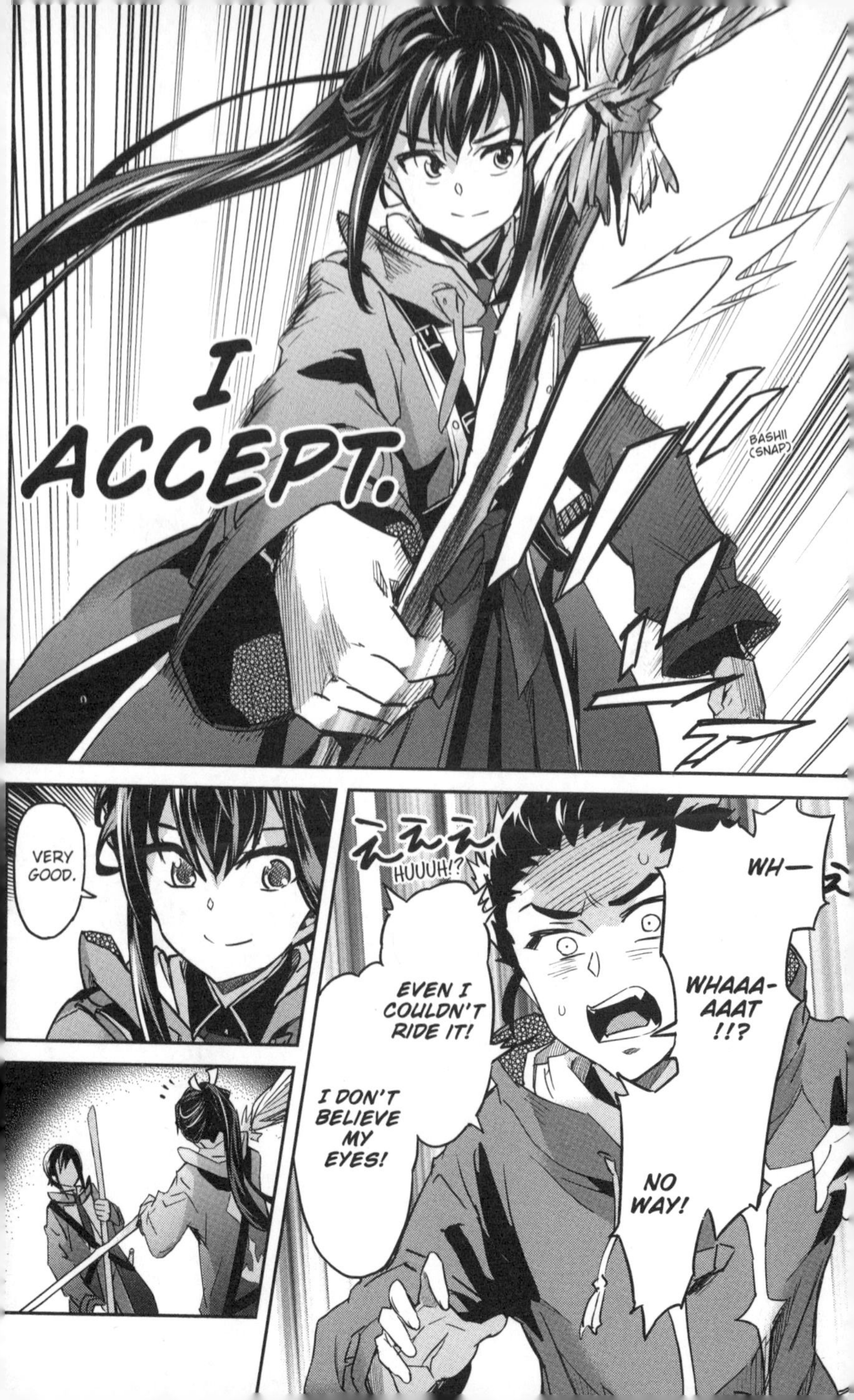
I ACCEPT.
BASHII (SNAP)
WH—
えええ HUUUH!?
WHAAAA-AAAT!!?
EVEN I COULDN'T RIDE IT!
NO WAY!
I DON'T BELIEVE MY EYES!
VERY GOOD.

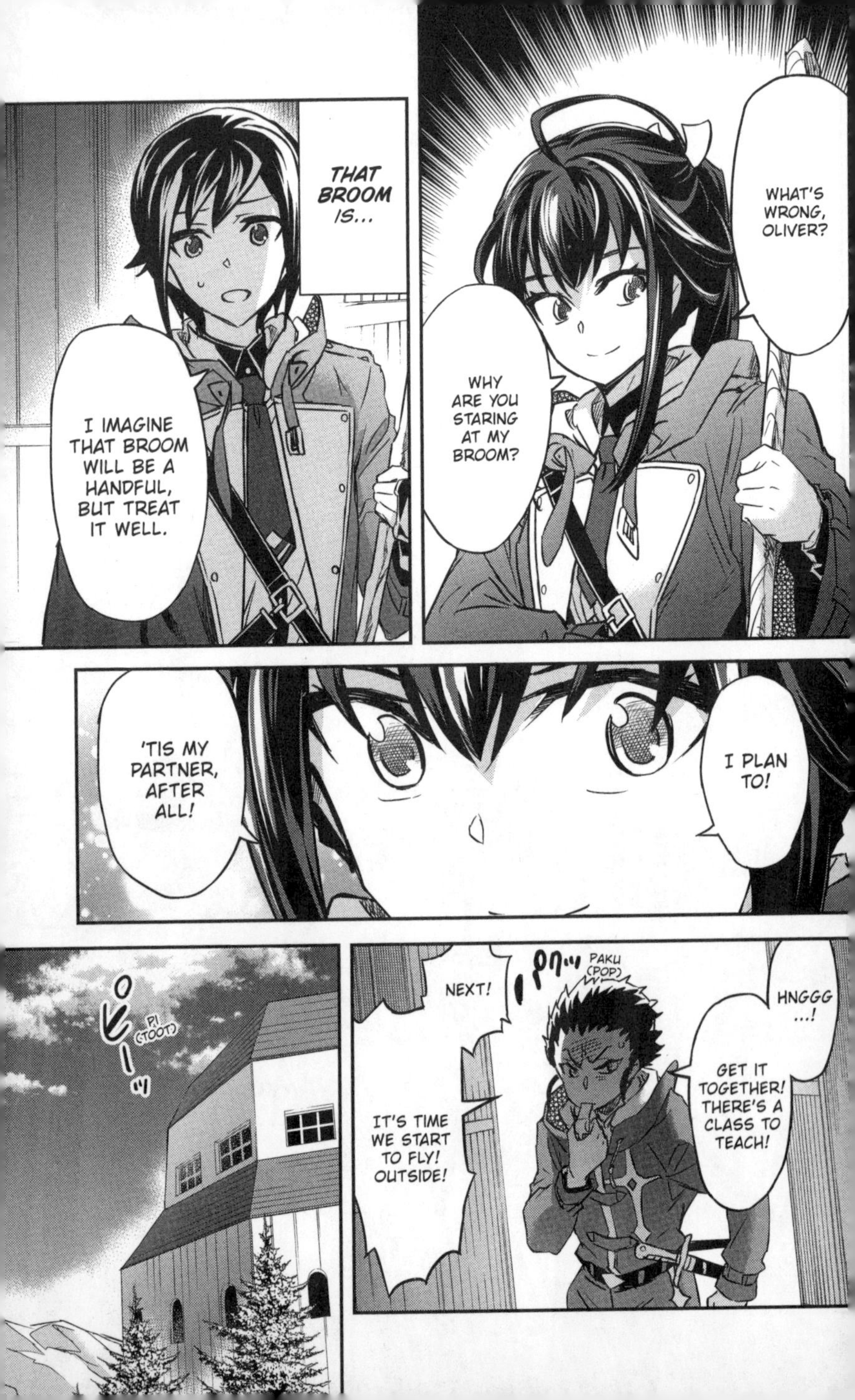
WHAT'S WRONG, OLIVER?
WHY ARE YOU STARING AT MY BROOM?
THAT BROOM IS...
I IMAGINE THAT BROOM WILL BE A HANDFUL, BUT TREAT IT WELL.
I PLAN TO!
'TIS MY PARTNER, AFTER ALL!
HNGGG ...!
GET IT TOGETHER! THERE'S A CLASS TO TEACH!
PAKU (POP)
NEXT!
IT'S TIME WE START TO FLY! OUTSIDE!
PI (TOOT)

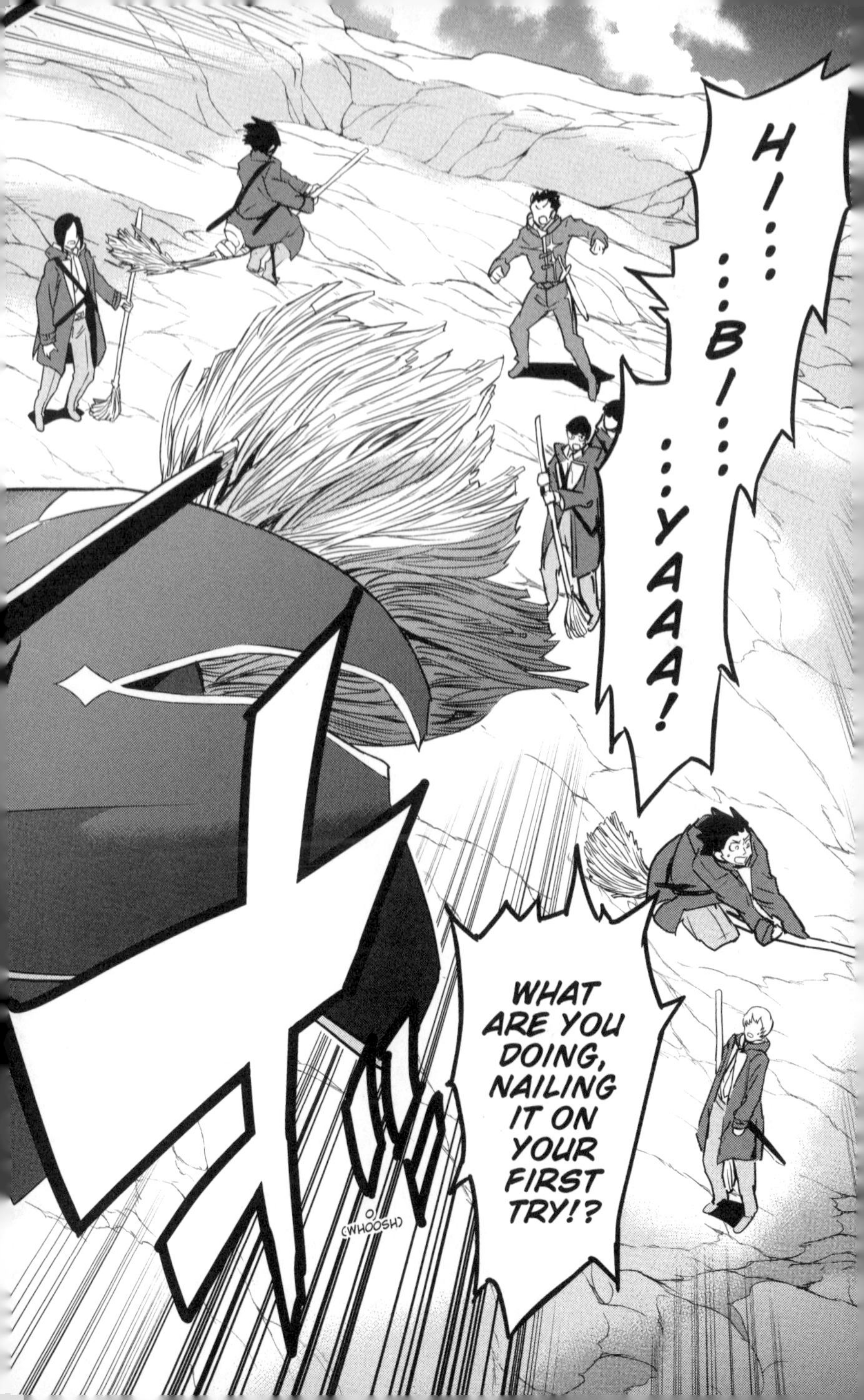
HI... ...BI... ...YAAAA!
WHAT ARE YOU DOING, NAILING IT ON YOUR FIRST TRY!?
O (WHOOSH)

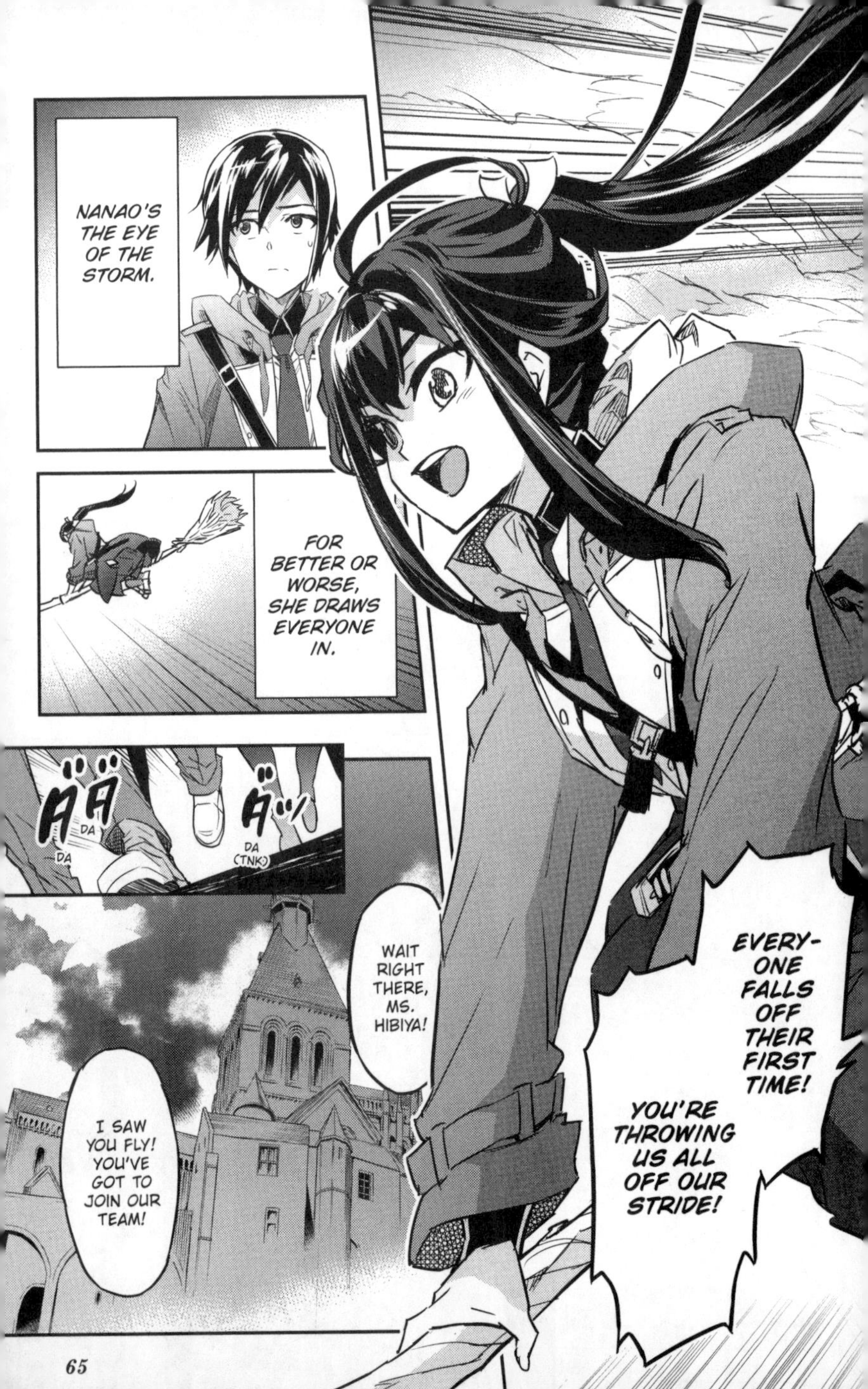
EVERY-ONE FALLS OFF THEIR FIRST TIME!
YOU'RE THROWING US ALL OFF OUR STRIDE!
NANAO'S THE EYE OF THE STORM.
FOR BETTER OR WORSE, SHE DRAWS EVERYONE IN.
DA
DA
DA (TNK)
WAIT RIGHT THERE, MS. HIBIYA!
I SAW YOU FLY! YOU'VE GOT TO JOIN OUR TEAM!

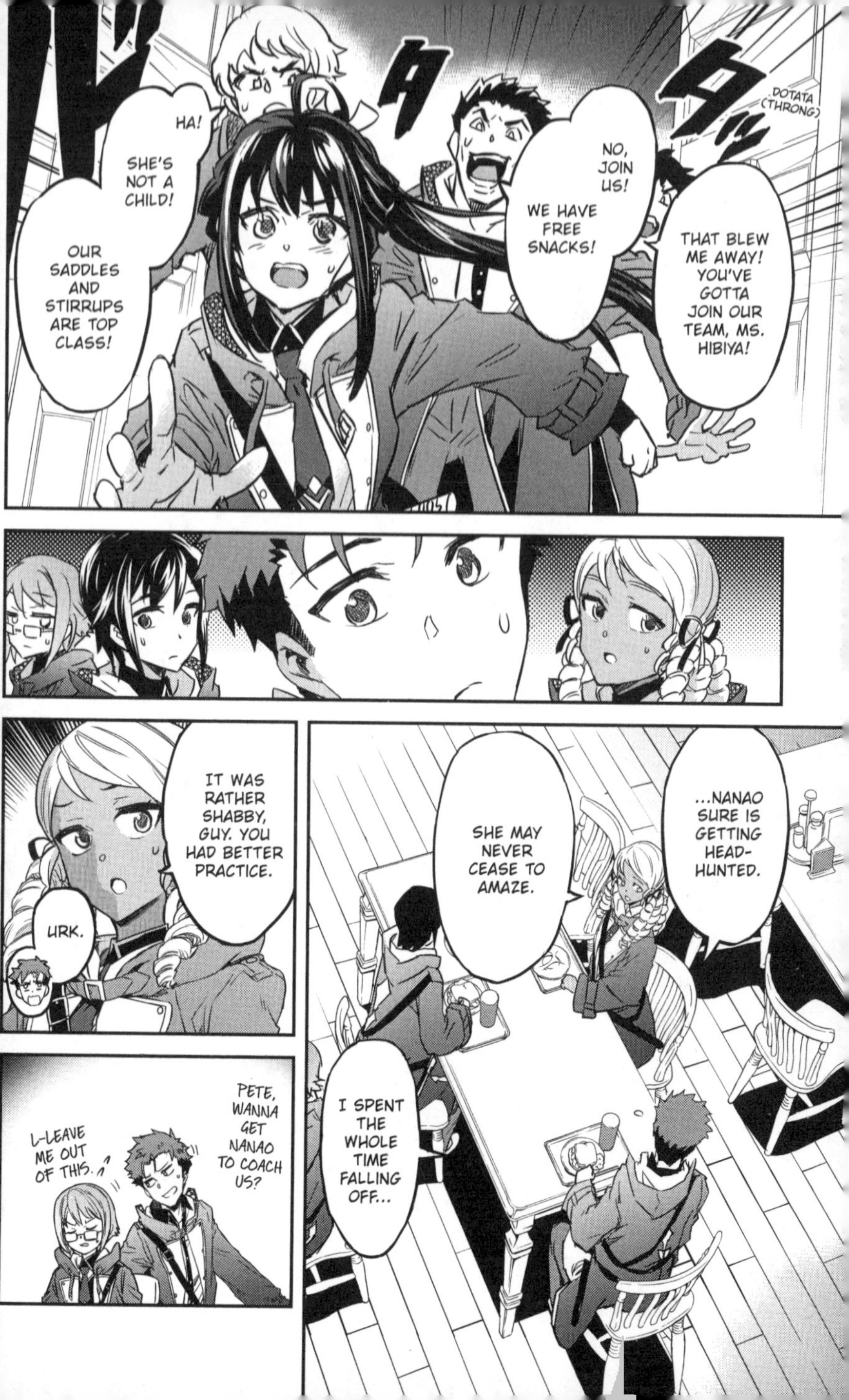
DOTATA (THRONG)
THAT BLEW ME AWAY! YOU'VE GOTTA JOIN OUR TEAM, MS. HIBIYA!
NO, JOIN US!
WE HAVE FREE SNACKS!
HA!
SHE'S NOT A CHILD!
OUR SADDLES AND STIRRUPS ARE TOP CLASS!
...NANAO SURE IS GETTING HEAD-HUNTED.
SHE MAY NEVER CEASE TO AMAZE.
I SPENT THE WHOLE TIME FALLING OFF...
IT WAS RATHER SHABBY, GUY. YOU HAD BETTER PRACTICE.
URK.
PETE, WANNA GET NANAO TO COACH US?
L-LEAVE ME OUT OF THIS.

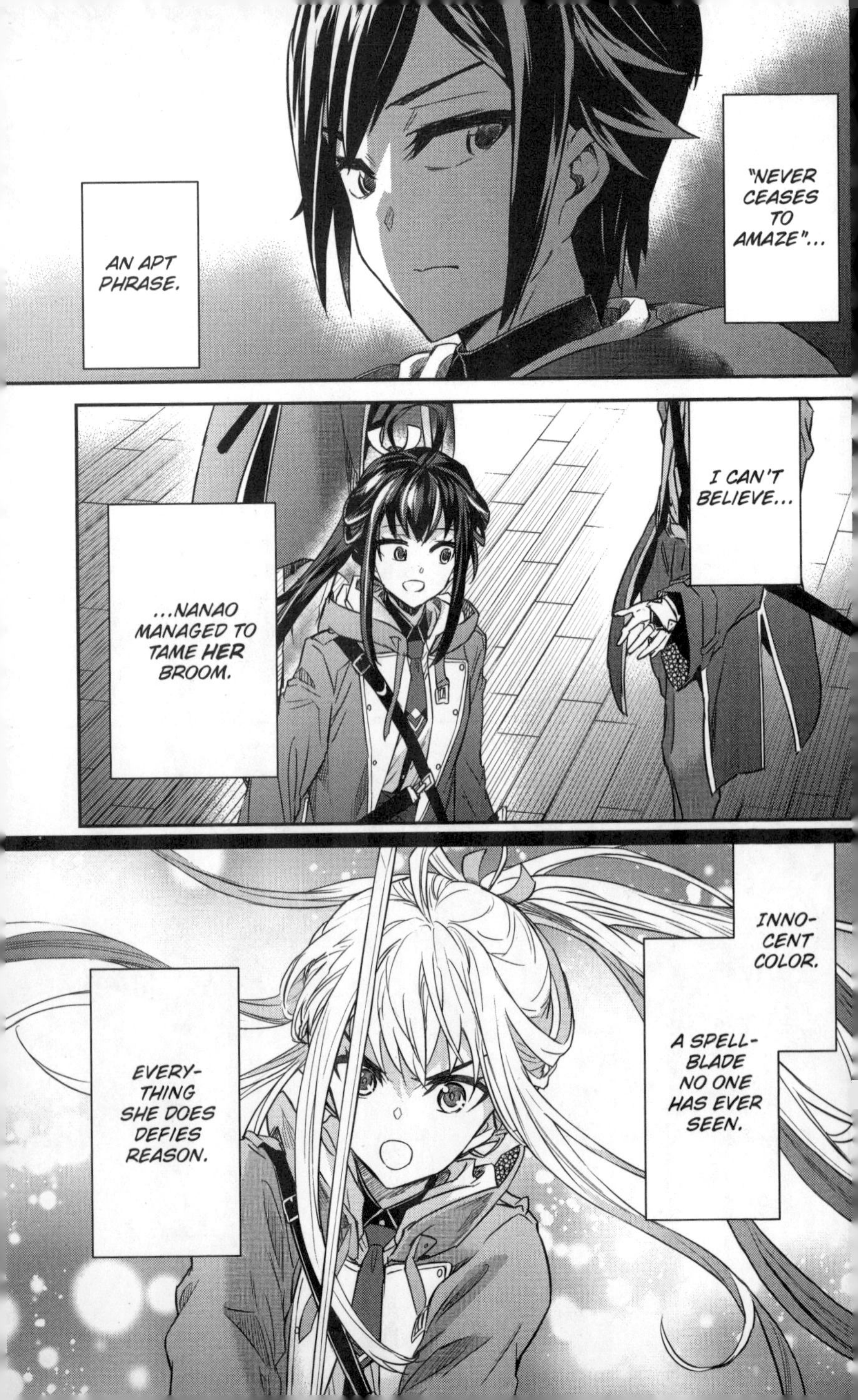
"NEVER CEASES TO AMAZE"...
AN APT PHRASE.
I CAN'T BELIEVE...
...NANAO MANAGED TO TAME HER BROOM.
INNOCENT COLOR.
A SPELLBLADE NO ONE HAS EVER SEEN.
EVERYTHING SHE DOES DEFIES REASON.

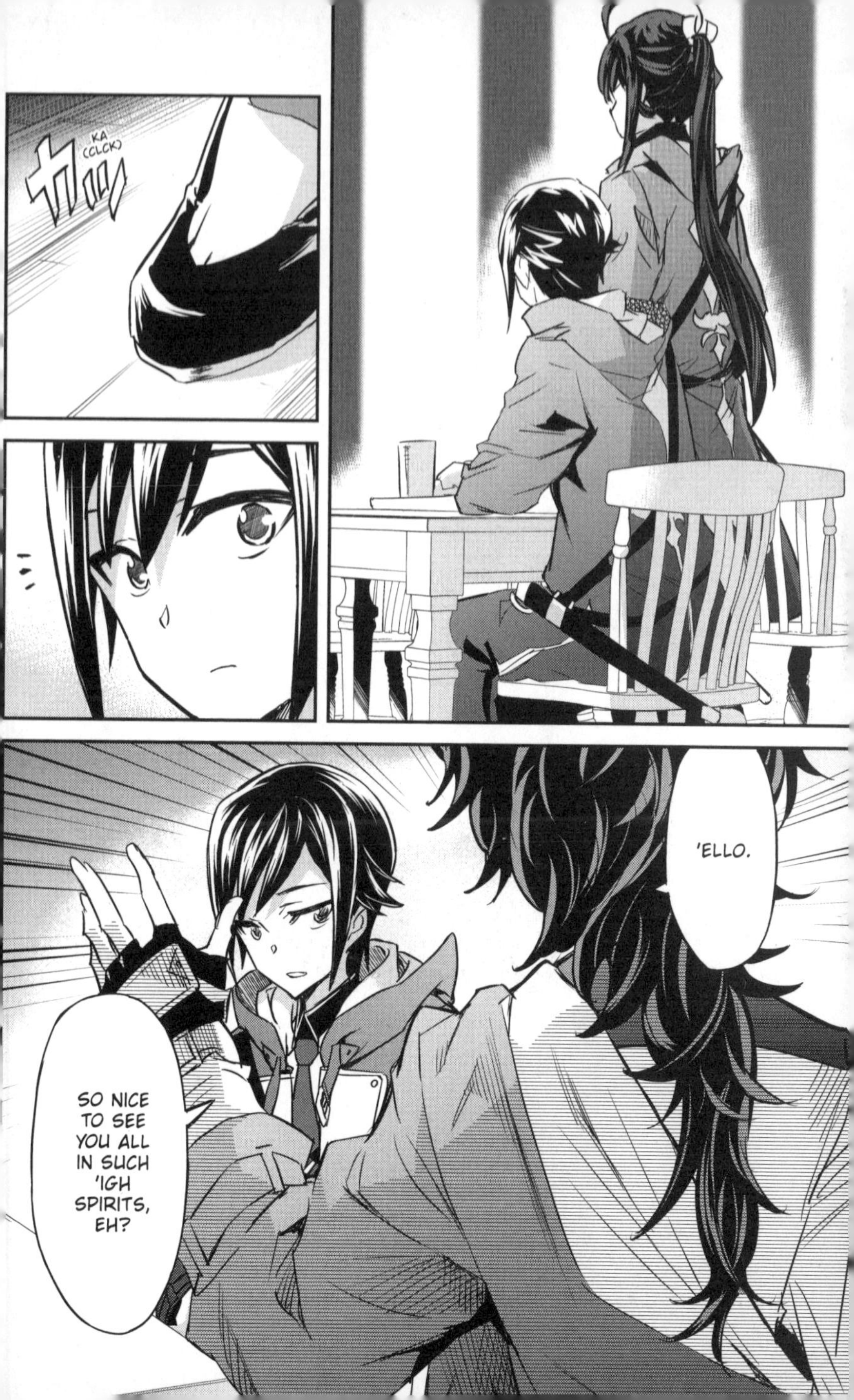
カッ
KA (CLCK)
'ELLO.
SO NICE TO SEE YOU ALL IN SUCH 'IGH SPIRITS, EH?

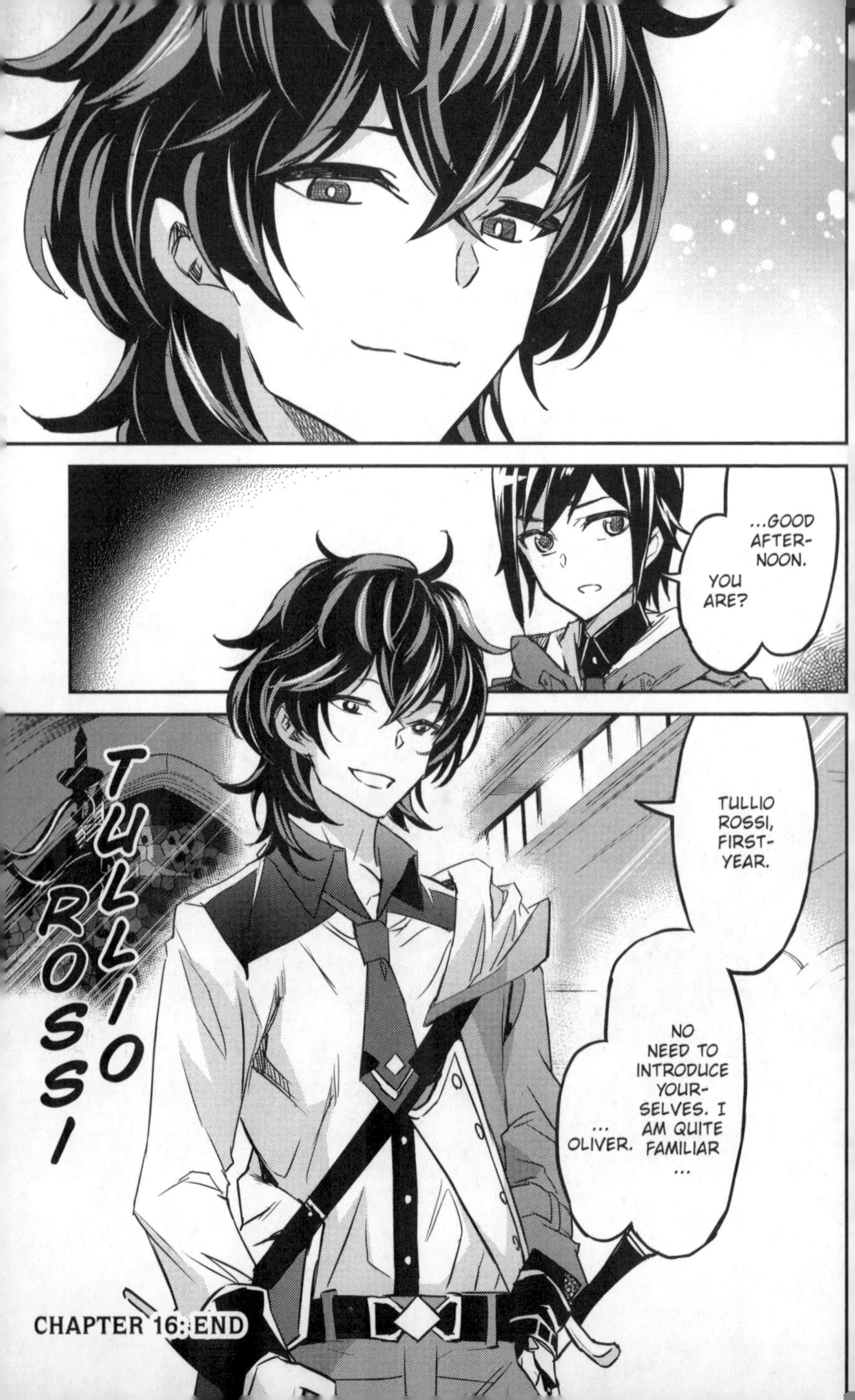
...GOOD AFTER-NOON.
YOU ARE?
TULLIO ROSSI, FIRST-YEAR.
NO NEED TO INTRODUCE YOUR-SELVES. I AM QUITE FAMILIAR ...
... OLIVER.
TULLIO ROSSI
CHAPTER 16: END

Reign of the Seven Spellblades

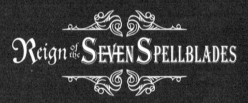

CHAPTER 17: MAGIC AND TEMPERAMENT

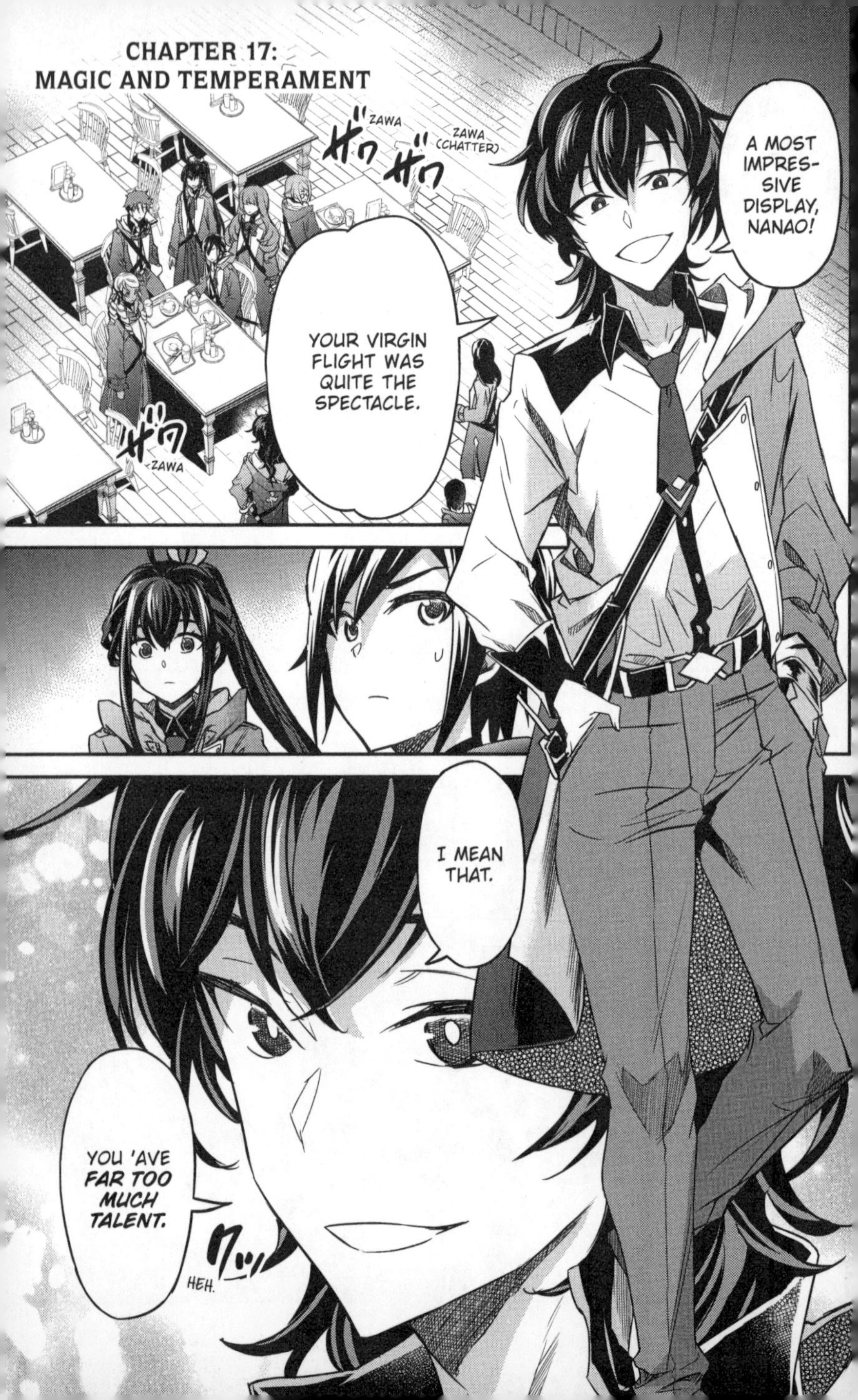
A MOST IMPRESSIVE DISPLAY, NANAO!
ZAWA (CHATTER)
ZAWA
YOUR VIRGIN FLIGHT WAS QUITE THE SPECTACLE.
ZAWA
I MEAN THAT.
YOU 'AVE FAR TOO MUCH TALENT.
HEH.

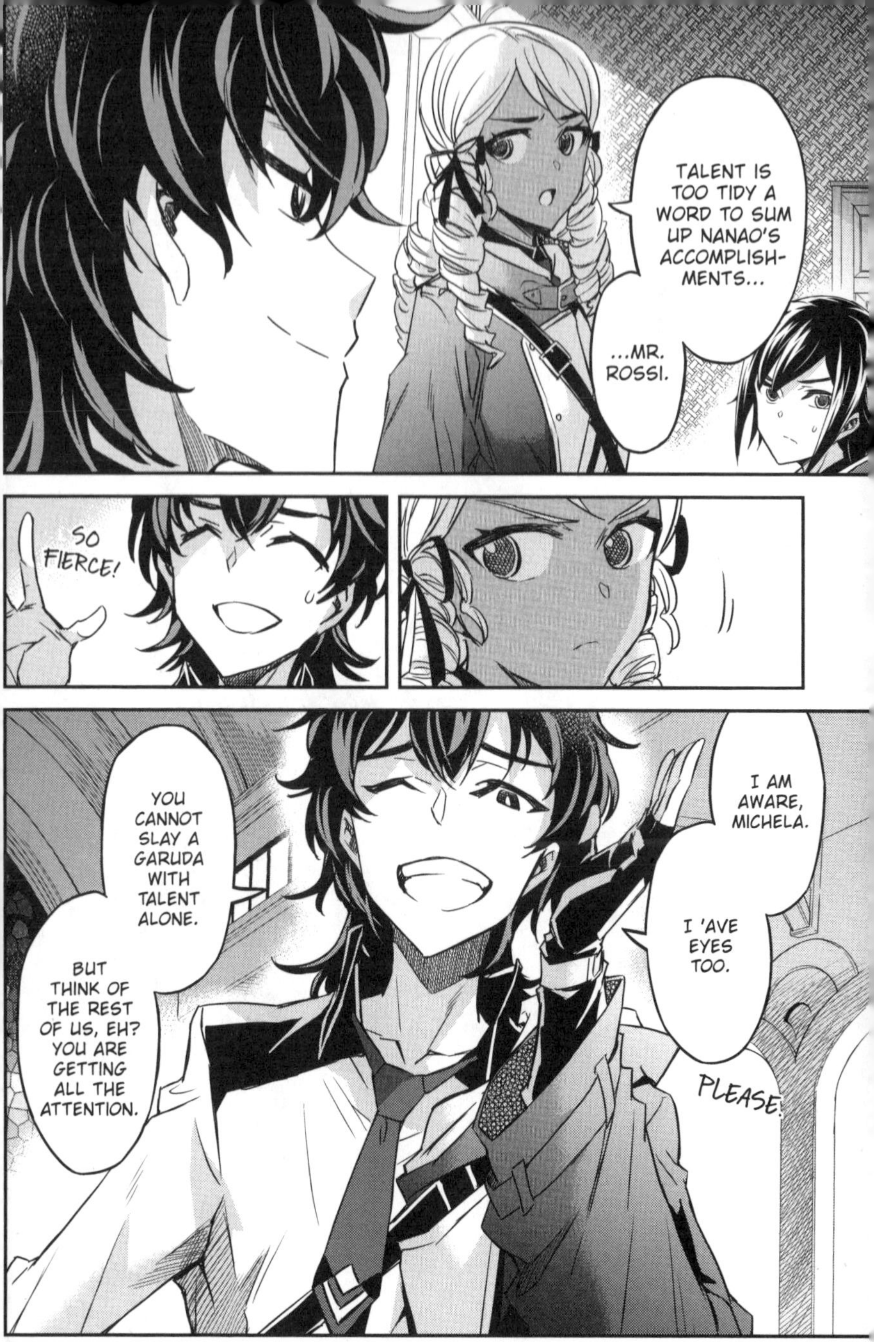
TALENT IS TOO TIDY A WORD TO SUM UP NANAO'S ACCOMPLISH-MENTS...
...MR. ROSSI.
SO FIERCE!
I AM AWARE, MICHELA.
I 'AVE EYES TOO.
YOU CANNOT SLAY A GARUDA WITH TALENT ALONE.
BUT THINK OF THE REST OF US, EH? YOU ARE GETTING ALL THE ATTENTION.
PLEASE.

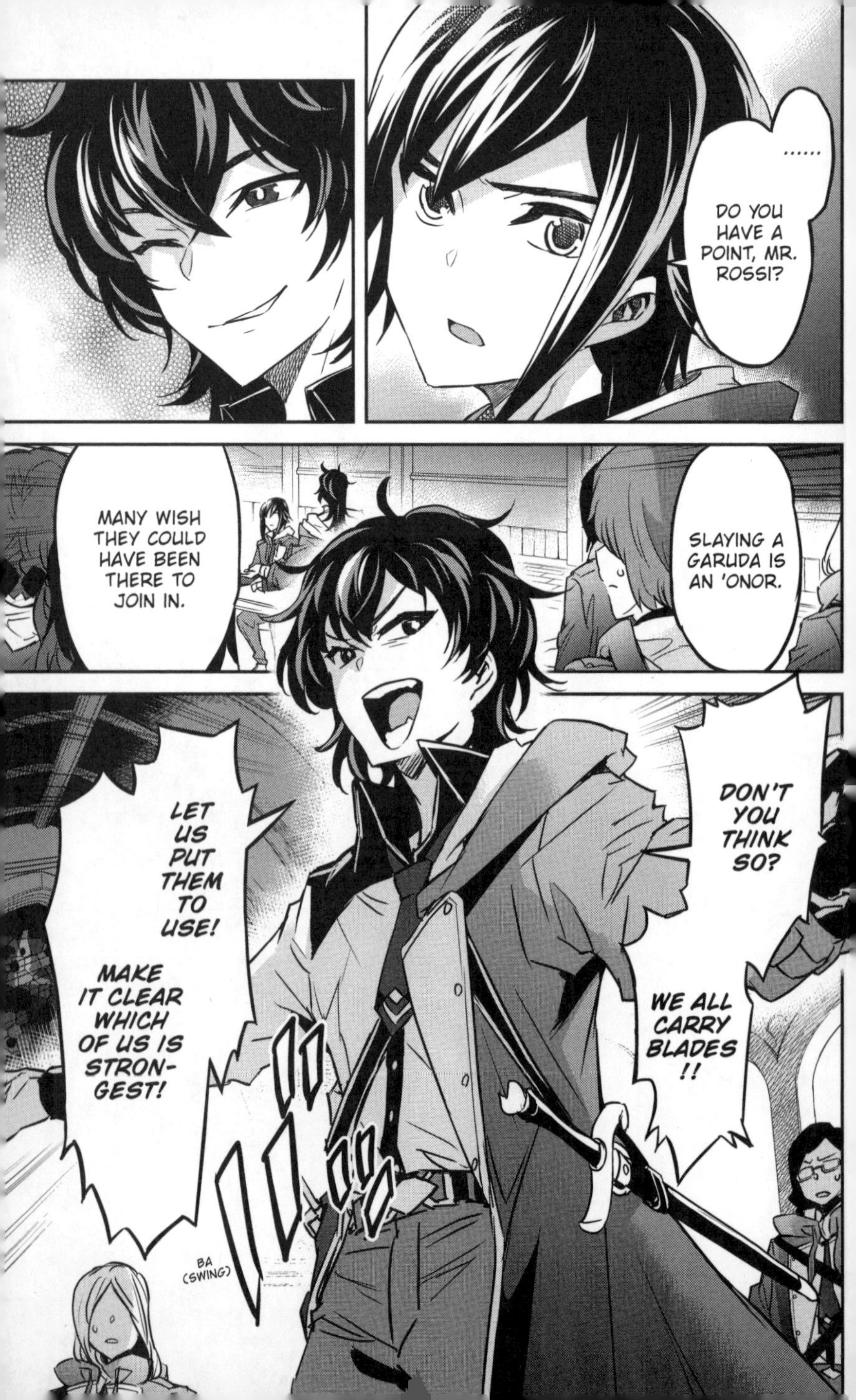
......
DO YOU HAVE A POINT, MR. ROSSI?
SLAYING A GARUDA IS AN 'ONOR.
MANY WISH THEY COULD HAVE BEEN THERE TO JOIN IN.
DON'T YOU THINK SO?
WE ALL CARRY BLADES!!
LET US PUT THEM TO USE!
MAKE IT CLEAR WHICH OF US IS STRONGEST!
BA (SWING)

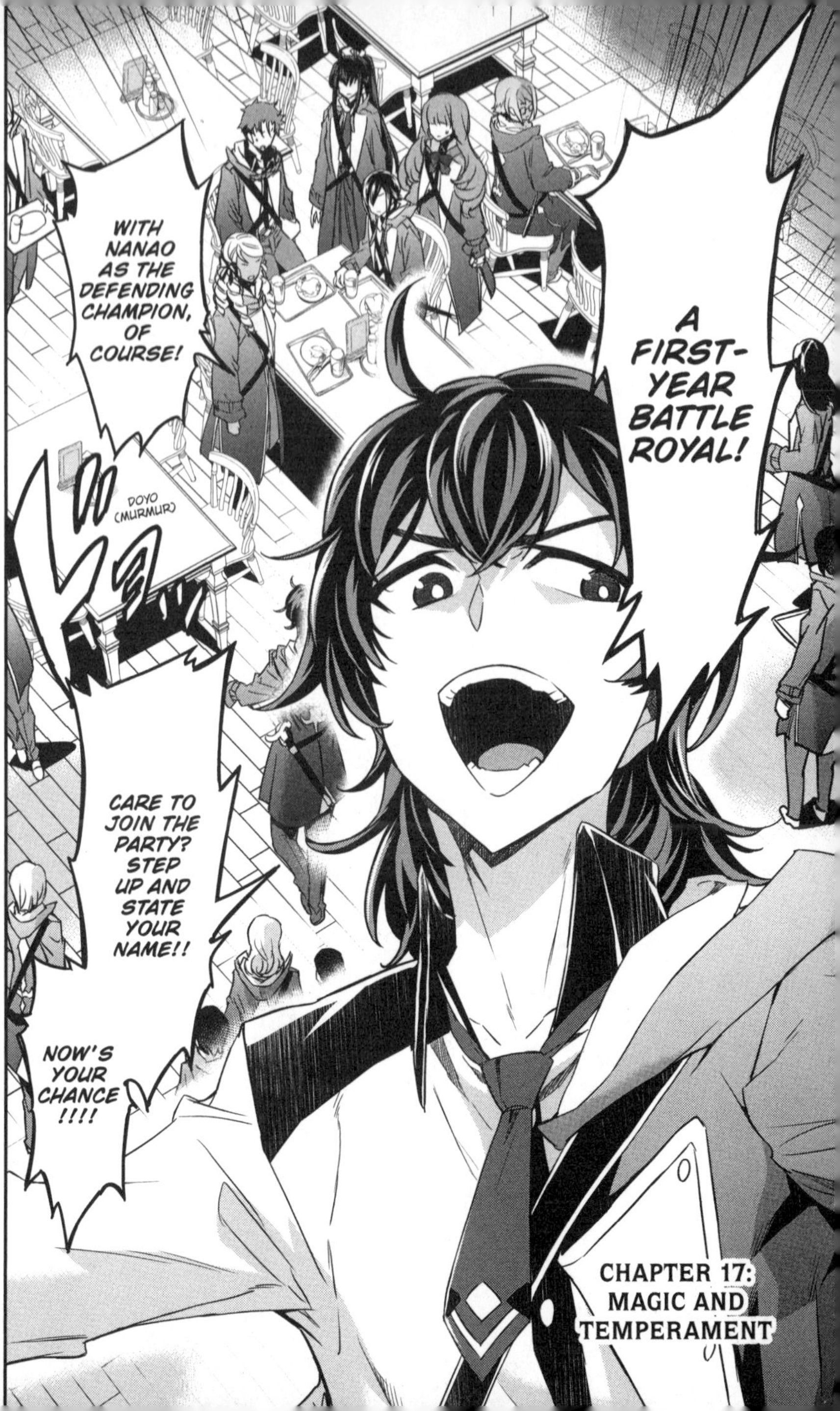
A FIRST-YEAR BATTLE ROYAL!
WITH NANAO AS THE DEFENDING CHAMPION, OF COURSE!
DOYO (MURMUR)
CARE TO JOIN THE PARTY? STEP UP AND STATE YOUR NAME!!
NOW'S YOUR CHANCE !!!!

CHAPTER 17: MAGIC AND TEMPERAMENT

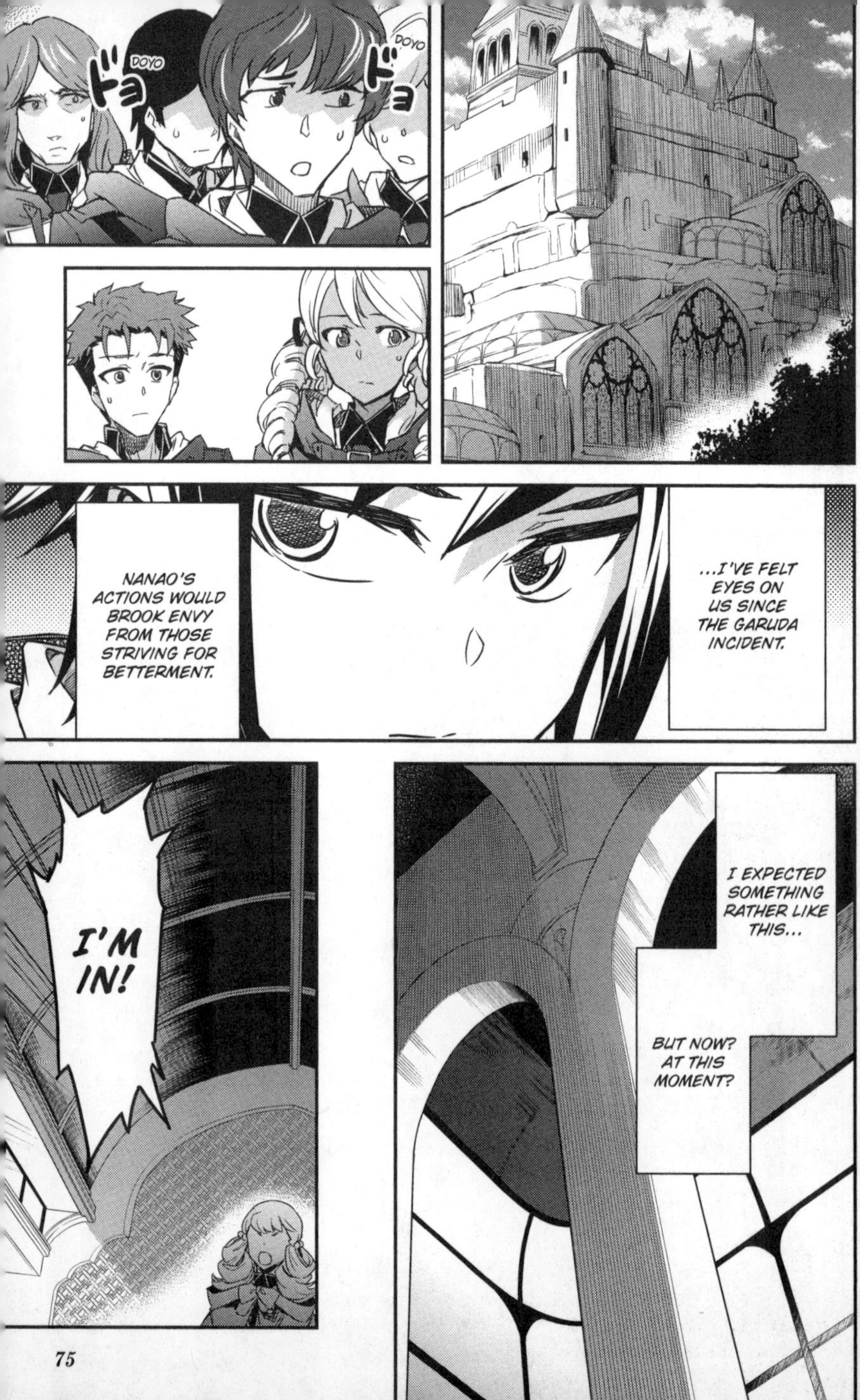
ドヨ DOYO
ドヨ DOYO
...I'VE FELT EYES ON US SINCE THE GARUDA INCIDENT.
NANAO'S ACTIONS WOULD BROOK ENVY FROM THOSE STRIVING FOR BETTERMENT.
I EXPECTED SOMETHING RATHER LIKE THIS...
BUT NOW? AT THIS MOMENT?
I'M IN!

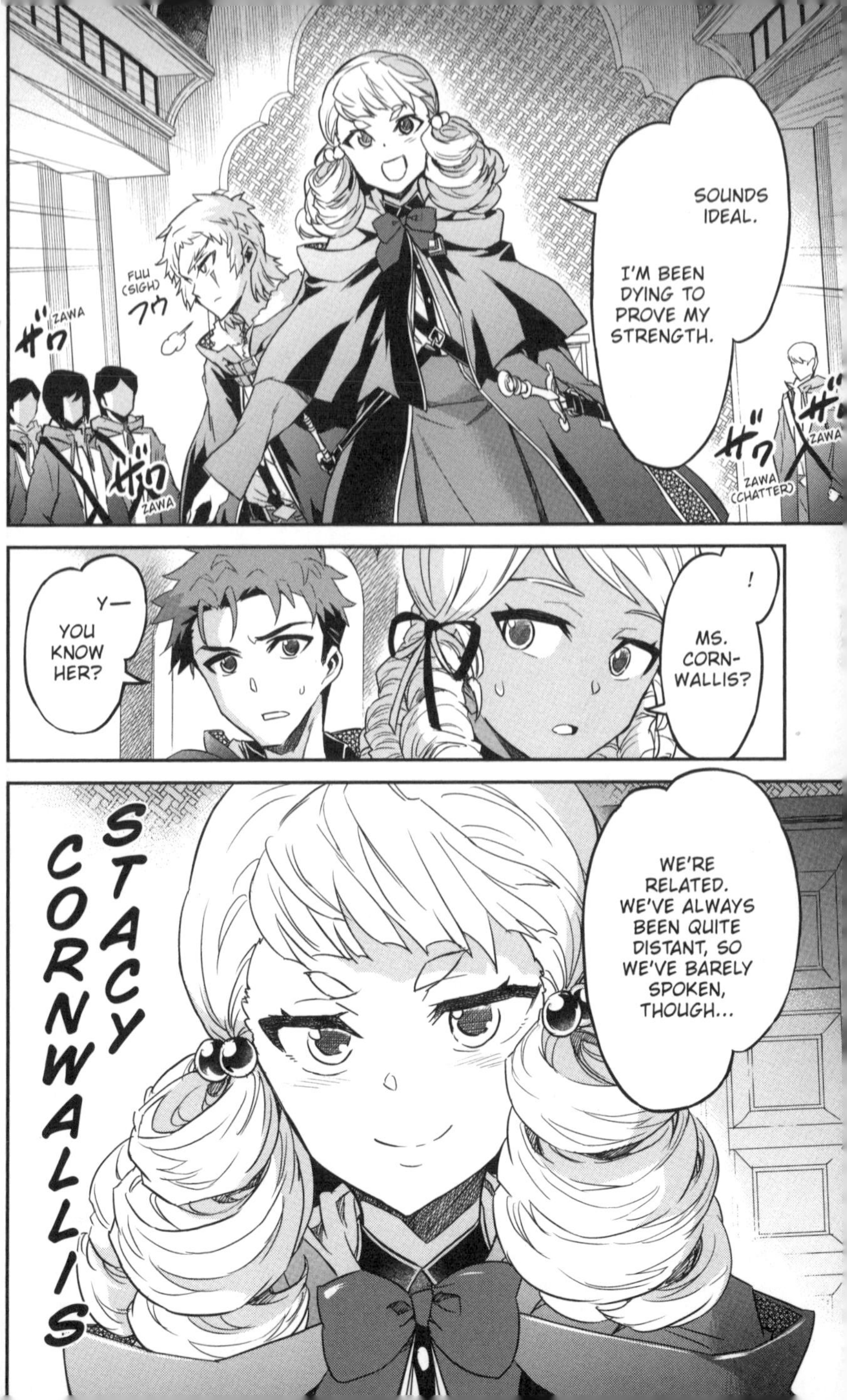
SOUNDS IDEAL.
I'M BEEN DYING TO PROVE MY STRENGTH.
ザワ ZAWA
ザワ ZAWA (CHATTER)
フウ FUU (SIGH)
ザワ ZAWA
ザワ ZAWA
! MS. CORN-WALLIS?
Y— YOU KNOW HER?
WE'RE RELATED. WE'VE ALWAYS BEEN QUITE DISTANT, SO WE'VE BARELY SPOKEN, THOUGH...
STACY CORNWALLIS

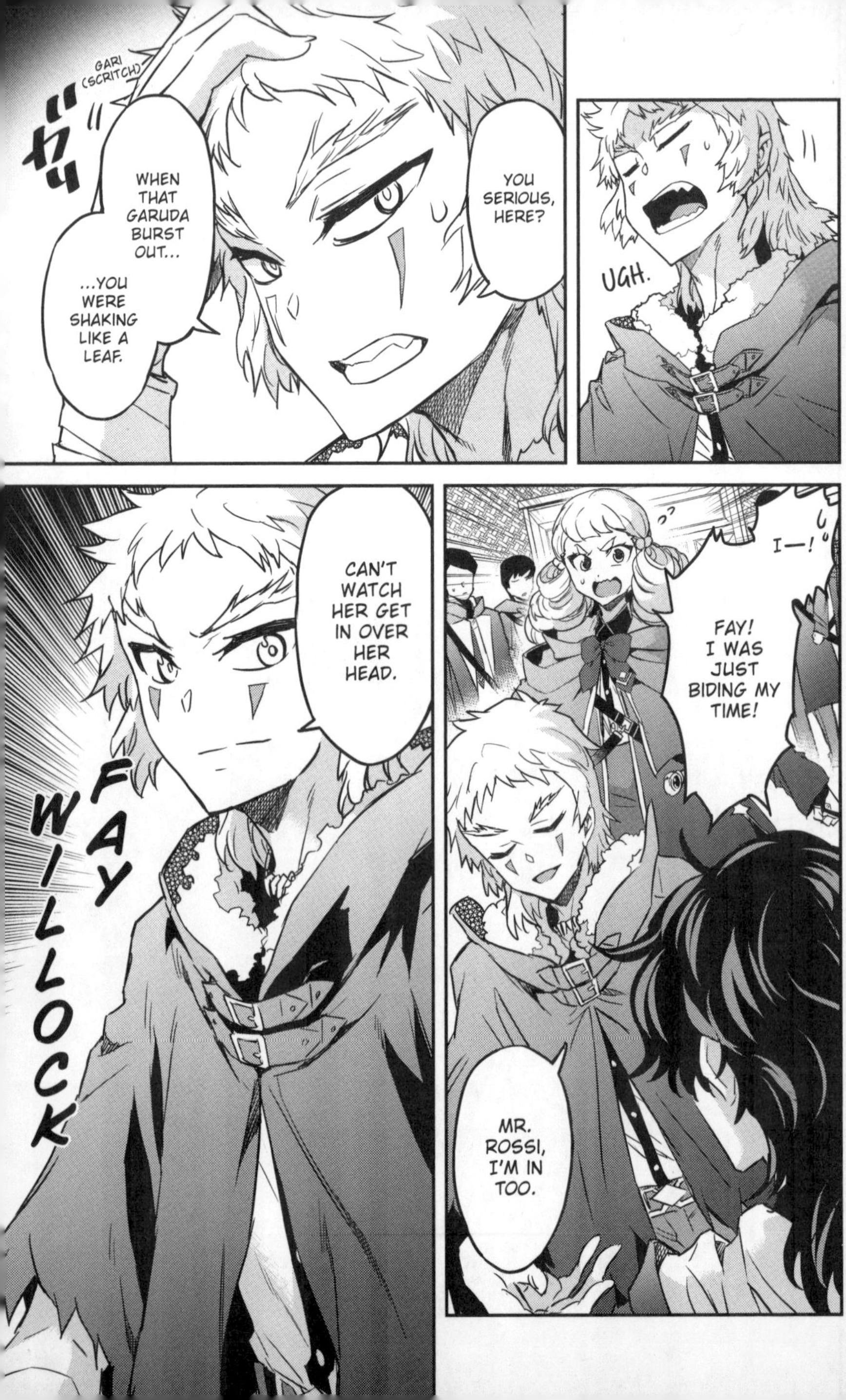
UGH.
YOU SERIOUS, HERE?
GARI (SCRITCH)
WHEN THAT GARUDA BURST OUT...
...YOU WERE SHAKING LIKE A LEAF.
I—!
FAY! I WAS JUST BIDING MY TIME!
MR. ROSSI, I'M IN TOO.
CAN'T WATCH HER GET IN OVER HER HEAD.
FAY WILLOCK

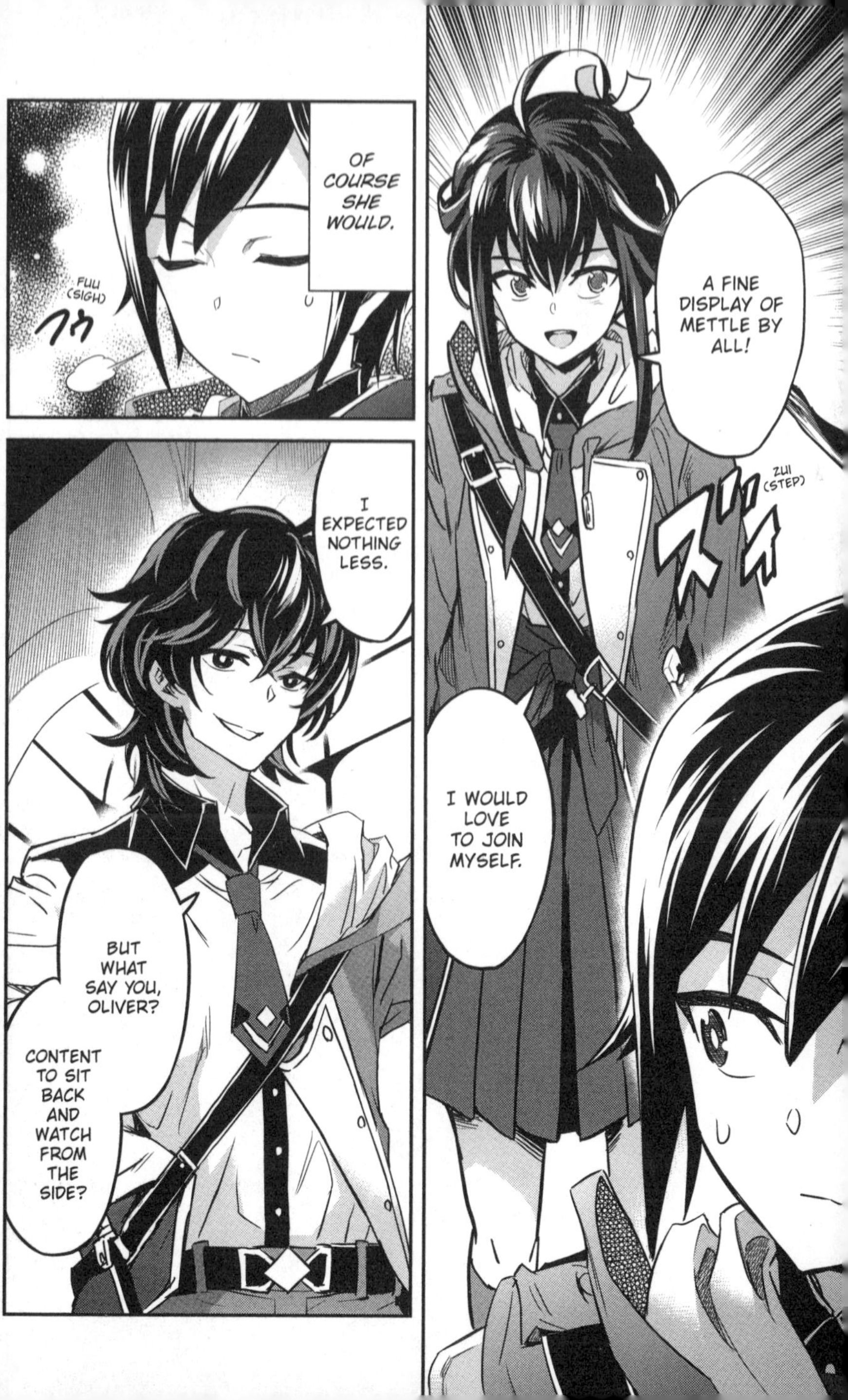
A FINE DISPLAY OF METTLE BY ALL!
ZUI (STEP)
I WOULD LOVE TO JOIN MYSELF.
OF COURSE SHE WOULD.
FUU (SIGH)
I EXPECTED NOTHING LESS.
BUT WHAT SAY YOU, OLIVER?
CONTENT TO SIT BACK AND WATCH FROM THE SIDE?

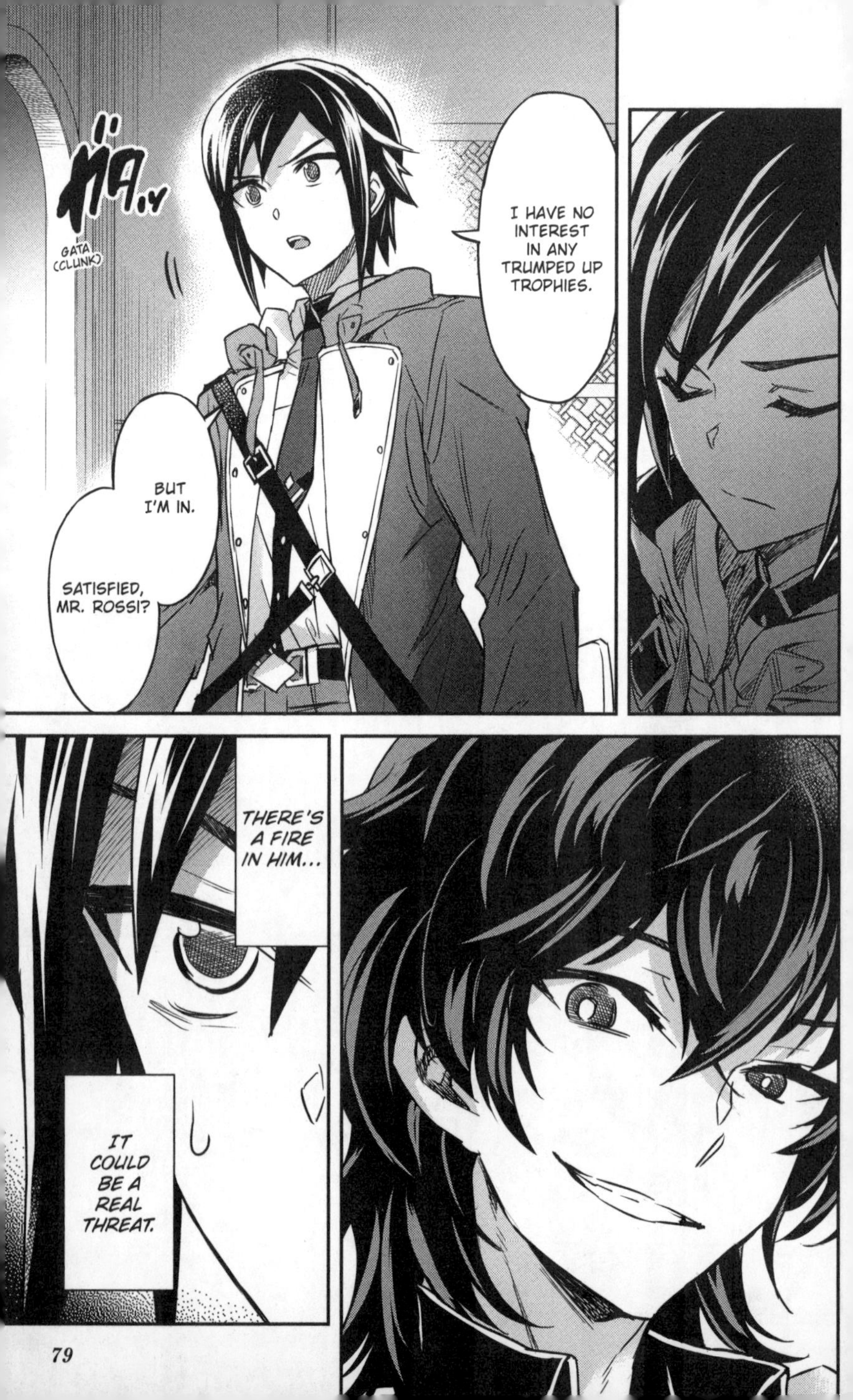
I HAVE NO INTEREST IN ANY TRUMPED UP TROPHIES.
GATA (CLUNK)
BUT I'M IN.
SATISFIED, MR. ROSSI?
THERE'S A FIRE IN HIM...
IT COULD BE A REAL THREAT.

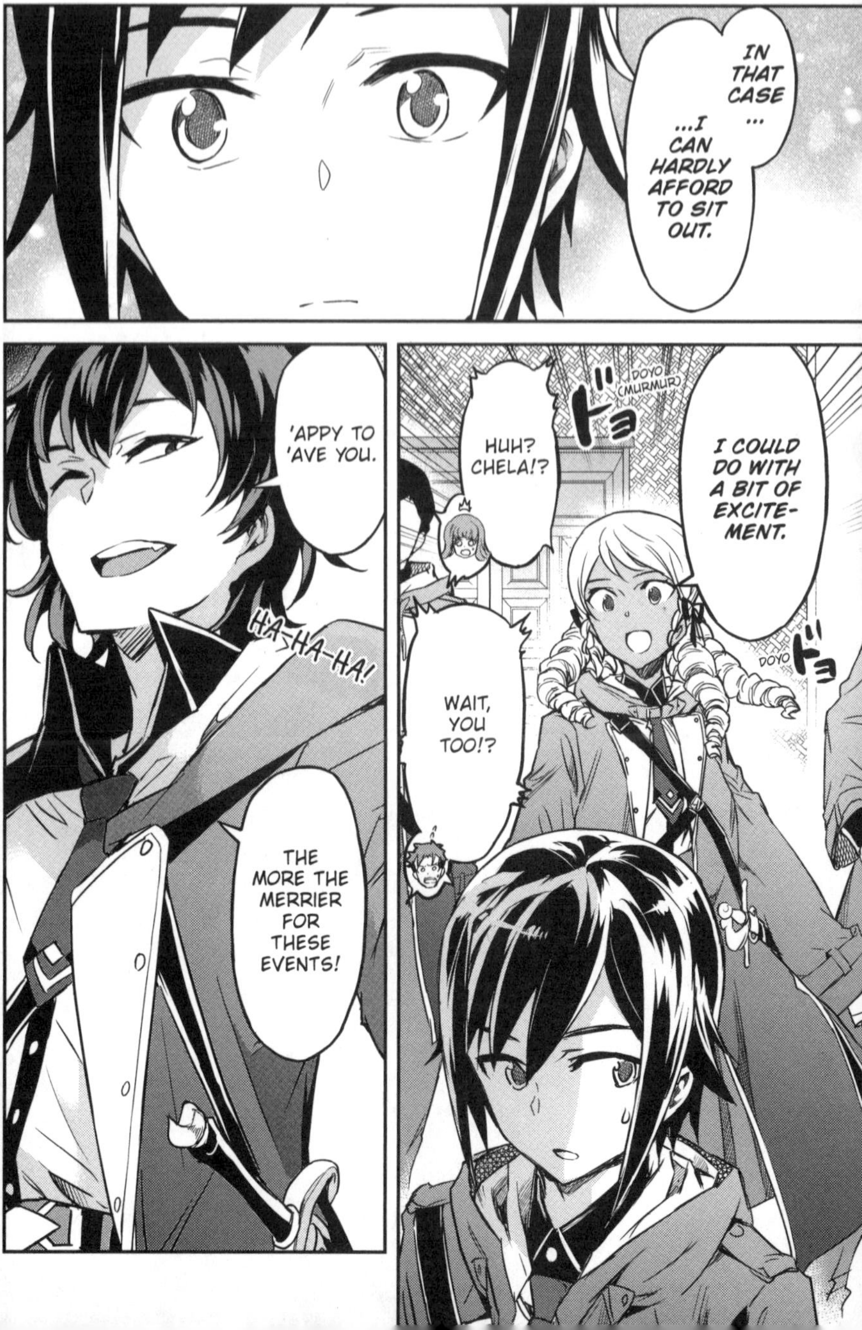
IN THAT CASE...
...I CAN HARDLY AFFORD TO SIT OUT.
DOYO (MURMUR)
ドョ
I COULD DO WITH A BIT OF EXCITE-MENT.
HUH? CHELA!?
DOYO
ドョ
WAIT, YOU TOO!?
'APPY TO 'AVE YOU.
HA-HA-HA!
THE MORE THE MERRIER FOR THESE EVENTS!

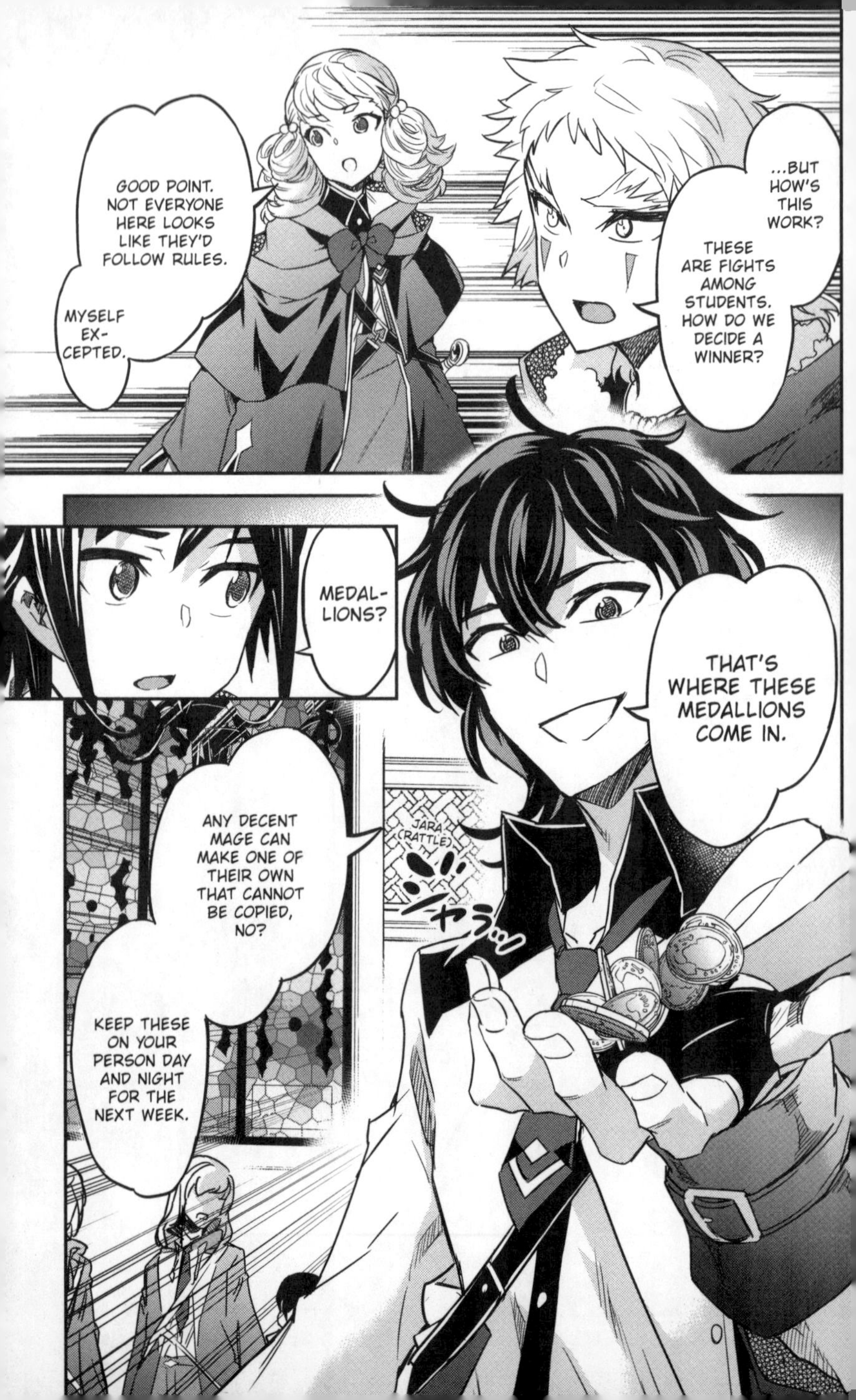
...BUT HOW'S THIS WORK?
THESE ARE FIGHTS AMONG STUDENTS. HOW DO WE DECIDE A WINNER?
GOOD POINT. NOT EVERYONE HERE LOOKS LIKE THEY'D FOLLOW RULES.
MYSELF EX-CEPTED.
THAT'S WHERE THESE MEDALLIONS COME IN.
JARA (RATTLE)
MEDAL-LIONS?
ANY DECENT MAGE CAN MAKE ONE OF THEIR OWN THAT CANNOT BE COPIED, NO?
KEEP THESE ON YOUR PERSON DAY AND NIGHT FOR THE NEXT WEEK.

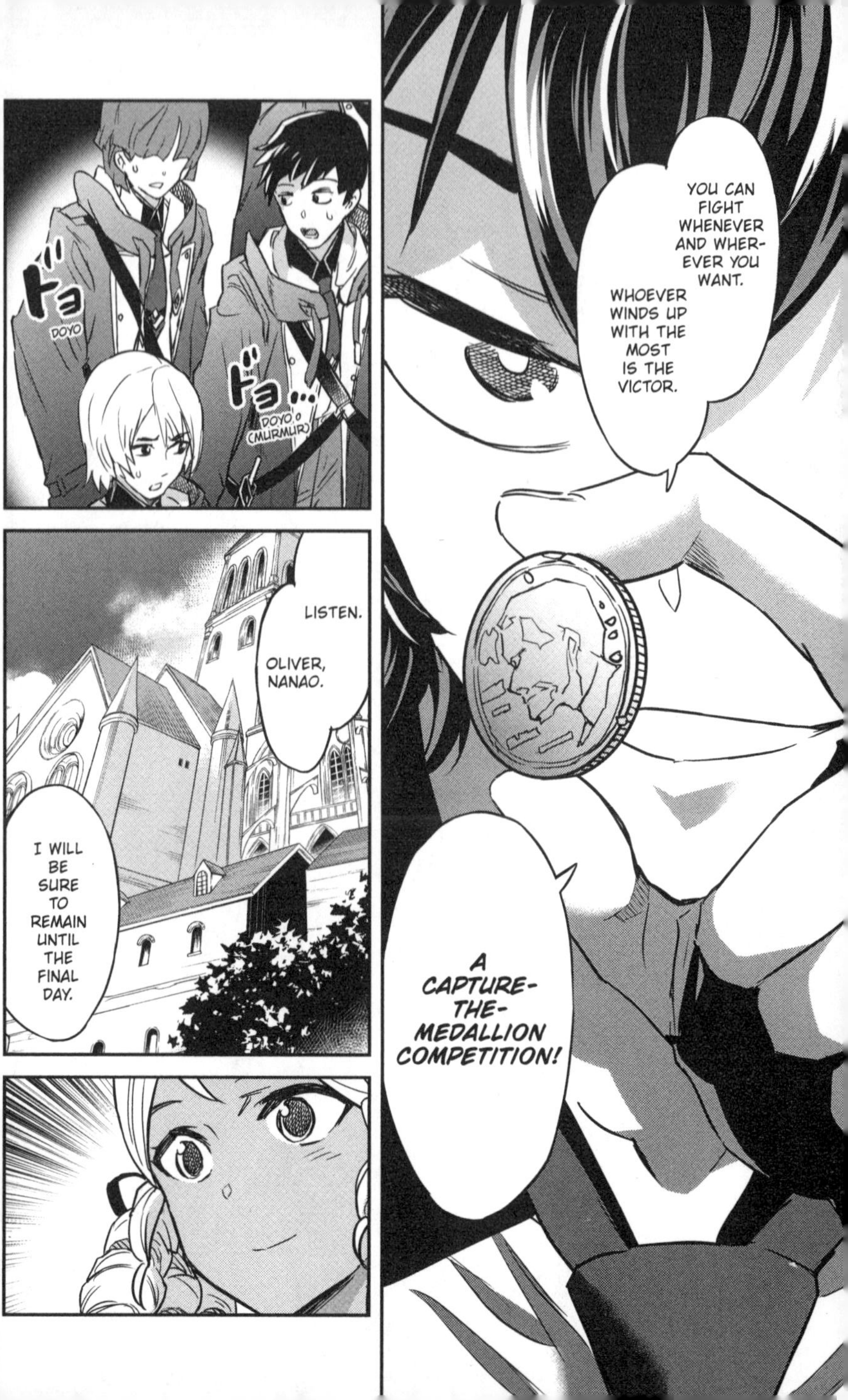
YOU CAN FIGHT WHENEVER AND WHER-EVER YOU WANT.
WHOEVER WINDS UP WITH THE MOST IS THE VICTOR.
A CAPTURE-THE-MEDALLION COMPETITION!
ドョ
DOYO
ドョ…
DOYO (MURMUR)
LISTEN.
OLIVER, NANAO.
I WILL BE SURE TO REMAIN UNTIL THE FINAL DAY.

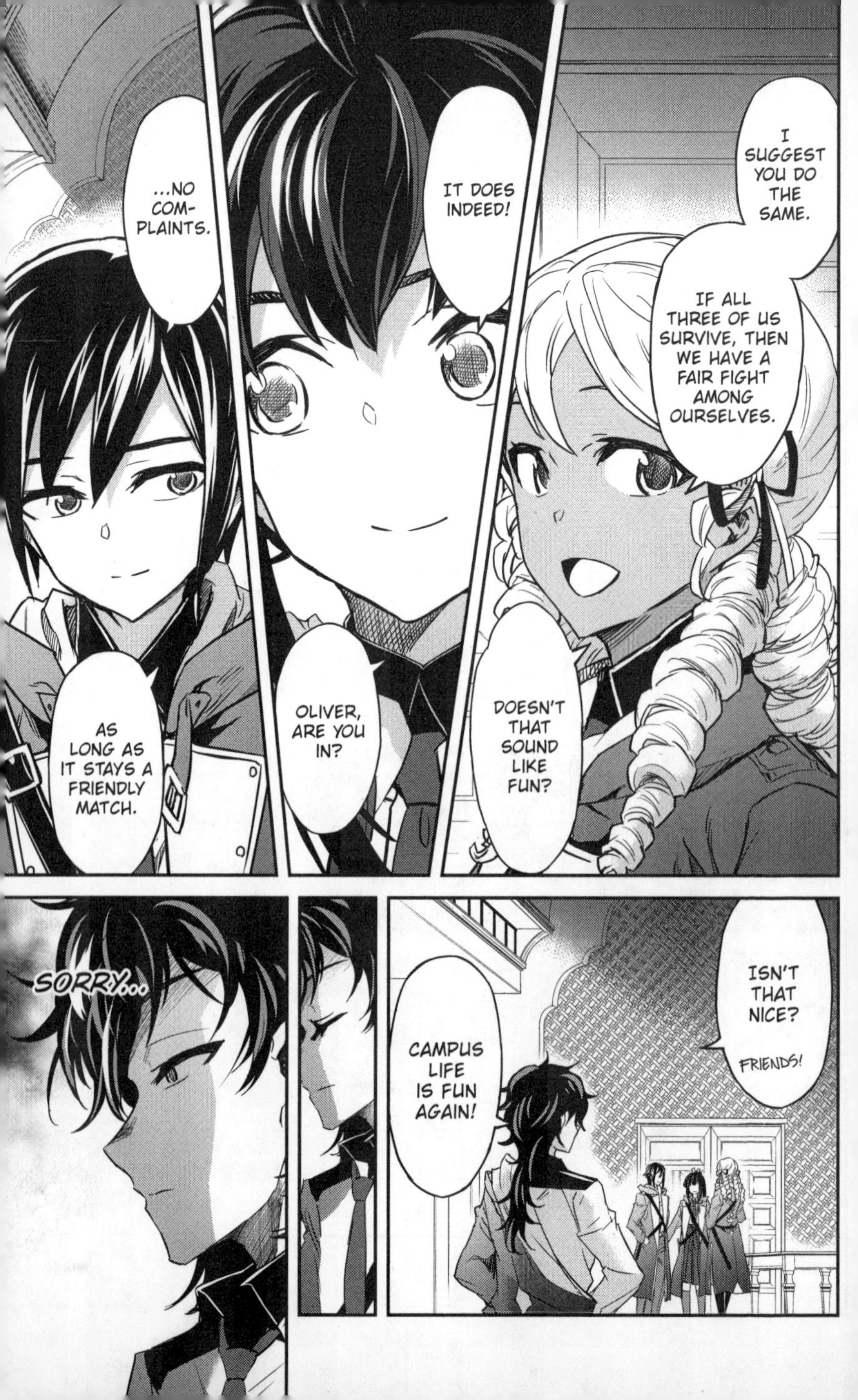
I SUGGEST YOU DO THE SAME.
IF ALL THREE OF US SURVIVE, THEN WE HAVE A FAIR FIGHT AMONG OURSELVES.
DOESN'T THAT SOUND LIKE FUN?
IT DOES INDEED!
OLIVER, ARE YOU IN?
...NO COM-PLAINTS.
AS LONG AS IT STAYS A FRIENDLY MATCH.
ISN'T THAT NICE?
FRIENDS!
CAMPUS LIFE IS FUN AGAIN!
SORRY...

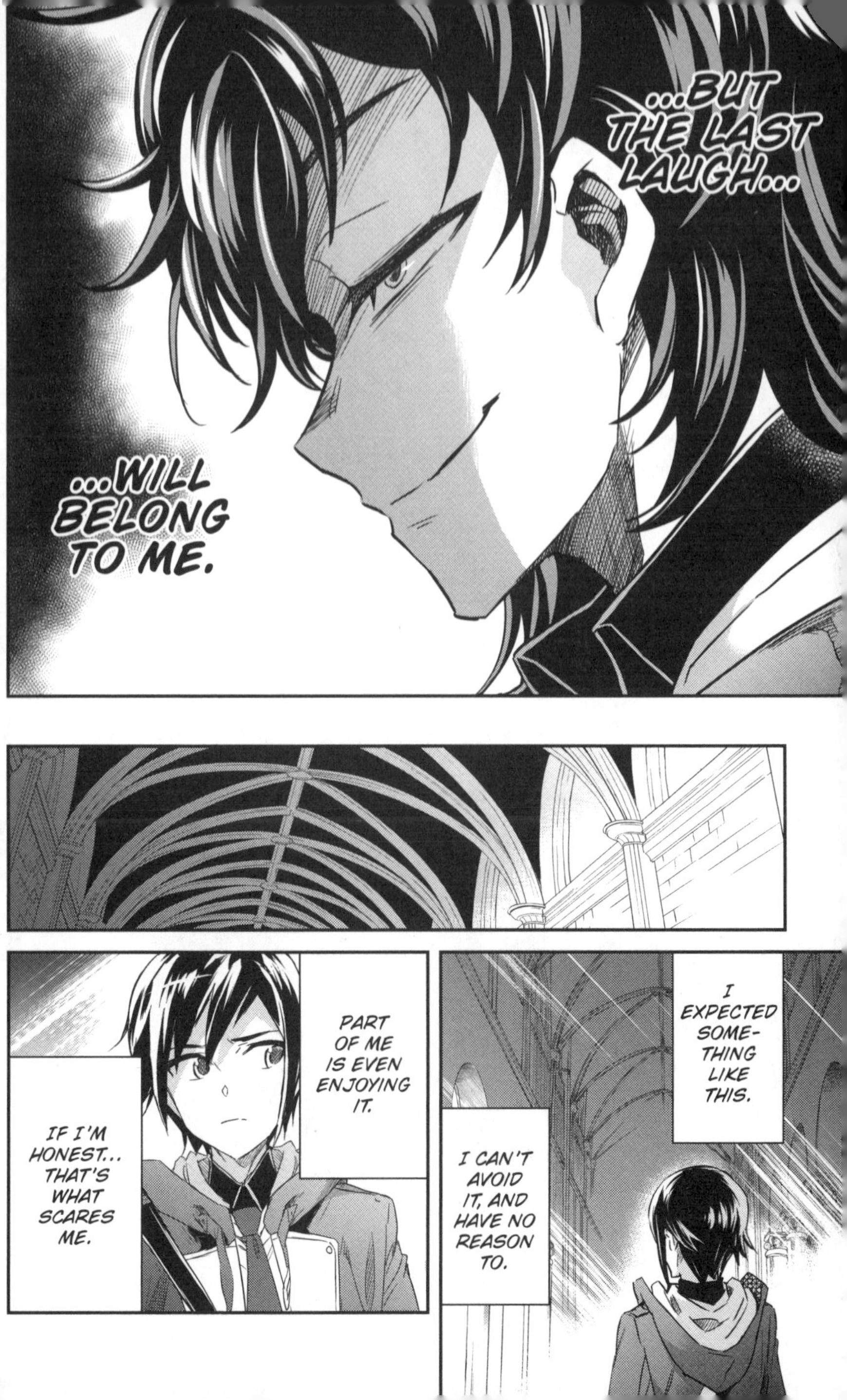
...BUT THE LAST LAUGH...
...WILL BELONG TO ME.
I EXPECTED SOME-THING LIKE THIS.
I CAN'T AVOID IT, AND HAVE NO REASON TO.
PART OF ME IS EVEN ENJOYING IT.
IF I'M HONEST... THAT'S WHAT SCARES ME.

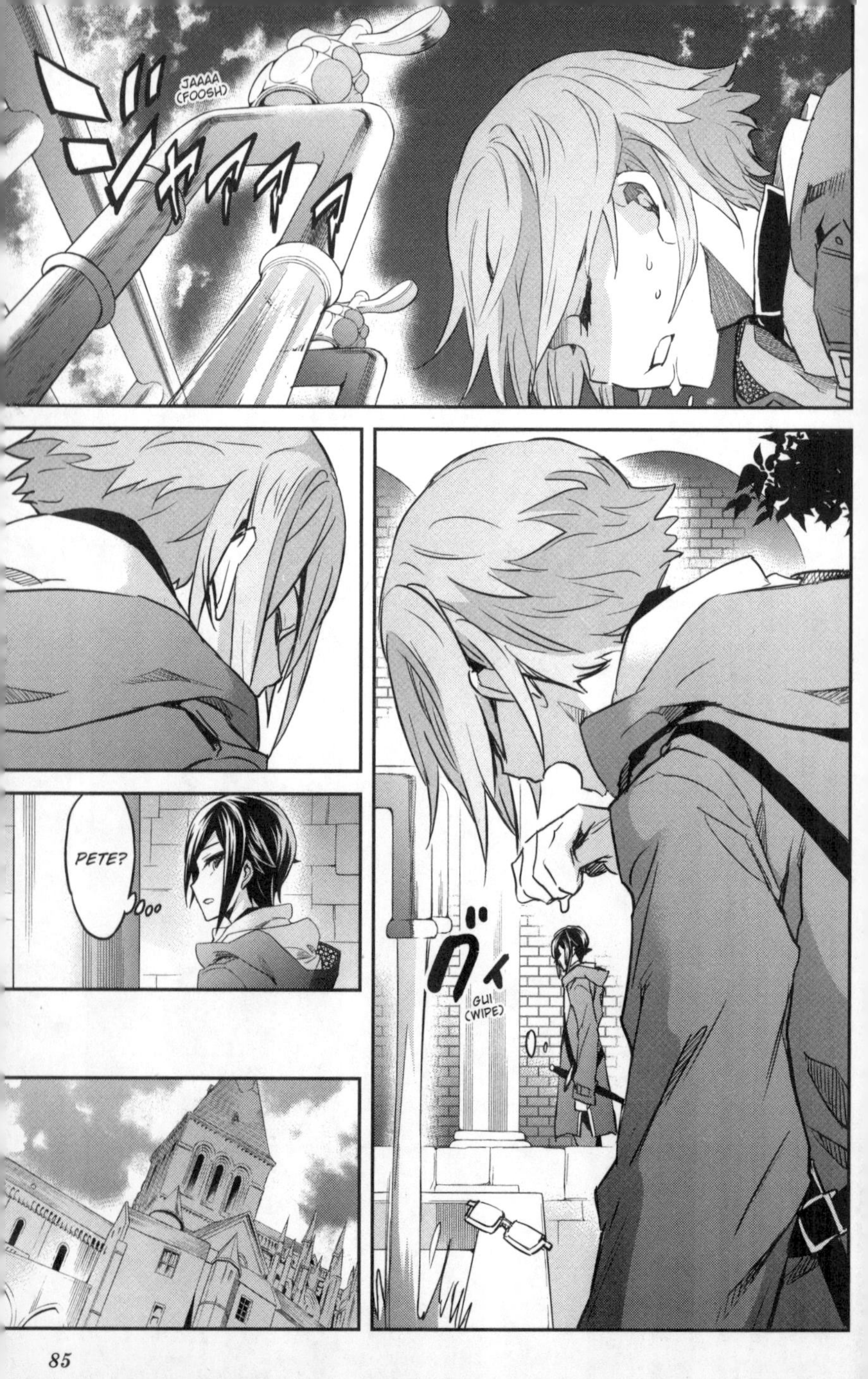
ジャアアア
JAAAA (FOOSH)
グイ
GUI (WIPE)
PETE?

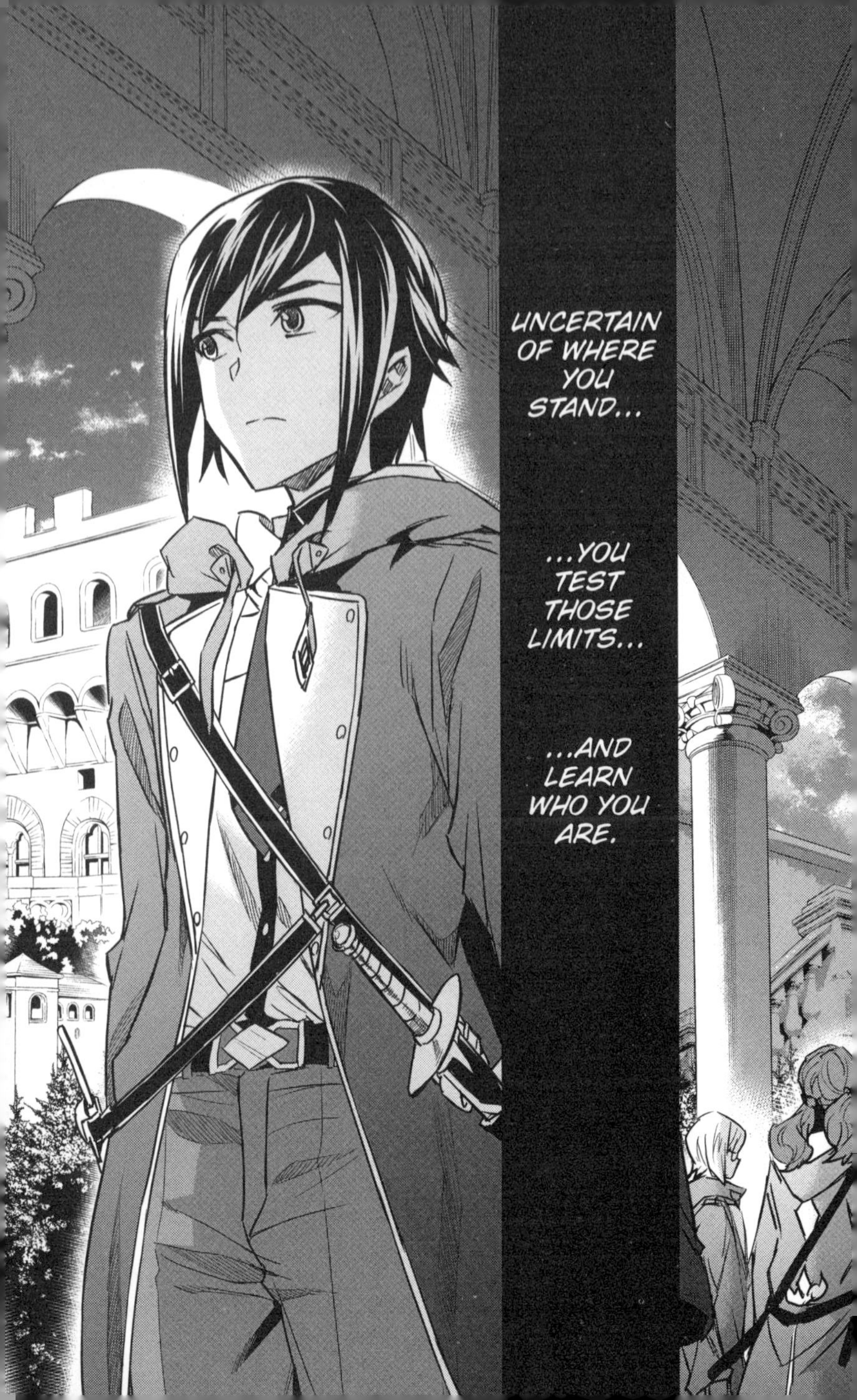
UNCERTAIN OF WHERE YOU STAND...
...YOU TEST THOSE LIMITS...
...AND LEARN WHO YOU ARE.

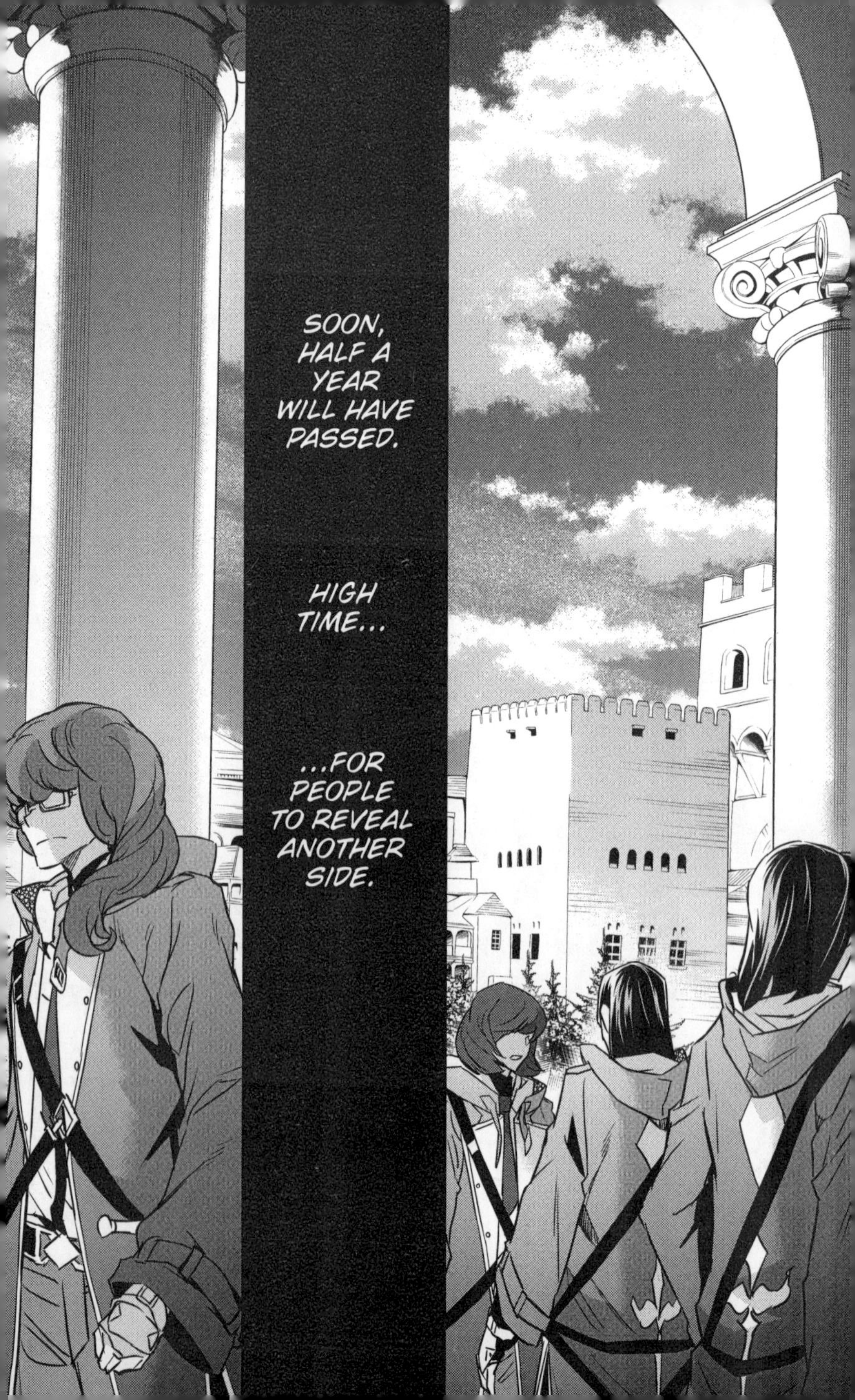
SOON, HALF A YEAR WILL HAVE PASSED.
HIGH TIME...
...FOR PEOPLE TO REVEAL ANOTHER SIDE.

MAGICAL ENGI-NEERING

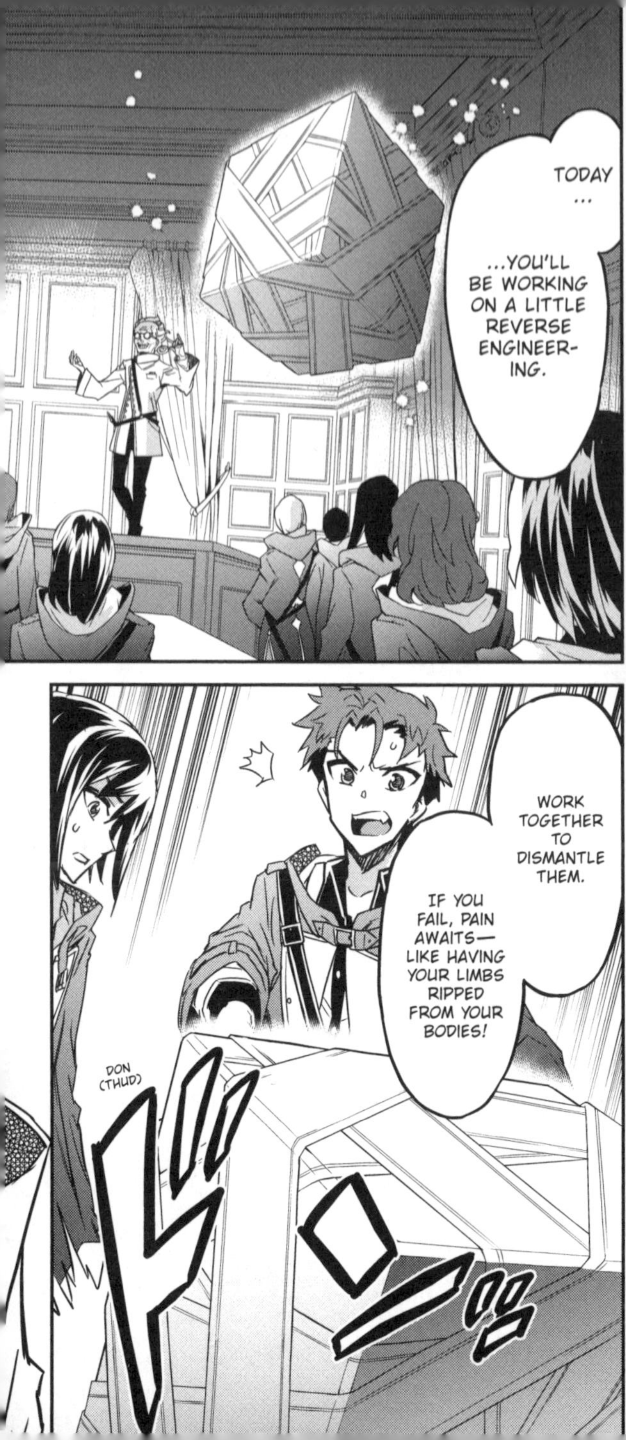
TODAY ...
...YOU'LL BE WORKING ON A LITTLE REVERSE ENGINEERING.
WORK TOGETHER TO DISMANTLE THEM.
IF YOU FAIL, PAIN AWAITS—LIKE HAVING YOUR LIMBS RIPPED FROM YOUR BODIES!
DON (THUD)

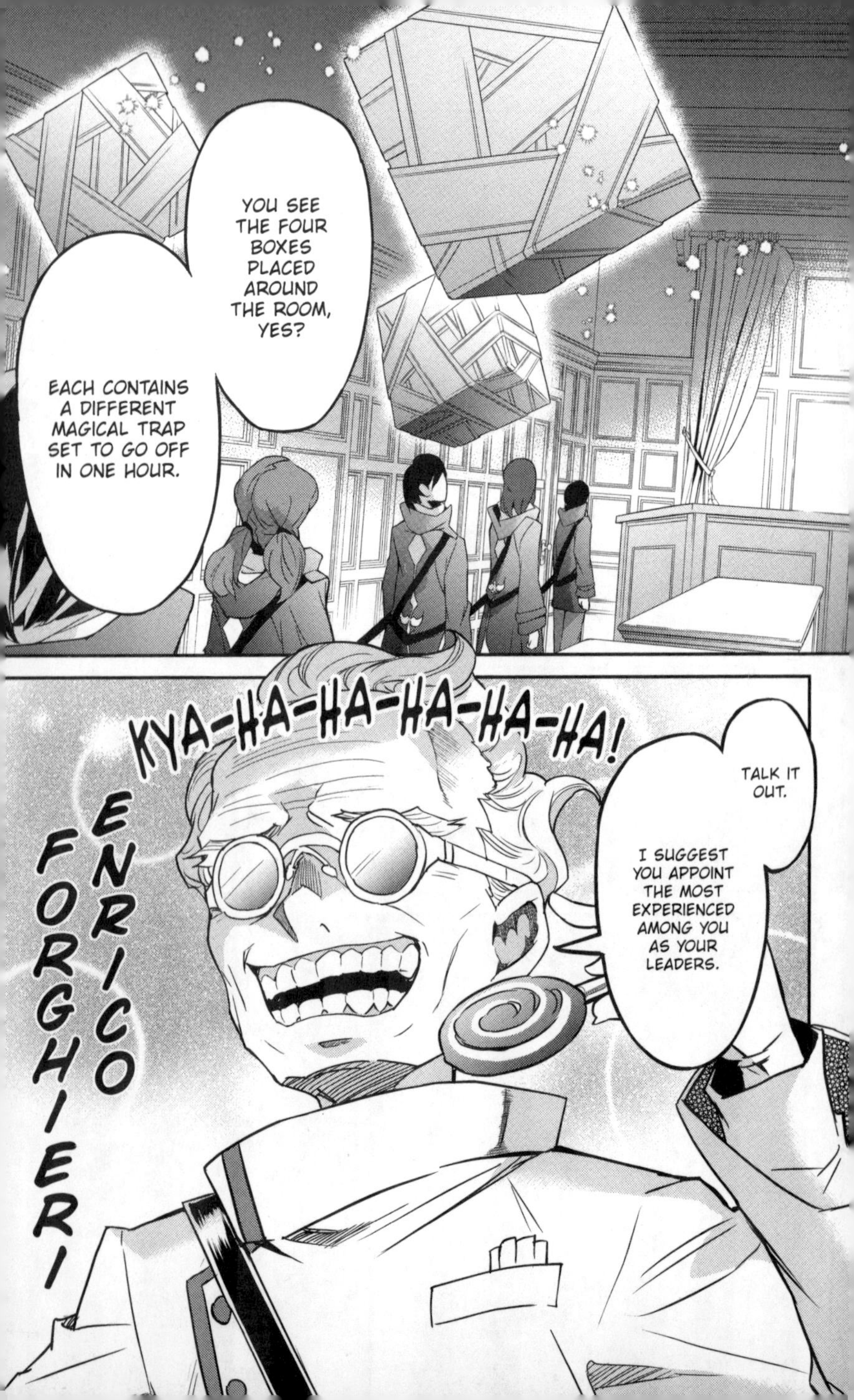
YOU SEE THE FOUR BOXES PLACED AROUND THE ROOM, YES?
EACH CONTAINS A DIFFERENT MAGICAL TRAP SET TO GO OFF IN ONE HOUR.
TALK IT OUT.
I SUGGEST YOU APPOINT THE MOST EXPERIENCED AMONG YOU AS YOUR LEADERS.
KYA-HA-HA-HA-HA-HA-HA!
ENRICO FORGHIERI

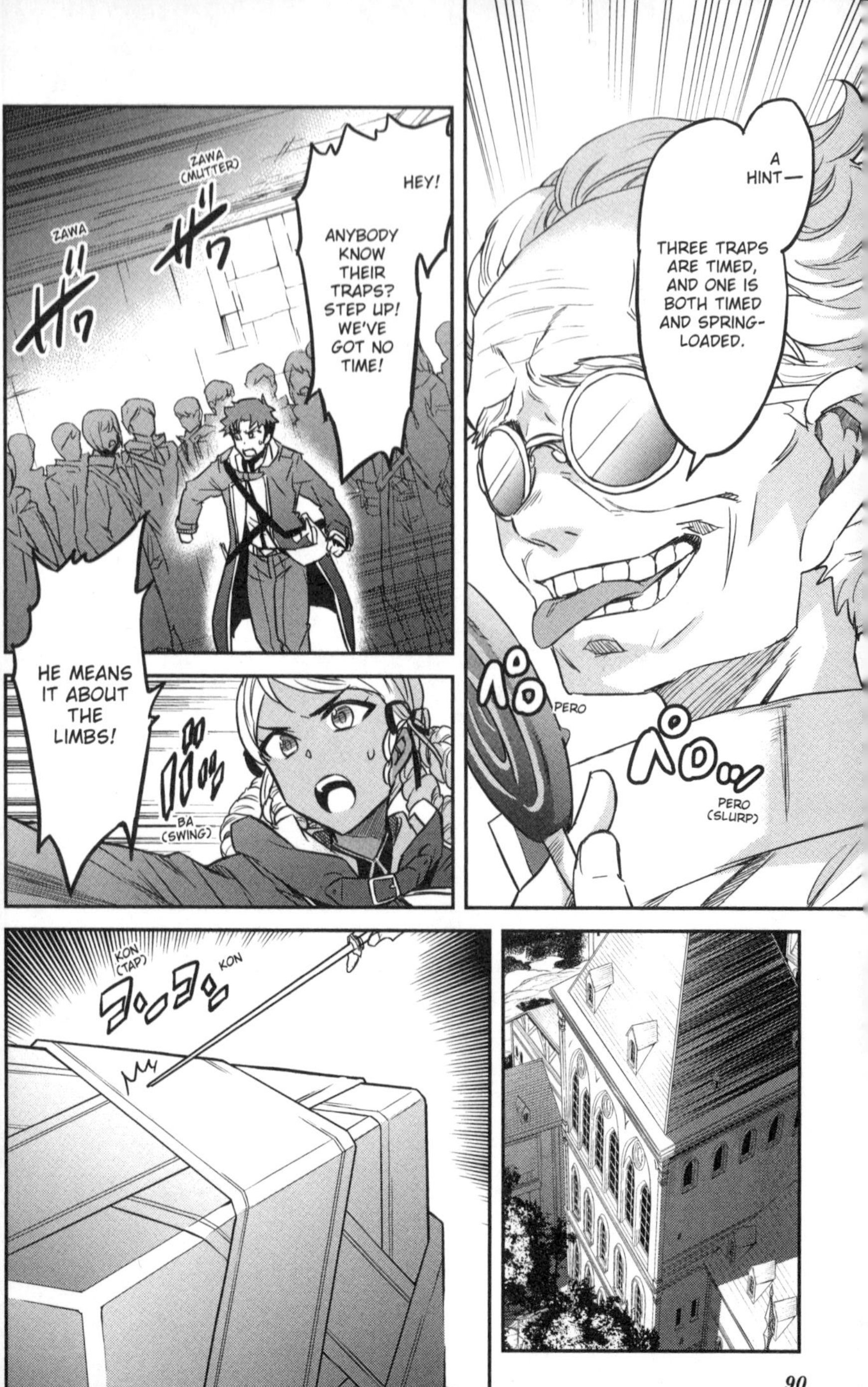
A HINT—
THREE TRAPS ARE TIMED, AND ONE IS BOTH TIMED AND SPRING-LOADED.
PERO
PERO (SLURP)
ZAWA (MUTTER)
ZAWA
HEY!
ANYBODY KNOW THEIR TRAPS? STEP UP! WE'VE GOT NO TIME!
HE MEANS IT ABOUT THE LIMBS!
BA (SWING)
KON (TAP)
KON

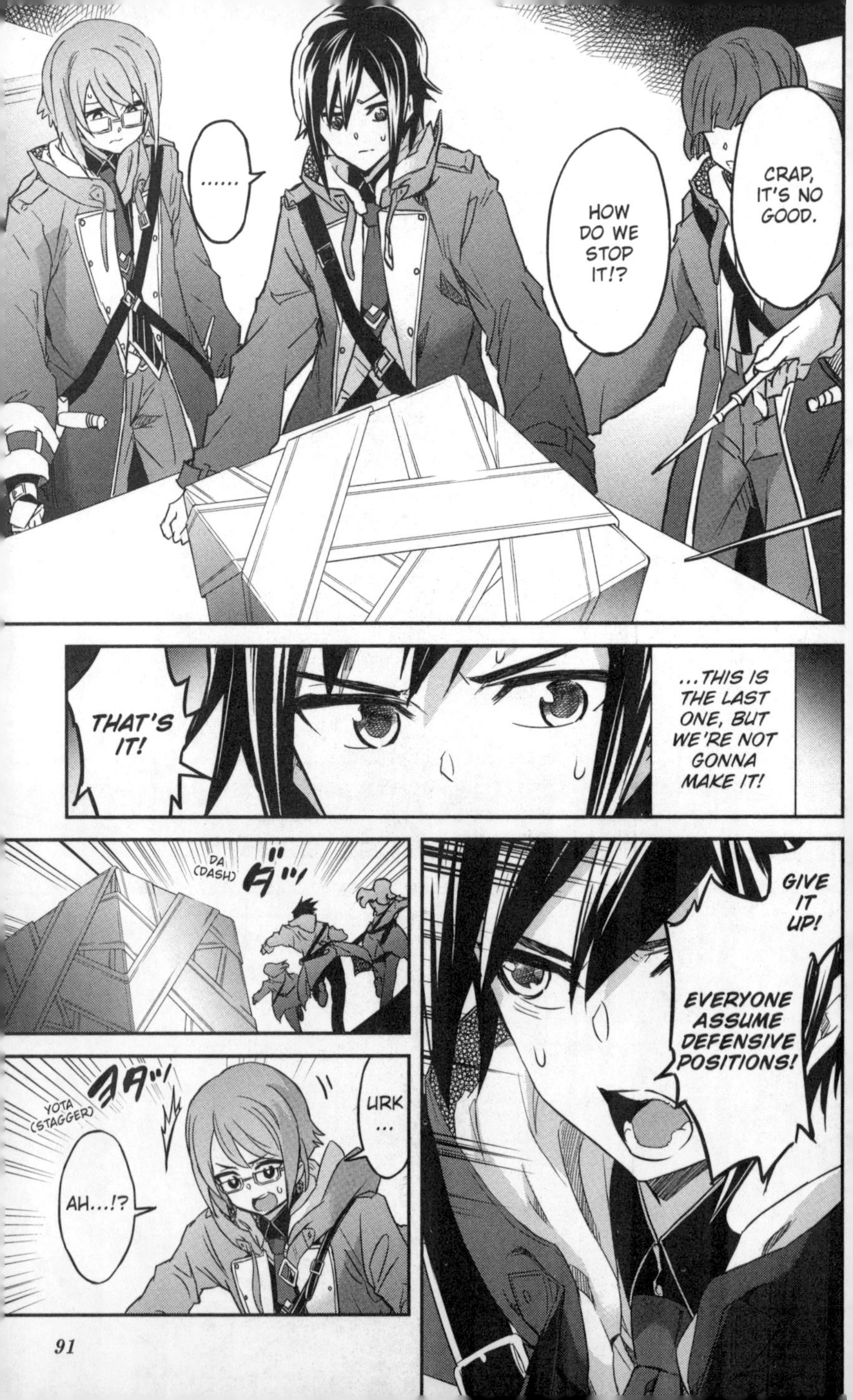
CRAP, IT'S NO GOOD.
HOW DO WE STOP IT!?
......
...THIS IS THE LAST ONE, BUT WE'RE NOT GONNA MAKE IT!
THAT'S IT!
GIVE IT UP!
EVERYONE ASSUME DEFENSIVE POSITIONS!
DA (DASH)
URK ...
YOTA (STAGGER)
AH...!?

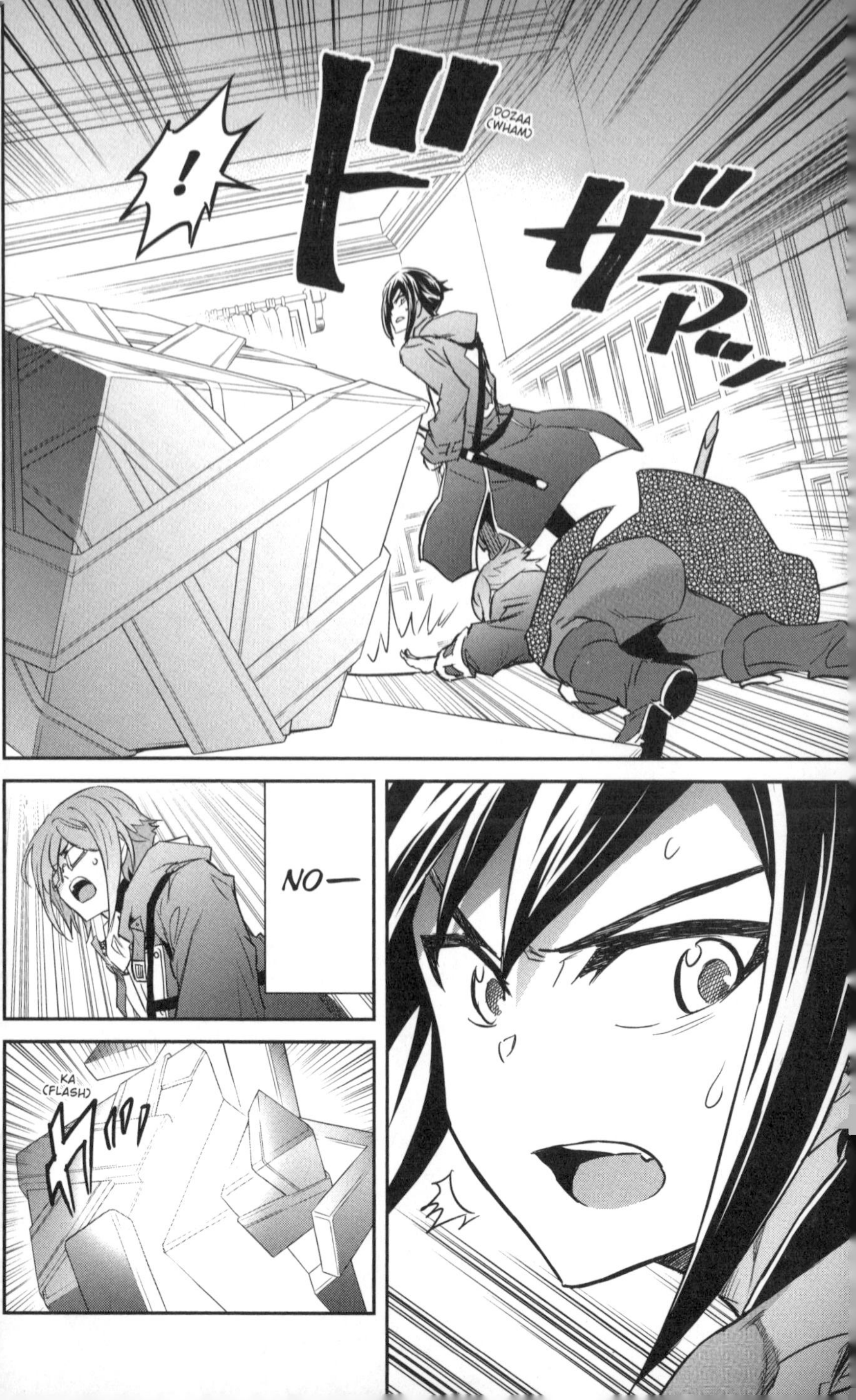
!
DOZAA (WHAM)
NO—
KA (FLASH)

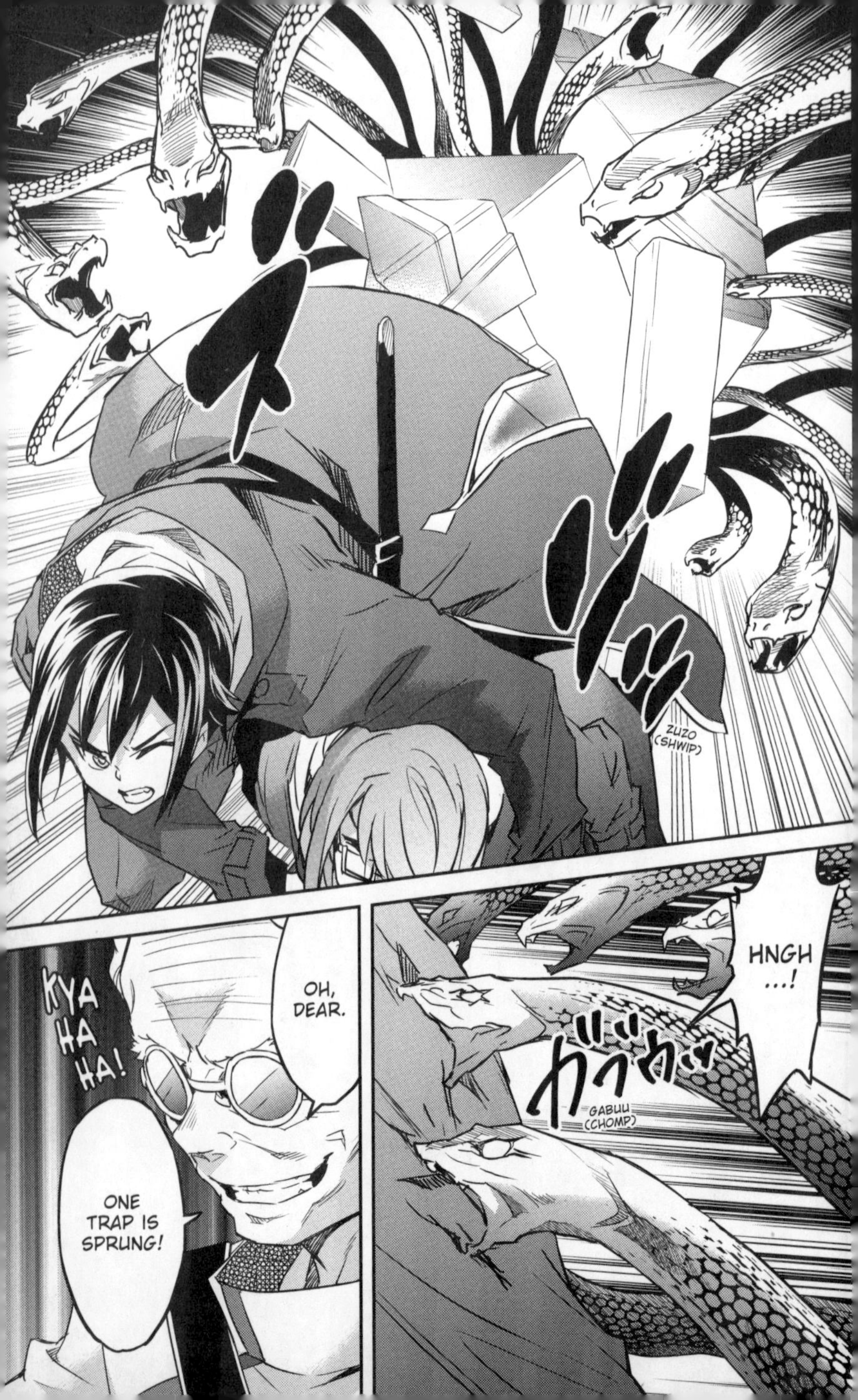
ZUZO (SHWIP)
HNGH ...!
GABUU (CHOMP)
OH, DEAR.
KYA HA HA!
ONE TRAP IS SPRUNG!

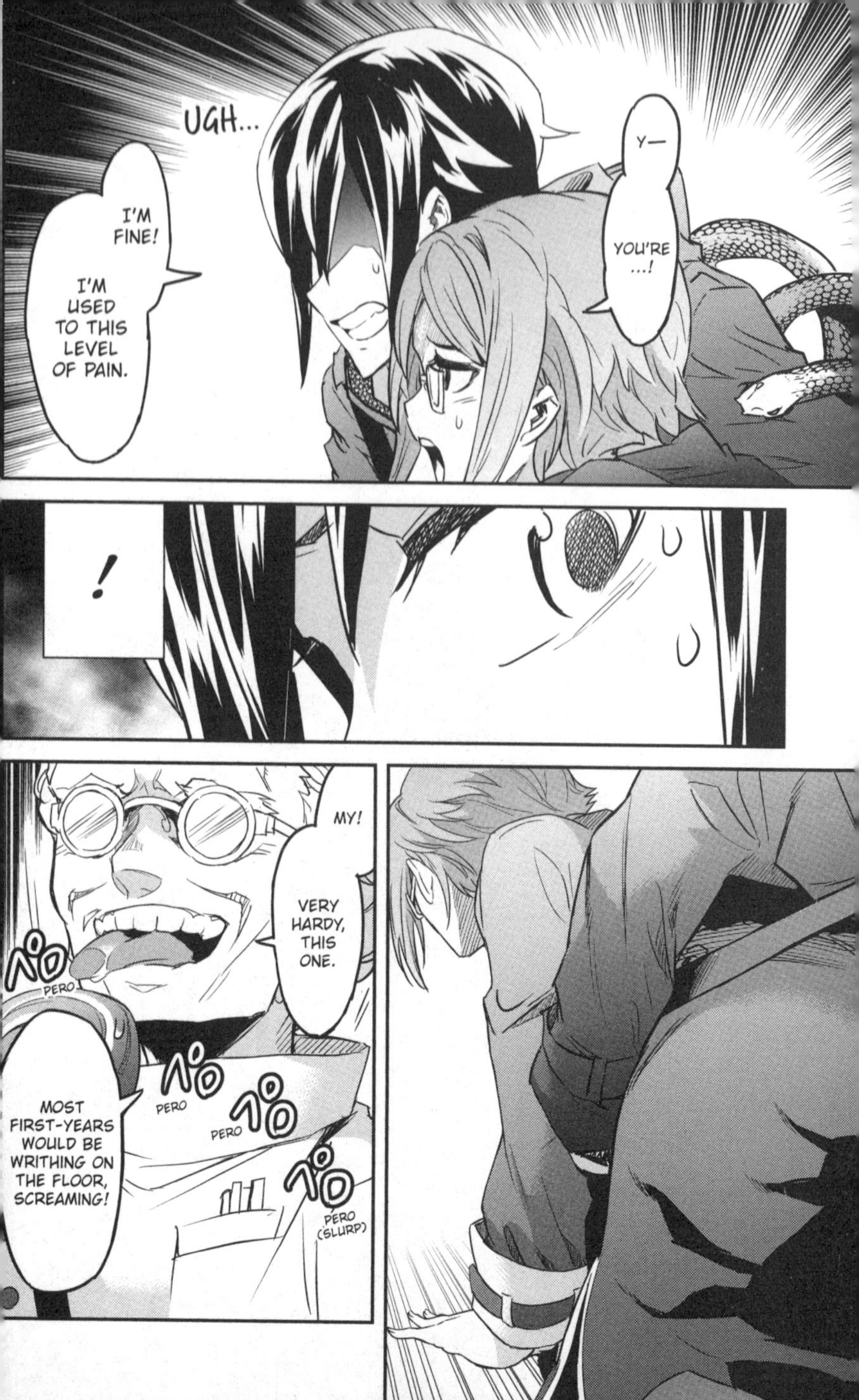
Y—
YOU'RE ...!
UGH...
I'M FINE!
I'M USED TO THIS LEVEL OF PAIN.
!
MY!
VERY HARDY, THIS ONE.
ペロ
PERO
MOST FIRST-YEARS WOULD BE WRITHING ON THE FLOOR, SCREAMING!
ペロ
PERO
ペロ
PERO
ペロ
PERO (SLURP)

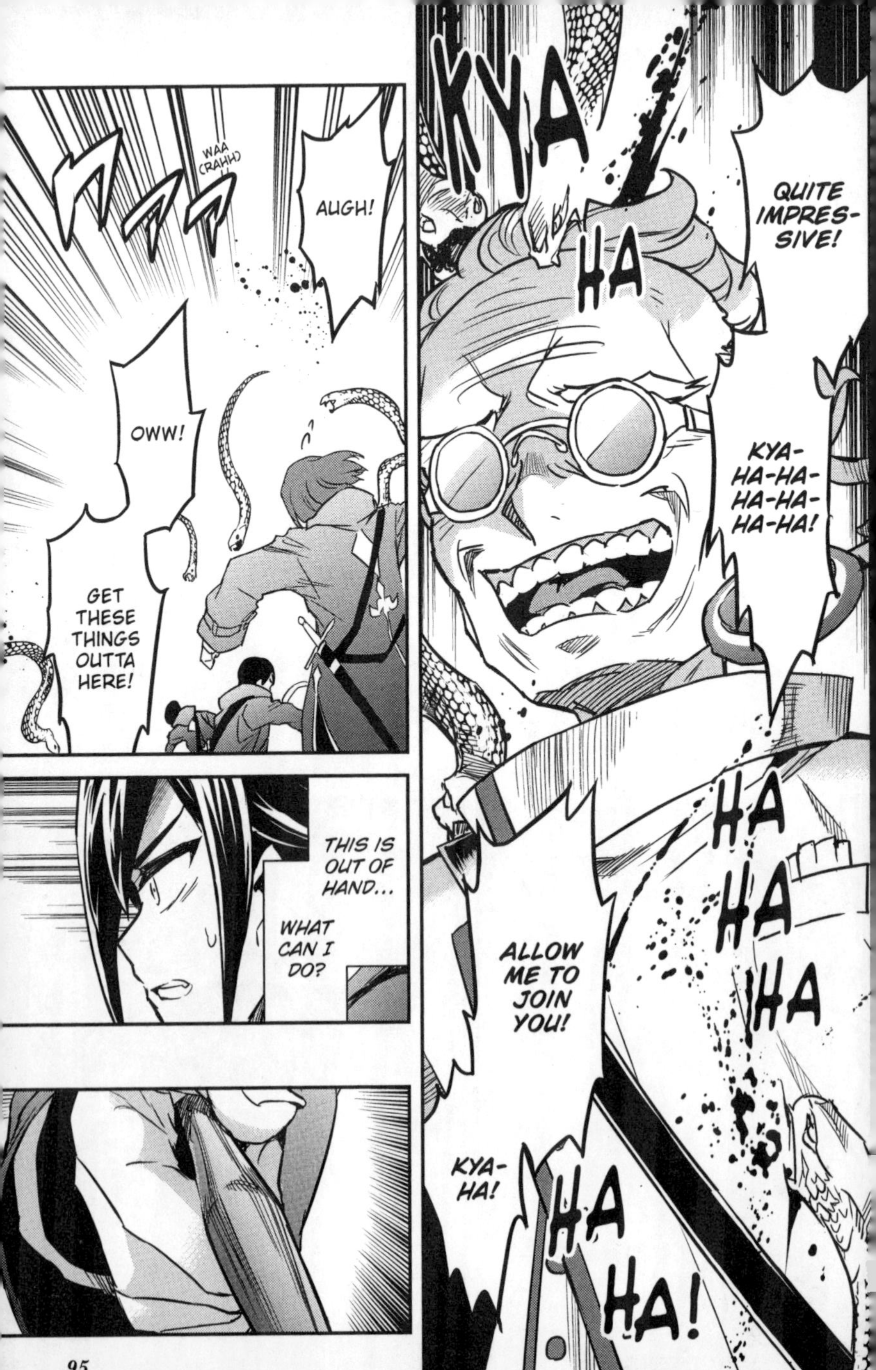
KYA
HA
QUITE IMPRES-SIVE!
KYA-HA-HA-HA-HA-HA-HA!
HA HA HA HA
ALLOW ME TO JOIN YOU!
KYA-HA!
HA HA!
AUGH!
WAA (RAHH)
OWW!
GET THESE THINGS OUTTA HERE!
THIS IS OUT OF HAND...
WHAT CAN I DO?

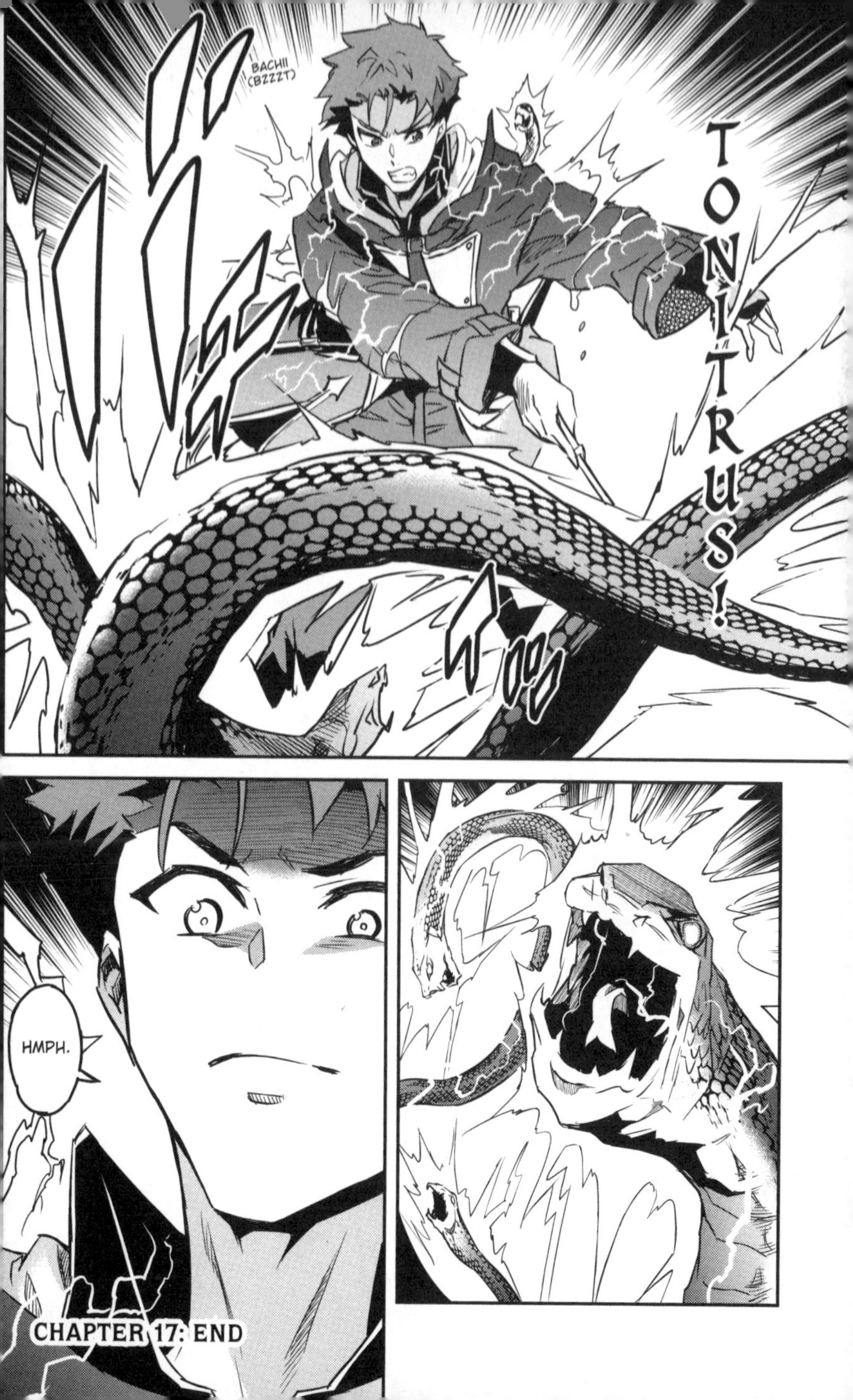
TONITRUS!
BACHII (BZZZT)
HMPH.
CHAPTER 17: END

CHAPTER 18: REVERSI

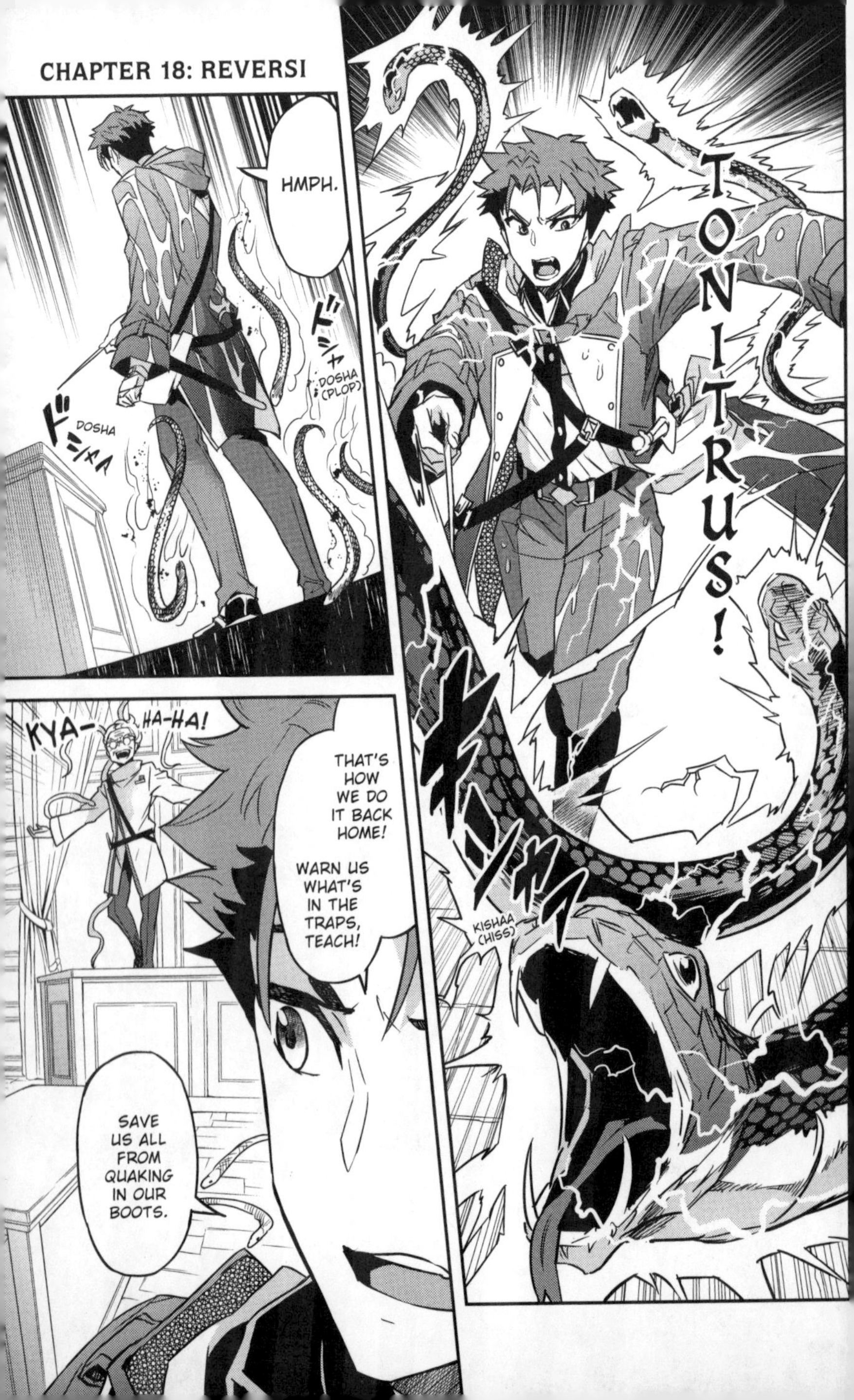

TONITRUS!
KISHAA (HISS)
HMPH.
DOSHA (PLOP)
DOSHA
KYA-HA-HA!
THAT'S HOW WE DO IT BACK HOME!
WARN US WHAT'S IN THE TRAPS, TEACH!
SAVE US ALL FROM QUAKING IN OUR BOOTS.

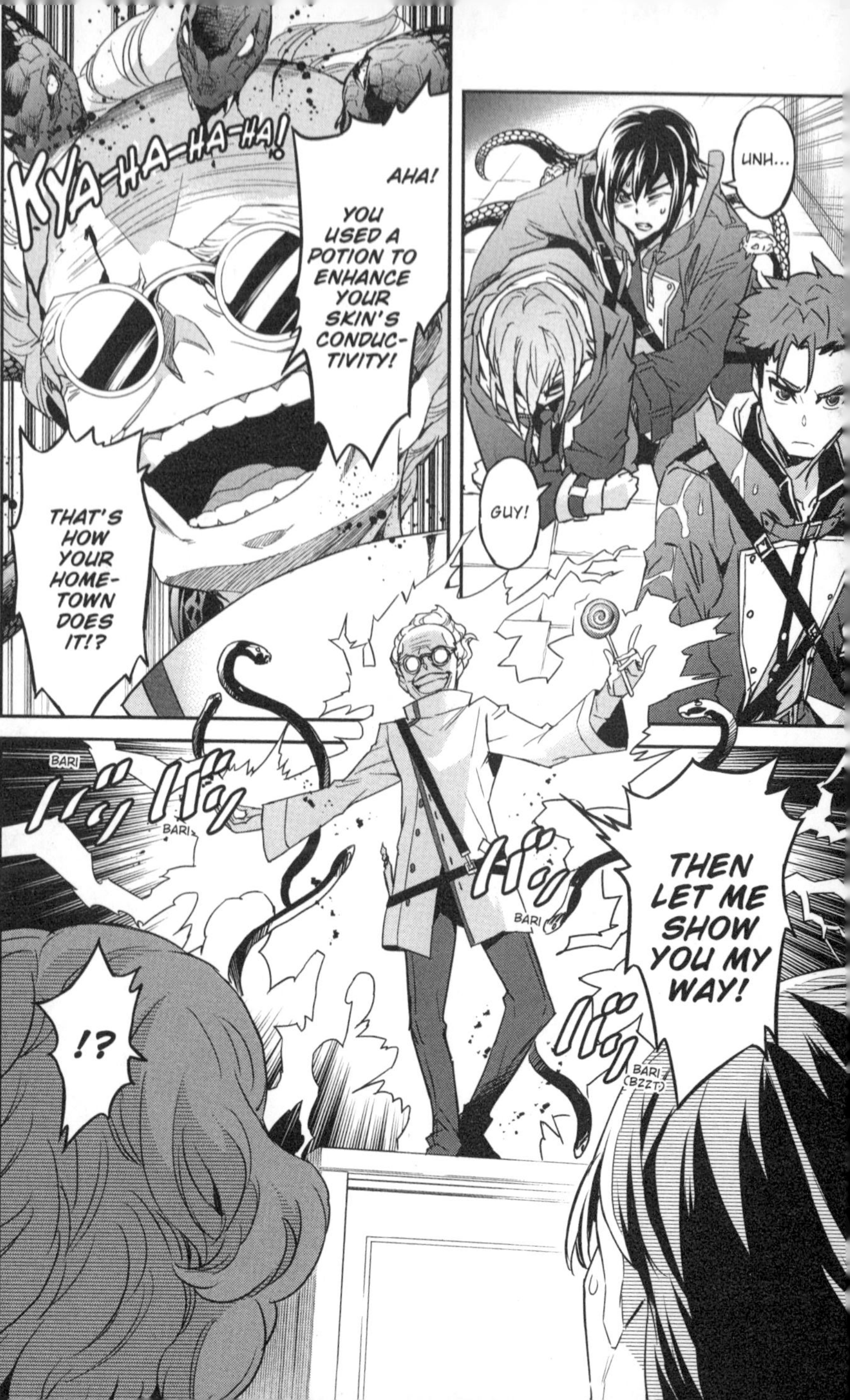

UNH...
GUY!
KYA-HA-HA-HA!
AHA!
YOU USED A POTION TO ENHANCE YOUR SKIN'S CONDUC-TIVITY!
THAT'S HOW YOUR HOME-TOWN DOES IT!?
THEN LET ME SHOW YOU MY WAY!
BARI (BZZT)
BARI
!?
BARI
BARI

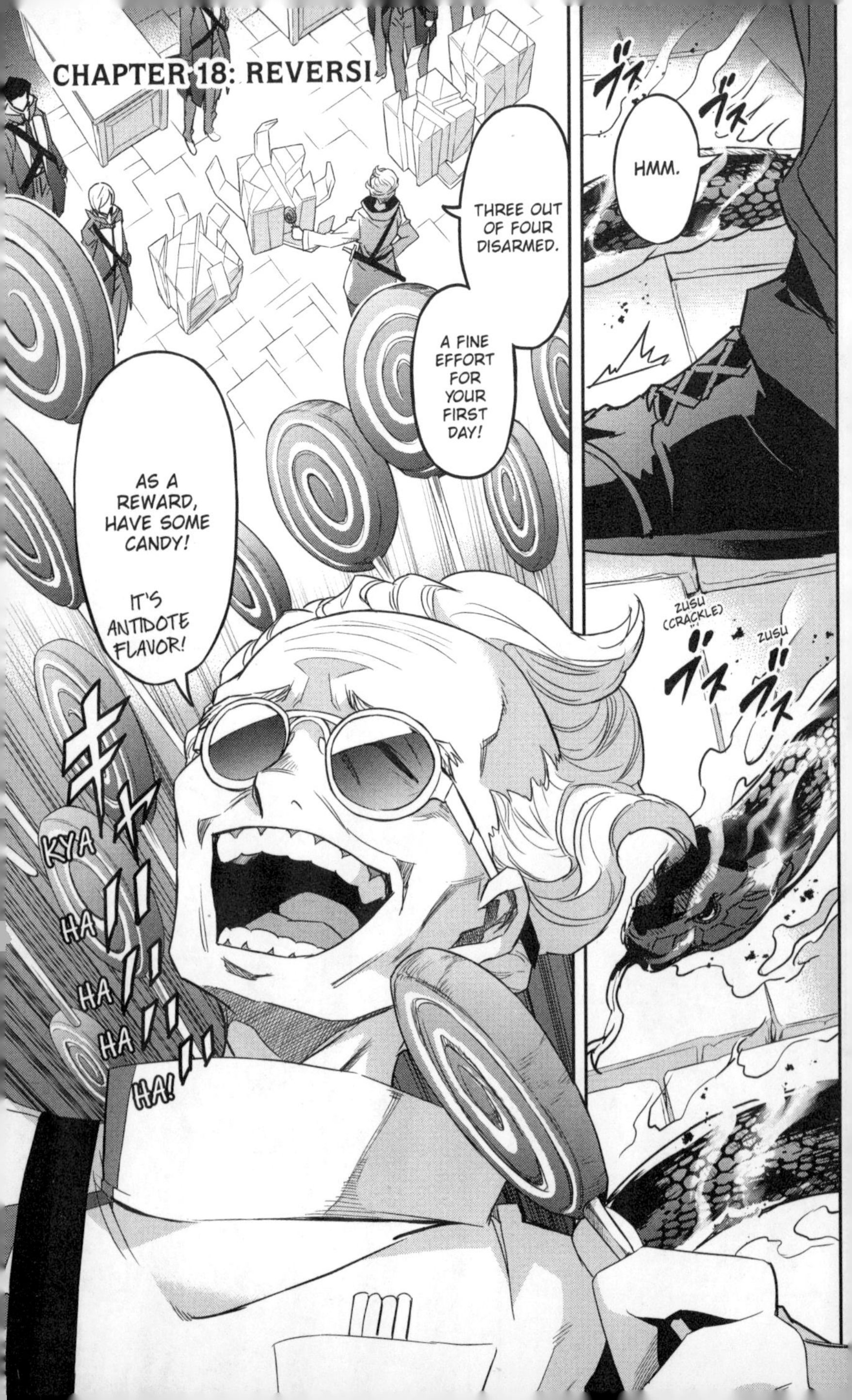
HMM.
ZUSU (CRACKLE)
ZUSU
CHAPTER 18: REVERSI
THREE OUT OF FOUR DISARMED.
A FINE EFFORT FOR YOUR FIRST DAY!
AS A REWARD, HAVE SOME CANDY!
IT'S ANTIDOTE FLAVOR!
KYA HA HA HA HA!

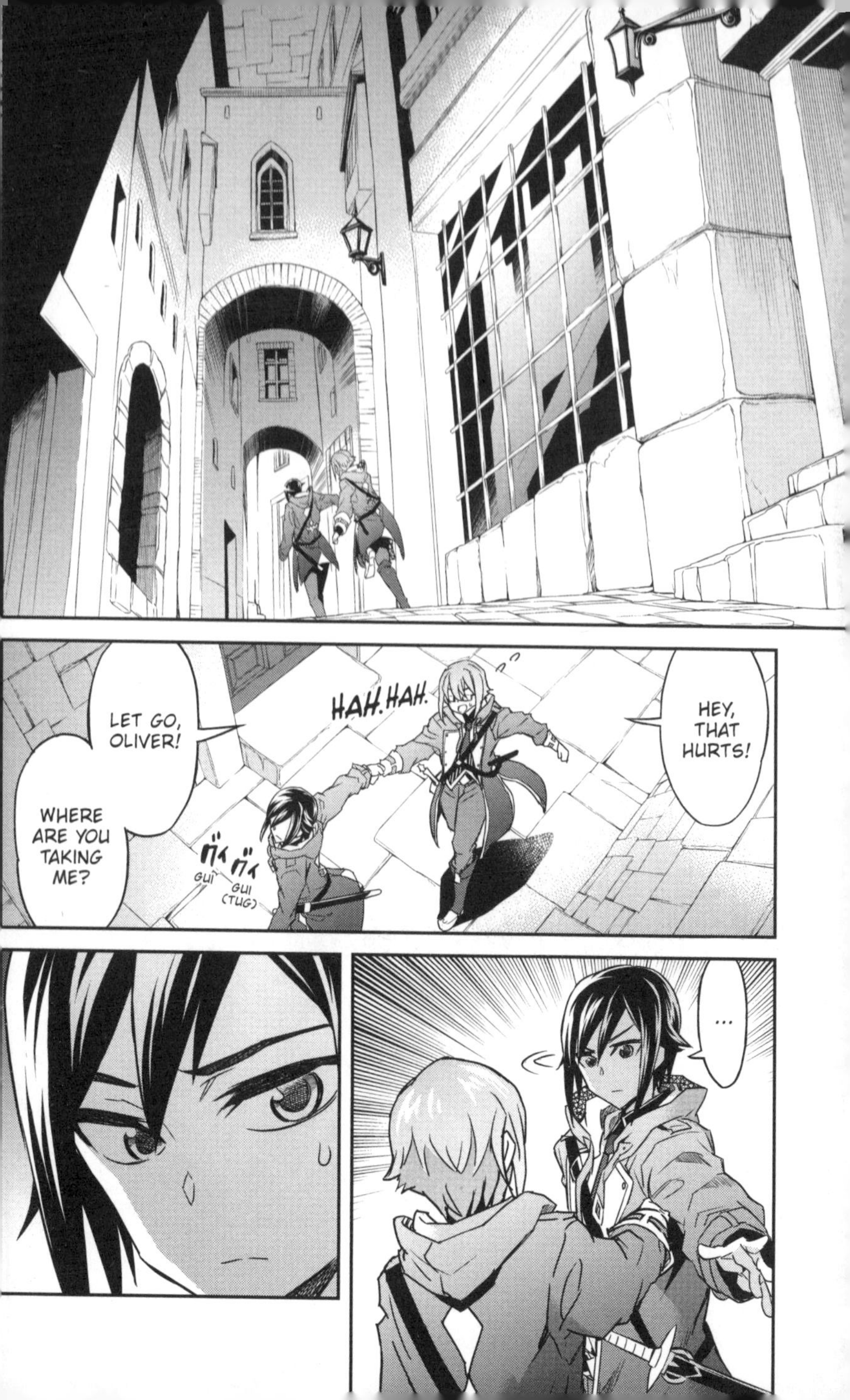
HEY, THAT HURTS!
HAH. HAH.
LET GO, OLIVER!
WHERE ARE YOU TAKING ME?
グィ グィ
GUI GUI (TUG)
...

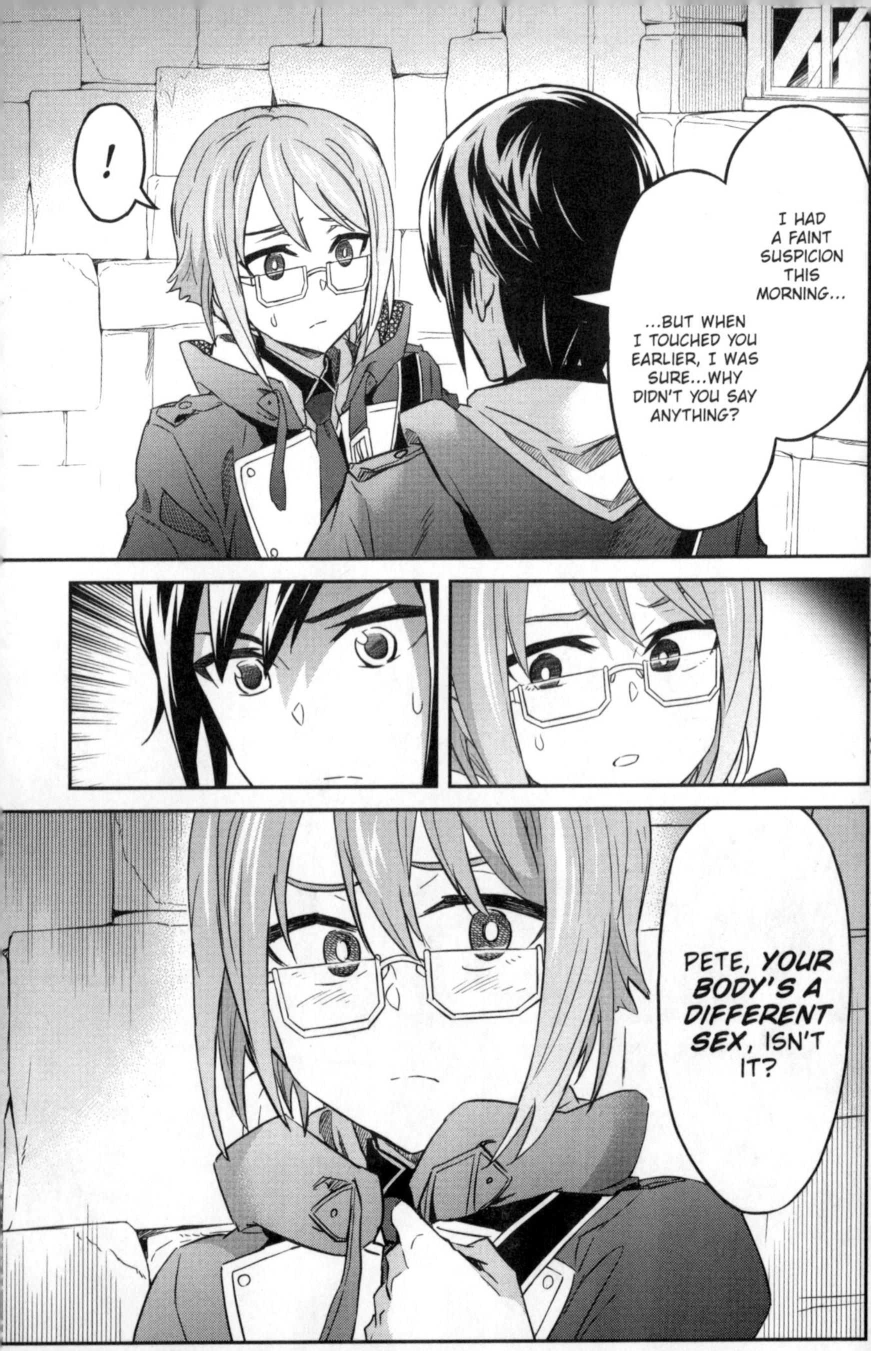
I HAD A FAINT SUSPICION THIS MORNING...
...BUT WHEN I TOUCHED YOU EARLIER, I WAS SURE...WHY DIDN'T YOU SAY ANYTHING?
!
PETE, YOUR BODY'S A DIFFERENT SEX, ISN'T IT?

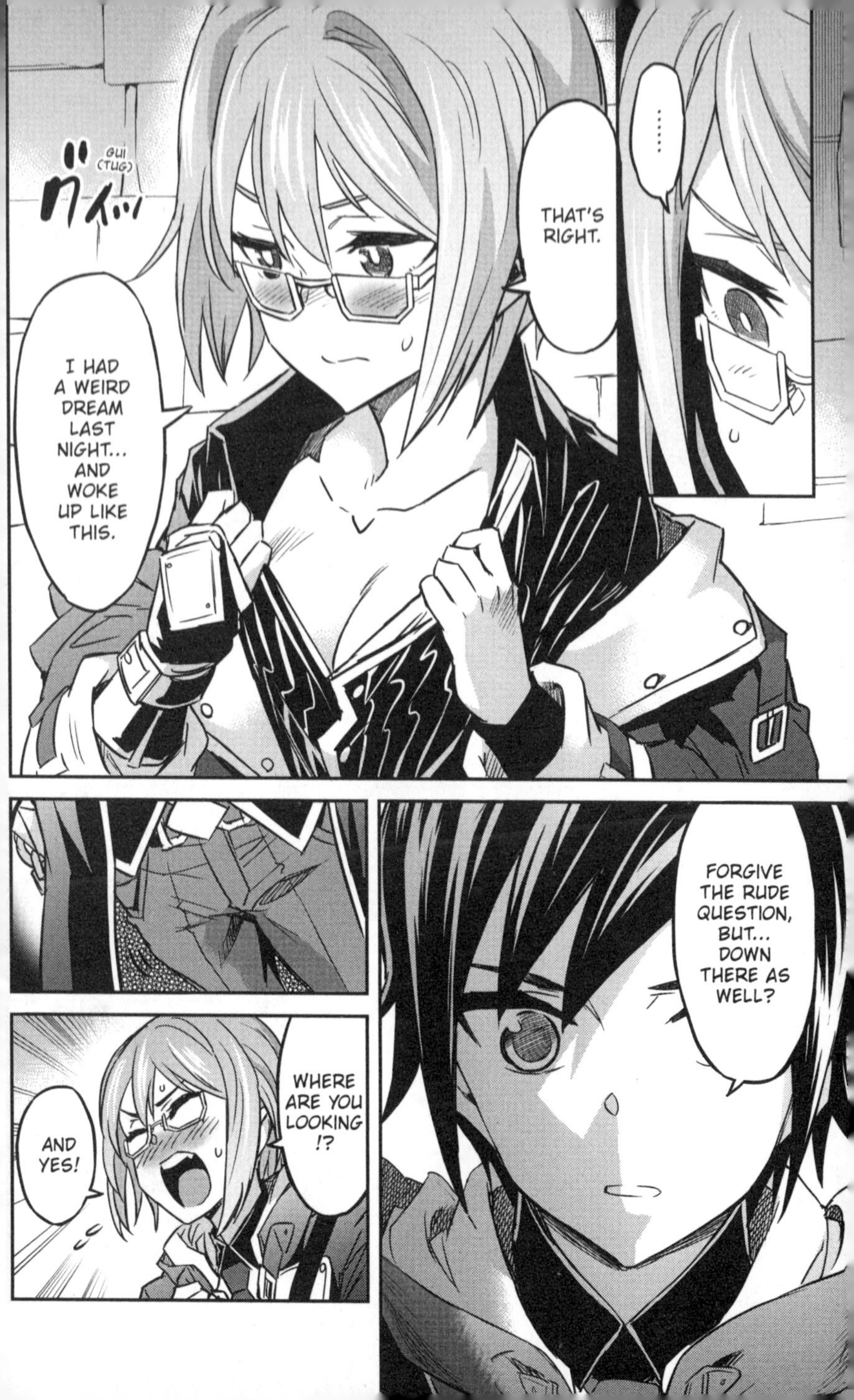
......
THAT'S RIGHT.
GUI (TUG)
I HAD A WEIRD DREAM LAST NIGHT... AND WOKE UP LIKE THIS.
FORGIVE THE RUDE QUESTION, BUT... DOWN THERE AS WELL?
WHERE ARE YOU LOOKING!?
AND YES!

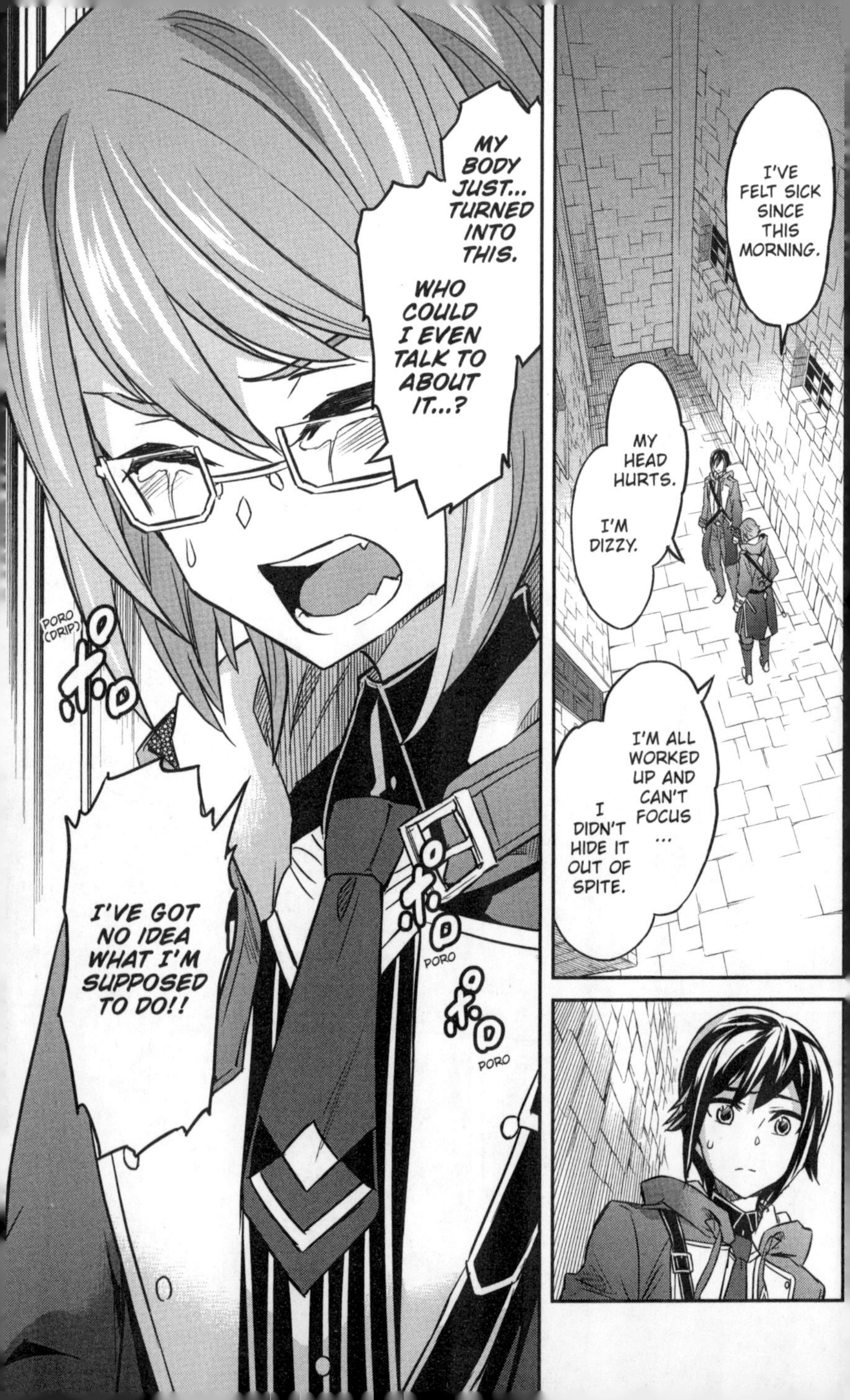
I'VE FELT SICK SINCE THIS MORNING.
MY HEAD HURTS.
I'M DIZZY.
I'M ALL WORKED UP AND CAN'T FOCUS ...
I DIDN'T HIDE IT OUT OF SPITE.
MY BODY JUST... TURNED INTO THIS.
WHO COULD I EVEN TALK TO ABOUT IT...?
PORO (DRIP)
I'VE GOT NO IDEA WHAT I'M SUPPOSED TO DO!!
PORO
PORO

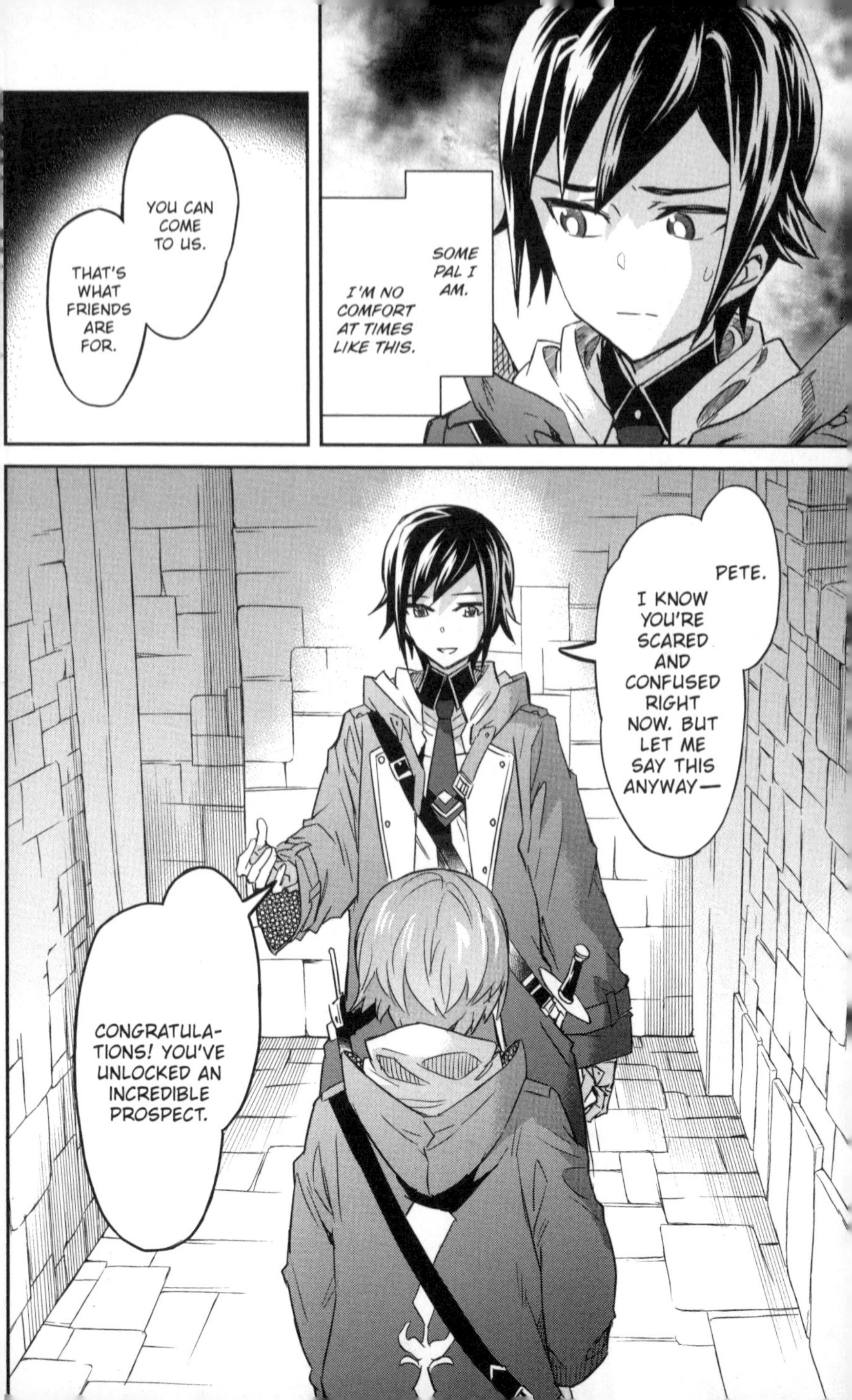
SOME PAL I AM.
I'M NO COMFORT AT TIMES LIKE THIS.
YOU CAN COME TO US.
THAT'S WHAT FRIENDS ARE FOR.
PETE.
I KNOW YOU'RE SCARED AND CONFUSED RIGHT NOW. BUT LET ME SAY THIS ANYWAY—
CONGRATULA-TIONS! YOU'VE UNLOCKED AN INCREDIBLE PROSPECT.

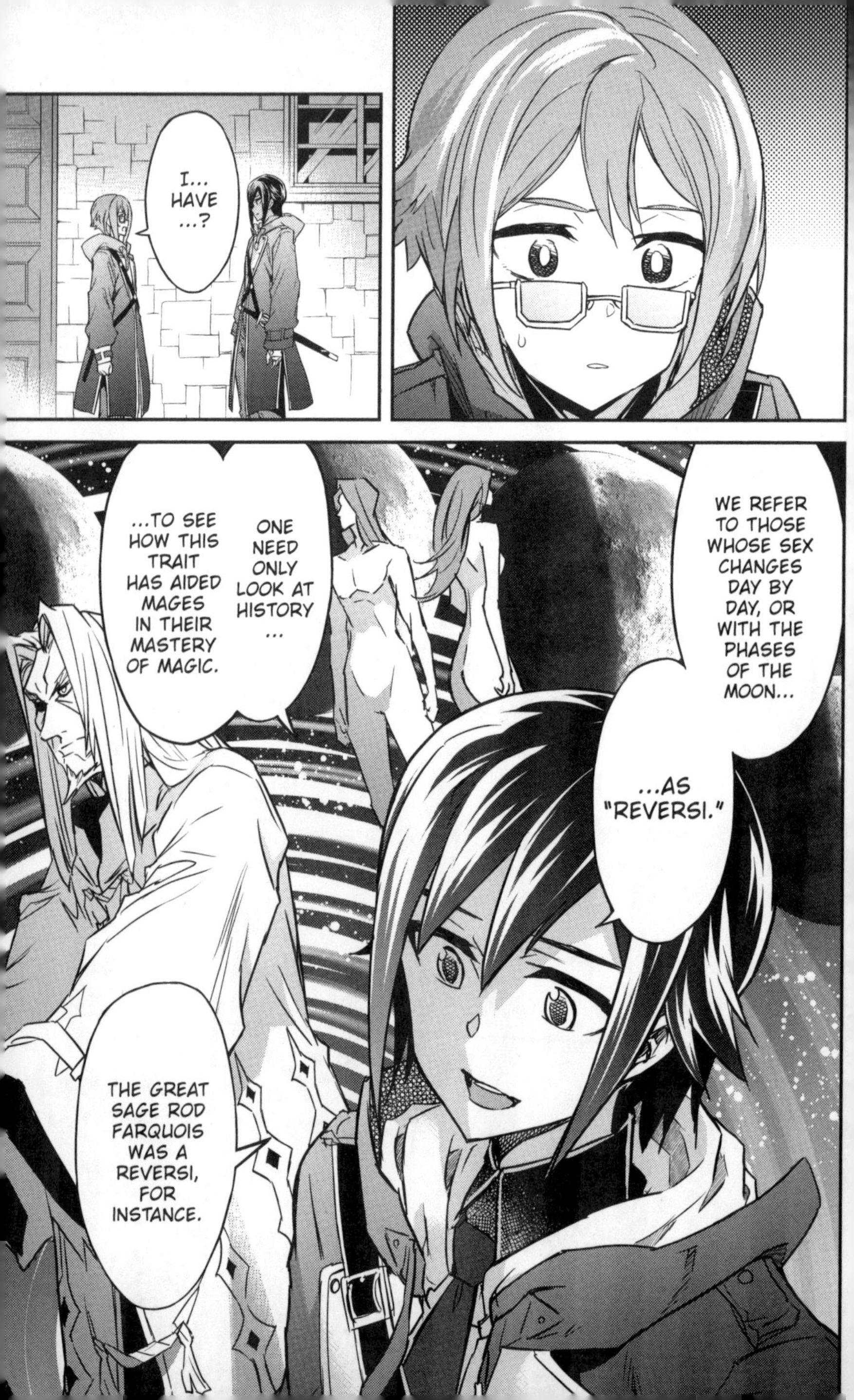
I... HAVE ...?
WE REFER TO THOSE WHOSE SEX CHANGES DAY BY DAY, OR WITH THE PHASES OF THE MOON...
...AS "REVERSI."
ONE NEED ONLY LOOK AT HISTORY ...
...TO SEE HOW THIS TRAIT HAS AIDED MAGES IN THEIR MASTERY OF MAGIC.
THE GREAT SAGE ROD FARQUOIS WAS A REVERSI, FOR INSTANCE.

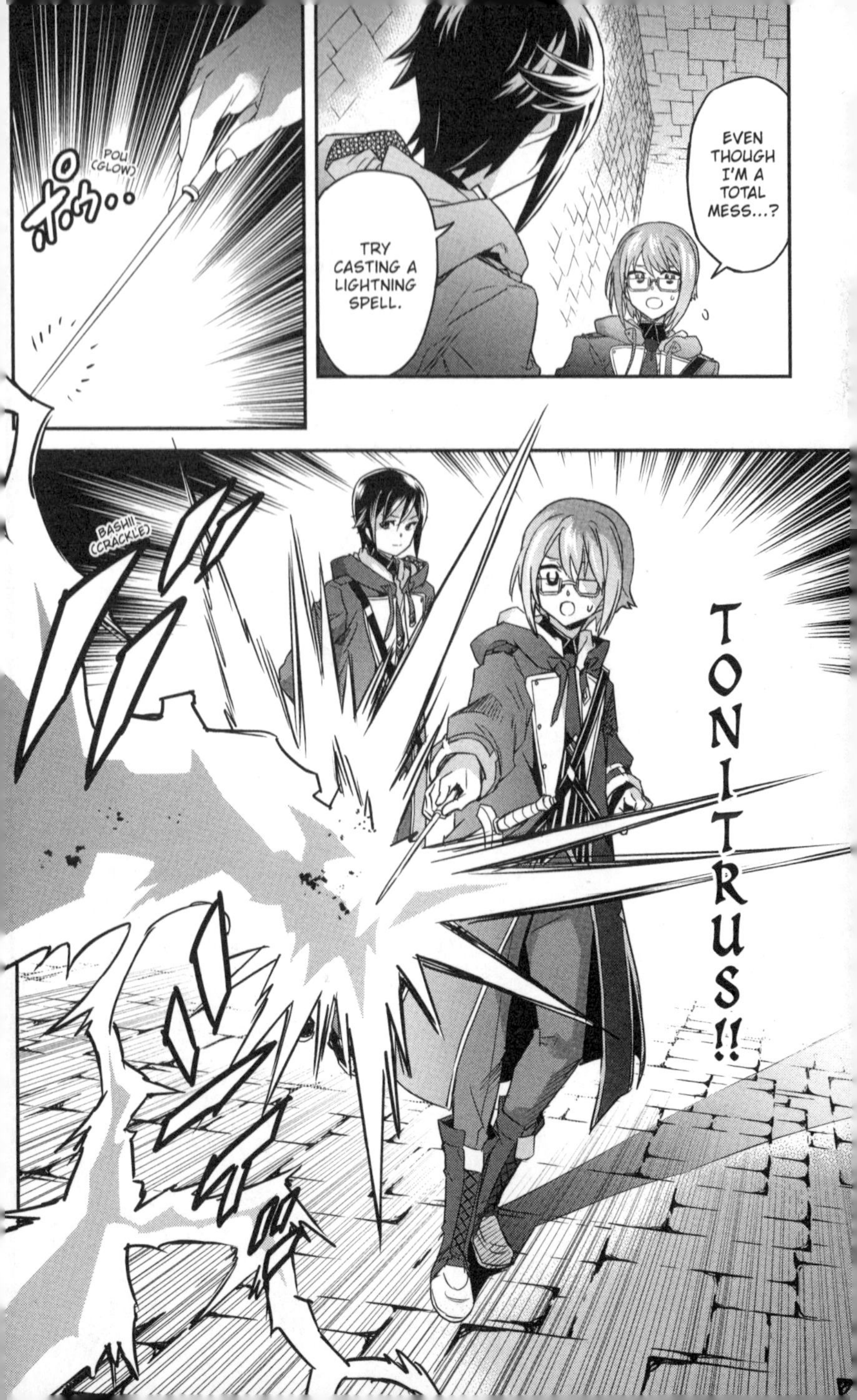
EVEN THOUGH I'M A TOTAL MESS...?
TRY CASTING A LIGHTNING SPELL.
POU (GLOW)
ポゥ・・
BASHI (CRACKLE)
TONITRUS!!

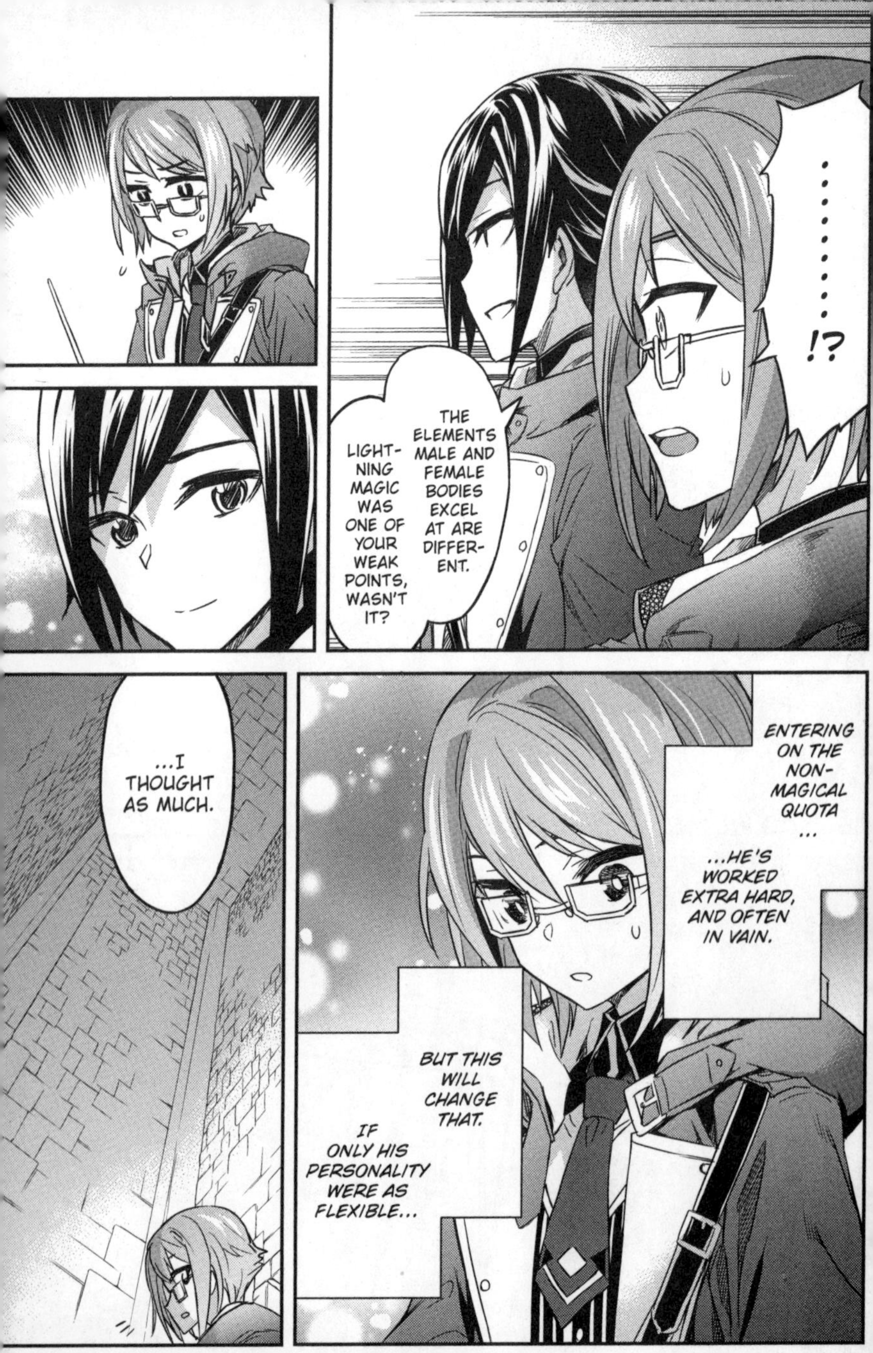
......!?
THE ELEMENTS MALE AND FEMALE BODIES EXCEL AT ARE DIFFERENT.
LIGHTNING MAGIC WAS ONE OF YOUR WEAK POINTS, WASN'T IT?
ENTERING ON THE NON-MAGICAL QUOTA...
...HE'S WORKED EXTRA HARD, AND OFTEN IN VAIN.
BUT THIS WILL CHANGE THAT.
IF ONLY HIS PERSONALITY WERE AS FLEXIBLE...
...I THOUGHT AS MUCH.

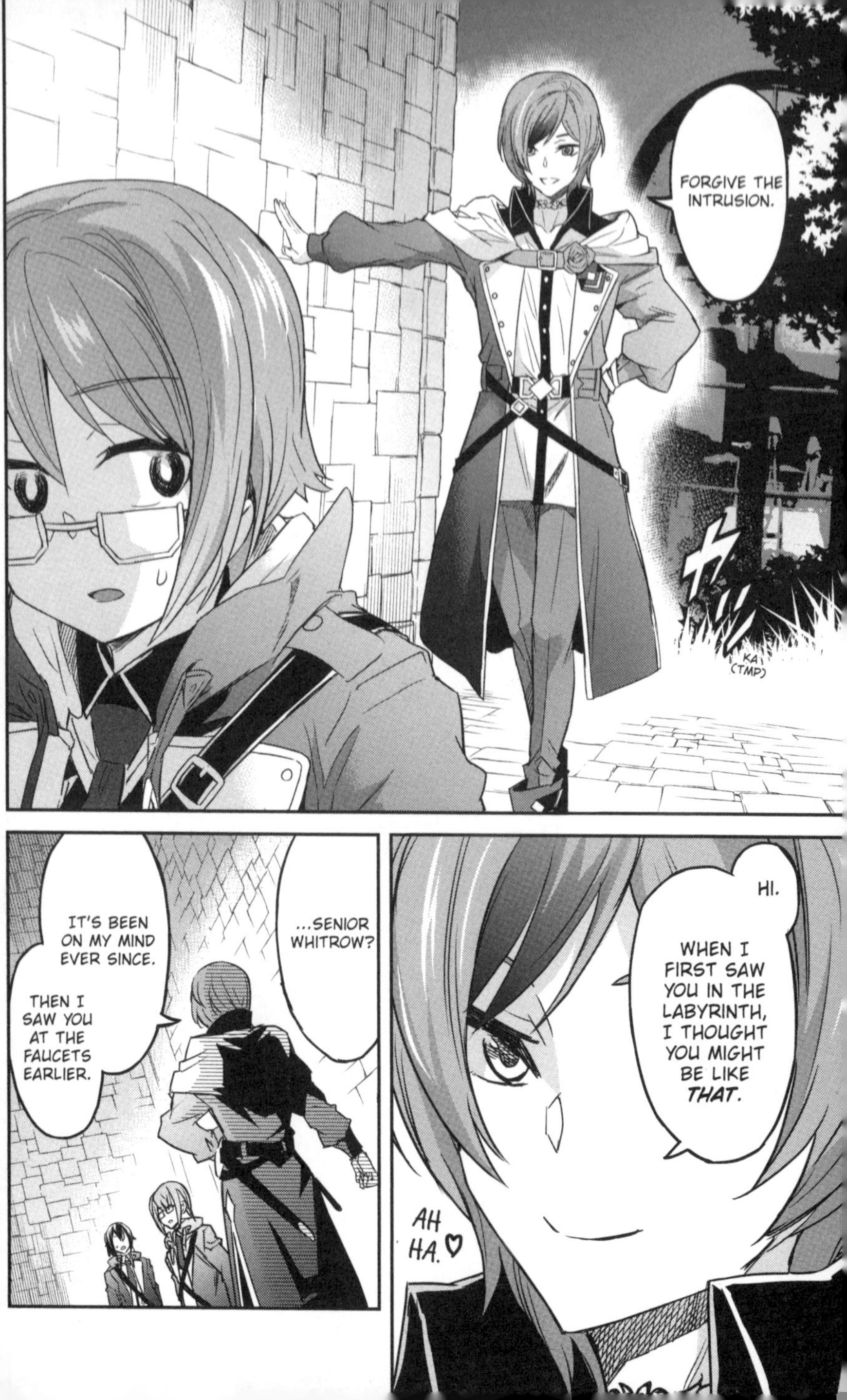
FORGIVE THE INTRUSION.
KA (TMP)
HI.
WHEN I FIRST SAW YOU IN THE LABYRINTH, I THOUGHT YOU MIGHT BE LIKE *THAT*.
AH HA. ♡
...SENIOR WHITROW?
IT'S BEEN ON MY MIND EVER SINCE.
THEN I SAW YOU AT THE FAUCETS EARLIER.

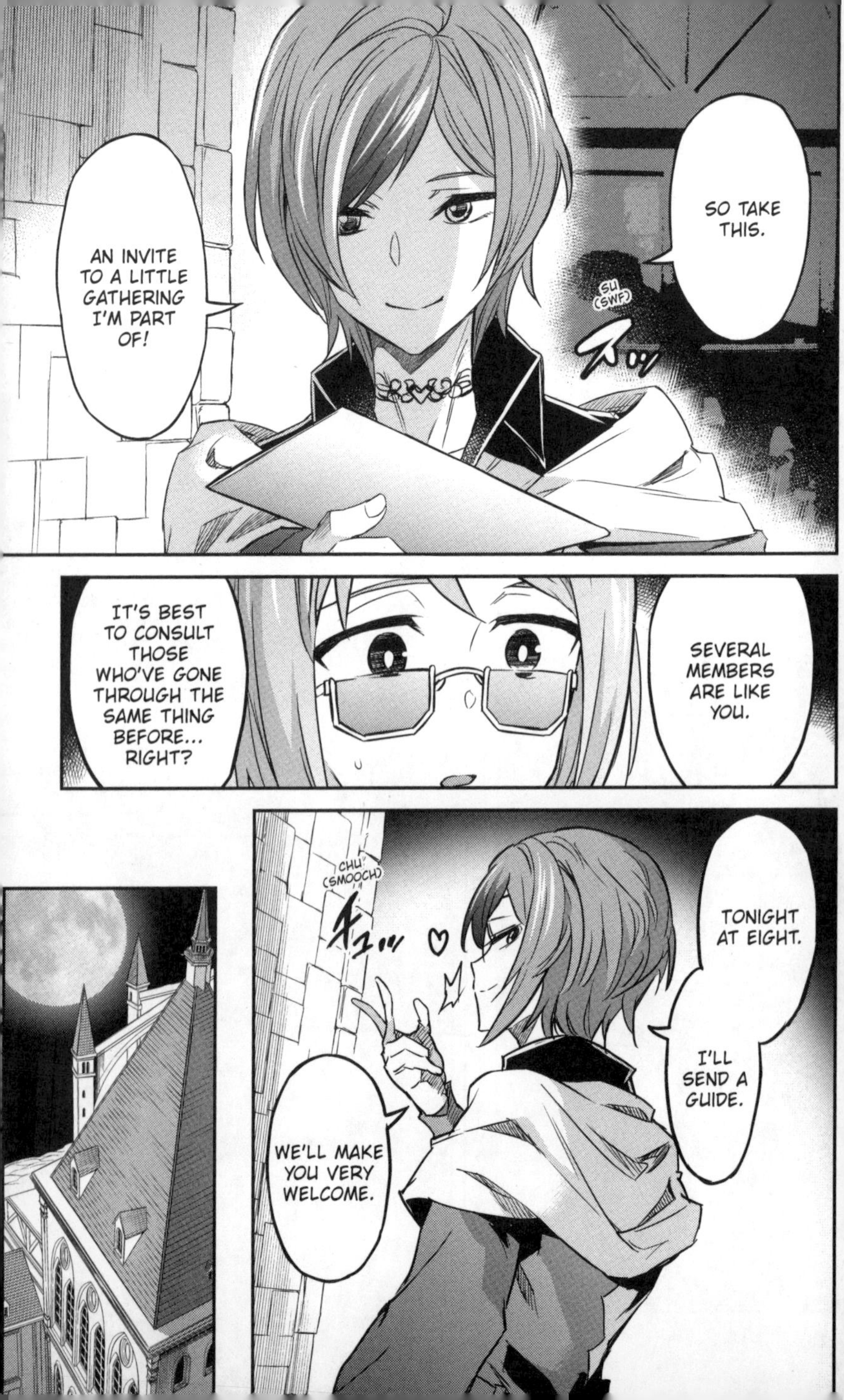
SO TAKE THIS.
SU (SWF)
AN INVITE TO A LITTLE GATHERING I'M PART OF!
SEVERAL MEMBERS ARE LIKE YOU.
IT'S BEST TO CONSULT THOSE WHO'VE GONE THROUGH THE SAME THING BEFORE... RIGHT?
TONIGHT AT EIGHT.
I'LL SEND A GUIDE.
CHU (SMOOCH)
WE'LL MAKE YOU VERY WELCOME.

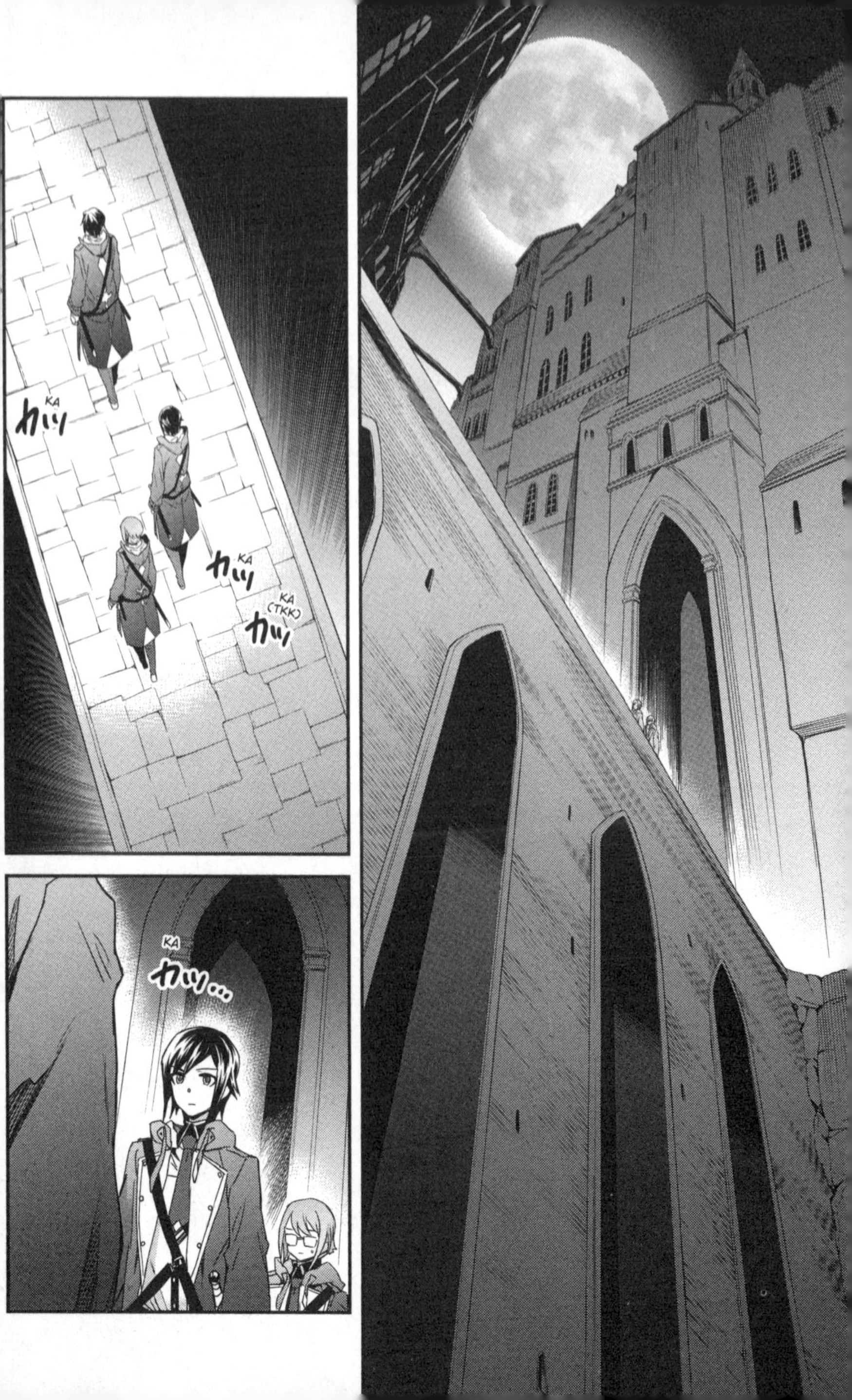
KA
カッ
KA
カッ
KA
(TKK)
カッ
KA
カッ…

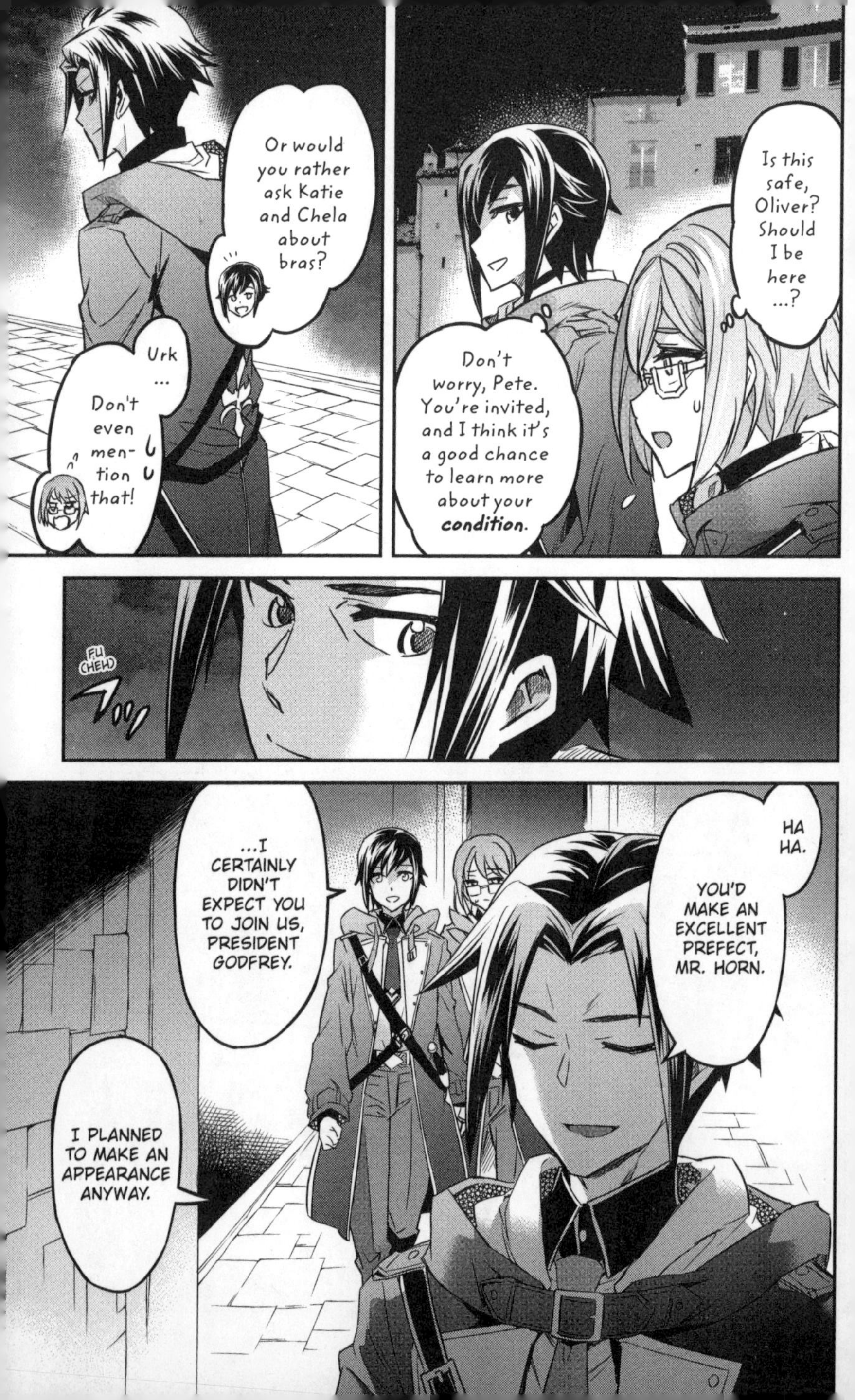
Is this safe, Oliver? Should I be here ...?
Don't worry, Pete. You're invited, and I think it's a good chance to learn more about your **condition**.
Or would you rather ask Katie and Chela about bras?
Urk ... Don't even men-tion that!
FU CHEH
HA HA.
YOU'D MAKE AN EXCELLENT PREFECT, MR. HORN.
...I CERTAINLY DIDN'T EXPECT YOU TO JOIN US, PRESIDENT GODFREY.
I PLANNED TO MAKE AN APPEARANCE ANYWAY.

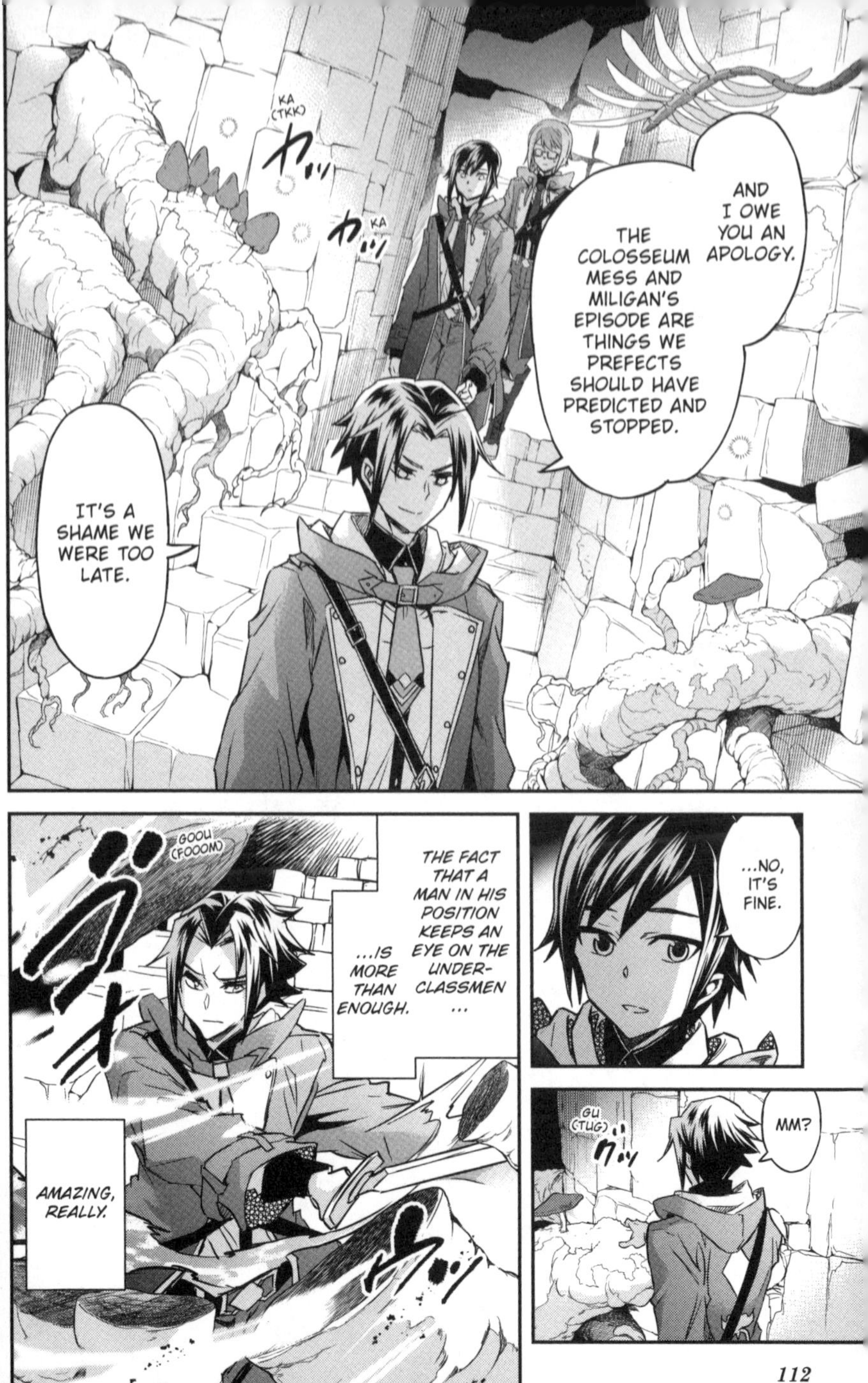
KA (TKK)
KA
THE COLOSSEUM MESS AND MILIGAN'S EPISODE ARE THINGS WE PREFECTS SHOULD HAVE PREDICTED AND STOPPED.
AND I OWE YOU AN APOLOGY.
IT'S A SHAME WE WERE TOO LATE.
...NO, IT'S FINE.
GU (TUG)
MM?
THE FACT THAT A MAN IN HIS POSITION KEEPS AN EYE ON THE UNDER-CLASSMEN ...
...IS MORE THAN ENOUGH.
GOOU (FOOOM)
AMAZING, REALLY.

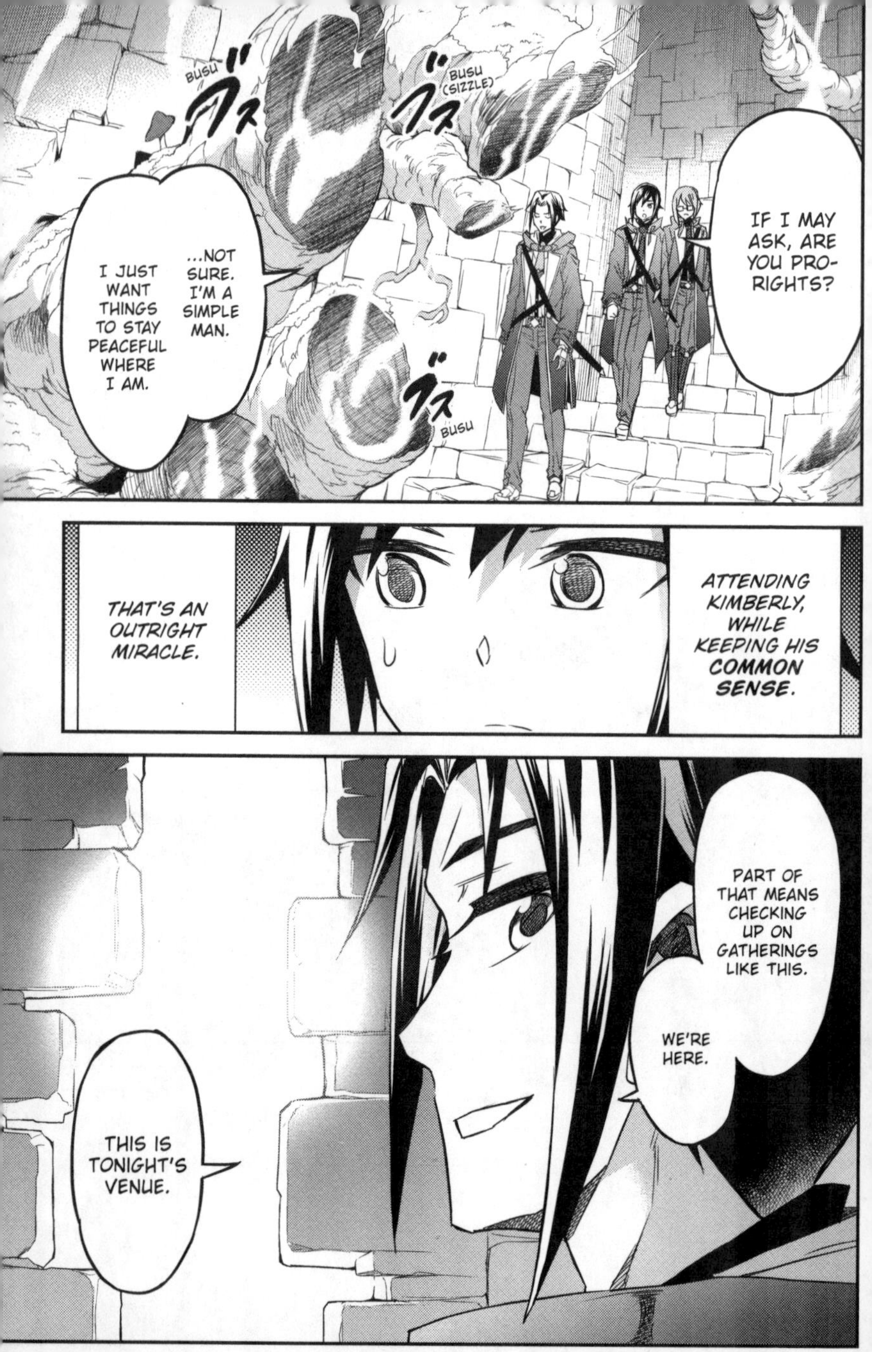
BUSU (SIZZLE)
BUSU
IF I MAY ASK, ARE YOU PRO-RIGHTS?
...NOT SURE. I'M A SIMPLE MAN.
I JUST WANT THINGS TO STAY PEACEFUL WHERE I AM.
BUSU
ATTENDING KIMBERLY, WHILE KEEPING HIS COMMON SENSE.
THAT'S AN OUTRIGHT MIRACLE.
PART OF THAT MEANS CHECKING UP ON GATHERINGS LIKE THIS.
WE'RE HERE.
THIS IS TONIGHT'S VENUE.

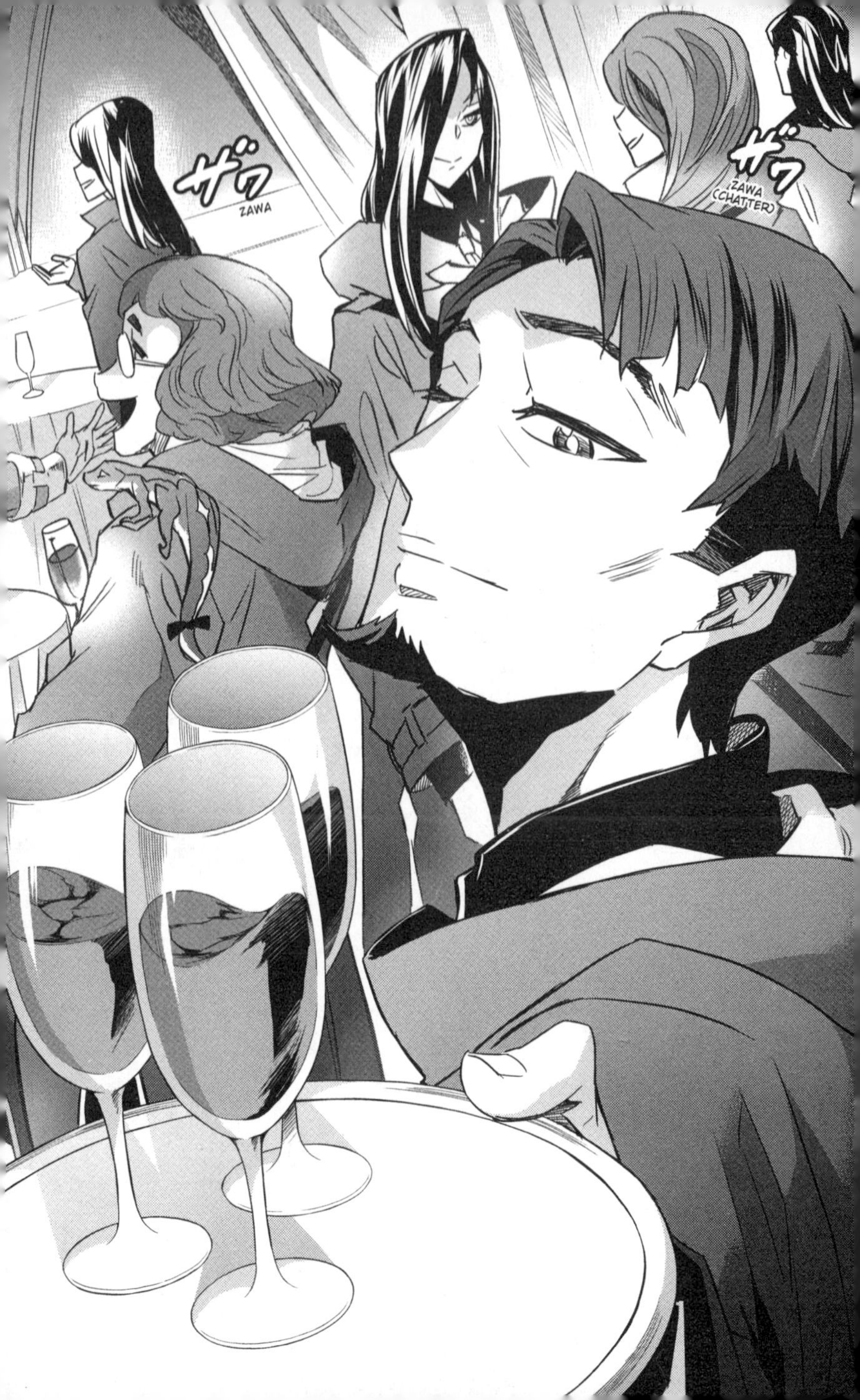
ザワ
ZAWA
(CHATTER)
ザワ
ZAWA

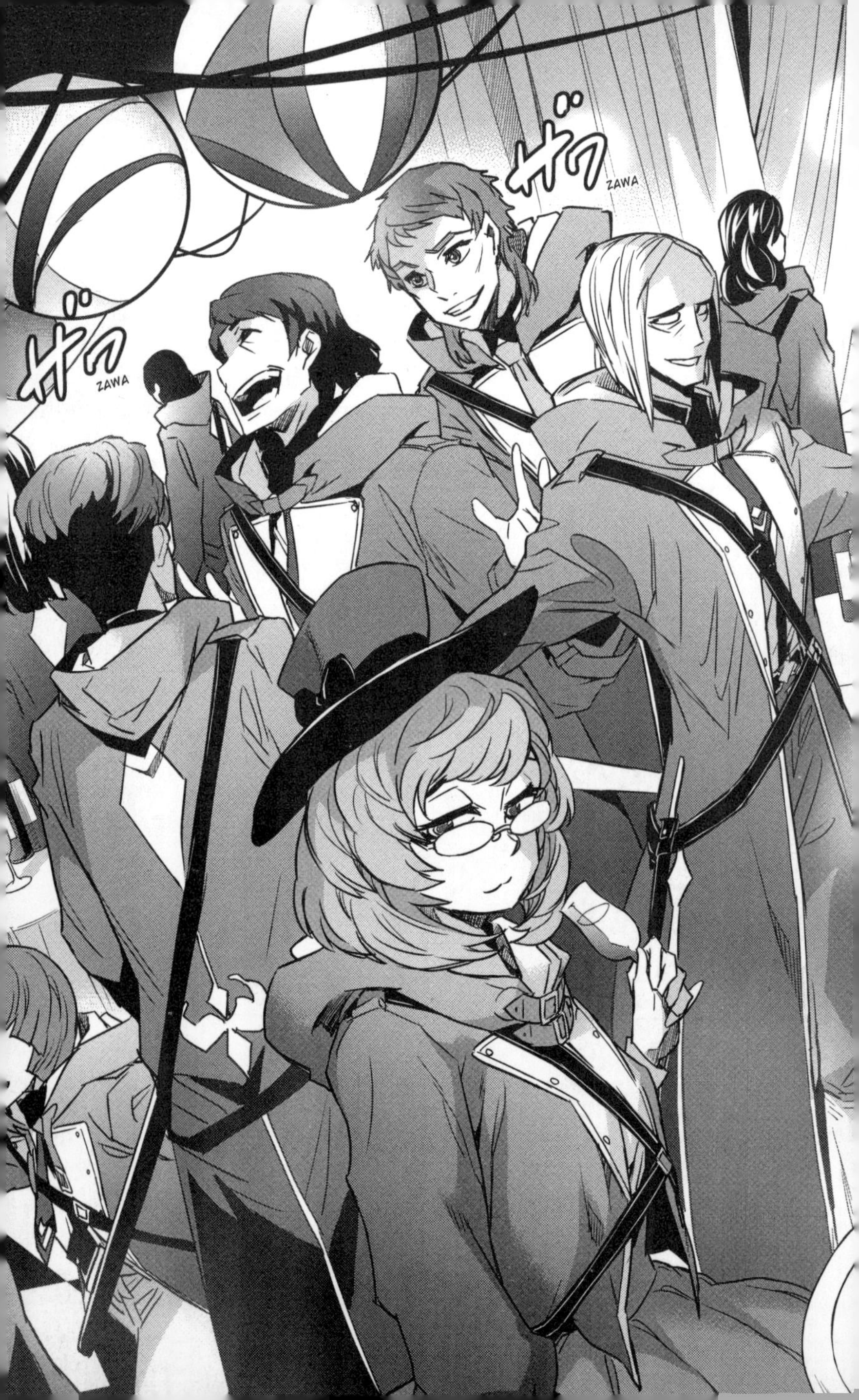
ザワ
ZAWA
ザワ
ZAWA

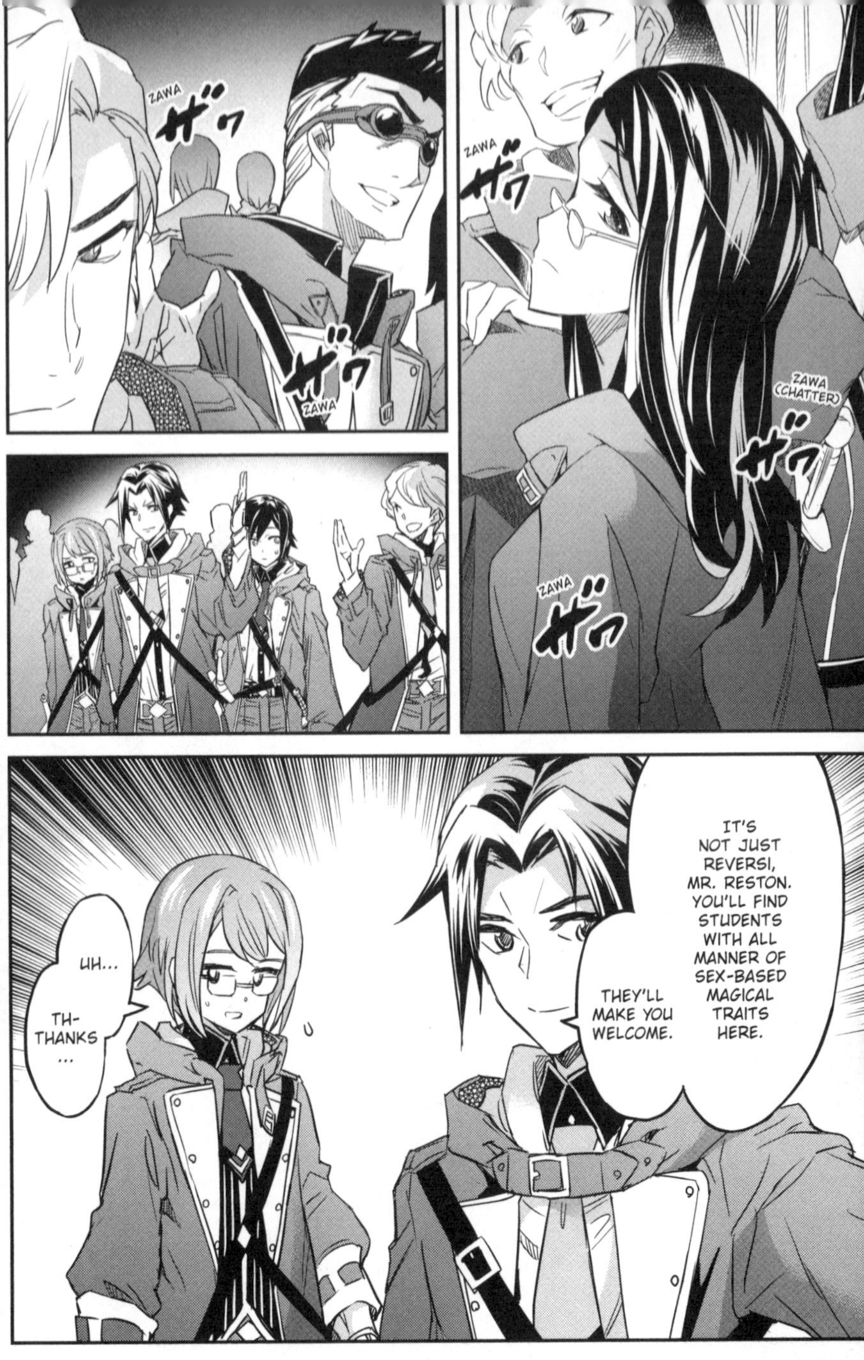
ZAWA
ZAWA (CHATTER)
ZAWA
ZAWA
ZAWA
IT'S NOT JUST REVERSI, MR. RESTON. YOU'LL FIND STUDENTS WITH ALL MANNER OF SEX-BASED MAGICAL TRAITS HERE.
THEY'LL MAKE YOU WELCOME.
UH...
TH-THANKS...

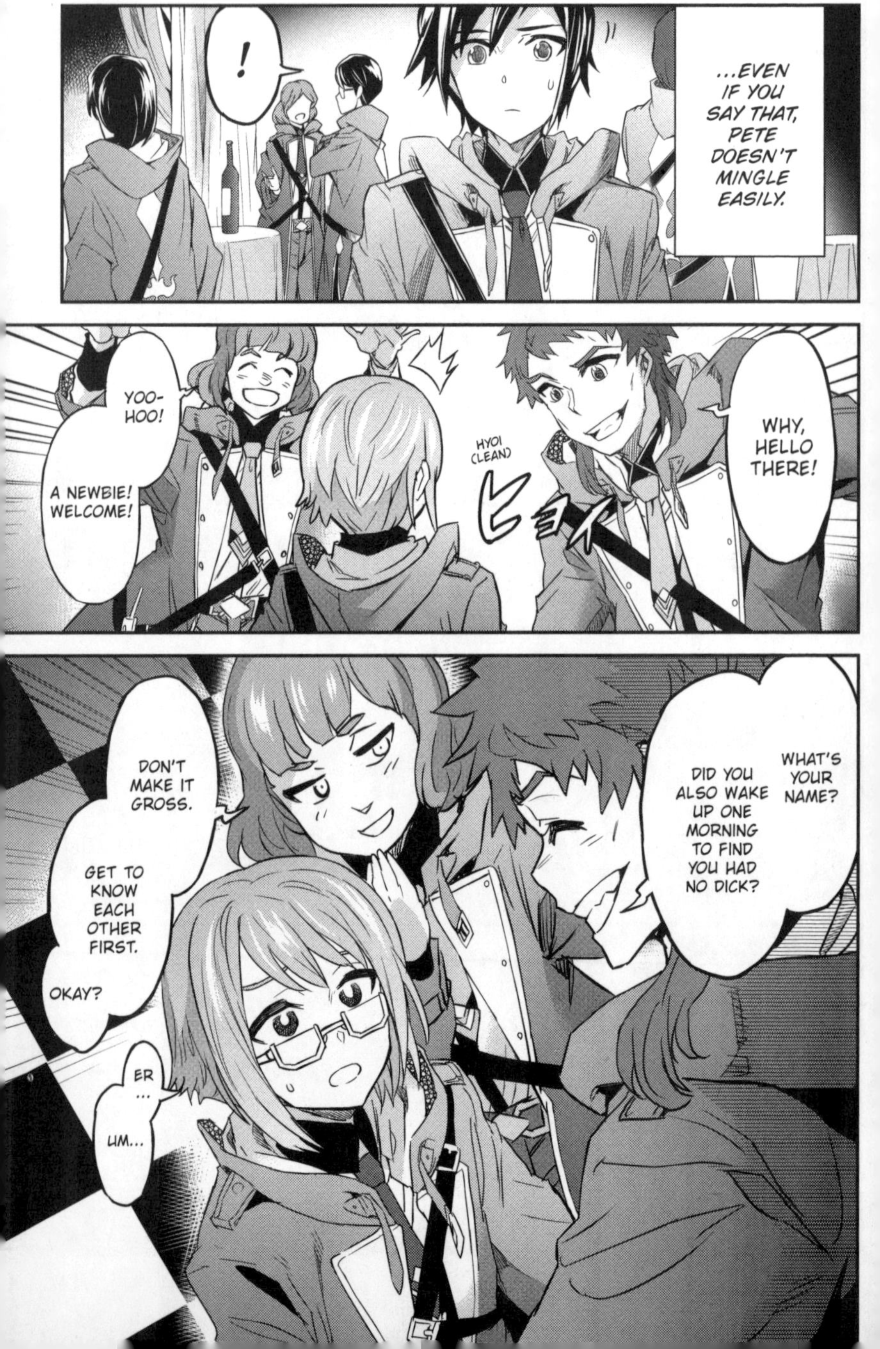
...EVEN IF YOU SAY THAT, PETE DOESN'T MINGLE EASILY.
!
WHY, HELLO THERE!
HYOI (LEAN)
ヒョイ
YOO-HOO!
A NEWBIE! WELCOME!
WHAT'S YOUR NAME?
DID YOU ALSO WAKE UP ONE MORNING TO FIND YOU HAD NO DICK?
DON'T MAKE IT GROSS.
GET TO KNOW EACH OTHER FIRST.
OKAY?
ER...
UM...

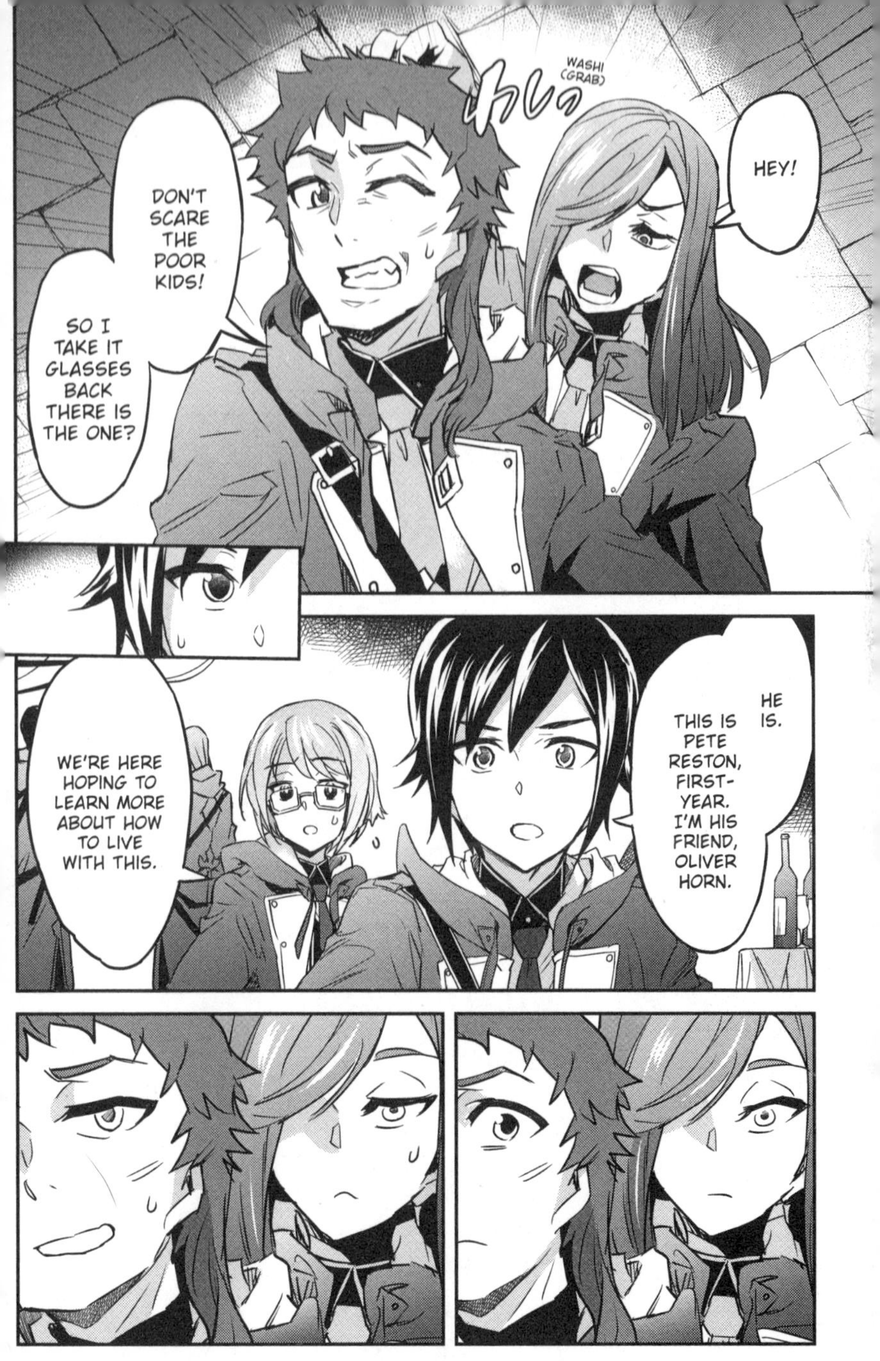
WASHI (GRAB)
HEY!
DON'T SCARE THE POOR KIDS!
SO I TAKE IT GLASSES BACK THERE IS THE ONE?
HE IS.
THIS IS PETE RESTON, FIRST-YEAR. I'M HIS FRIEND, OLIVER HORN.
WE'RE HERE HOPING TO LEARN MORE ABOUT HOW TO LIVE WITH THIS.

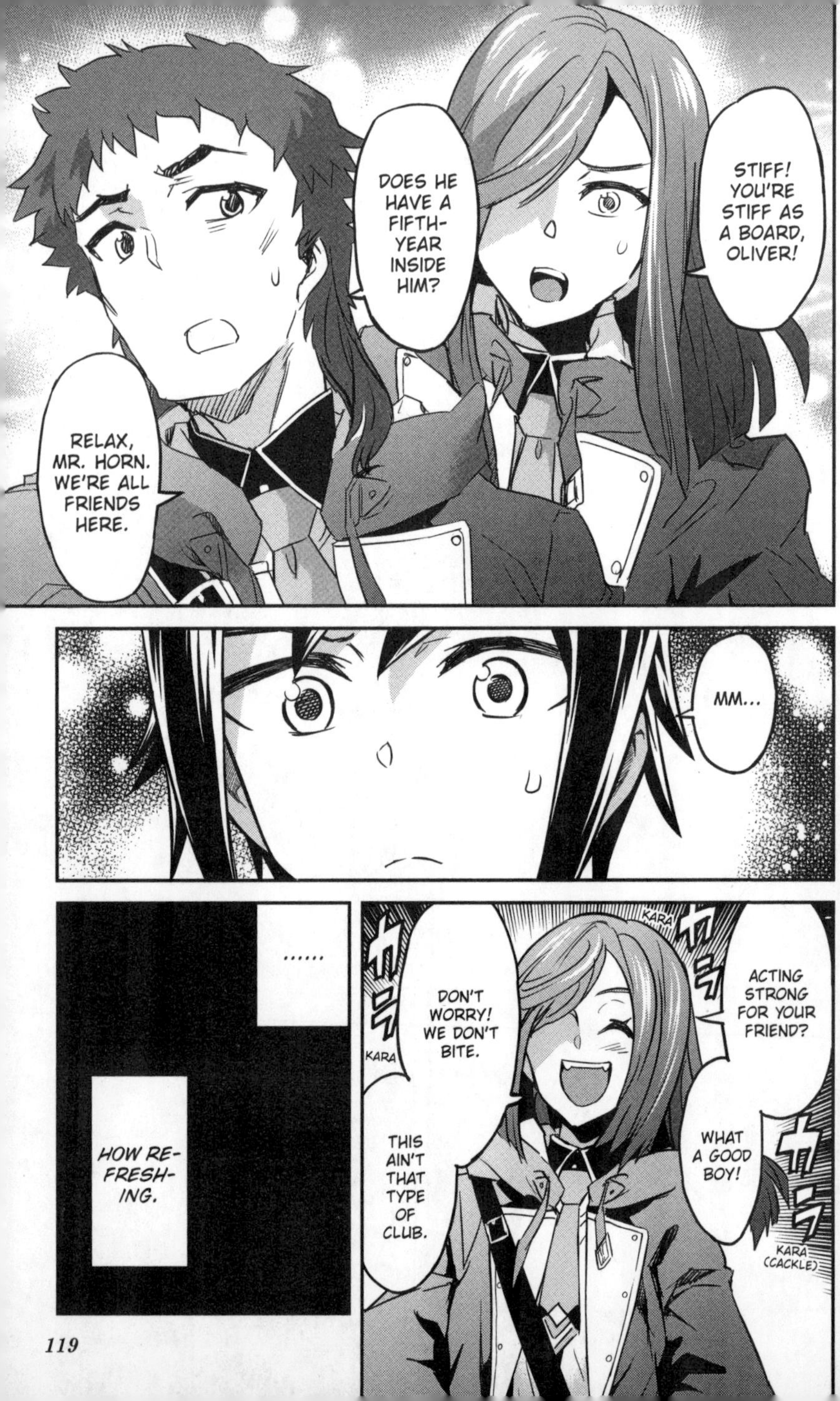
STIFF! YOU'RE STIFF AS A BOARD, OLIVER!
DOES HE HAVE A FIFTH-YEAR INSIDE HIM?
RELAX, MR. HORN. WE'RE ALL FRIENDS HERE.
MM...
KARA
ACTING STRONG FOR YOUR FRIEND?
DON'T WORRY! WE DON'T BITE.
KARA
WHAT A GOOD BOY!
KARA (CACKLE)
THIS AIN'T THAT TYPE OF CLUB.
......
HOW RE-FRESH-ING.

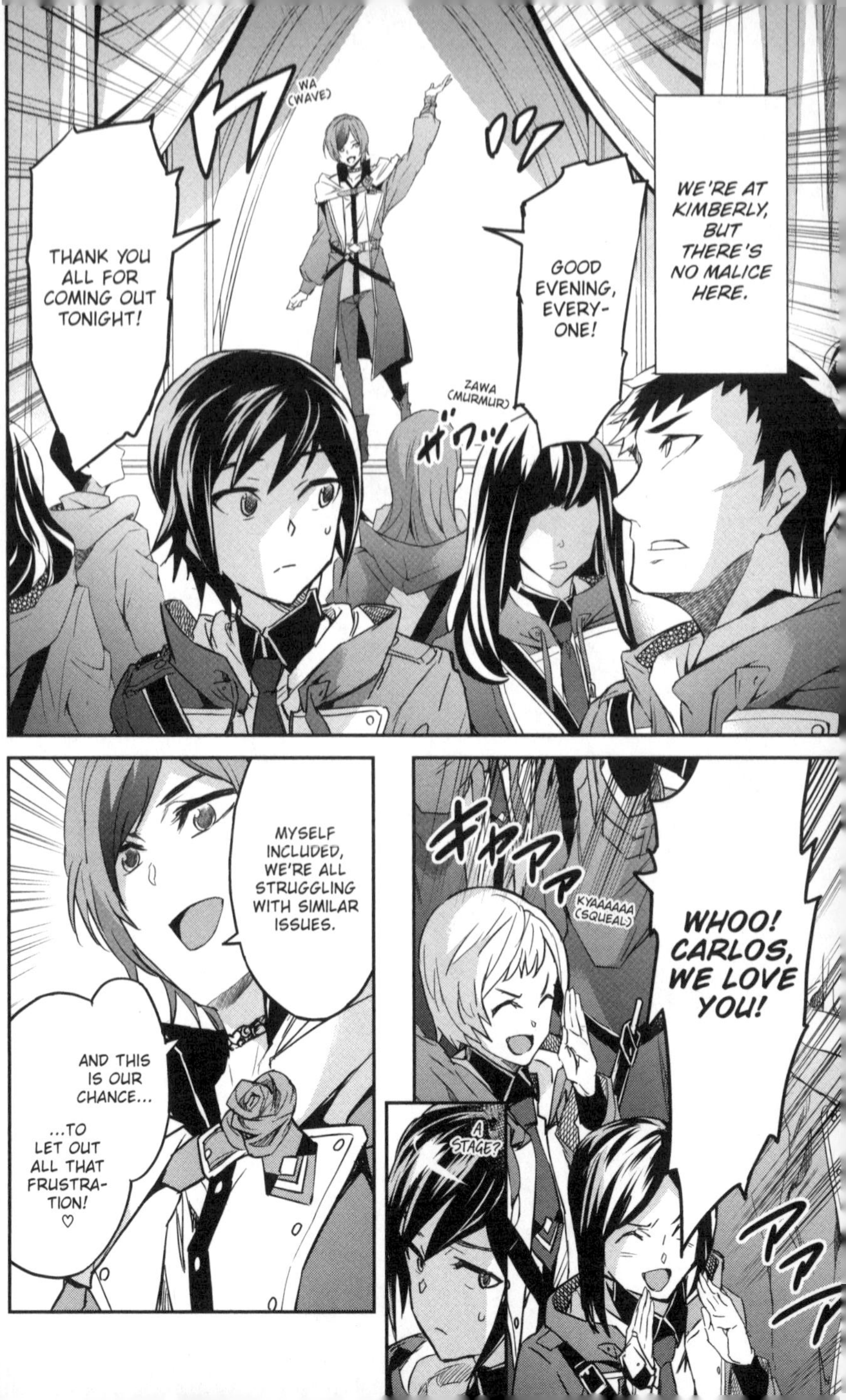
WE'RE AT KIMBERLY, BUT THERE'S NO MALICE HERE.
GOOD EVENING, EVERY-ONE!
WA (WAVE)
THANK YOU ALL FOR COMING OUT TONIGHT!
ZAWA (MURMUR)
WHOO! CARLOS, WE LOVE YOU!
KYAAAAAA (SQUEAL)
A STAGE?
MYSELF INCLUDED, WE'RE ALL STRUGGLING WITH SIMILAR ISSUES.
AND THIS IS OUR CHANCE...
...TO LET OUT ALL THAT FRUSTRA-TION! ♡

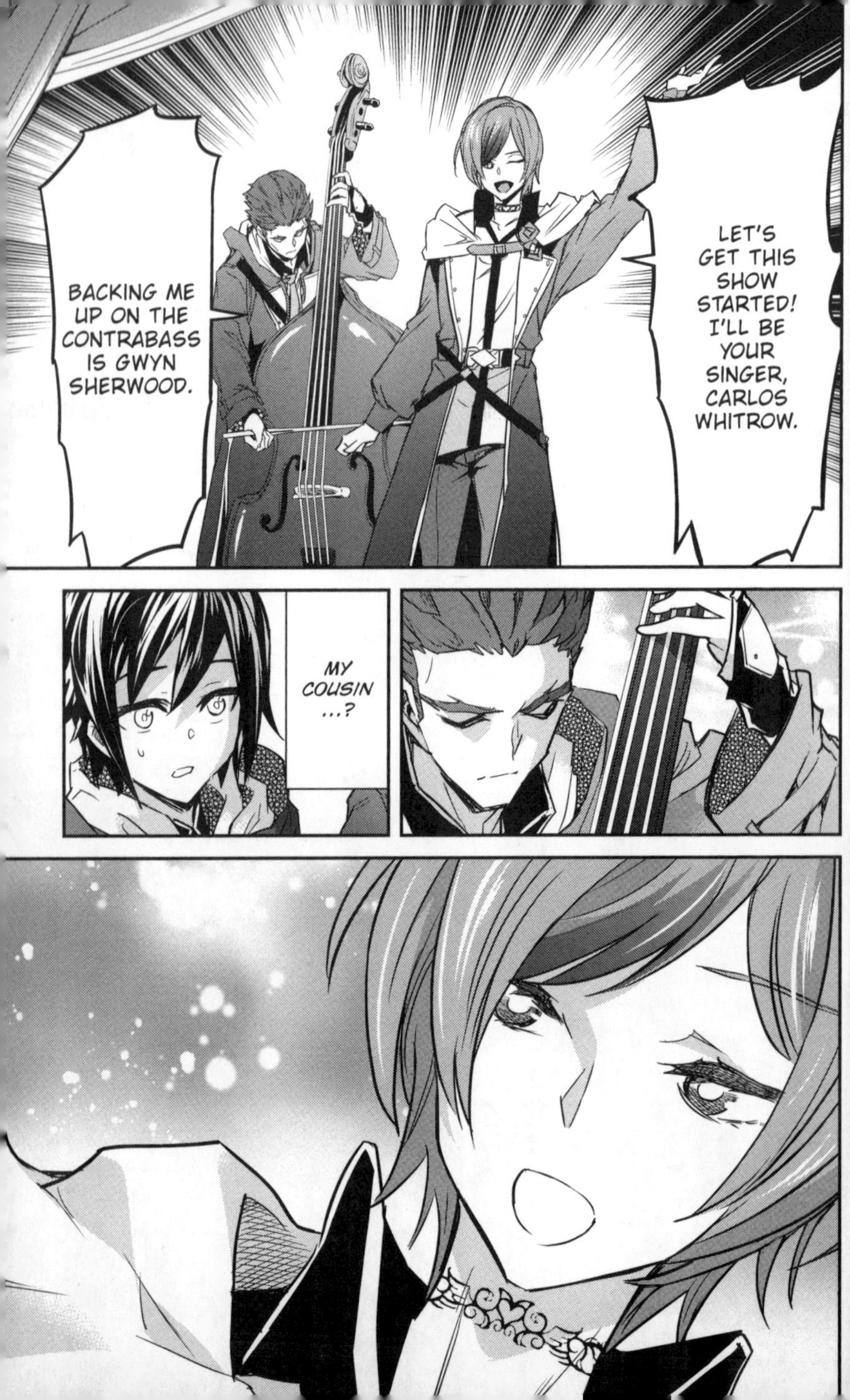
LET'S GET THIS SHOW STARTED! I'LL BE YOUR SINGER, CARLOS WHITROW.
BACKING ME UP ON THE CONTRABASS IS GWYN SHERWOOD.
MY COUSIN ...?

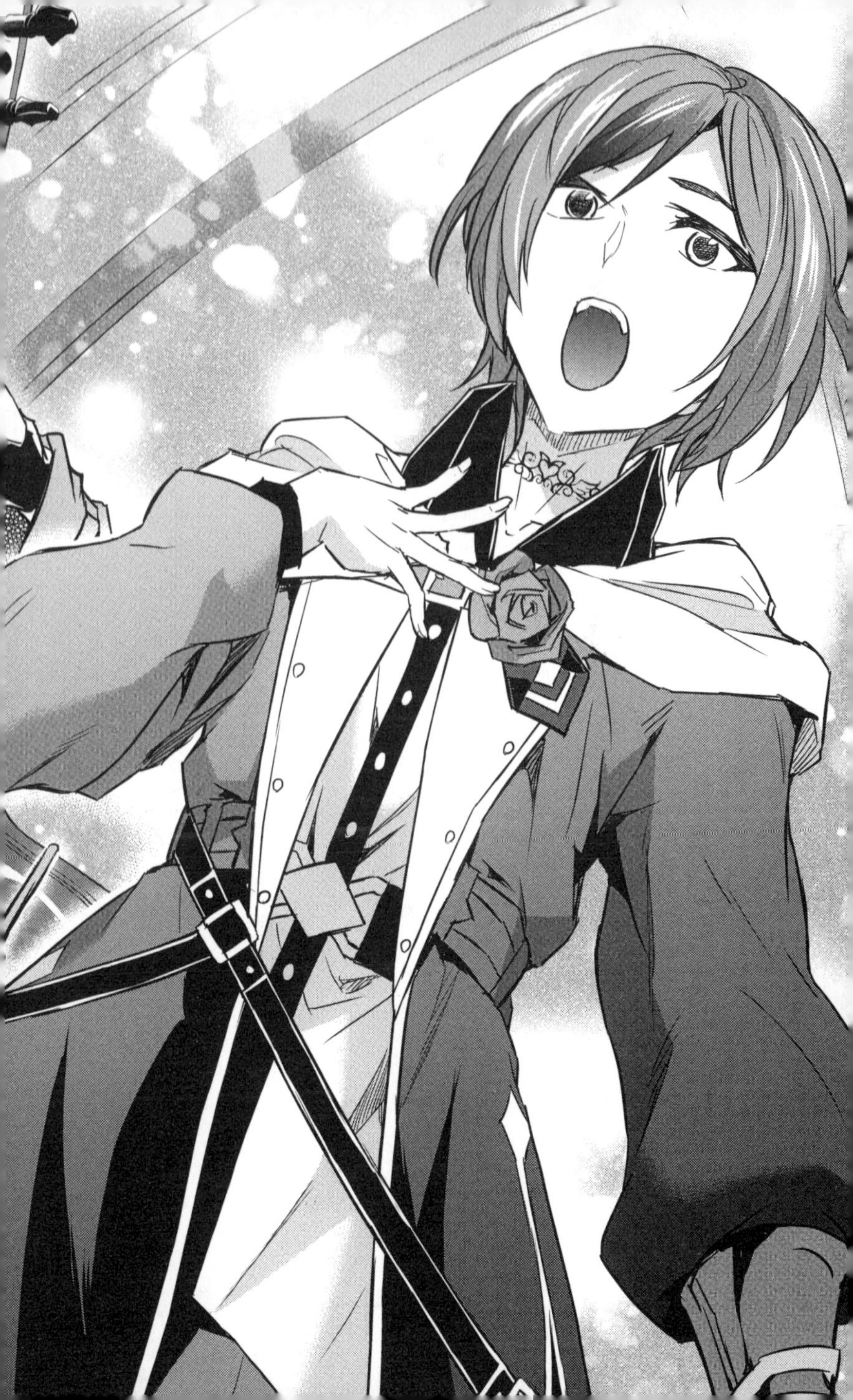

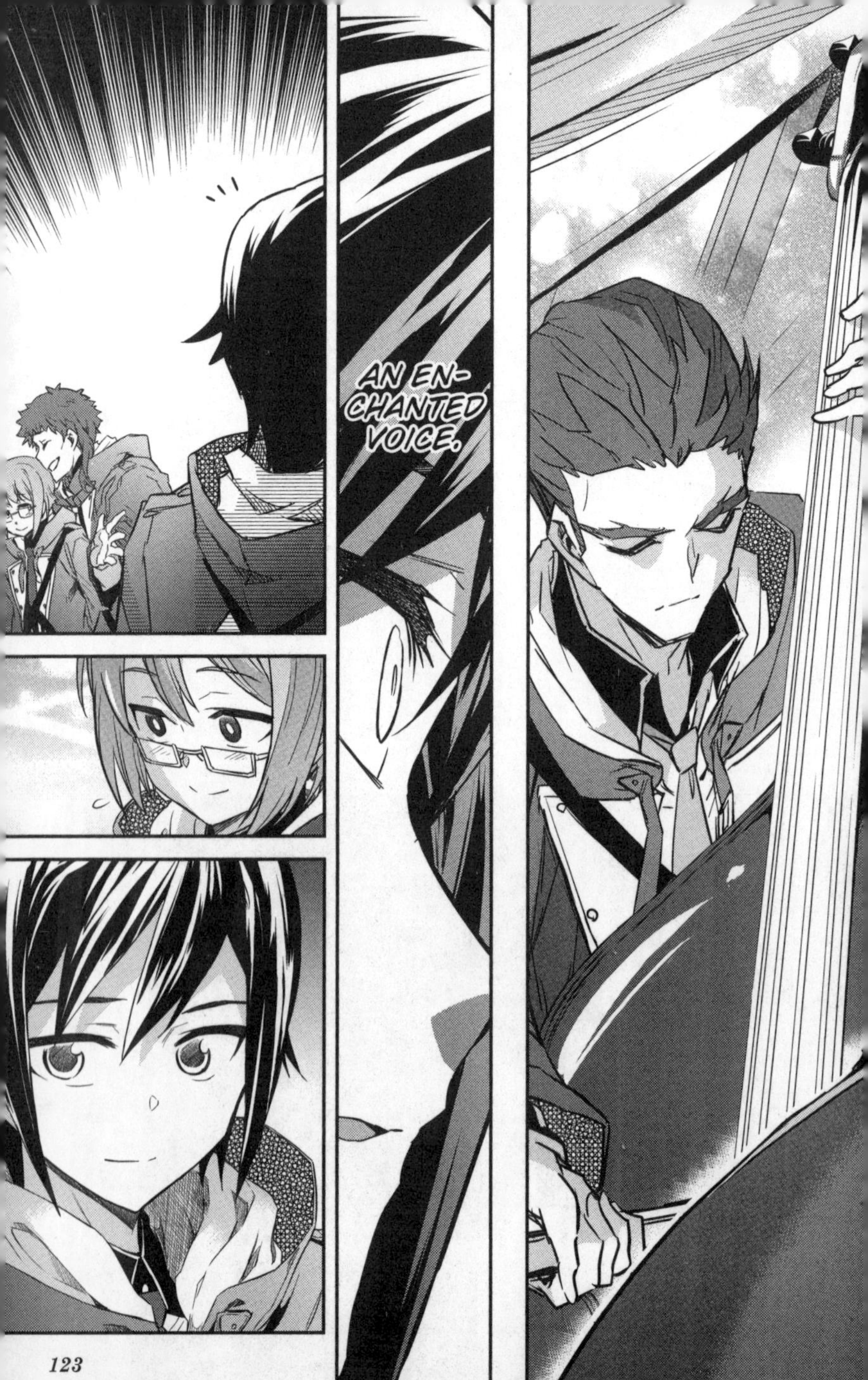
AN EN-
CHANTED
VOICE.

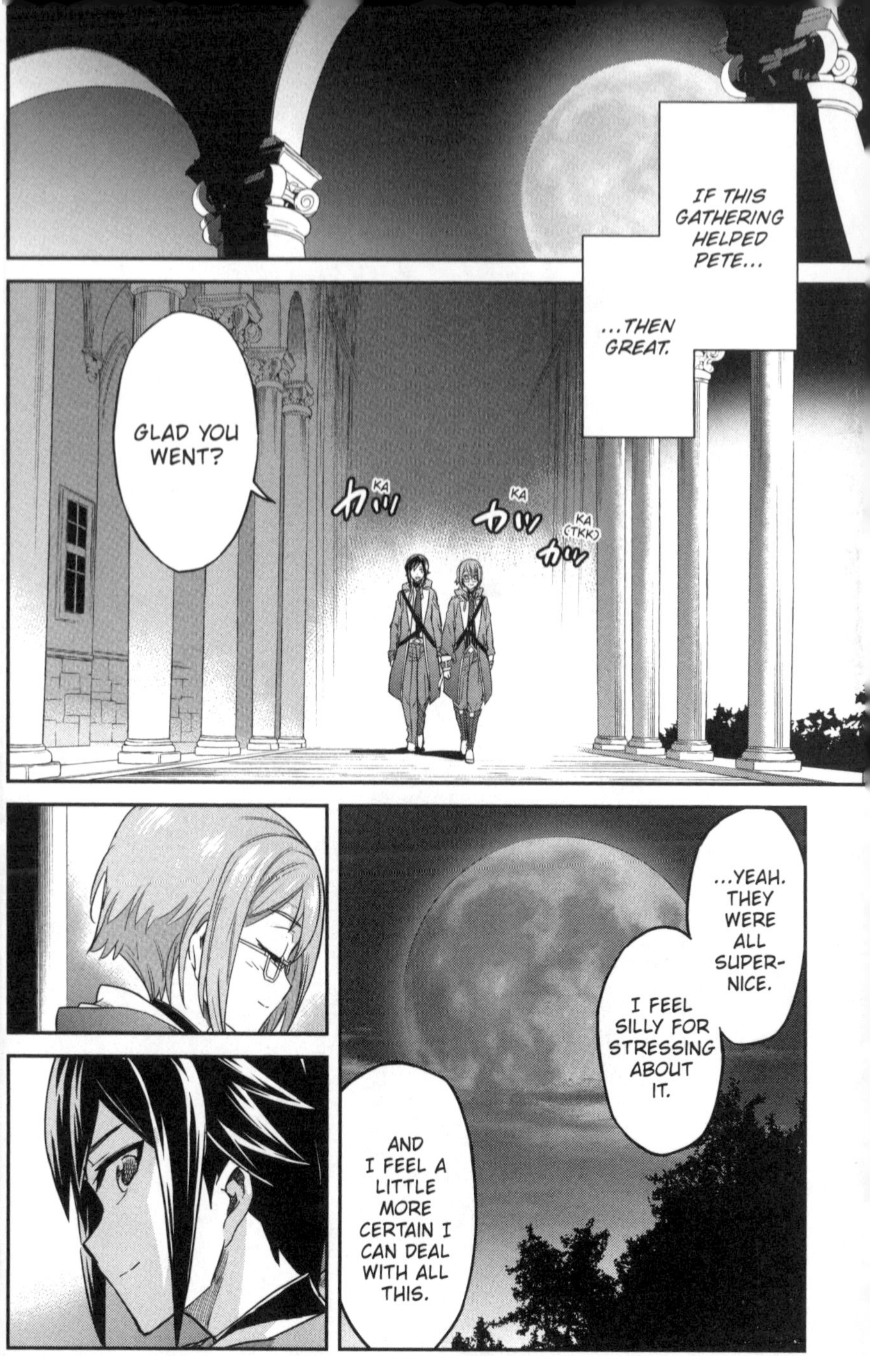
IF THIS GATHERING HELPED PETE...
...THEN GREAT.
GLAD YOU WENT?
KA (TKK)
KA
KA
...YEAH. THEY WERE ALL SUPER-NICE.
I FEEL SILLY FOR STRESSING ABOUT IT.
AND I FEEL A LITTLE MORE CERTAIN I CAN DEAL WITH ALL THIS.

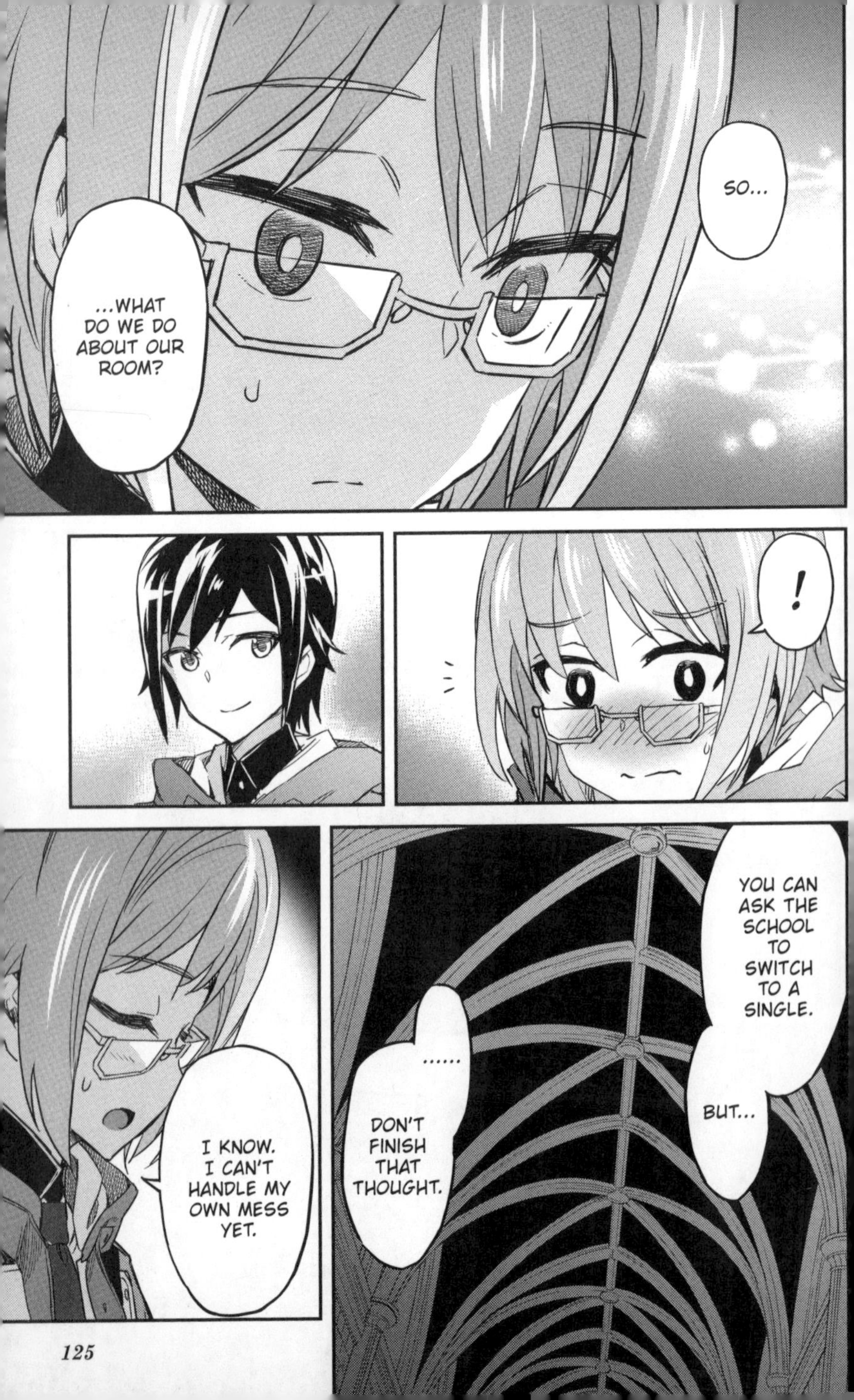
SO...
...WHAT DO WE DO ABOUT OUR ROOM?
!
YOU CAN ASK THE SCHOOL TO SWITCH TO A SINGLE.
BUT...
......
DON'T FINISH THAT THOUGHT.
I KNOW. I CAN'T HANDLE MY OWN MESS YET.

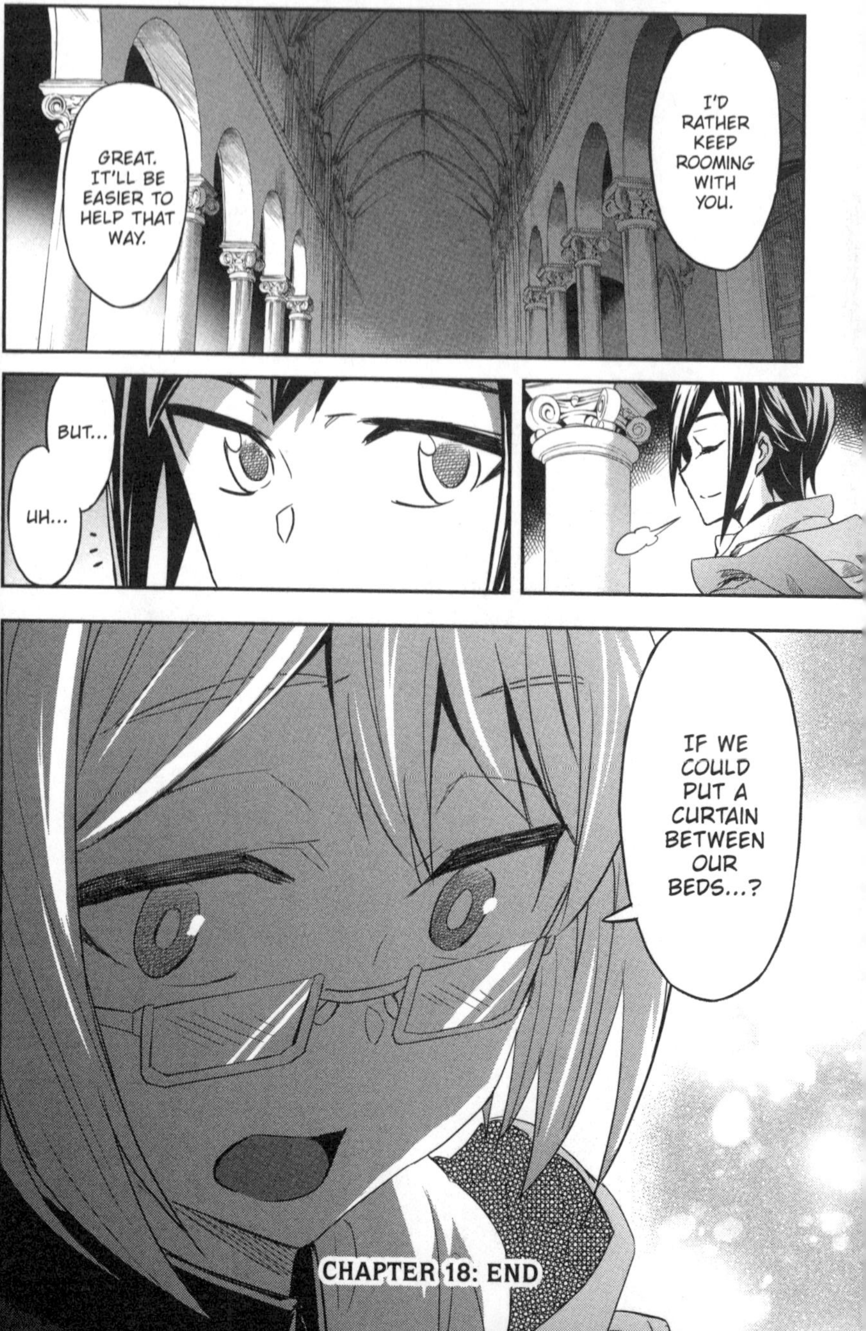
I'D RATHER KEEP ROOMING WITH YOU.
GREAT. IT'LL BE EASIER TO HELP THAT WAY.
BUT...
UH...
IF WE COULD PUT A CURTAIN BETWEEN OUR BEDS...?
CHAPTER 18: END

Reign of the Seven Spellblades

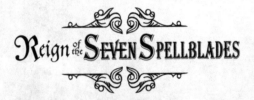

Reign of the SEVEN SPELLBLADES

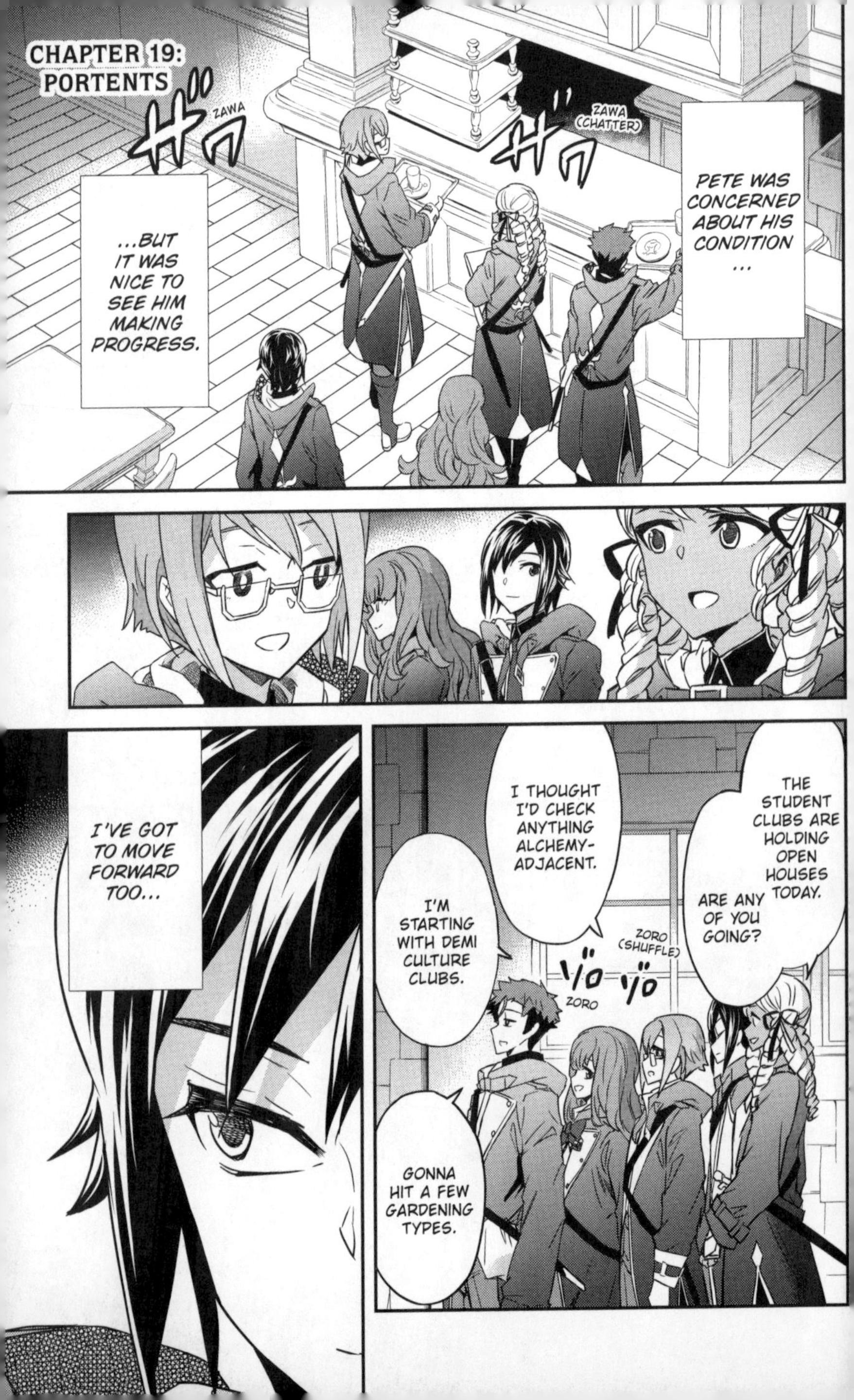
CHAPTER 19: PORTENTS
ZAWA (CHATTER)
ZAWA
PETE WAS CONCERNED ABOUT HIS CONDITION...
...BUT IT WAS NICE TO SEE HIM MAKING PROGRESS.
THE STUDENT CLUBS ARE HOLDING OPEN HOUSES TODAY.
ARE ANY OF YOU GOING?
I THOUGHT I'D CHECK ANYTHING ALCHEMY-ADJACENT.
I'M STARTING WITH DEMI CULTURE CLUBS.
ZORO (SHUFFLE)
ZORO
GONNA HIT A FEW GARDENING TYPES.
I'VE GOT TO MOVE FORWARD TOO...

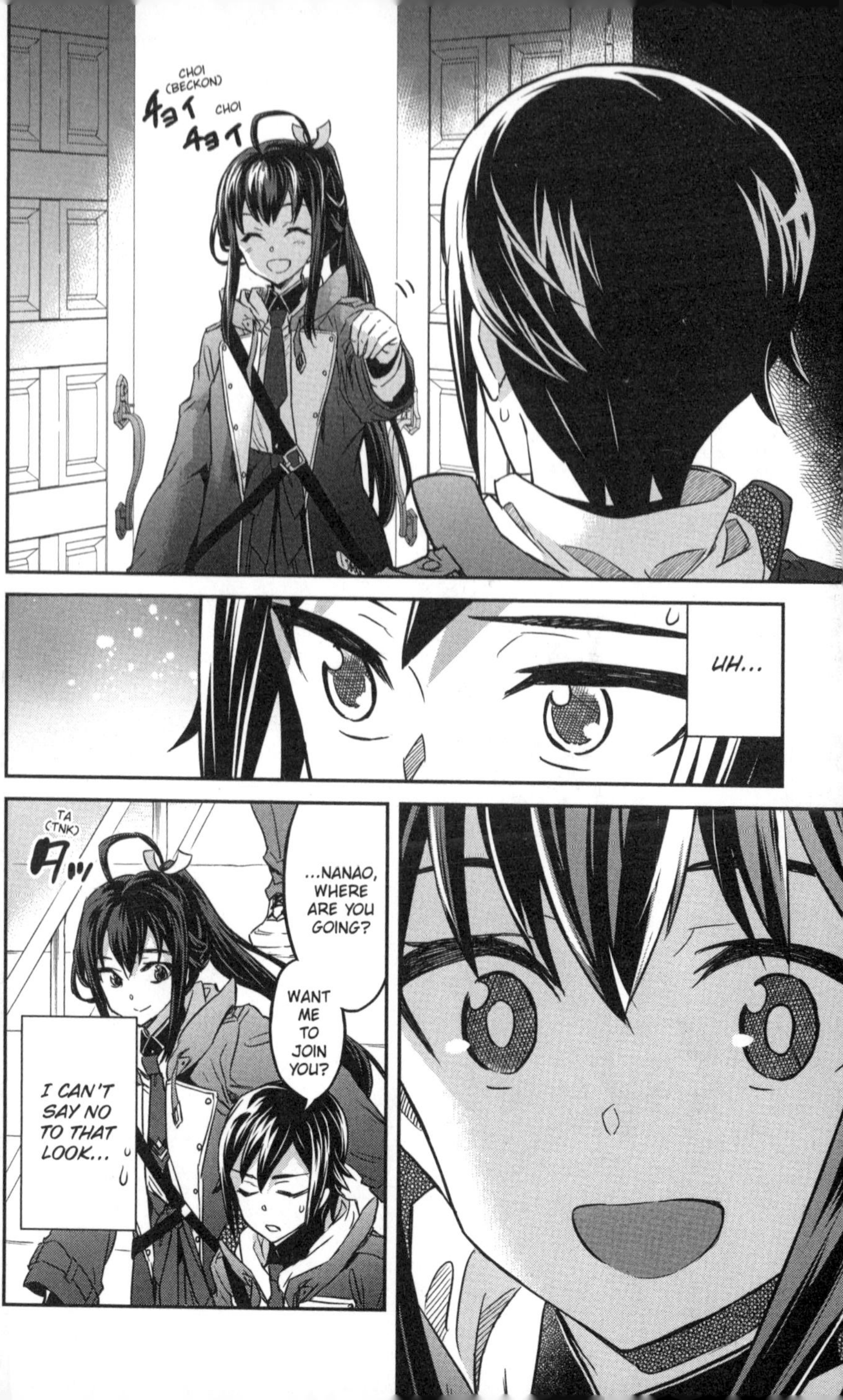
CHOI (BECKON)
チョイ
CHOI
チョイ
UH...
TA (TNK)
タッ
...NANAO, WHERE ARE YOU GOING?
WANT ME TO JOIN YOU?
I CAN'T SAY NO TO THAT LOOK...

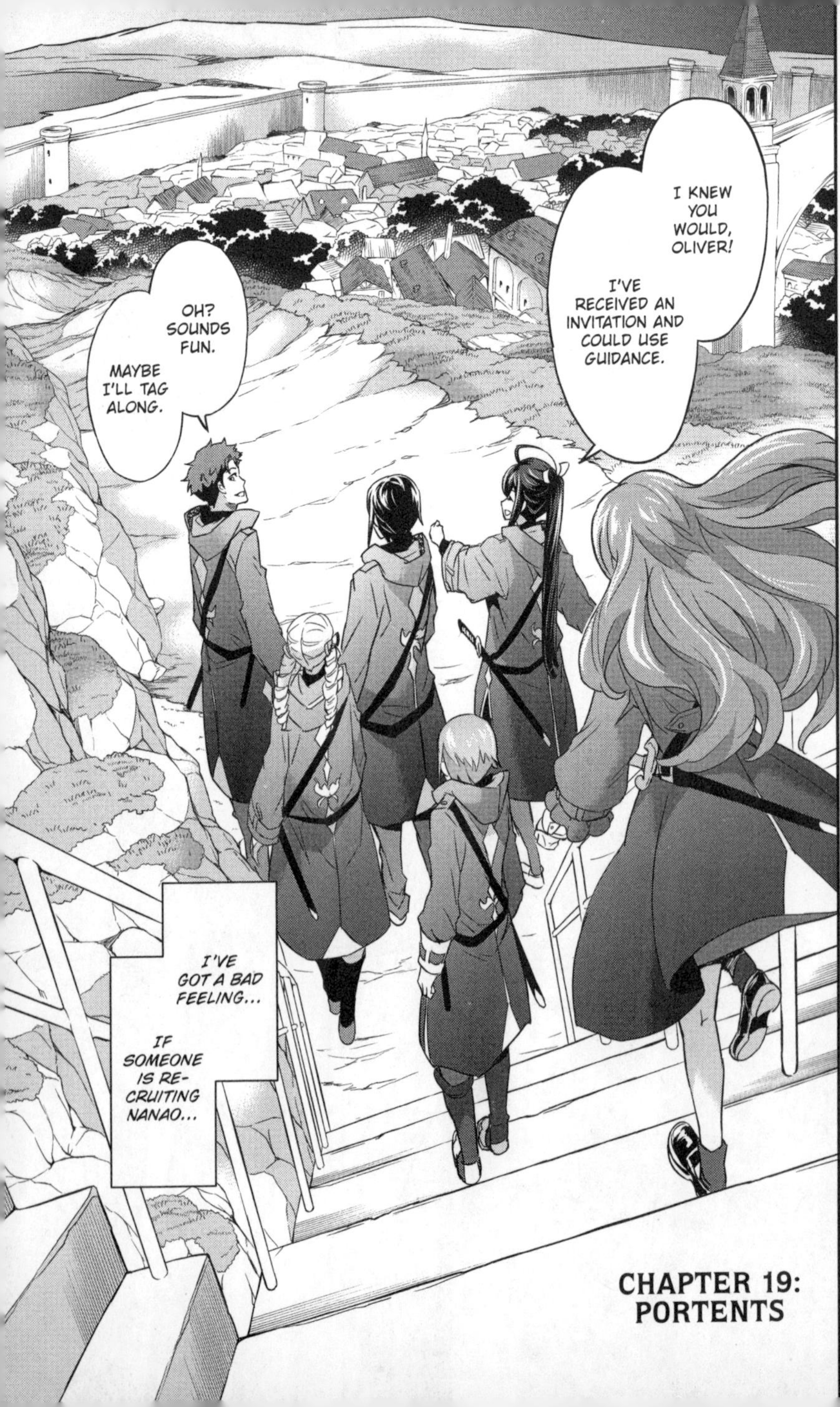
I KNEW YOU WOULD, OLIVER!
I'VE RECEIVED AN INVITATION AND COULD USE GUIDANCE.
OH? SOUNDS FUN.
MAYBE I'LL TAG ALONG.
I'VE GOT A BAD FEELING...
IF SOMEONE IS RE-CRUITING NANAO...

CHAPTER 19: PORTENTS

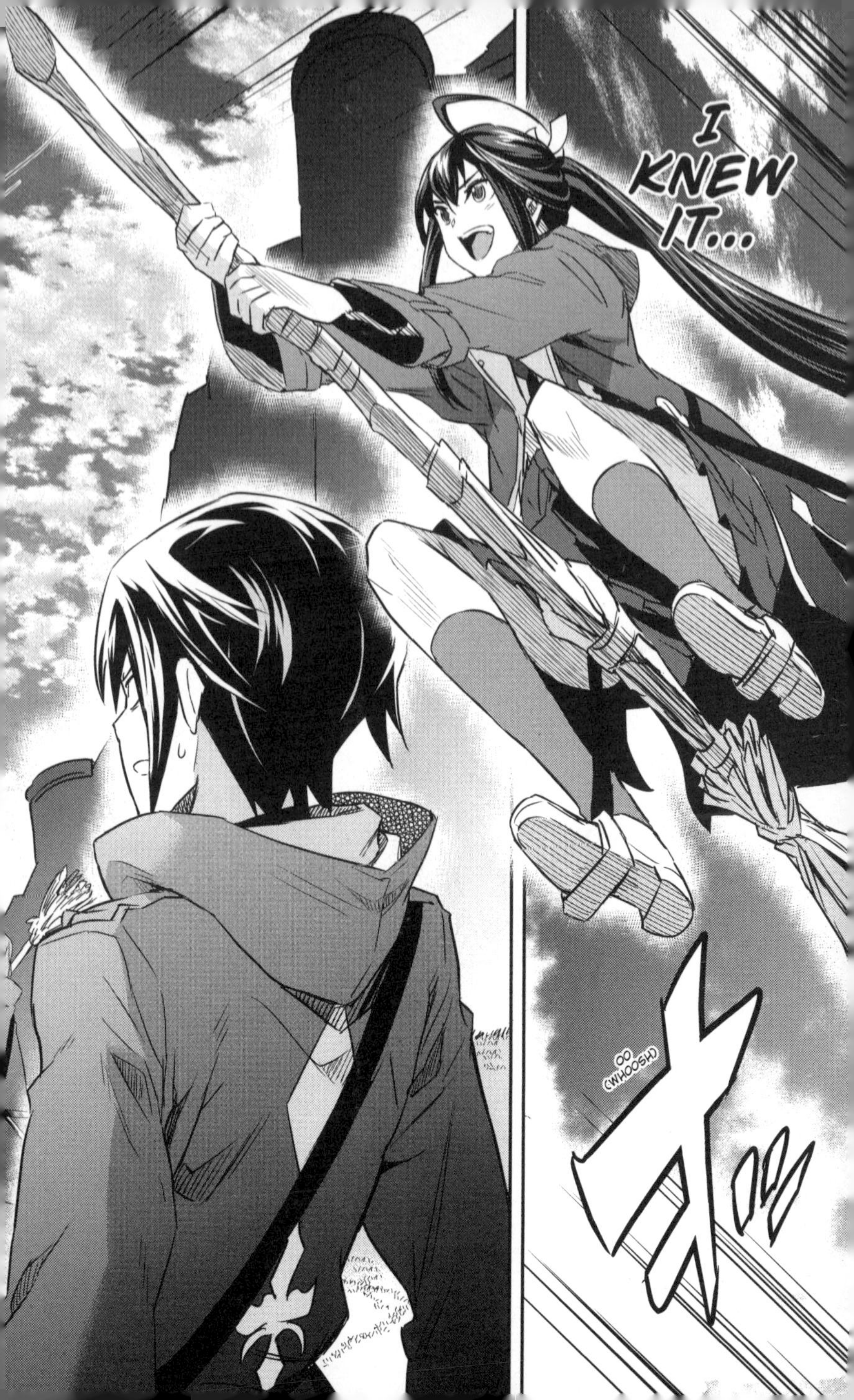
I KNEW IT...
OO
(WHOOSH)

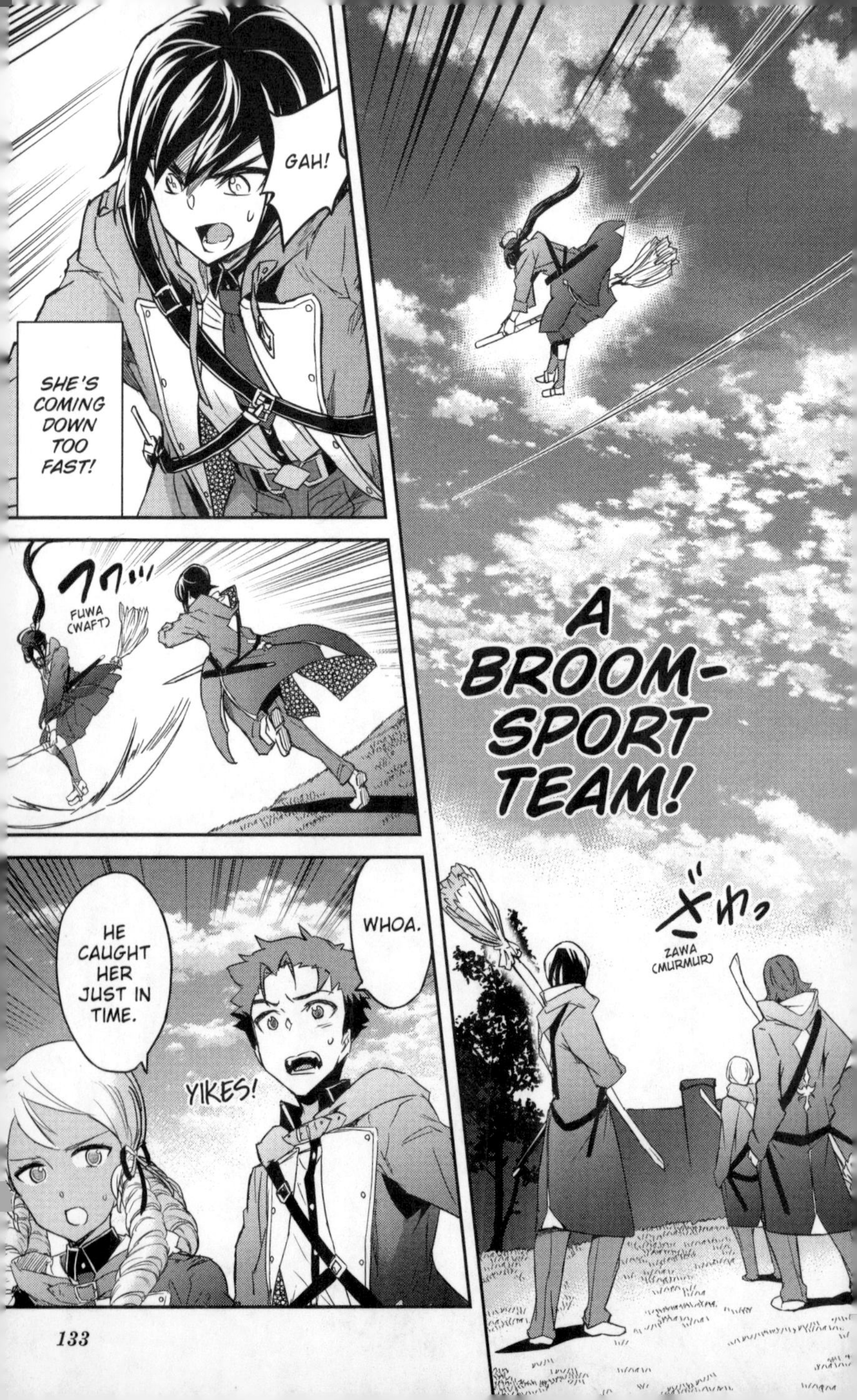
A BROOM-SPORT TEAM!
ZAWA (MURMUR)
GAH!
SHE'S COMING DOWN TOO FAST!
FUWA (WAFT)
WHOA.
HE CAUGHT HER JUST IN TIME.
YIKES!

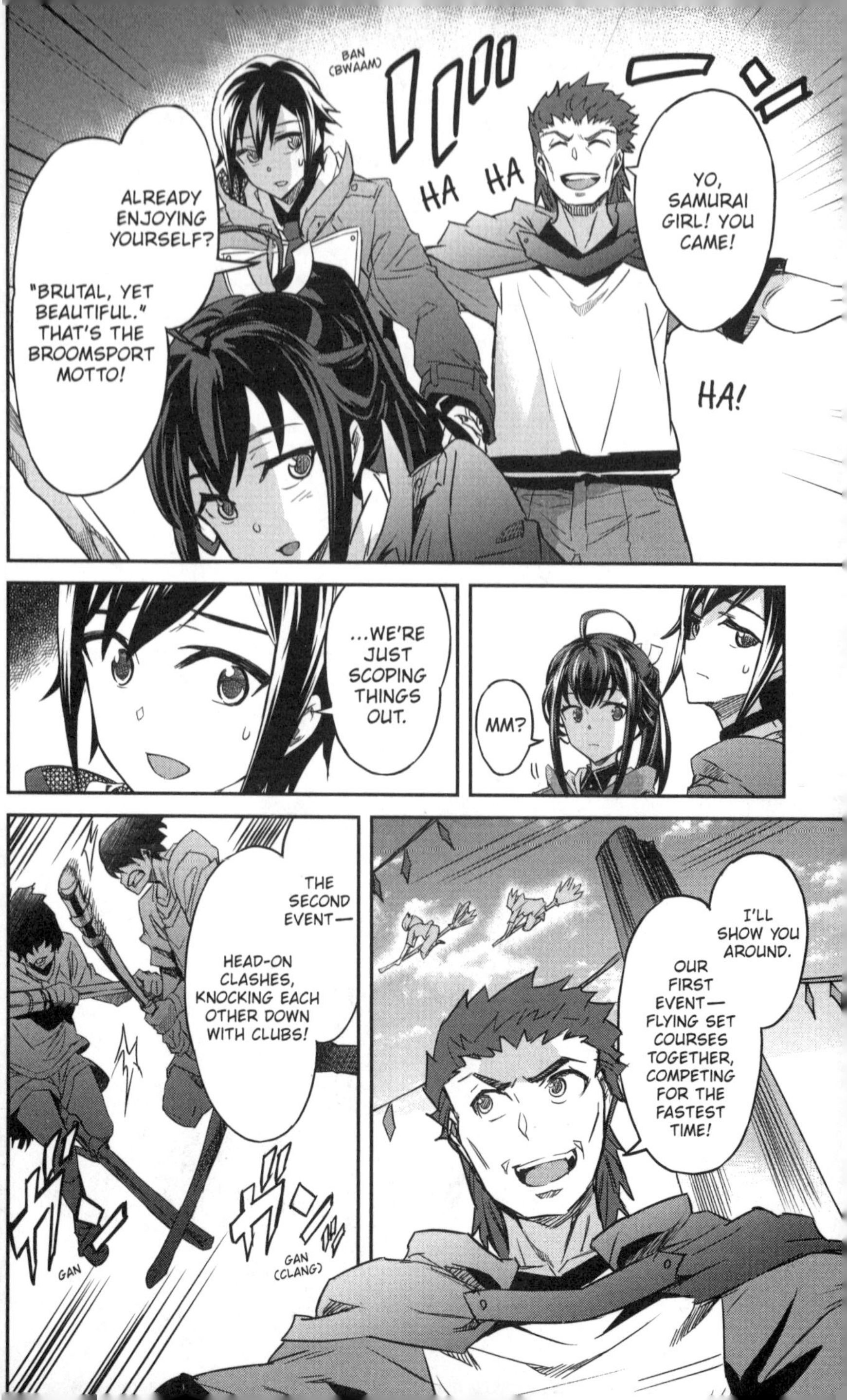

BAN (BWAAM)
YO, SAMURAI GIRL! YOU CAME!
HA HA
HA!
ALREADY ENJOYING YOURSELF?
"BRUTAL, YET BEAUTIFUL." THAT'S THE BROOMSPORT MOTTO!
MM?
...WE'RE JUST SCOPING THINGS OUT.
I'LL SHOW YOU AROUND.
OUR FIRST EVENT—FLYING SET COURSES TOGETHER, COMPETING FOR THE FASTEST TIME!
THE SECOND EVENT—
HEAD-ON CLASHES, KNOCKING EACH OTHER DOWN WITH CLUBS!
GAN (CLANG)
GAN

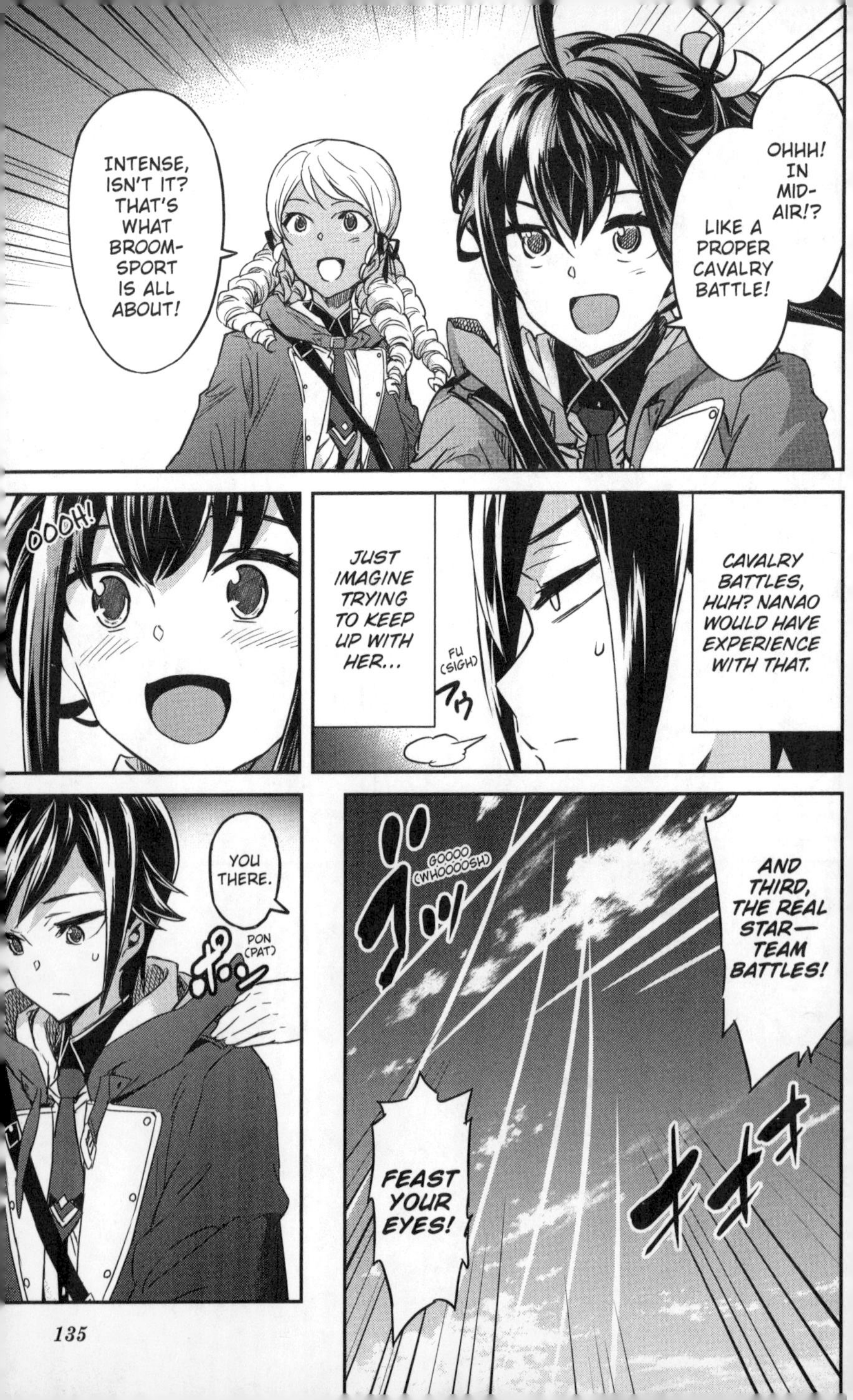
OHHH! IN MID-AIR!?
LIKE A PROPER CAVALRY BATTLE!
INTENSE, ISN'T IT? THAT'S WHAT BROOM-SPORT IS ALL ABOUT!
CAVALRY BATTLES, HUH? NANAO WOULD HAVE EXPERIENCE WITH THAT.
FU (SIGH)
JUST IMAGINE TRYING TO KEEP UP WITH HER...
OOOH!
AND THIRD, THE REAL STAR—TEAM BATTLES!
GOOOO (WHOOOOSH)
FEAST YOUR EYES!
YOU THERE.
PON (PAT)

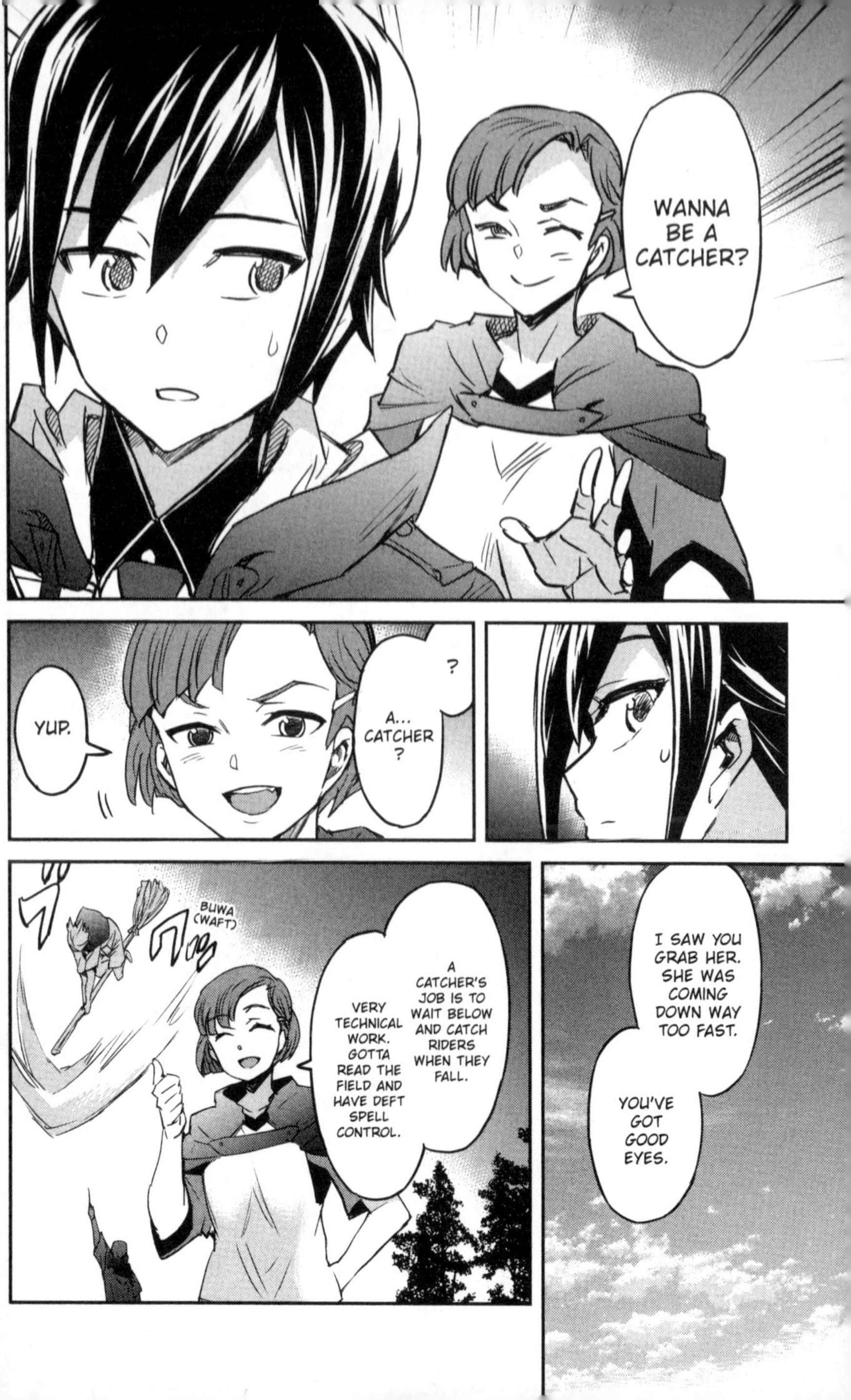
WANNA BE A CATCHER?
?
A... CATCHER ?
YUP.
I SAW YOU GRAB HER. SHE WAS COMING DOWN WAY TOO FAST.
YOU'VE GOT GOOD EYES.
BUWA (WAFT)
A CATCHER'S JOB IS TO WAIT BELOW AND CATCH RIDERS WHEN THEY FALL.
VERY TECHNICAL WORK. GOTTA READ THE FIELD AND HAVE DEFT SPELL CONTROL.

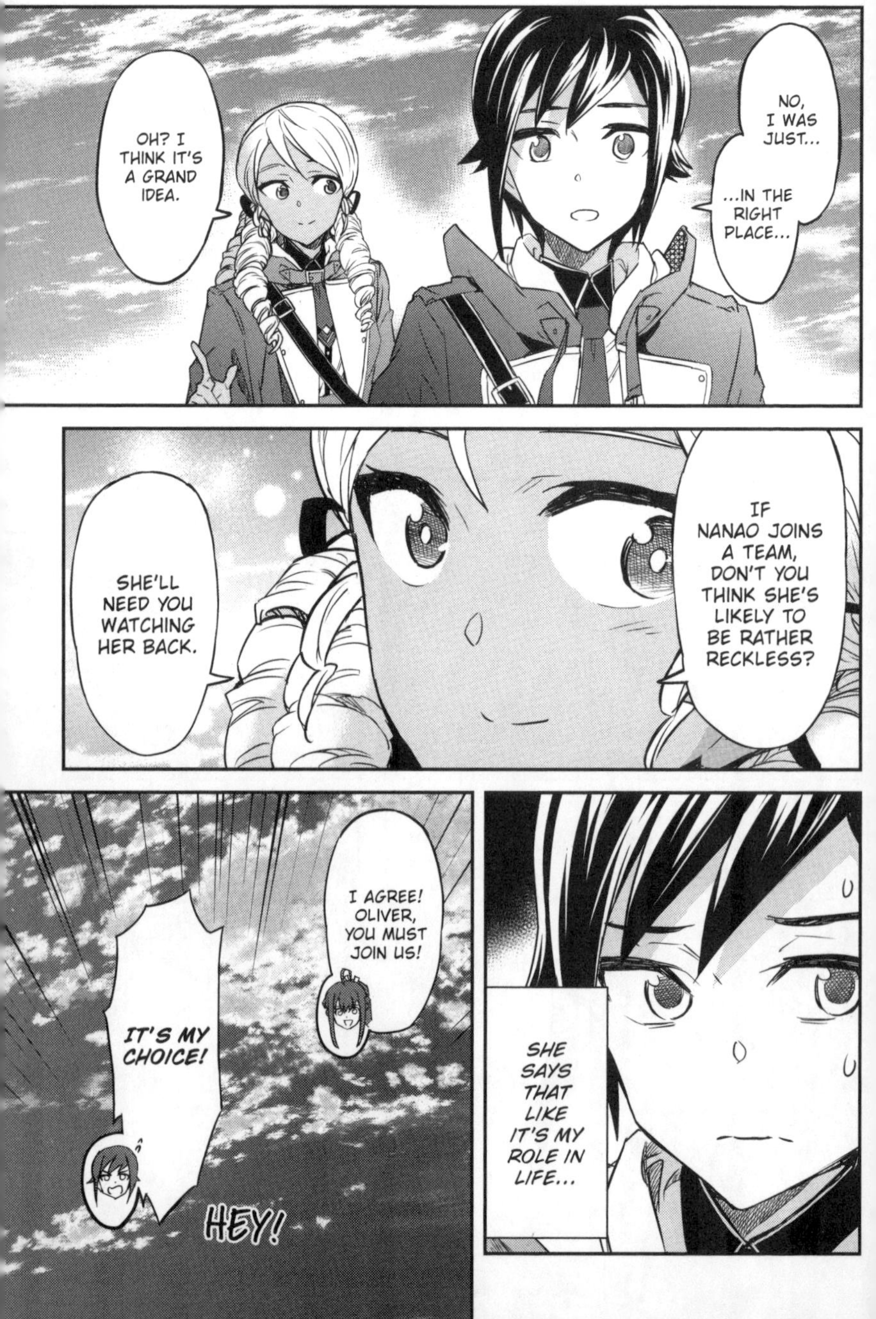
NO, I WAS JUST...
...IN THE RIGHT PLACE...
OH? I THINK IT'S A GRAND IDEA.
IF NANAO JOINS A TEAM, DON'T YOU THINK SHE'S LIKELY TO BE RATHER RECKLESS?
SHE'LL NEED YOU WATCHING HER BACK.
SHE SAYS THAT LIKE IT'S MY ROLE IN LIFE...
I AGREE! OLIVER, YOU MUST JOIN US!
IT'S MY CHOICE!
HEY!

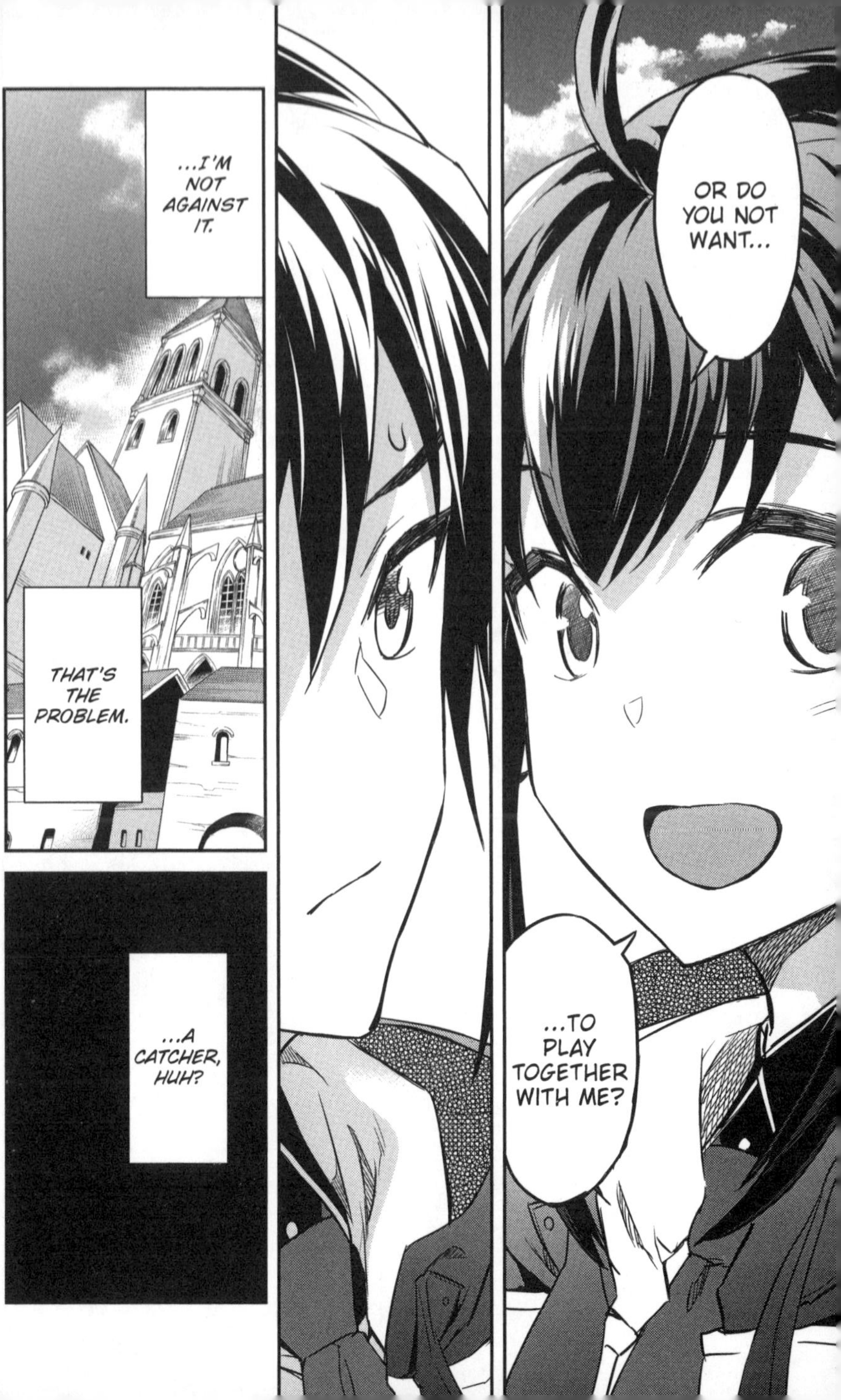
OR DO YOU NOT WANT...
...TO PLAY TOGETHER WITH ME?
...I'M NOT AGAINST IT.
THAT'S THE PROBLEM.
...A CATCHER, HUH?

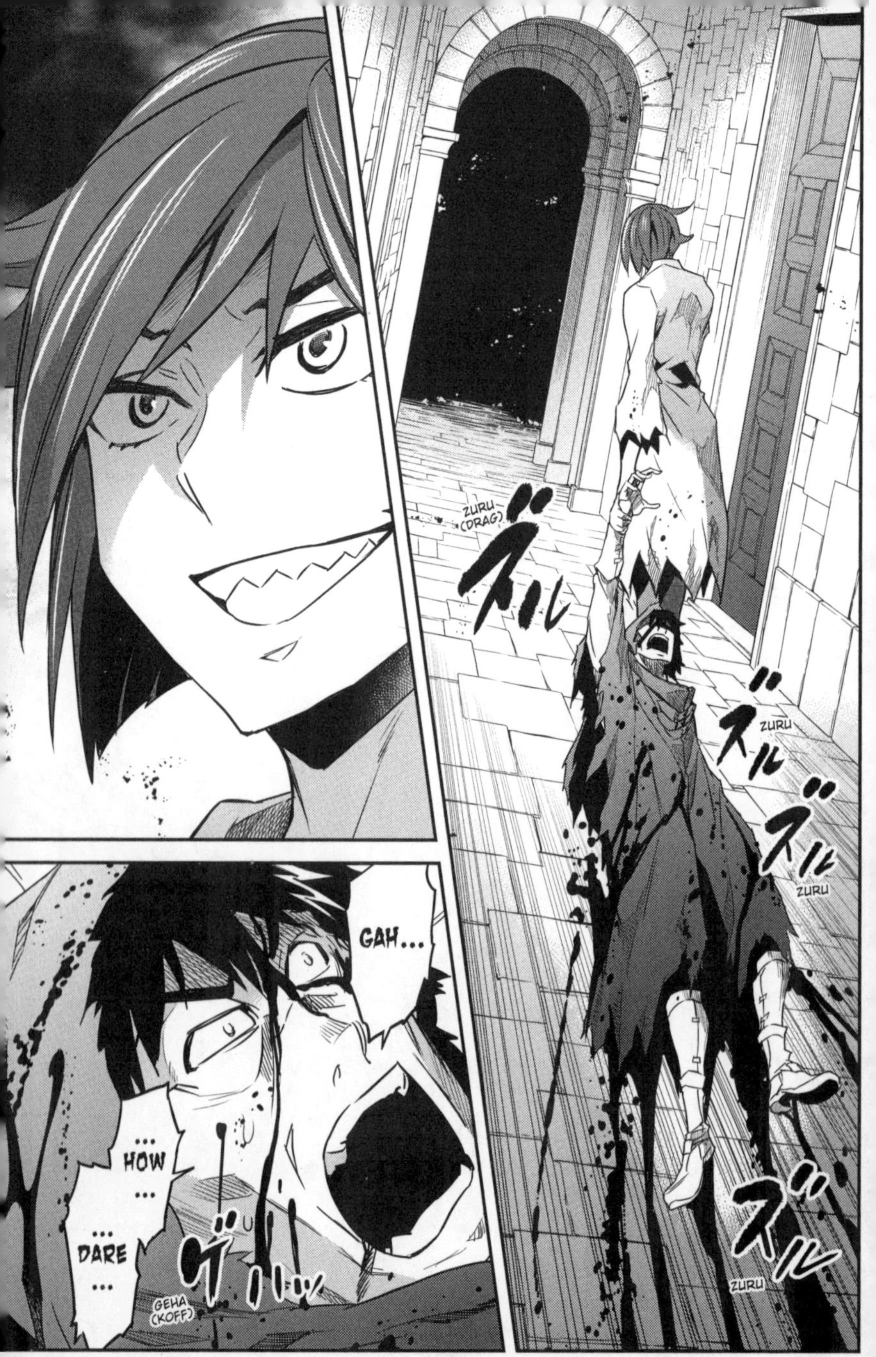
ズル
ZURU (DRAG)
ズル
ZURU
ズル
ZURU
ズル
ZURU
GAH...
...HOW... ...DARE...
GEHA (KOFF)

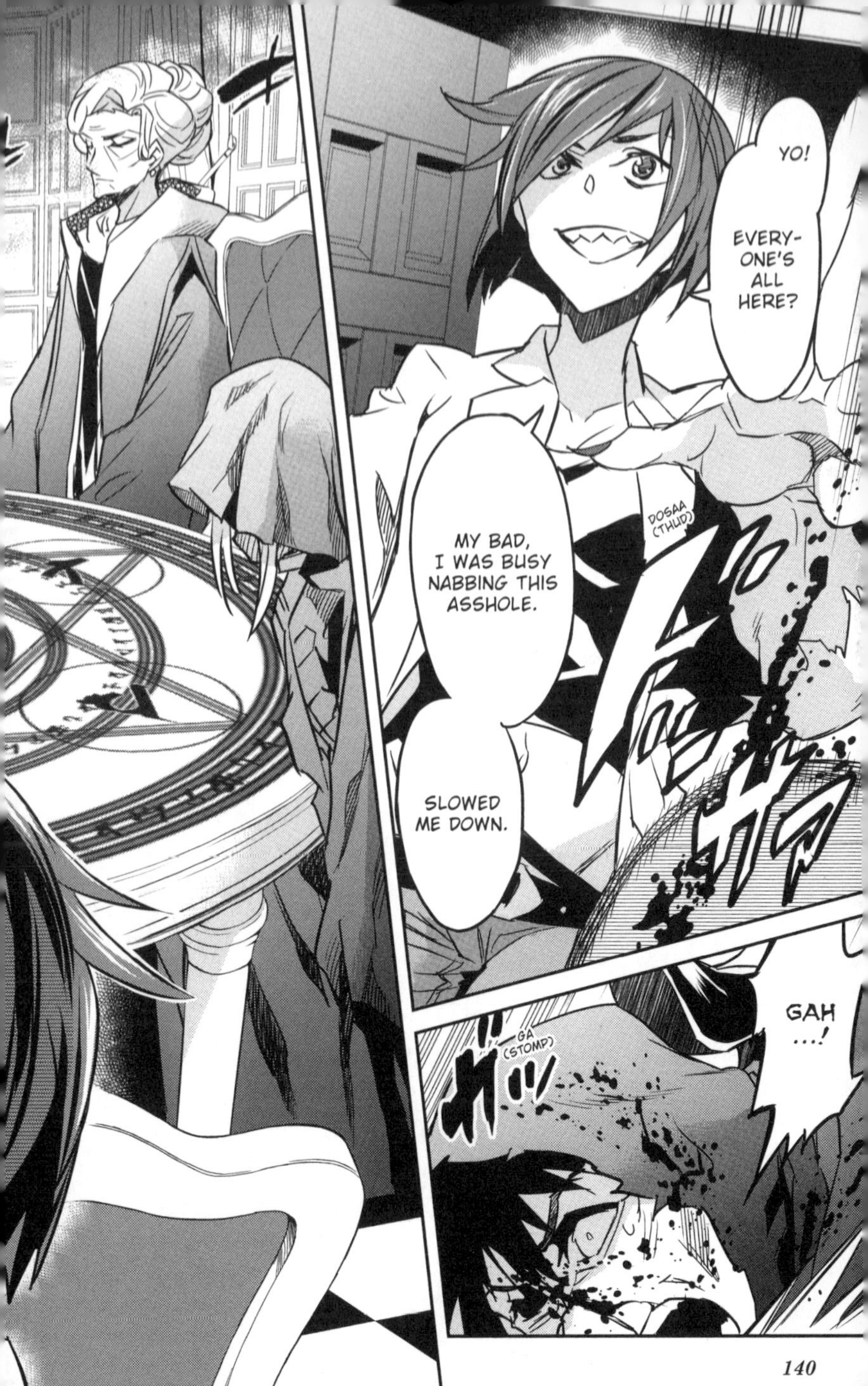
YO!
EVERY-ONE'S ALL HERE?
MY BAD, I WAS BUSY NABBING THIS ASSHOLE.
SLOWED ME DOWN.
DOSAA (THUD)
GAH ...!
GA (STOMP)

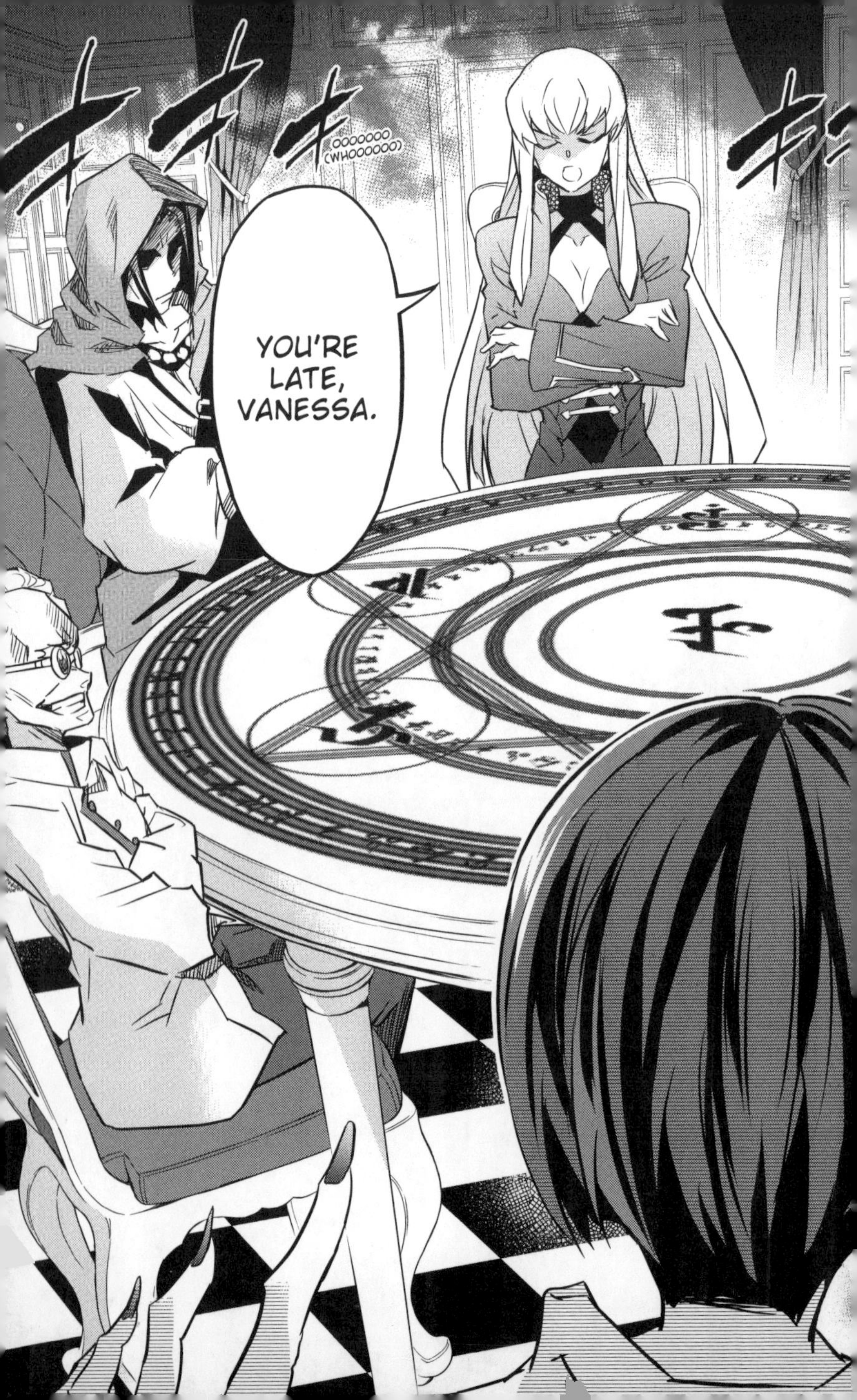
OOOOOOO
(WHOOOOOO)
YOU'RE LATE, VANESSA.

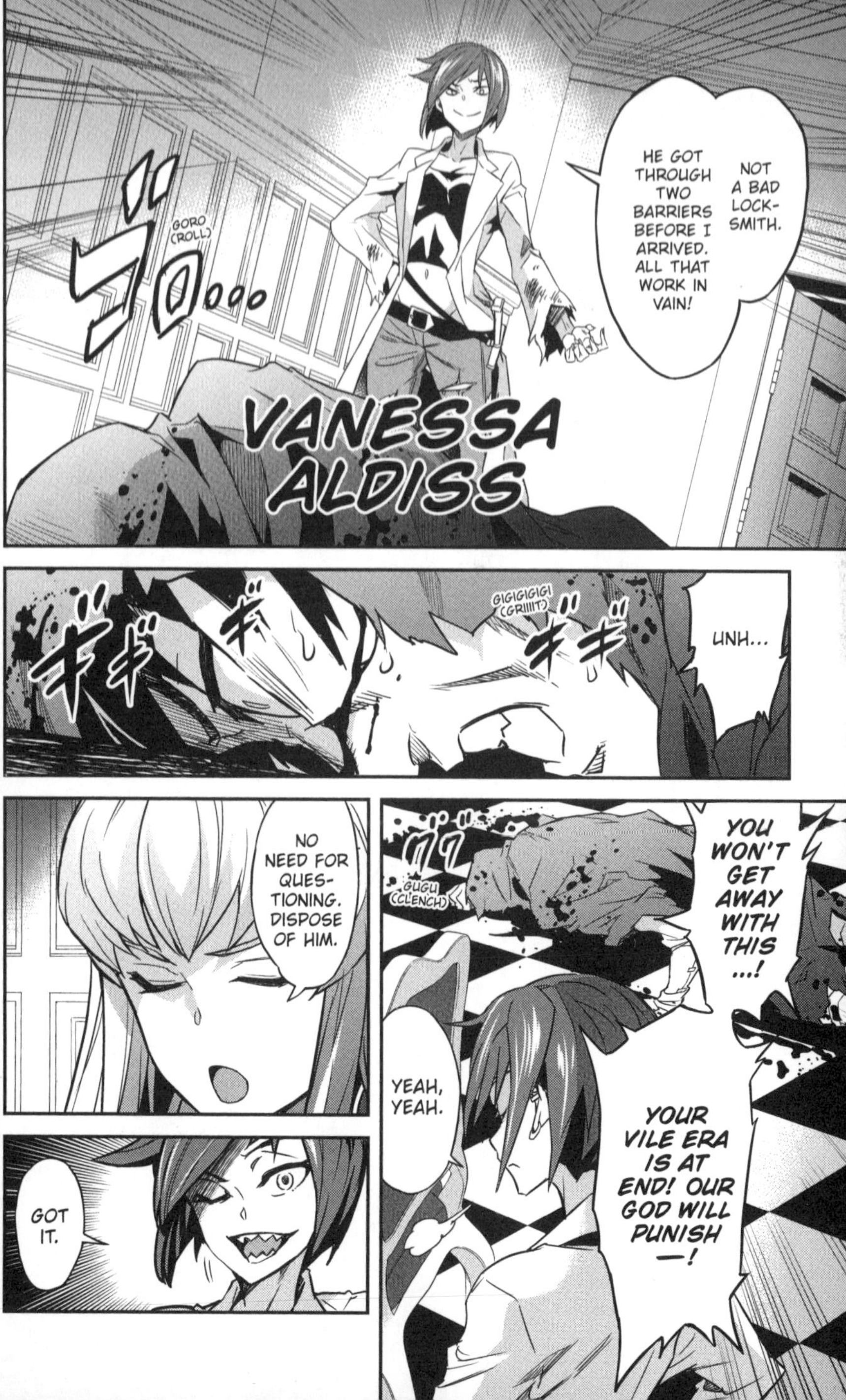
NOT A BAD LOCK-SMITH.
HE GOT THROUGH TWO BARRIERS BEFORE I ARRIVED. ALL THAT WORK IN VAIN!
GORO (ROLL)
VANESSA ALDISS
UNH...
GIGIGIGIGI (GRIIIIT)
YOU WON'T GET AWAY WITH THIS...!
GUGU (CLENCH)
YOUR VILE ERA IS AT END! OUR GOD WILL PUNISH—!
NO NEED FOR QUES-TIONING. DISPOSE OF HIM.
YEAH, YEAH.
GOT IT.

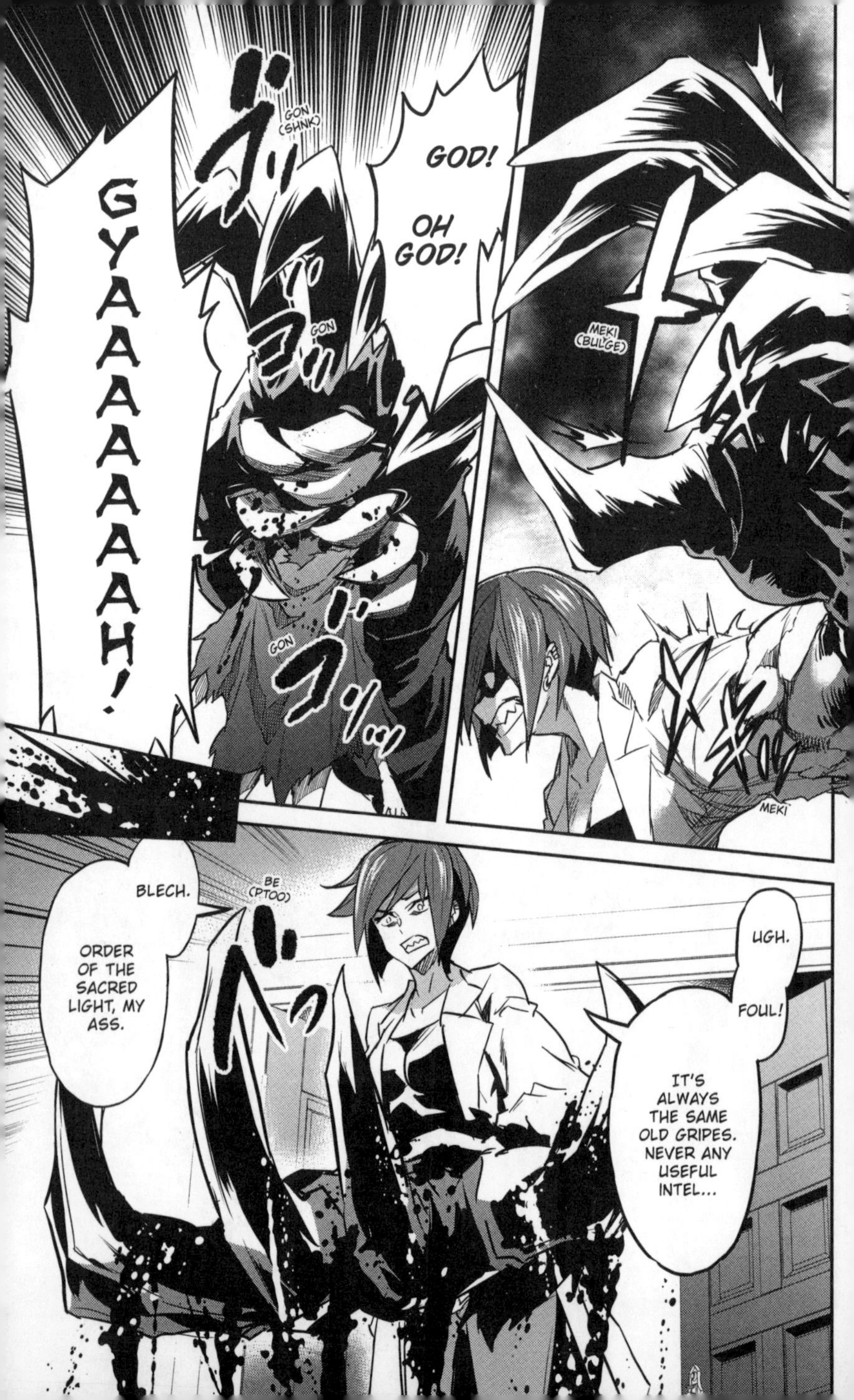
MEKI (BULGE)
MEKI
GOD!
OH GOD!
GON (SHNK)
GON
GON
GYAAAAAAAAH!
UGH.
FOUL!
IT'S ALWAYS THE SAME OLD GRIPES. NEVER ANY USEFUL INTEL...
BE (PTOO)
BLECH.
ORDER OF THE SACRED LIGHT, MY ASS.

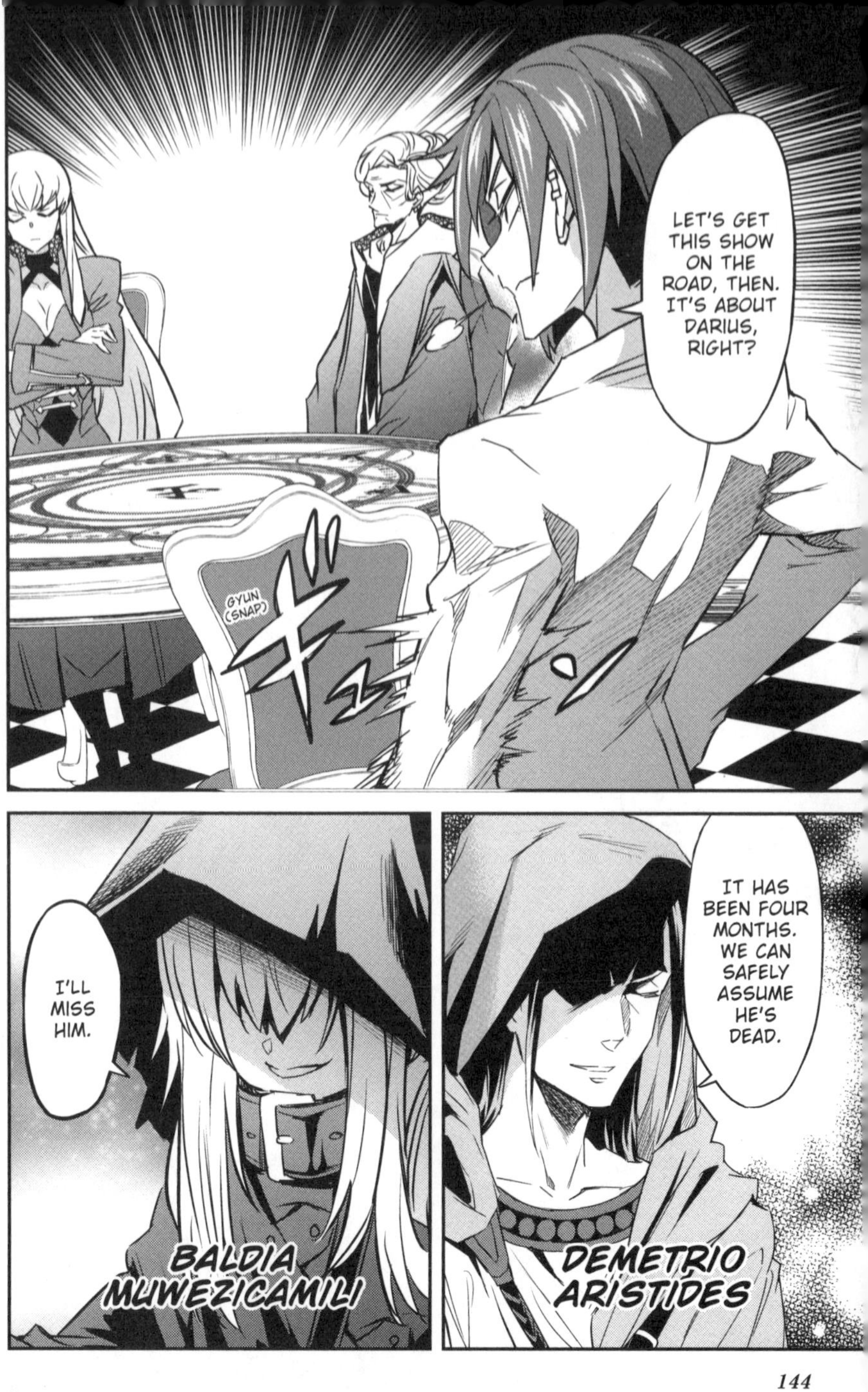
LET'S GET THIS SHOW ON THE ROAD, THEN. IT'S ABOUT DARIUS, RIGHT?
GYUN (SNAP)
IT HAS BEEN FOUR MONTHS. WE CAN SAFELY ASSUME HE'S DEAD.
DEMETRIO ARISTIDES
I'LL MISS HIM.
BALDIA MUWEZICAMILI

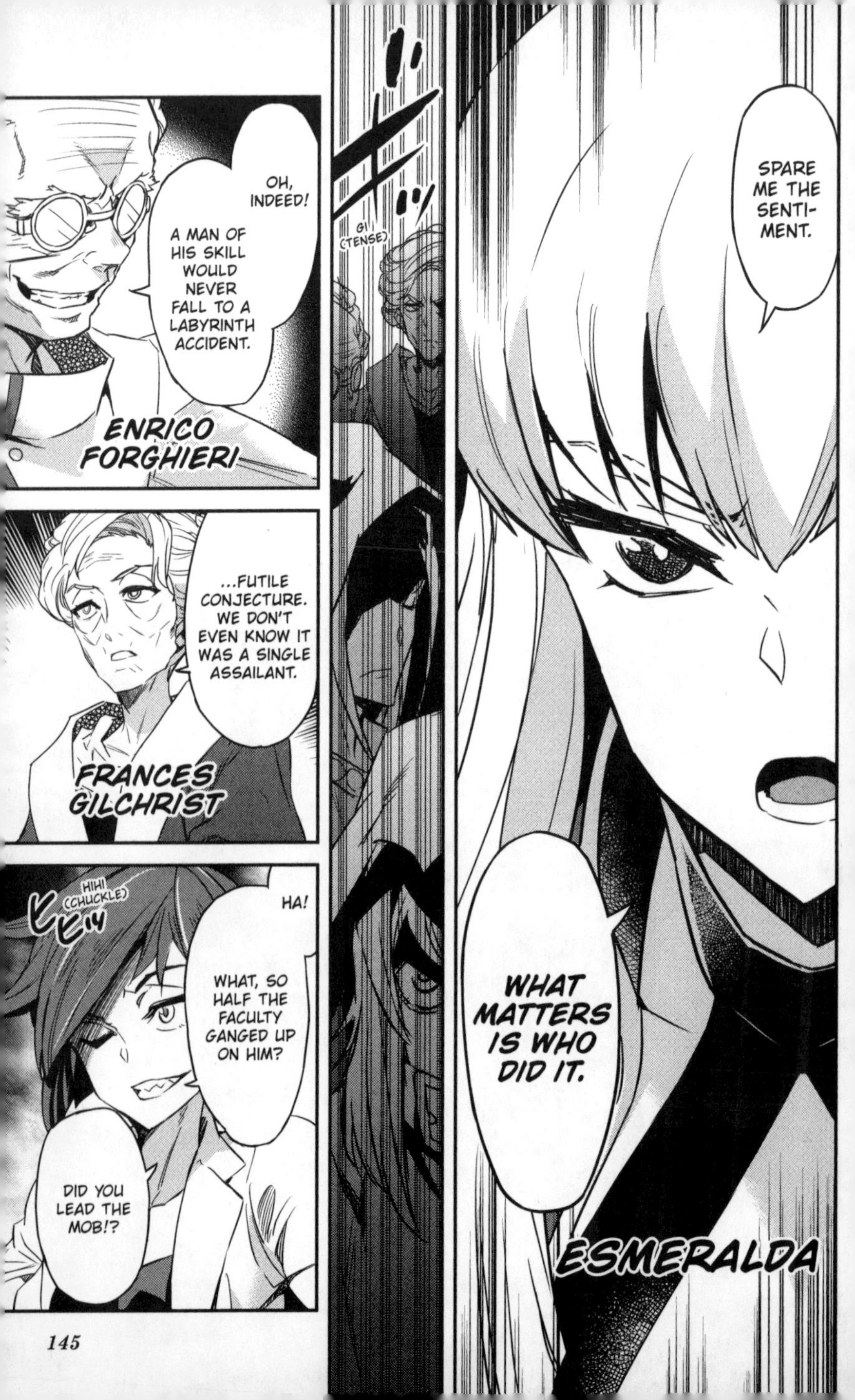
SPARE ME THE SENTI-MENT.
WHAT MATTERS IS WHO DID IT.
ESMERALDA
GI (TENSE)
OH, INDEED!
A MAN OF HIS SKILL WOULD NEVER FALL TO A LABYRINTH ACCIDENT.
ENRICO FORGHIERI
...FUTILE CONJECTURE. WE DON'T EVEN KNOW IT WAS A SINGLE ASSAILANT.
FRANCES GILCHRIST
HIHI (CHUCKLE)
HA!
WHAT, SO HALF THE FACULTY GANGED UP ON HIM?
DID YOU LEAD THE MOB!?

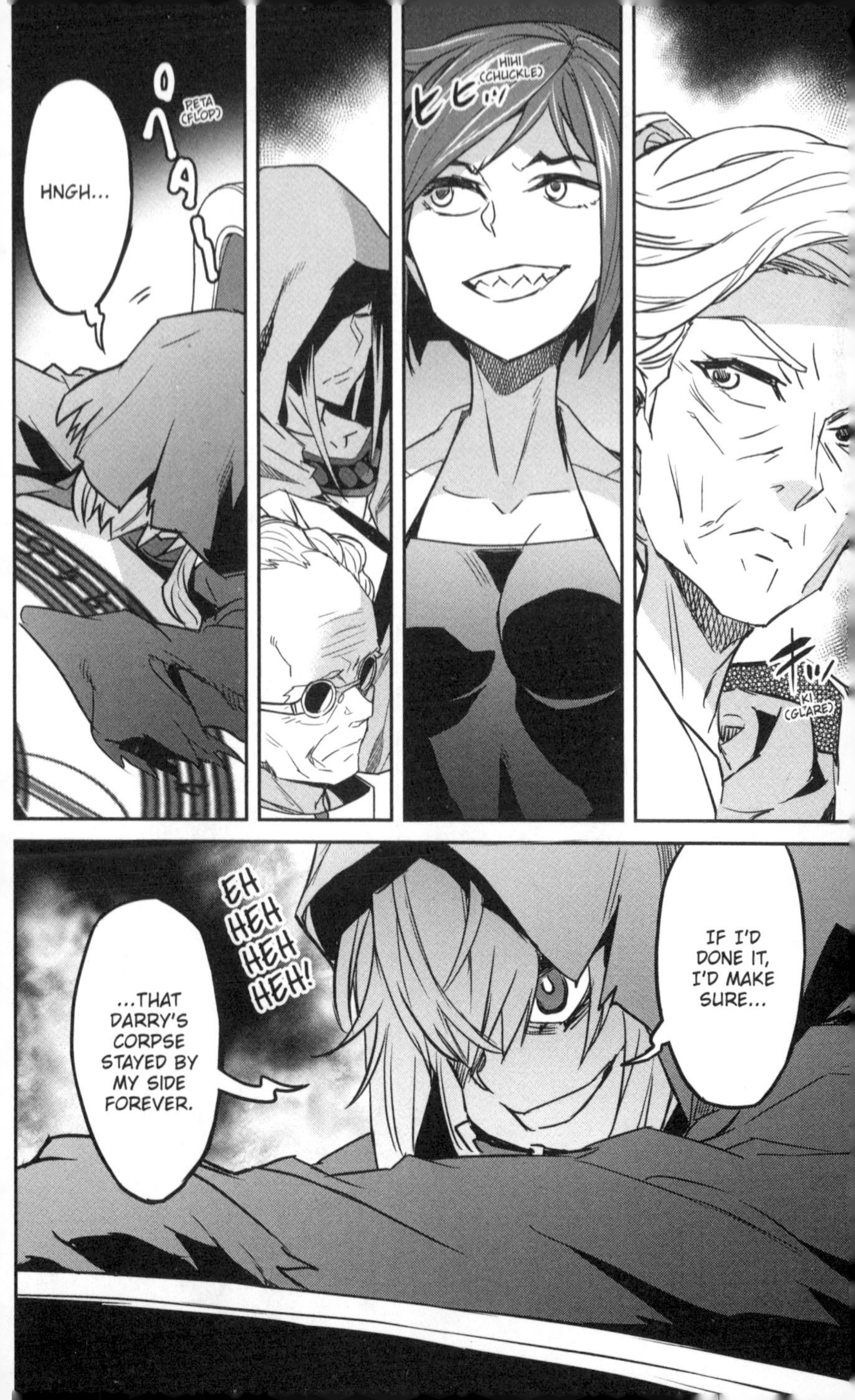
KI (GLARE)
HIHI (CHUCKLE)
PETA (FLOP)
HNGH...
IF I'D DONE IT, I'D MAKE SURE...
EH HEH HEH HEH!
...THAT DARRY'S CORPSE STAYED BY MY SIDE FOREVER.

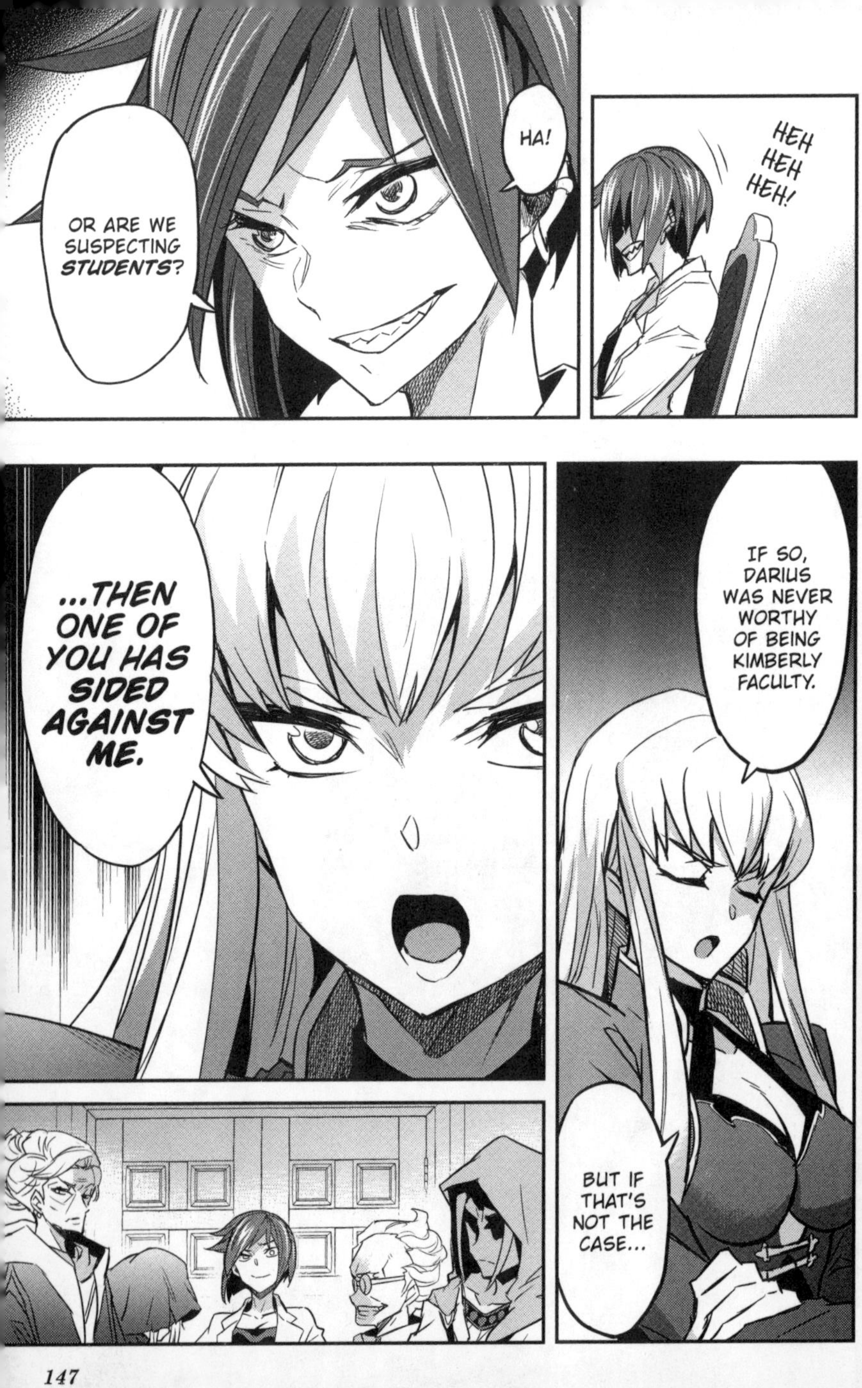
HEH HEH HEH!
HA!
OR ARE WE SUSPECTING STUDENTS?
IF SO, DARIUS WAS NEVER WORTHY OF BEING KIMBERLY FACULTY.
BUT IF THAT'S NOT THE CASE...
...THEN ONE OF YOU HAS SIDED AGAINST ME.

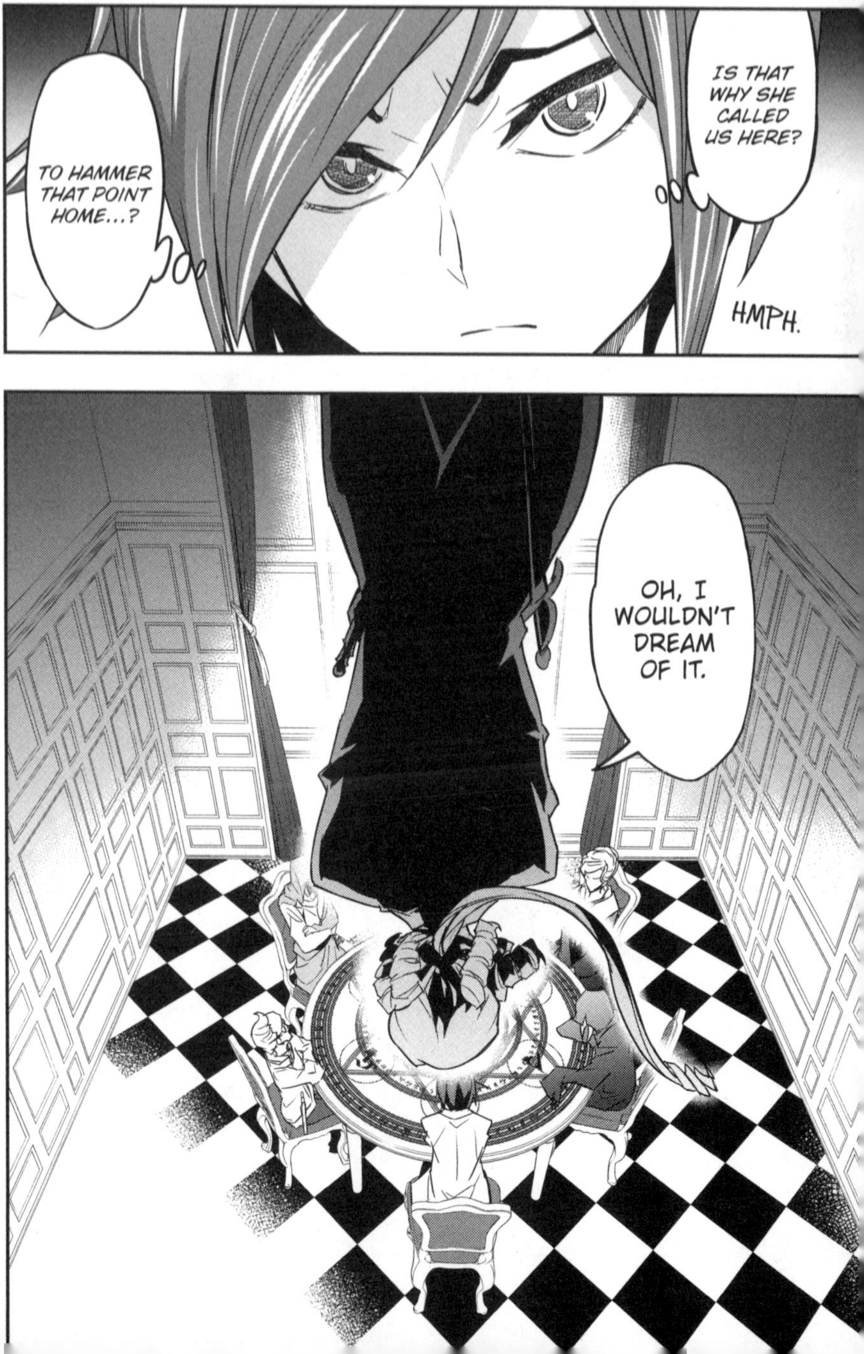
IS THAT WHY SHE CALLED US HERE?
TO HAMMER THAT POINT HOME...?
HMPH.
OH, I WOULDN'T DREAM OF IT.

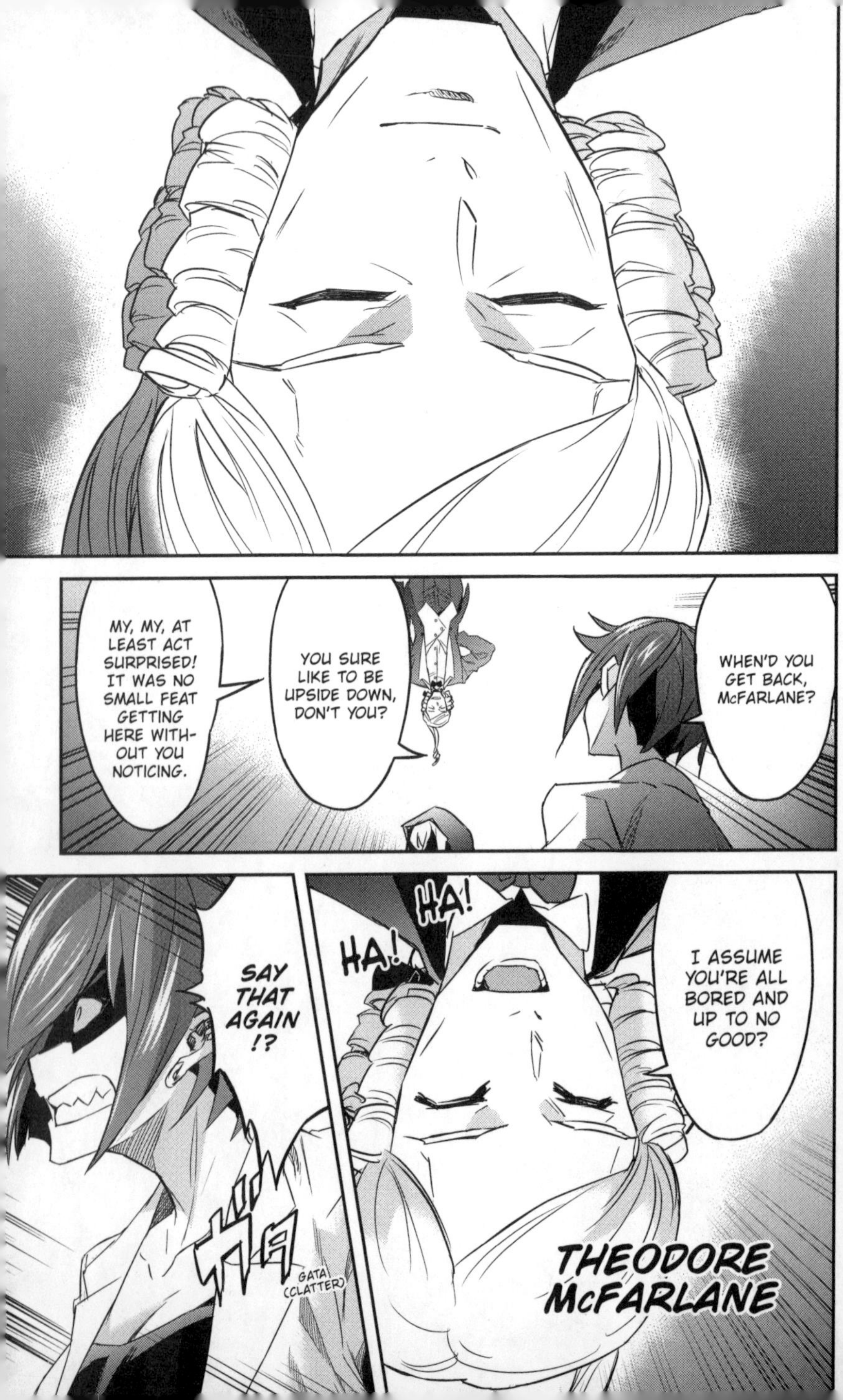
WHEN'D YOU GET BACK, McFARLANE?
YOU SURE LIKE TO BE UPSIDE DOWN, DON'T YOU?
MY, MY, AT LEAST ACT SURPRISED! IT WAS NO SMALL FEAT GETTING HERE WITHOUT YOU NOTICING.
I ASSUME YOU'RE ALL BORED AND UP TO NO GOOD?
HA! HA!
THEODORE McFARLANE
SAY THAT AGAIN!?
GATA (CLATTER)

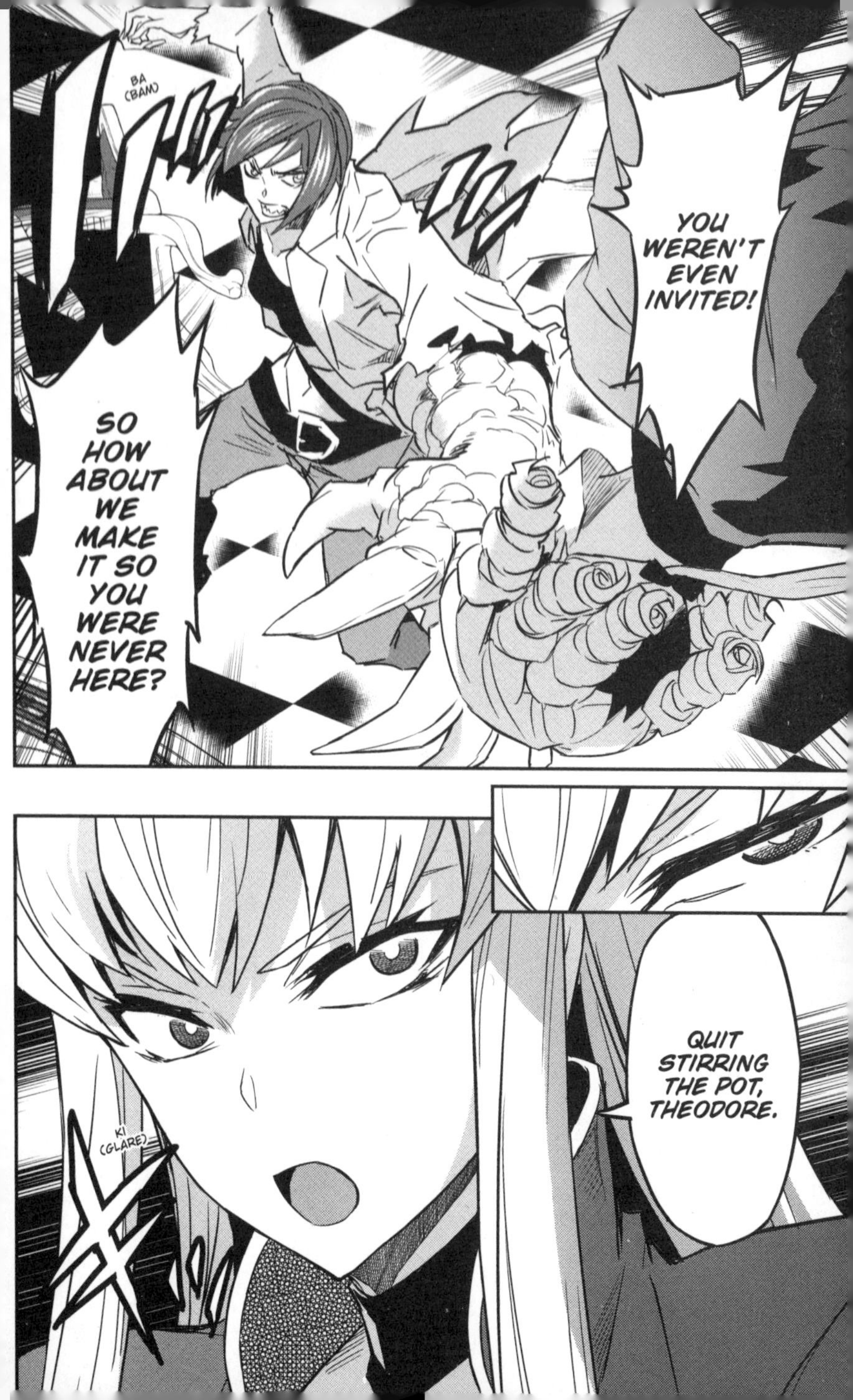
YOU WEREN'T EVEN INVITED!
BA (BAM)
SO HOW ABOUT WE MAKE IT SO YOU WERE NEVER HERE?
QUIT STIRRING THE POT, THEODORE.
KI (GLARE)

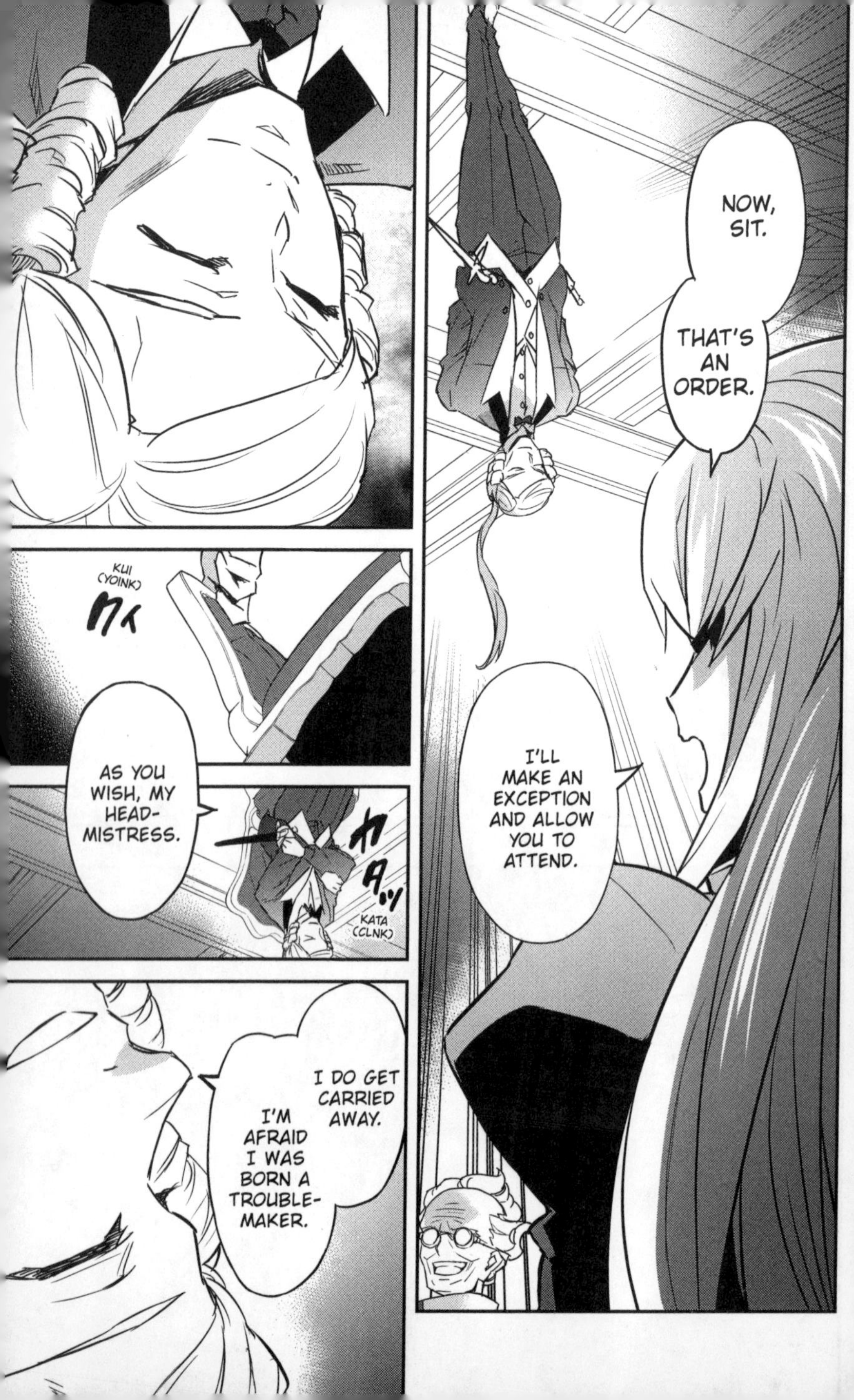
NOW, SIT.
THAT'S AN ORDER.
I'LL MAKE AN EXCEPTION AND ALLOW YOU TO ATTEND.
KUI (YOINK)
AS YOU WISH, MY HEAD-MISTRESS.
KATA (CLNK)
I DO GET CARRIED AWAY.
I'M AFRAID I WAS BORN A TROUBLE-MAKER.

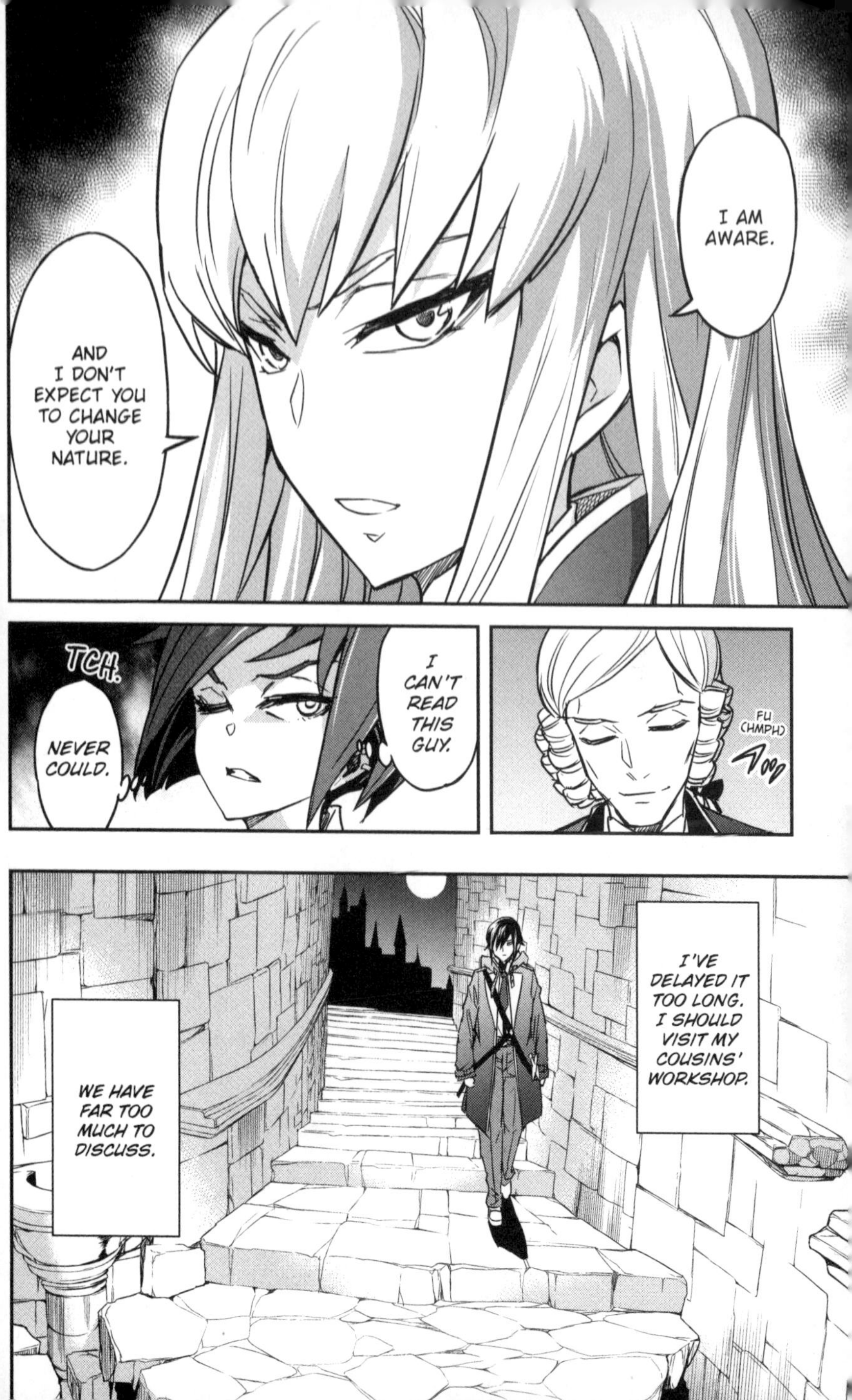
I AM AWARE.
AND I DON'T EXPECT YOU TO CHANGE YOUR NATURE.
FU (HMPH)
I CAN'T READ THIS GUY.
TCH.
NEVER COULD.
I'VE DELAYED IT TOO LONG. I SHOULD VISIT MY COUSINS' WORKSHOP.
WE HAVE FAR TOO MUCH TO DISCUSS.

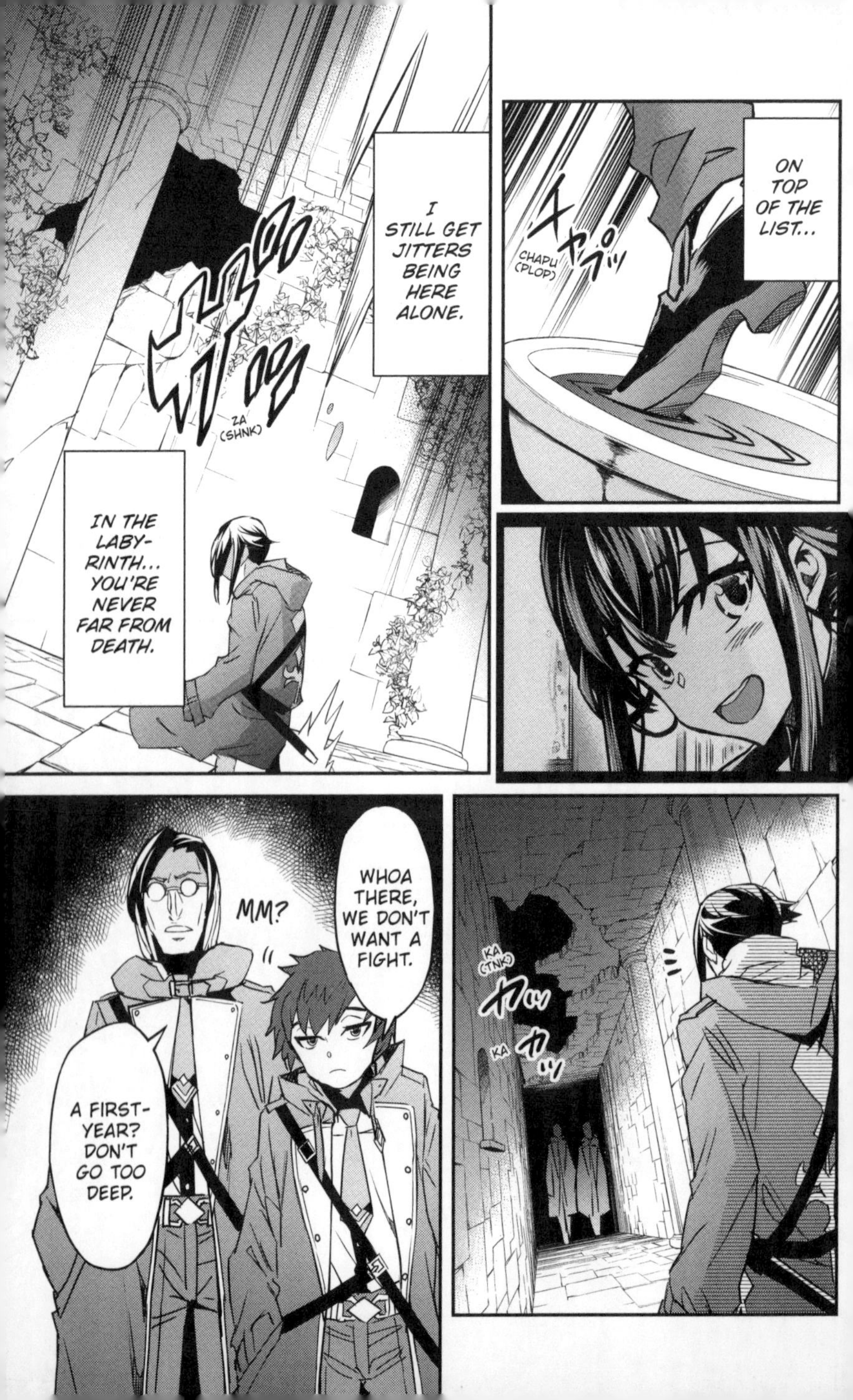
ON TOP OF THE LIST...
CHAPU (PLOP)
I STILL GET JITTERS BEING HERE ALONE.
ZA (SHNK)
IN THE LABY-RINTH... YOU'RE NEVER FAR FROM DEATH.
KA (TNK)
KA
WHOA THERE, WE DON'T WANT A FIGHT.
MM?
A FIRST-YEAR? DON'T GO TOO DEEP.

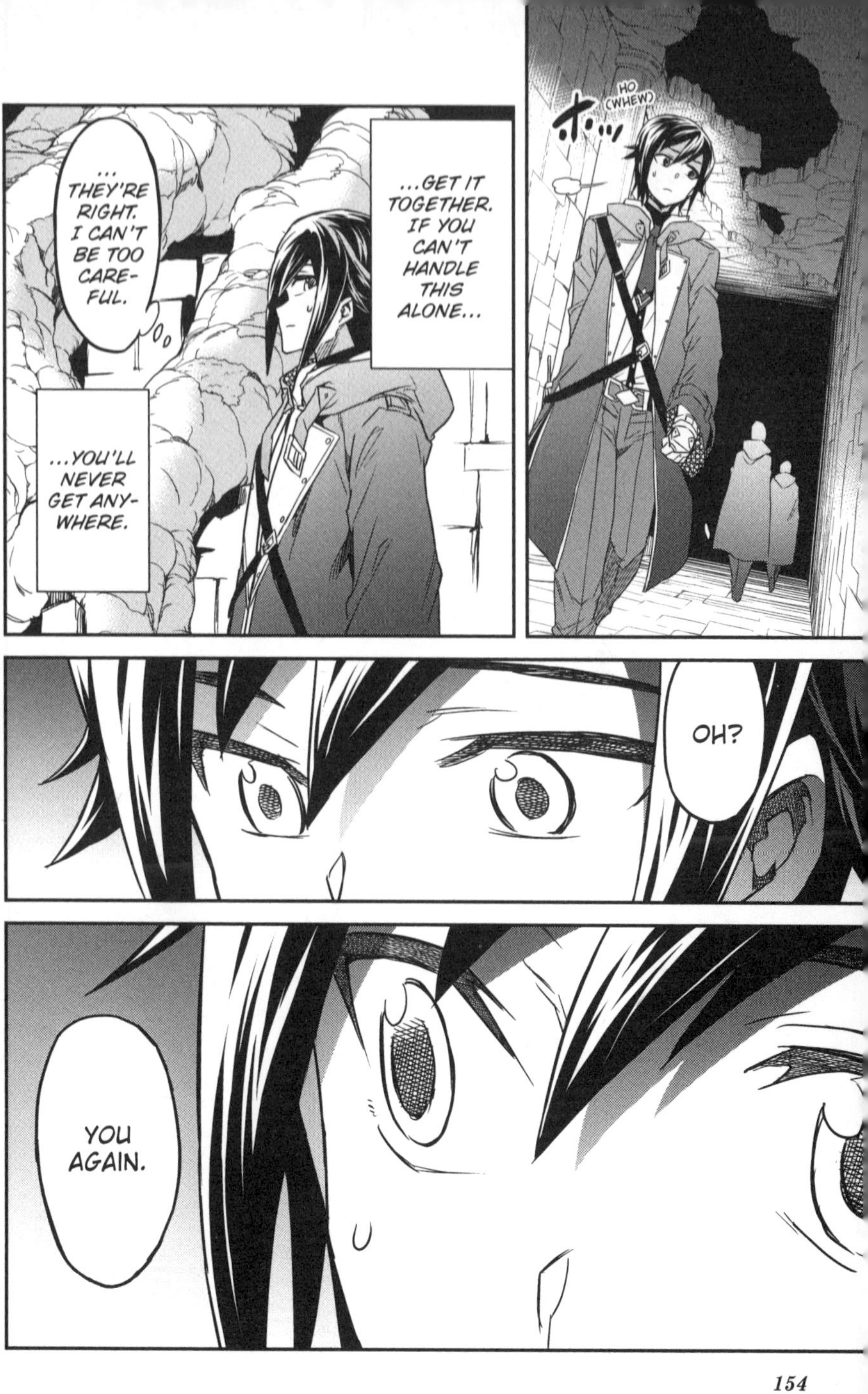
HO (WHEW)
...GET IT TOGETHER. IF YOU CAN'T HANDLE THIS ALONE...
... THEY'RE RIGHT. I CAN'T BE TOO CAREFUL.
...YOU'LL NEVER GET ANYWHERE.
OH?
YOU AGAIN.

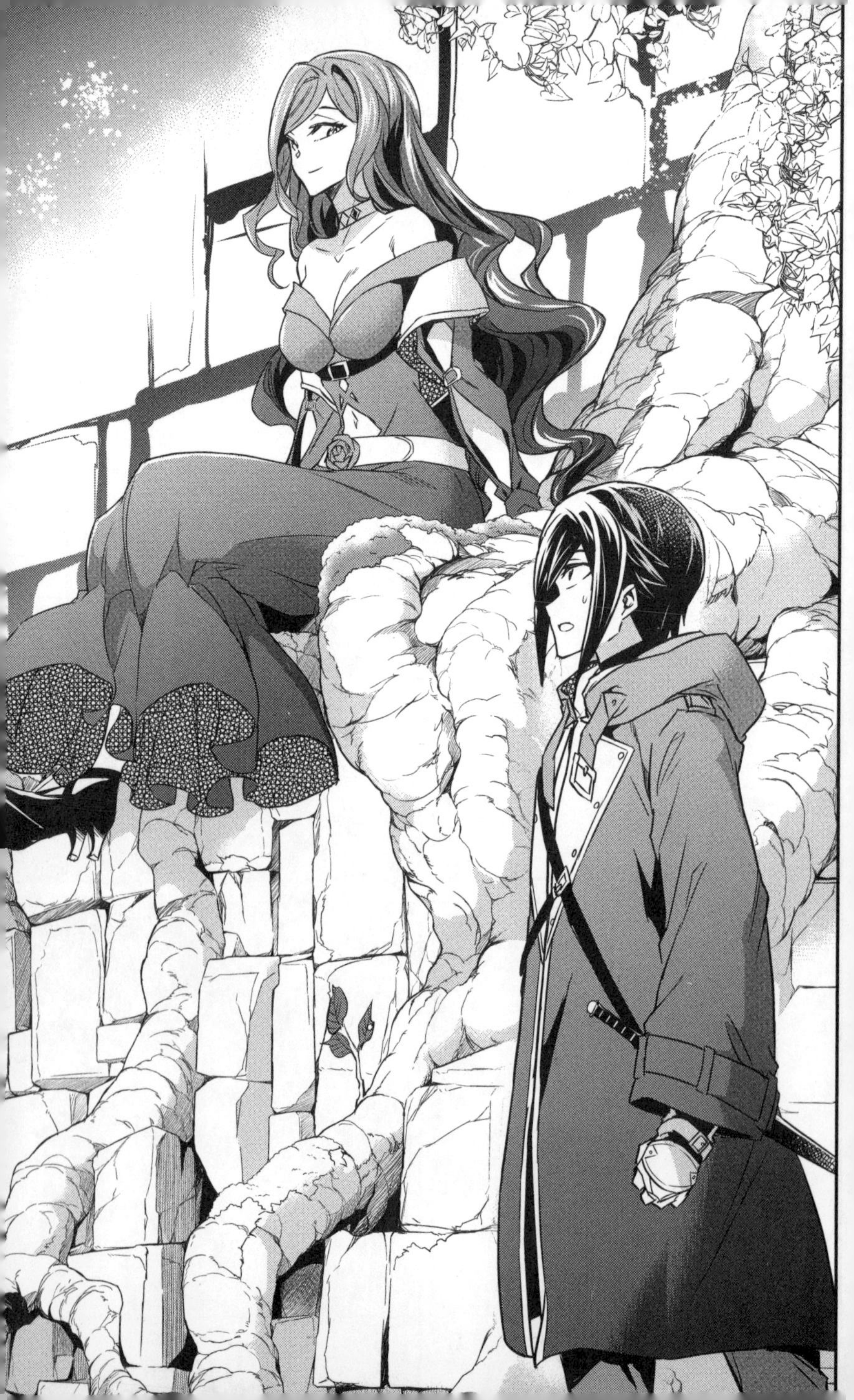

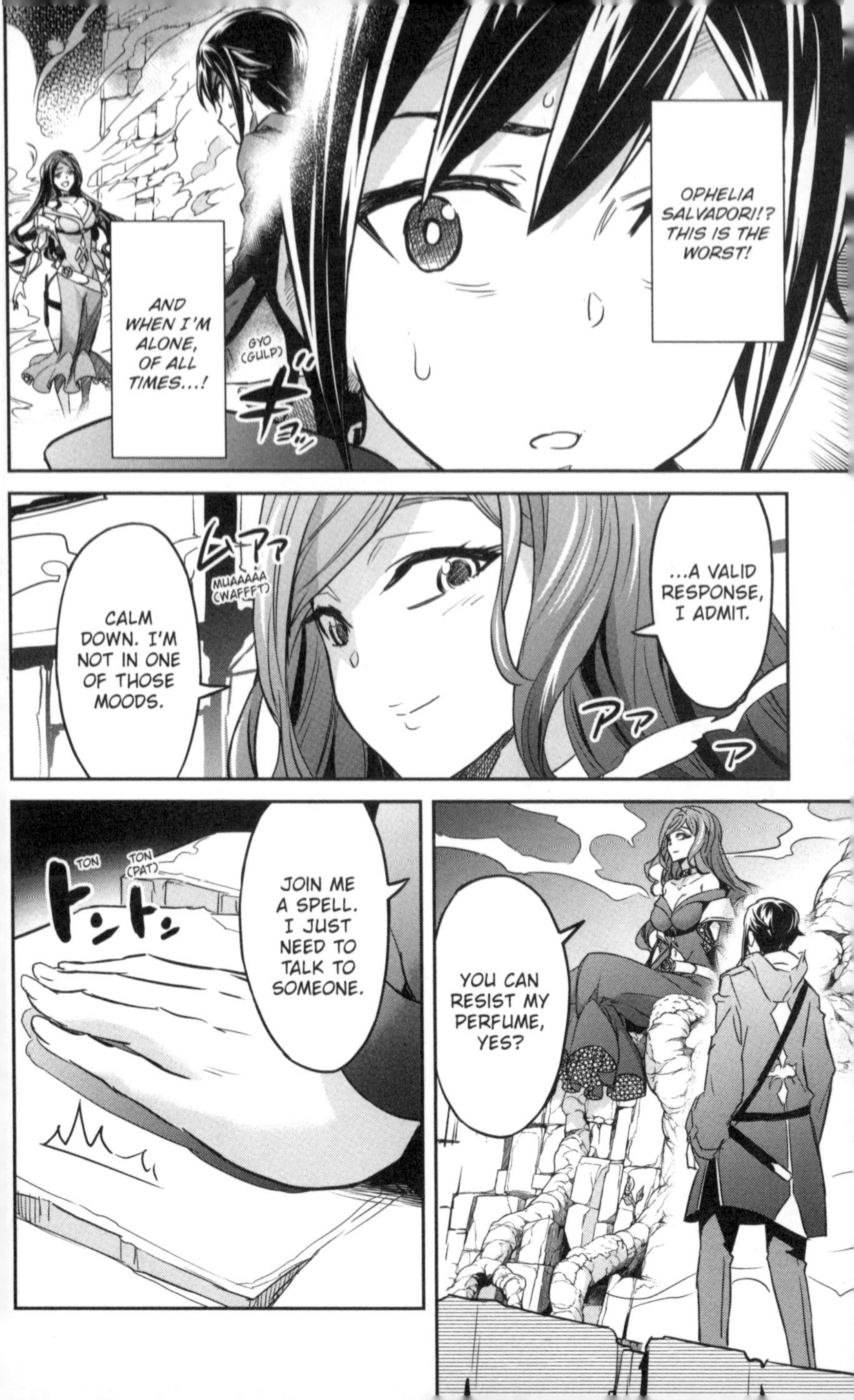
OPHELIA SALVADORI!? THIS IS THE WORST!
GYO (GULP)
AND WHEN I'M ALONE, OF ALL TIMES...!
...A VALID RESPONSE, I ADMIT.
MUAAAAA (WAFFFT)
CALM DOWN. I'M NOT IN ONE OF THOSE MOODS.
YOU CAN RESIST MY PERFUME, YES?
JOIN ME A SPELL. I JUST NEED TO TALK TO SOMEONE.
TON TON (PAT)

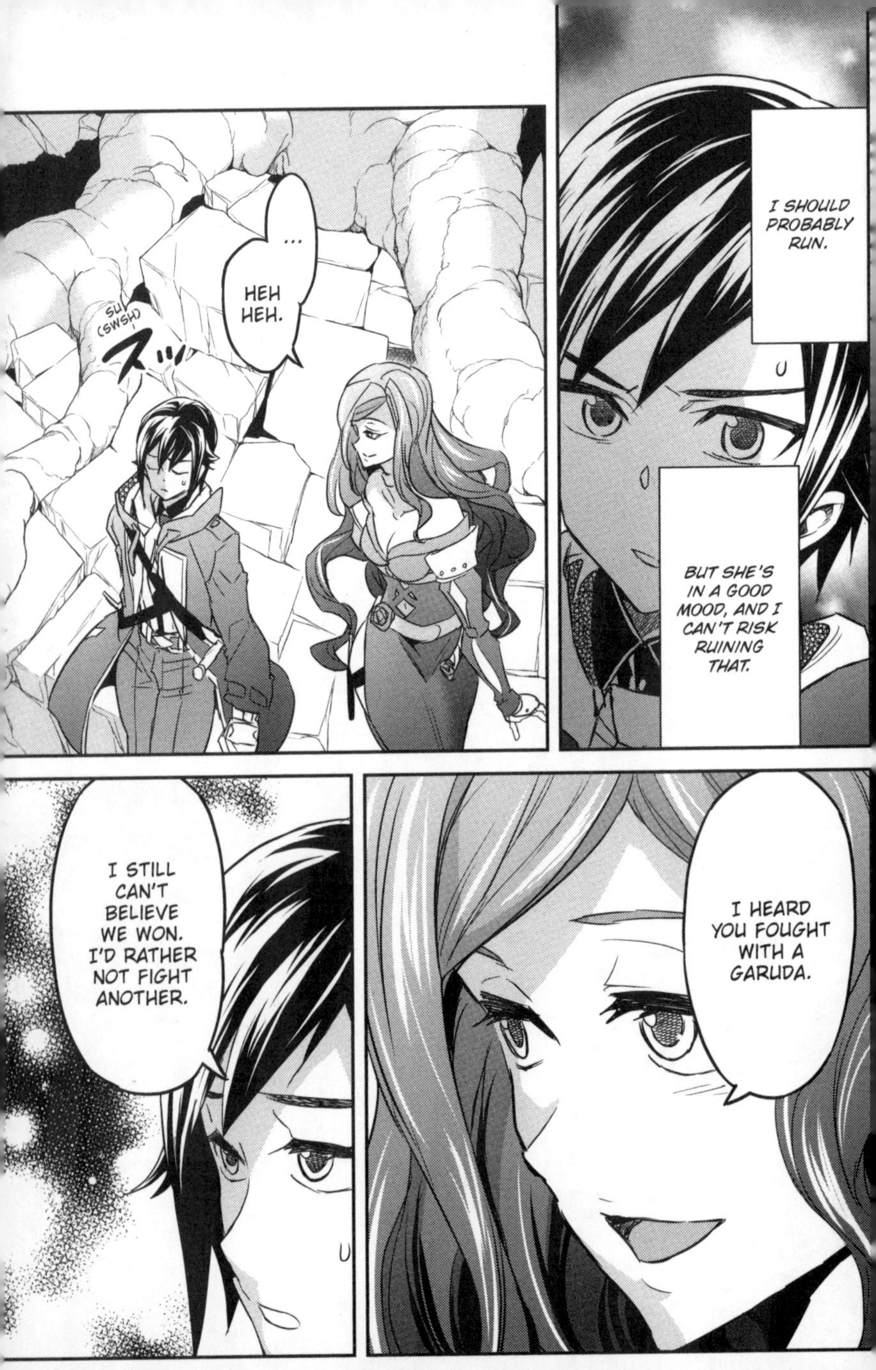
I SHOULD PROBABLY RUN.
BUT SHE'S IN A GOOD MOOD, AND I CAN'T RISK RUINING THAT.
...
HEH HEH.
SU (SWSH)
I HEARD YOU FOUGHT WITH A GARUDA.
I STILL CAN'T BELIEVE WE WON. I'D RATHER NOT FIGHT ANOTHER.

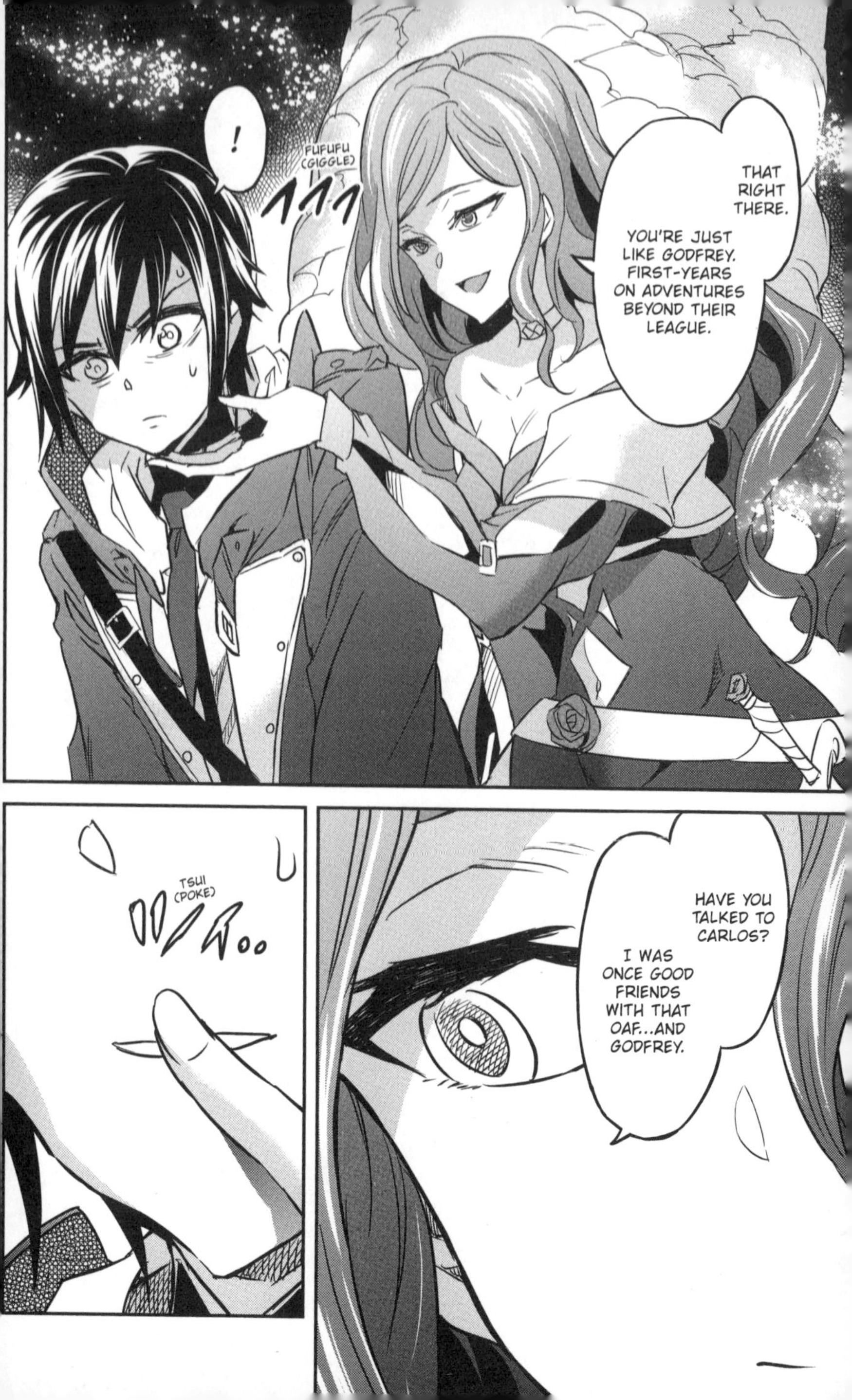
THAT RIGHT THERE.
YOU'RE JUST LIKE GODFREY. FIRST-YEARS ON ADVENTURES BEYOND THEIR LEAGUE.
FUFUFU (GIGGLE)
!
HAVE YOU TALKED TO CARLOS?
I WAS ONCE GOOD FRIENDS WITH THAT OAF...AND GODFREY.
TSUI (POKE)

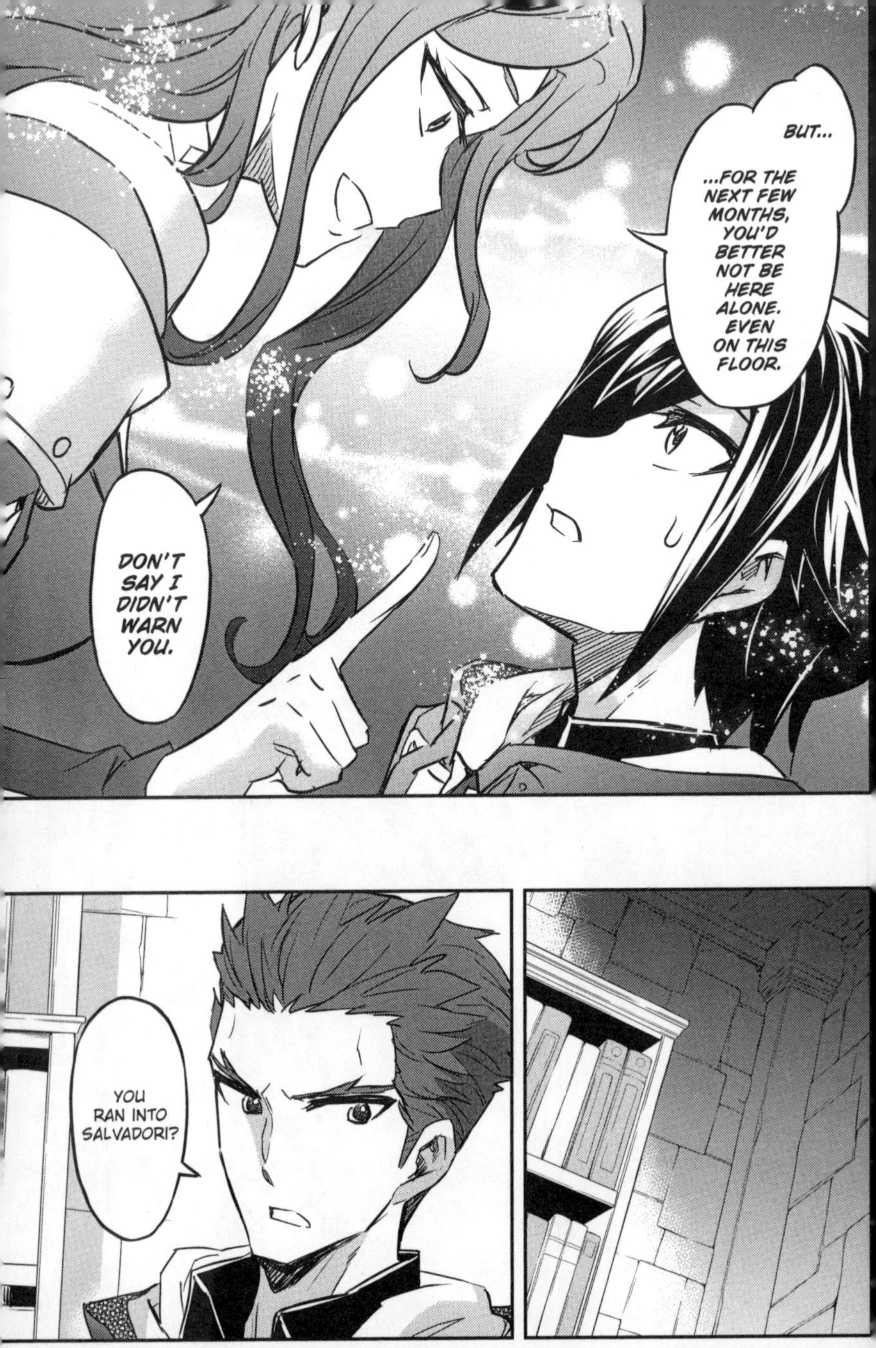
BUT...
...FOR THE NEXT FEW MONTHS, YOU'D BETTER NOT BE HERE ALONE. EVEN ON THIS FLOOR.
DON'T SAY I DIDN'T WARN YOU.
YOU RAN INTO SALVADORI?

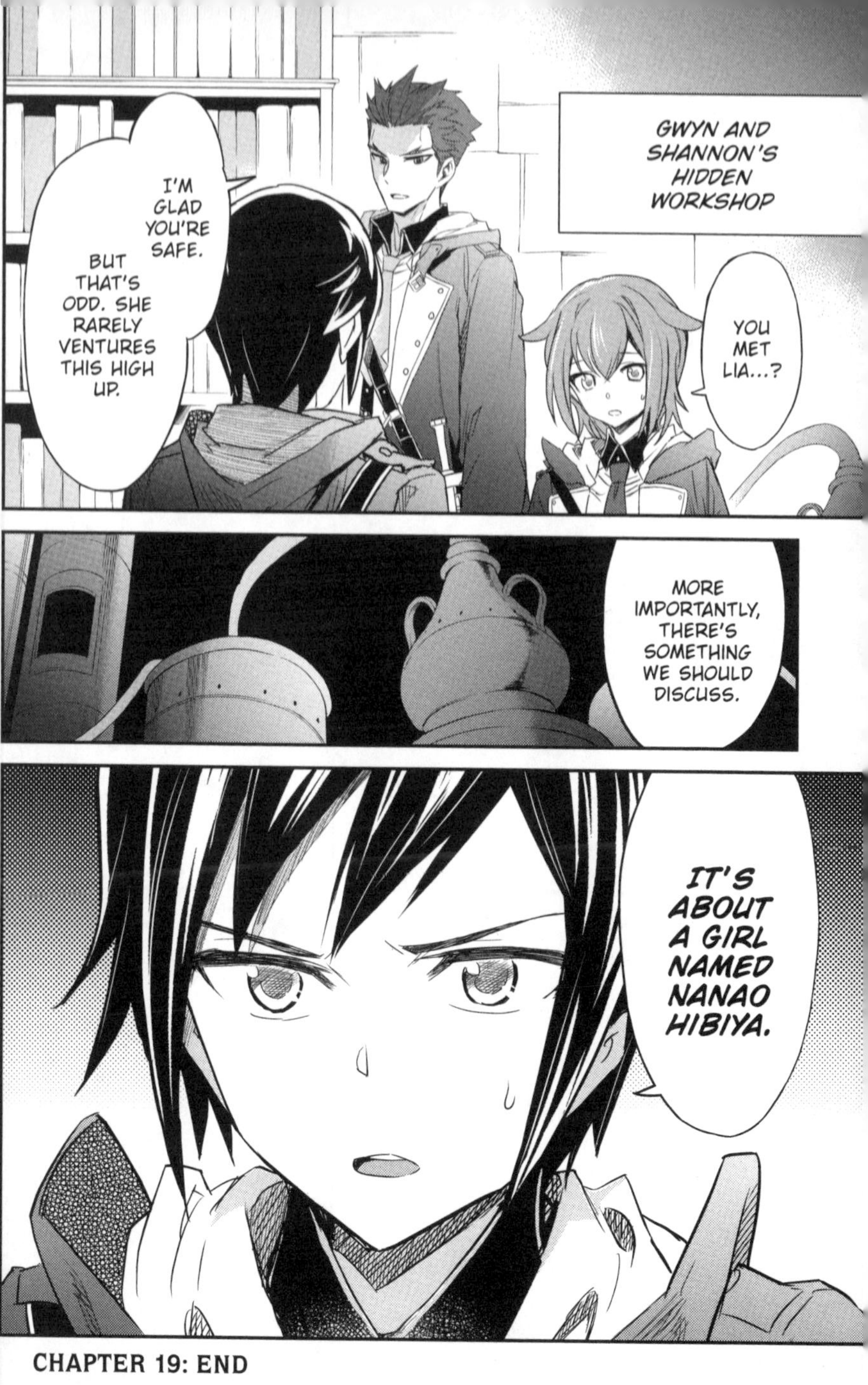
GWYN AND SHANNON'S HIDDEN WORKSHOP
YOU MET LIA...?
I'M GLAD YOU'RE SAFE.
BUT THAT'S ODD. SHE RARELY VENTURES THIS HIGH UP.
MORE IMPORTANTLY, THERE'S SOMETHING WE SHOULD DISCUSS.
IT'S ABOUT A GIRL NAMED NANAO HIBIYA.

CHAPTER 19: END

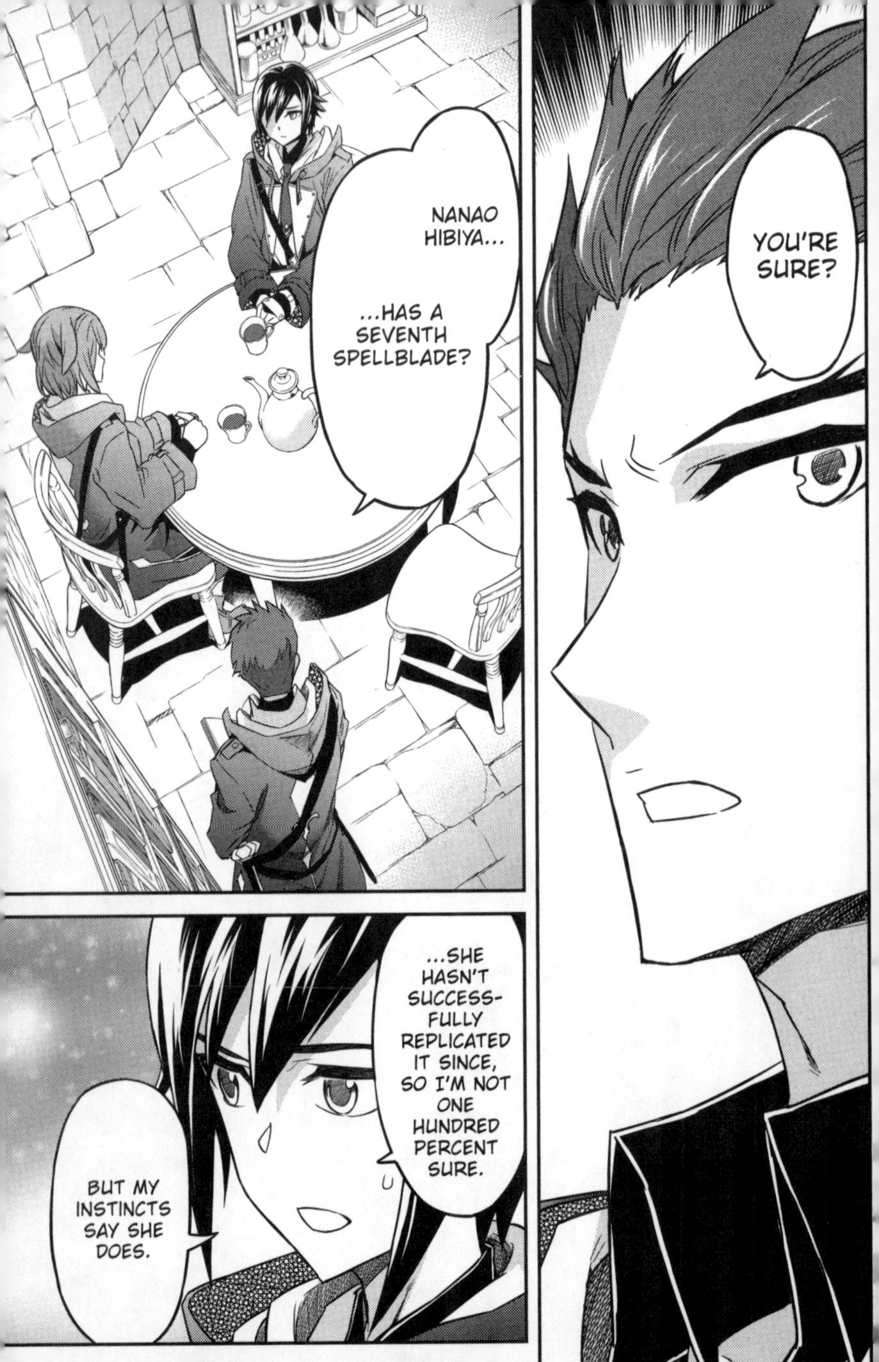
YOU'RE SURE?
NANAO HIBIYA...
...HAS A SEVENTH SPELLBLADE?
...SHE HASN'T SUCCESS-FULLY REPLICATED IT SINCE, SO I'M NOT ONE HUNDRED PERCENT SURE.
BUT MY INSTINCTS SAY SHE DOES.

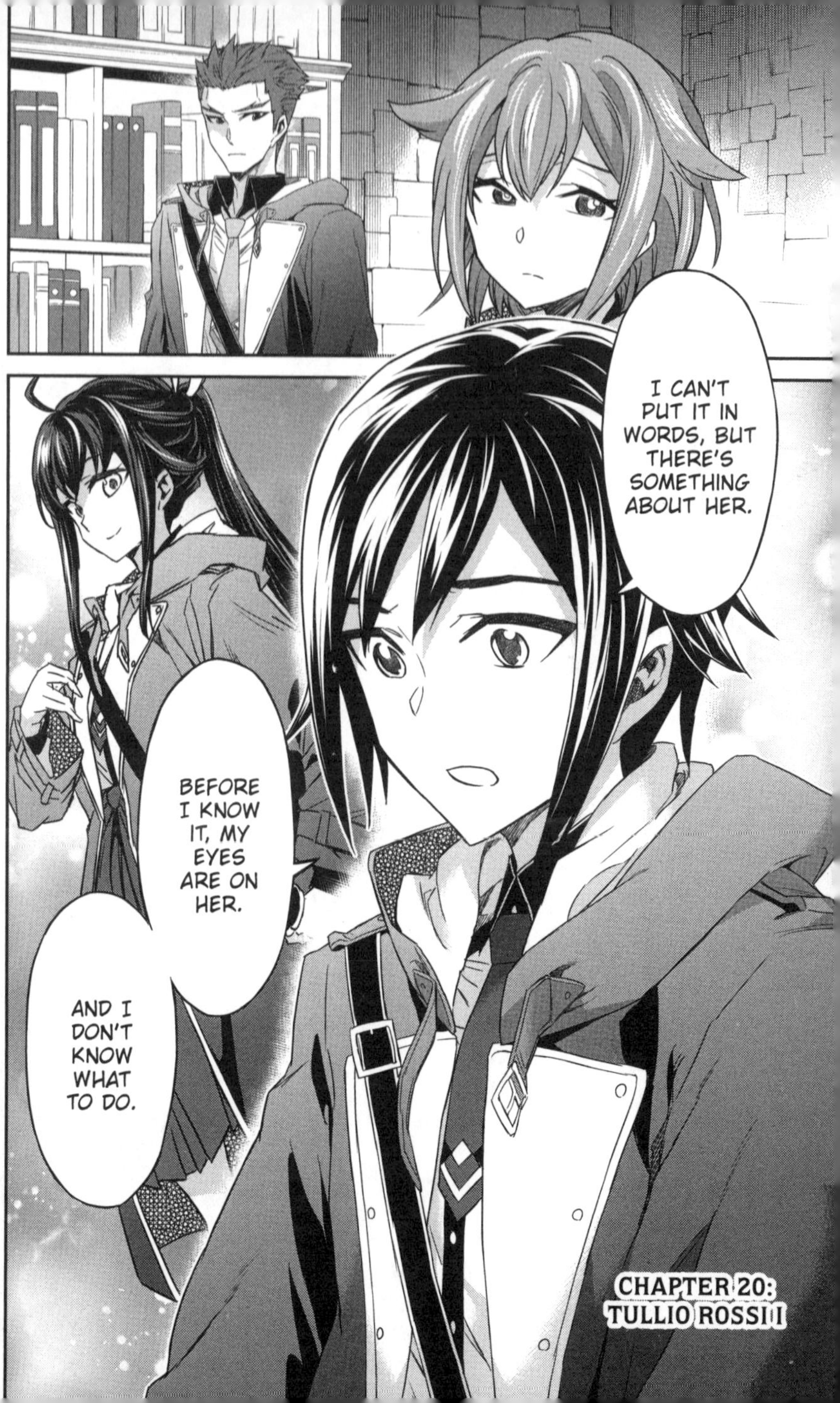
I CAN'T PUT IT IN WORDS, BUT THERE'S SOMETHING ABOUT HER.
BEFORE I KNOW IT, MY EYES ARE ON HER.
AND I DON'T KNOW WHAT TO DO.
CHAPTER 20: TULLIO ROSSI I

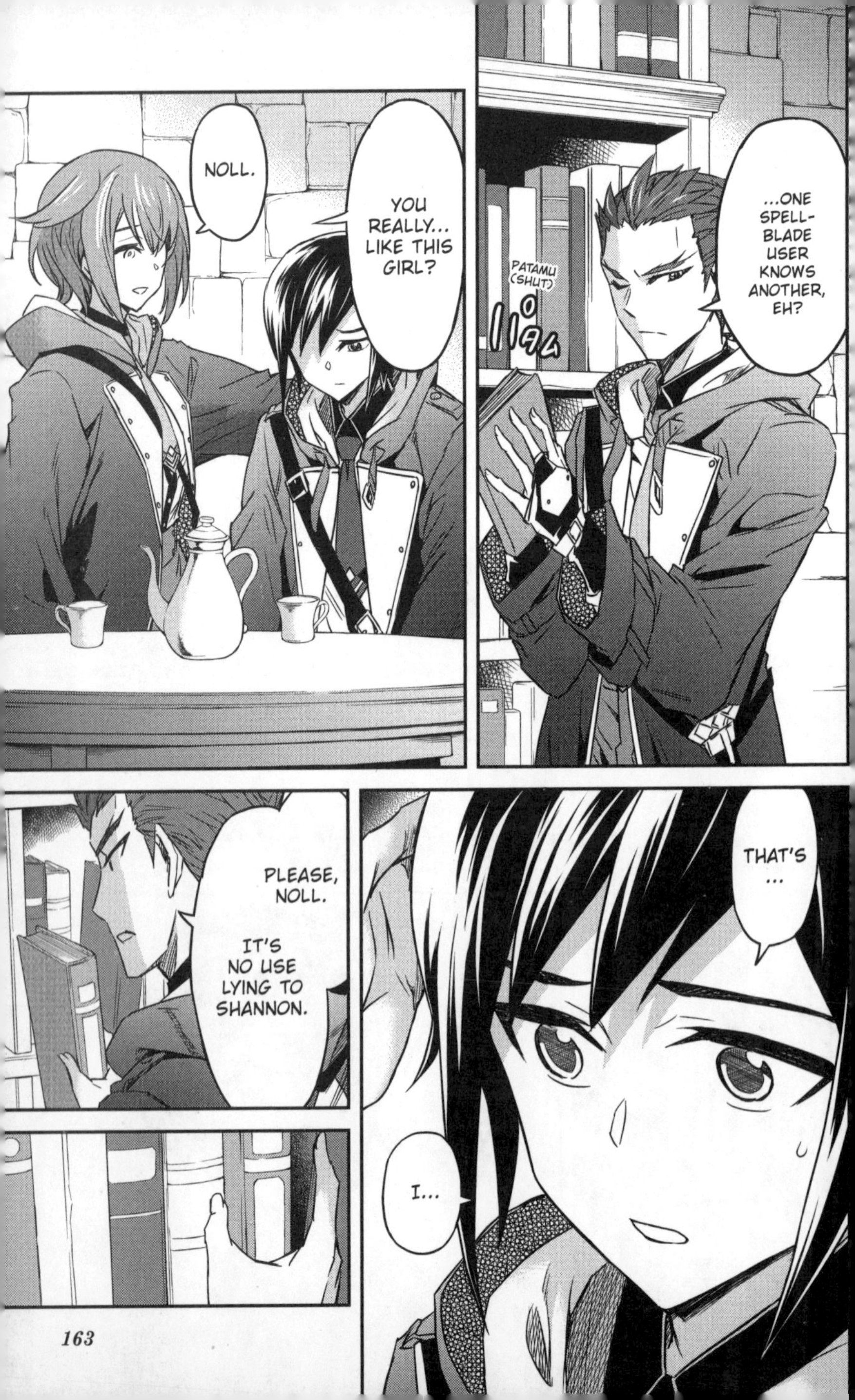
PATAMU (SHUT)
...ONE SPELL-BLADE USER KNOWS ANOTHER, EH?
NOLL.
YOU REALLY... LIKE THIS GIRL?
THAT'S...
I...
PLEASE, NOLL.
IT'S NO USE LYING TO SHANNON.

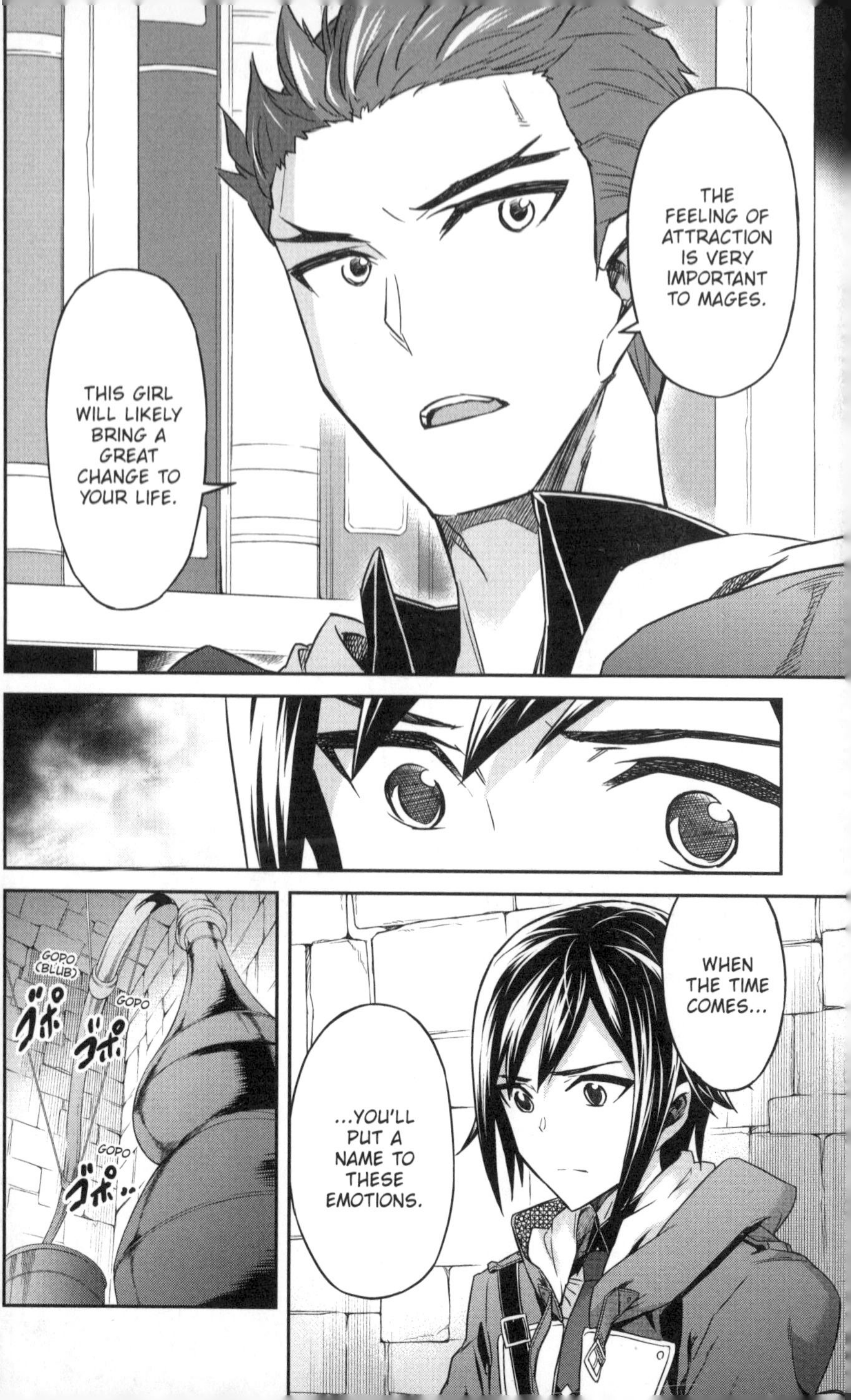
THE FEELING OF ATTRACTION IS VERY IMPORTANT TO MAGES.
THIS GIRL WILL LIKELY BRING A GREAT CHANGE TO YOUR LIFE.
WHEN THE TIME COMES...
...YOU'LL PUT A NAME TO THESE EMOTIONS.
ゴポ
GOPO (BLUB)
ゴポ
GOPO
ゴポ..
GOPO

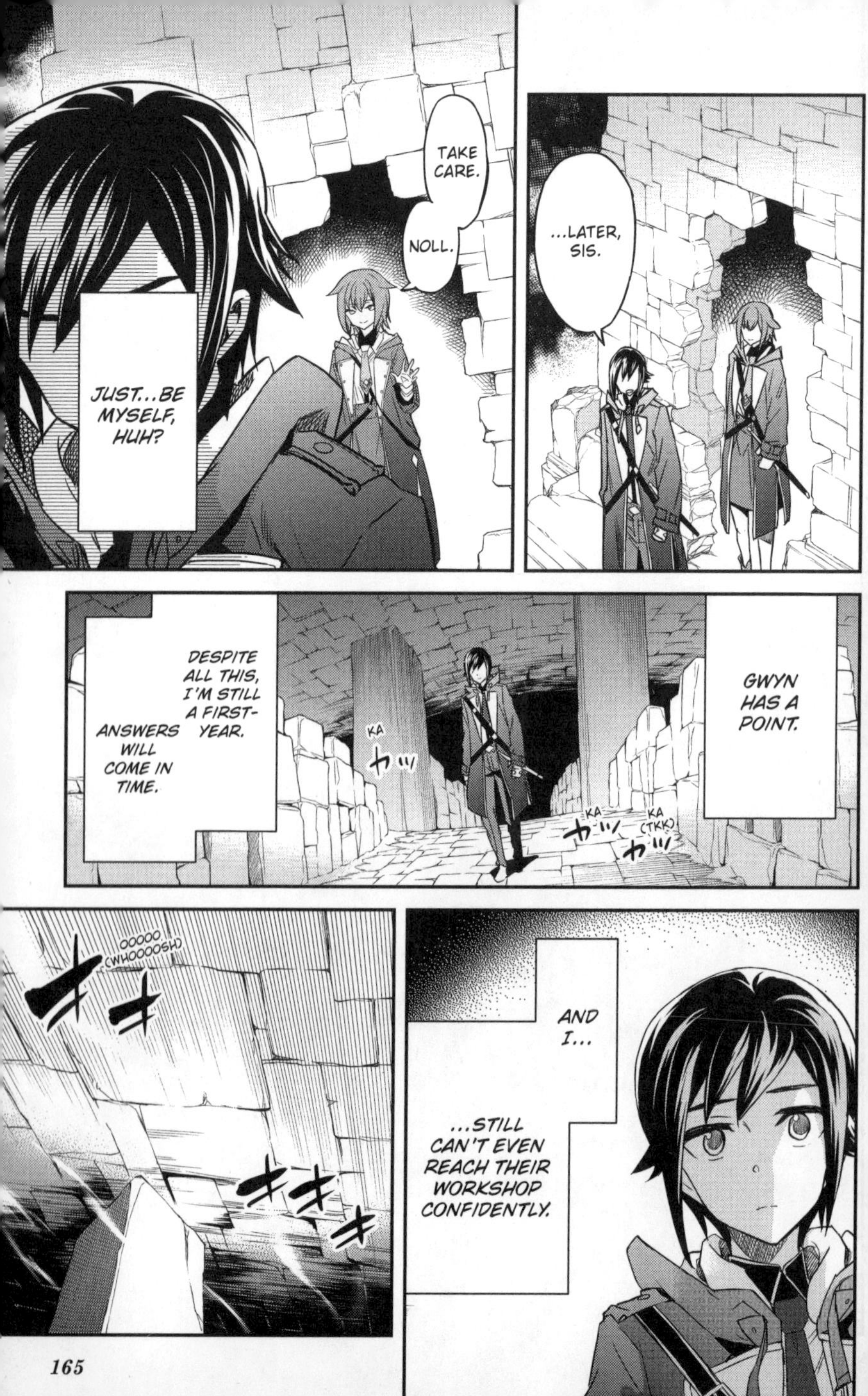
...LATER, SIS.
TAKE CARE.
NOLL.
JUST...BE MYSELF, HUH?
GWYN HAS A POINT.
KA (TKK)
KA
DESPITE ALL THIS, I'M STILL A FIRST-YEAR.
ANSWERS WILL COME IN TIME.
KA
AND I...
...STILL CAN'T EVEN REACH THEIR WORKSHOP CONFIDENTLY.
OOOOO (WHOOOOSH)

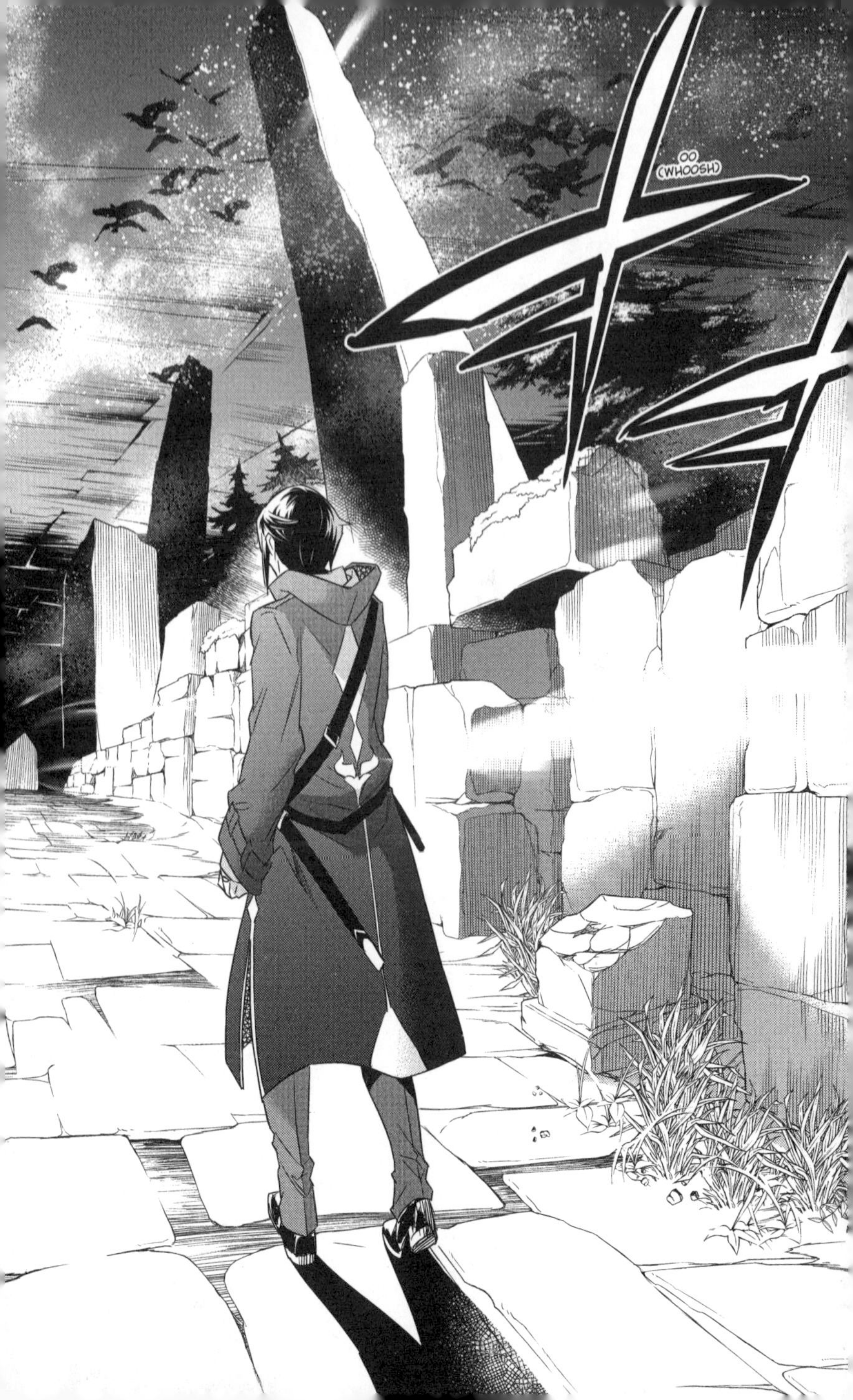
OO
(WHOOSH)

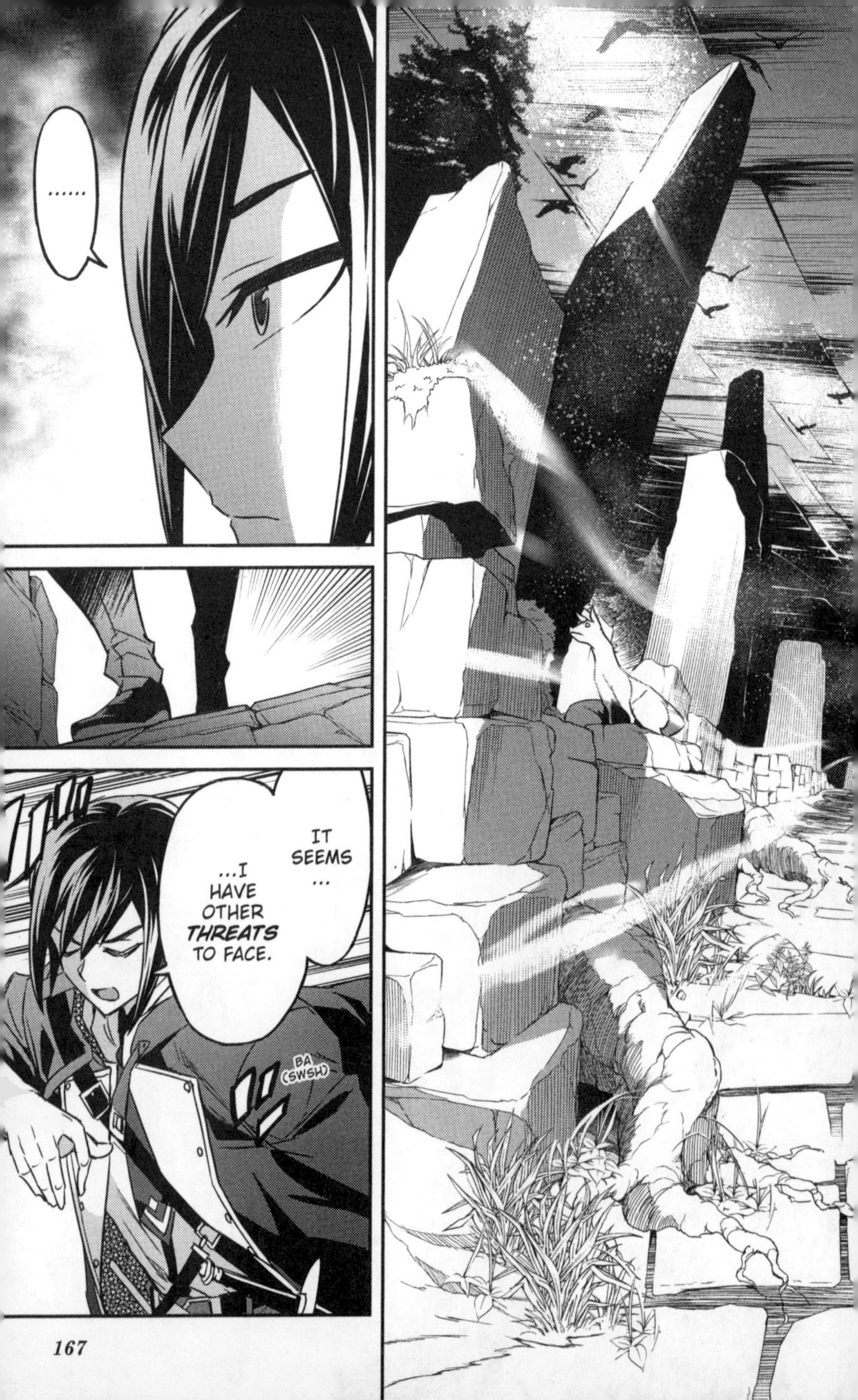
......
IT SEEMS... ...I HAVE OTHER THREATS TO FACE.
BA (SWSH)

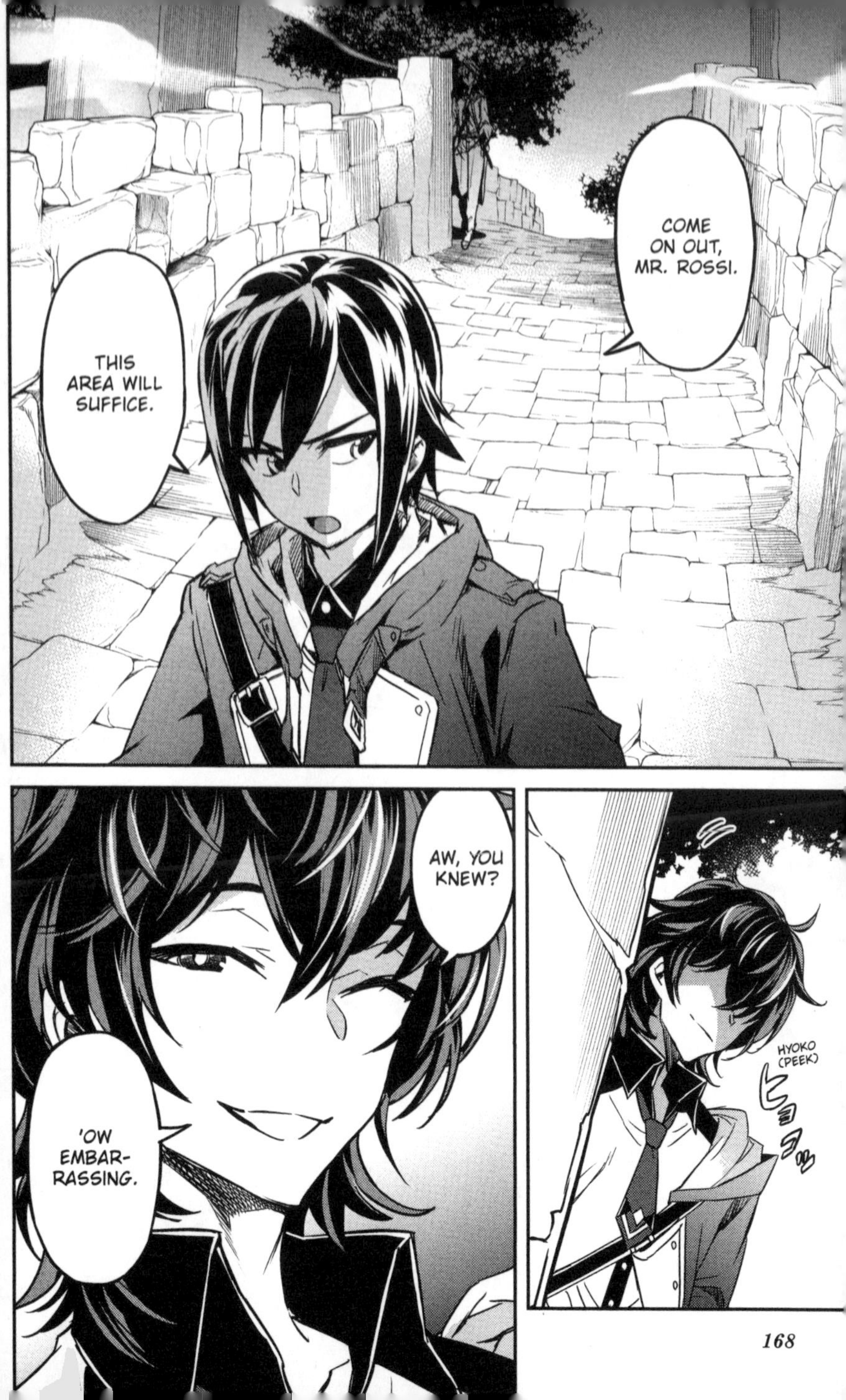
COME ON OUT, MR. ROSSI.
THIS AREA WILL SUFFICE.
HYOKO (PEEK)
AW, YOU KNEW?
'OW EMBAR-RASSING.

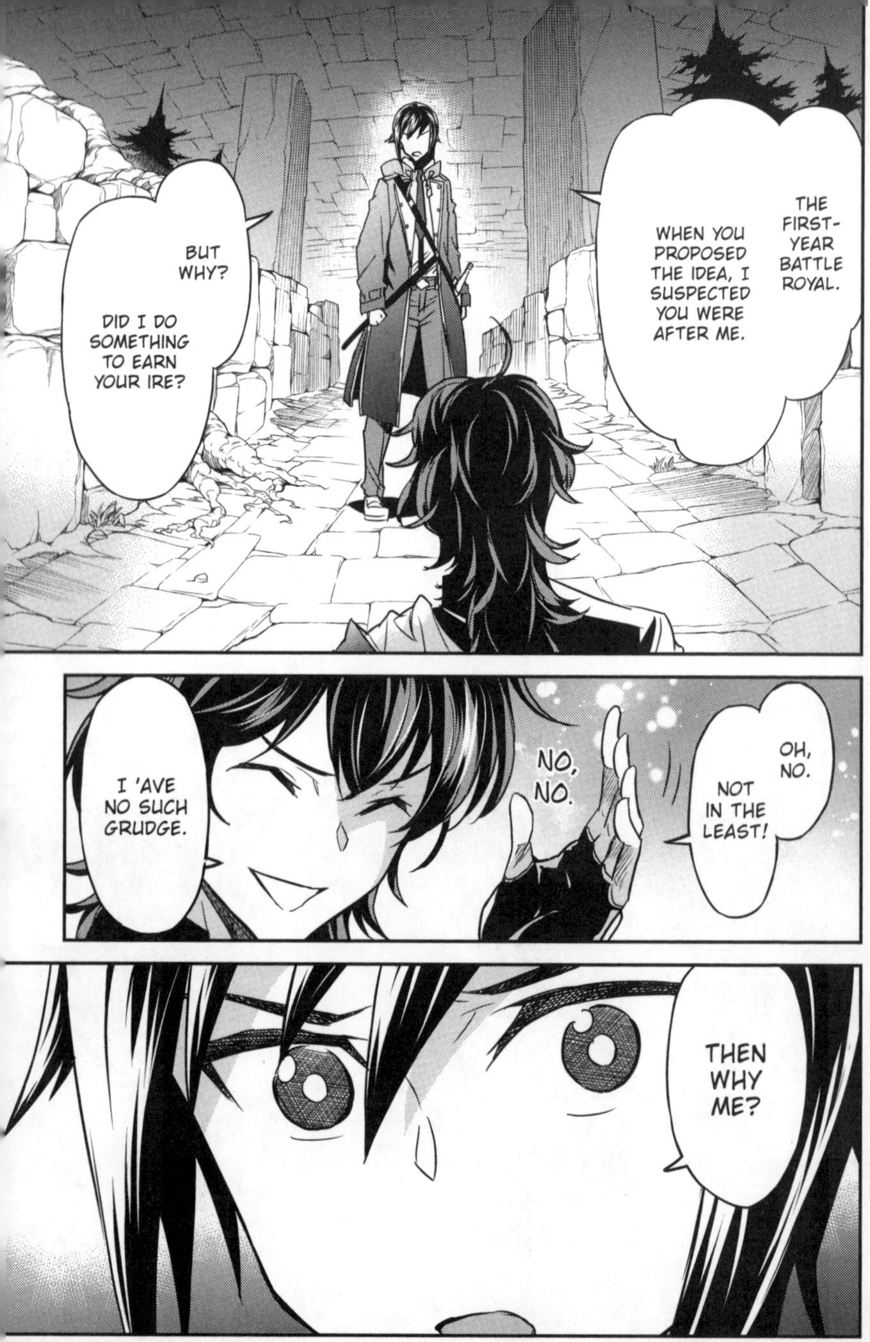
THE FIRST-YEAR BATTLE ROYAL.
WHEN YOU PROPOSED THE IDEA, I SUSPECTED YOU WERE AFTER ME.
BUT WHY?
DID I DO SOMETHING TO EARN YOUR IRE?
OH, NO.
NOT IN THE LEAST!
NO, NO.
I 'AVE NO SUCH GRUDGE.
THEN WHY ME?

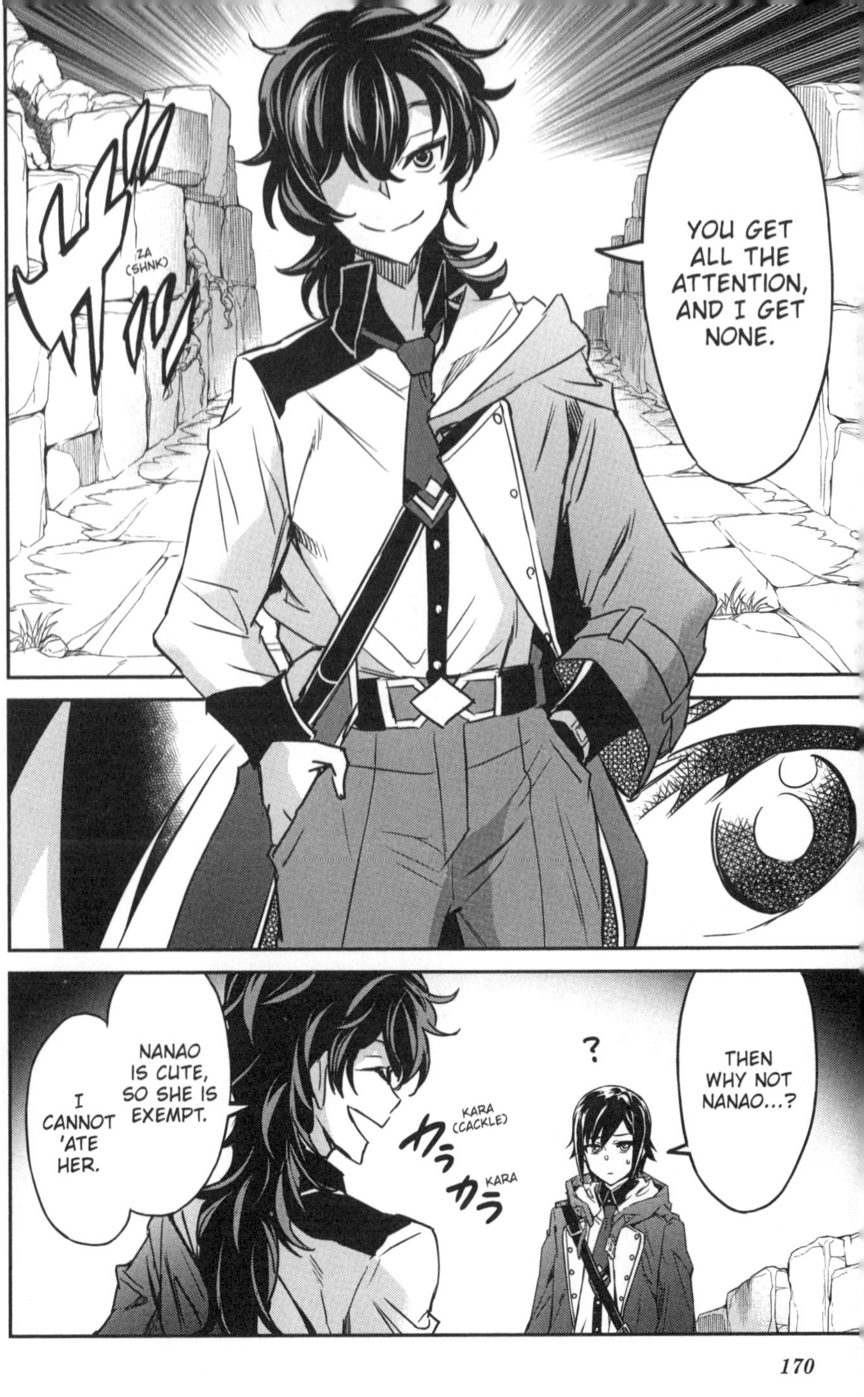
YOU GET ALL THE ATTENTION, AND I GET NONE.
ZA (SHNK)
THEN WHY NOT NANAO...?
?
KARA (CACKLE)
KARA
NANAO IS CUTE, SO SHE IS EXEMPT.
I CANNOT 'ATE HER.

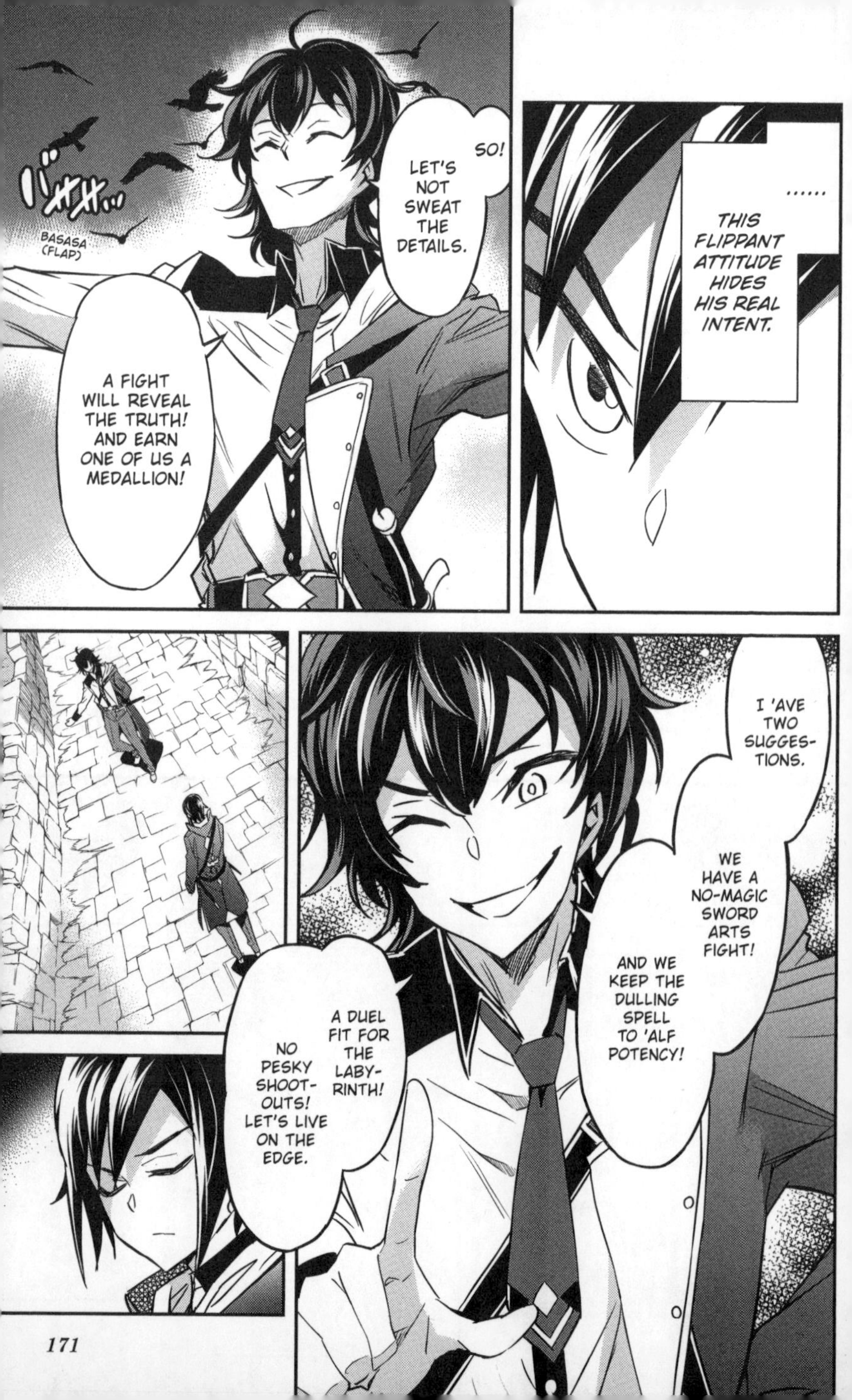
......
THIS FLIPPANT ATTITUDE HIDES HIS REAL INTENT.
SO!
LET'S NOT SWEAT THE DETAILS.
バサッ…
BASASA (FLAP)
A FIGHT WILL REVEAL THE TRUTH! AND EARN ONE OF US A MEDALLION!
I 'AVE TWO SUGGES-TIONS.
WE HAVE A NO-MAGIC SWORD ARTS FIGHT!
AND WE KEEP THE DULLING SPELL TO 'ALF POTENCY!
A DUEL FIT FOR THE LABY-RINTH!
NO PESKY SHOOT-OUTS! LET'S LIVE ON THE EDGE.

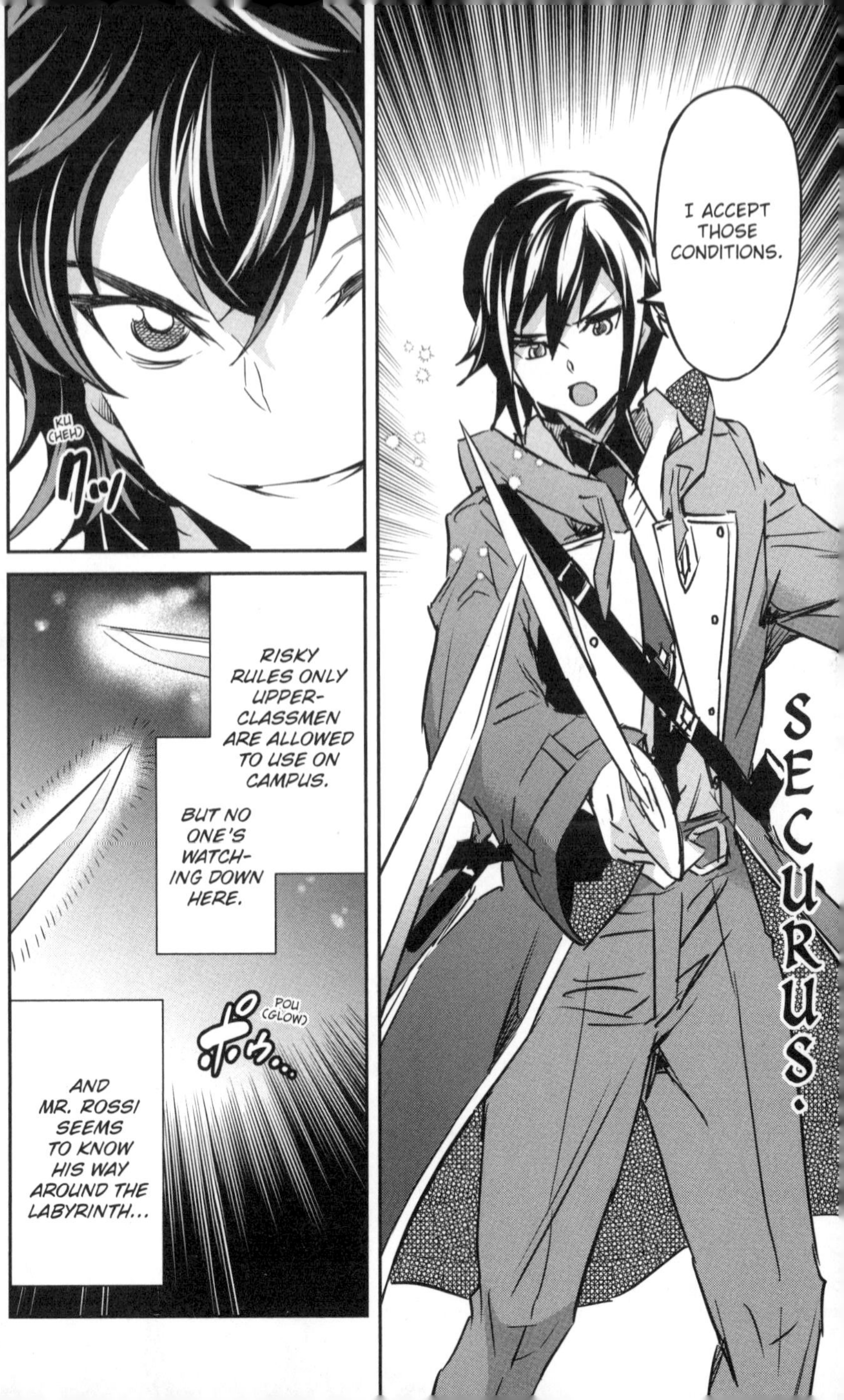
I ACCEPT THOSE CONDITIONS.
SECURUS.
KU (HEH)
RISKY RULES ONLY UPPER-CLASSMEN ARE ALLOWED TO USE ON CAMPUS.
BUT NO ONE'S WATCHING DOWN HERE.
POU (GLOW)
AND MR. ROSSI SEEMS TO KNOW HIS WAY AROUND THE LABYRINTH...

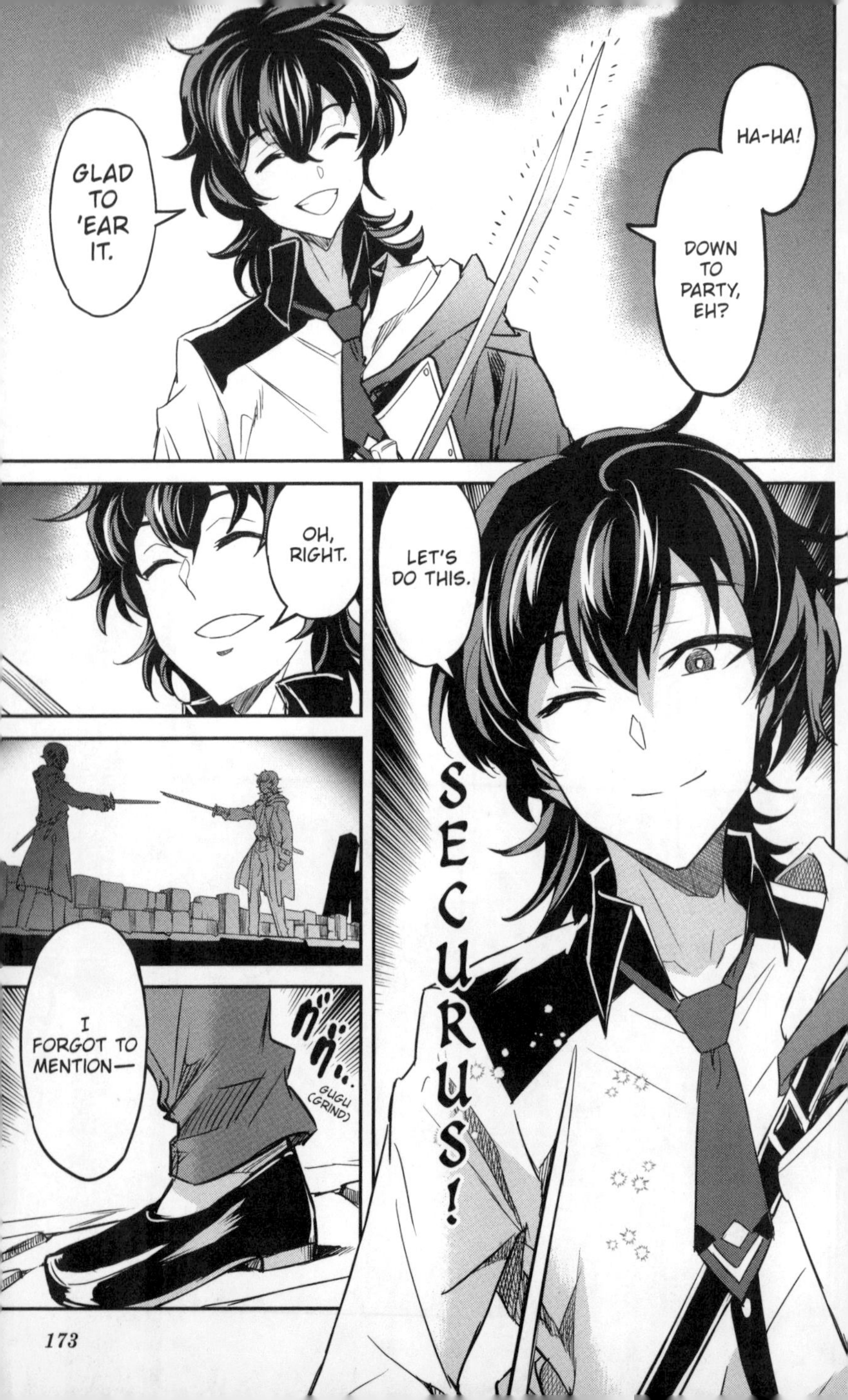
HA-HA!
DOWN TO PARTY, EH?
GLAD TO 'EAR IT.
LET'S DO THIS.
SECURUS!
OH, RIGHT.
I FORGOT TO MENTION—
GUGU (GRIND)

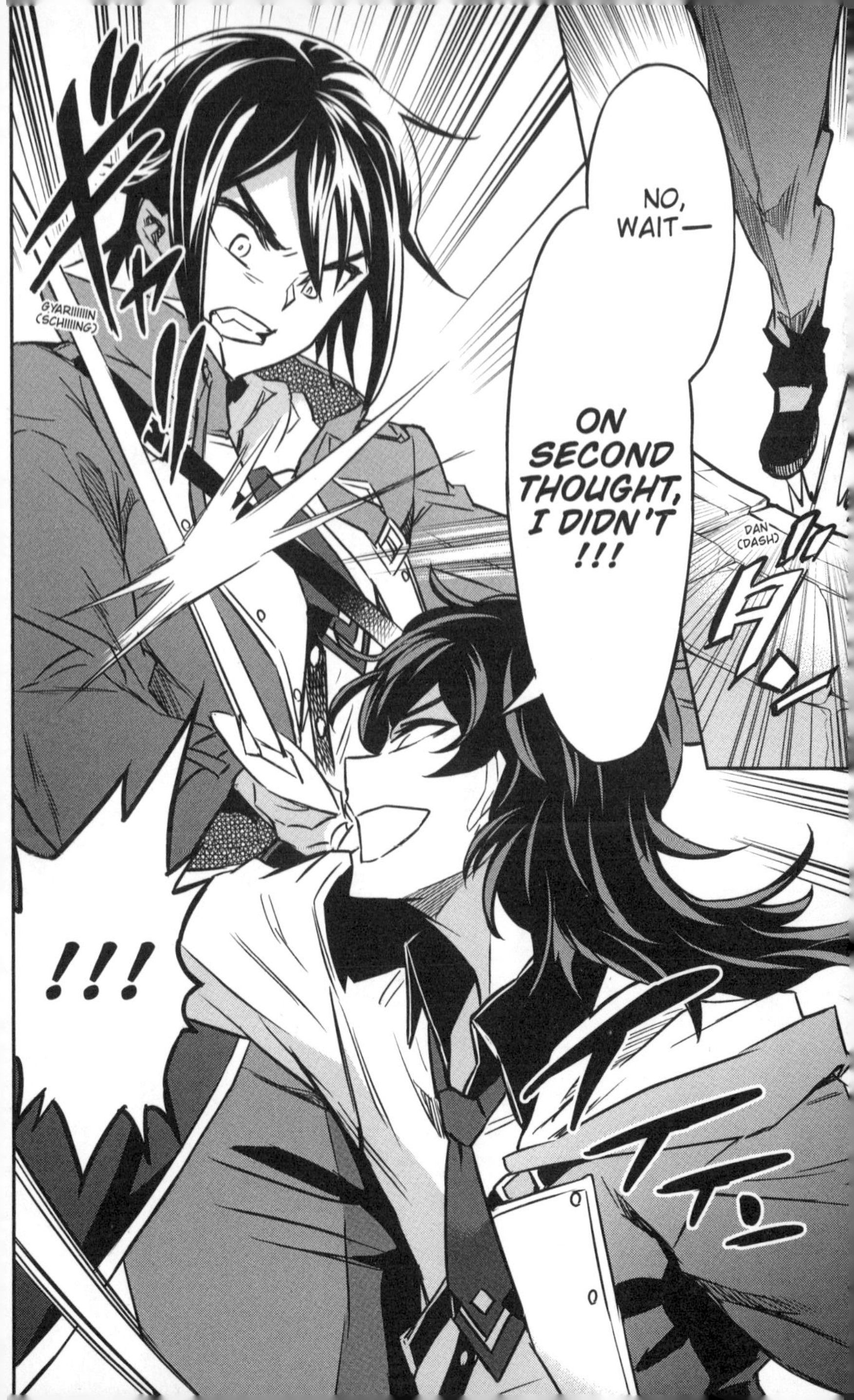
NO, WAIT—
ON SECOND THOUGHT, I DIDN'T !!!
DAN (DASH)
GYARIIIIIIN (SCHIIIING)
!!!

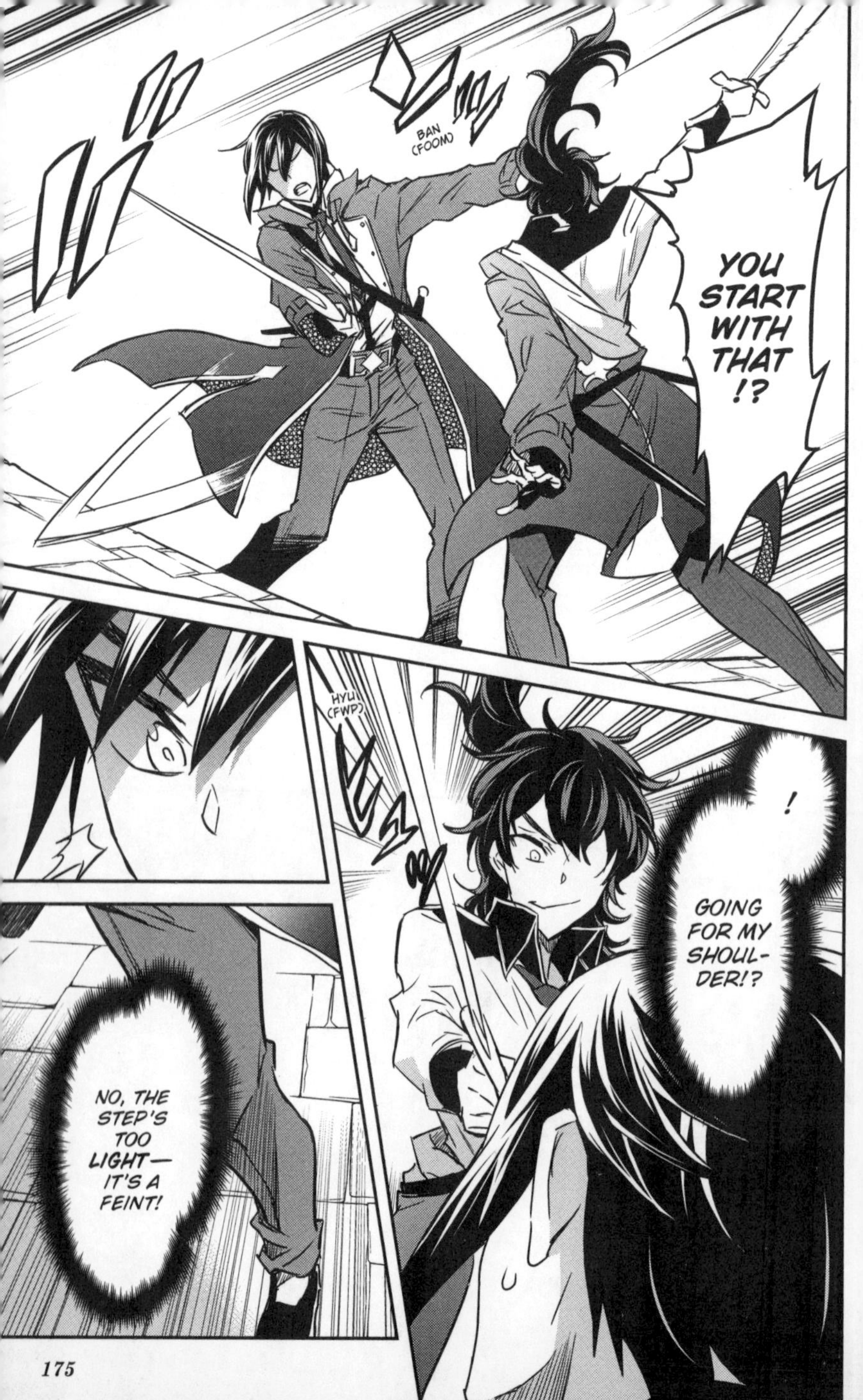
YOU START WITH THAT!?
BAN (FOOM)
HYU (FWP)
!
GOING FOR MY SHOULDER!?
NO, THE STEP'S TOO LIGHT— IT'S A FEINT!

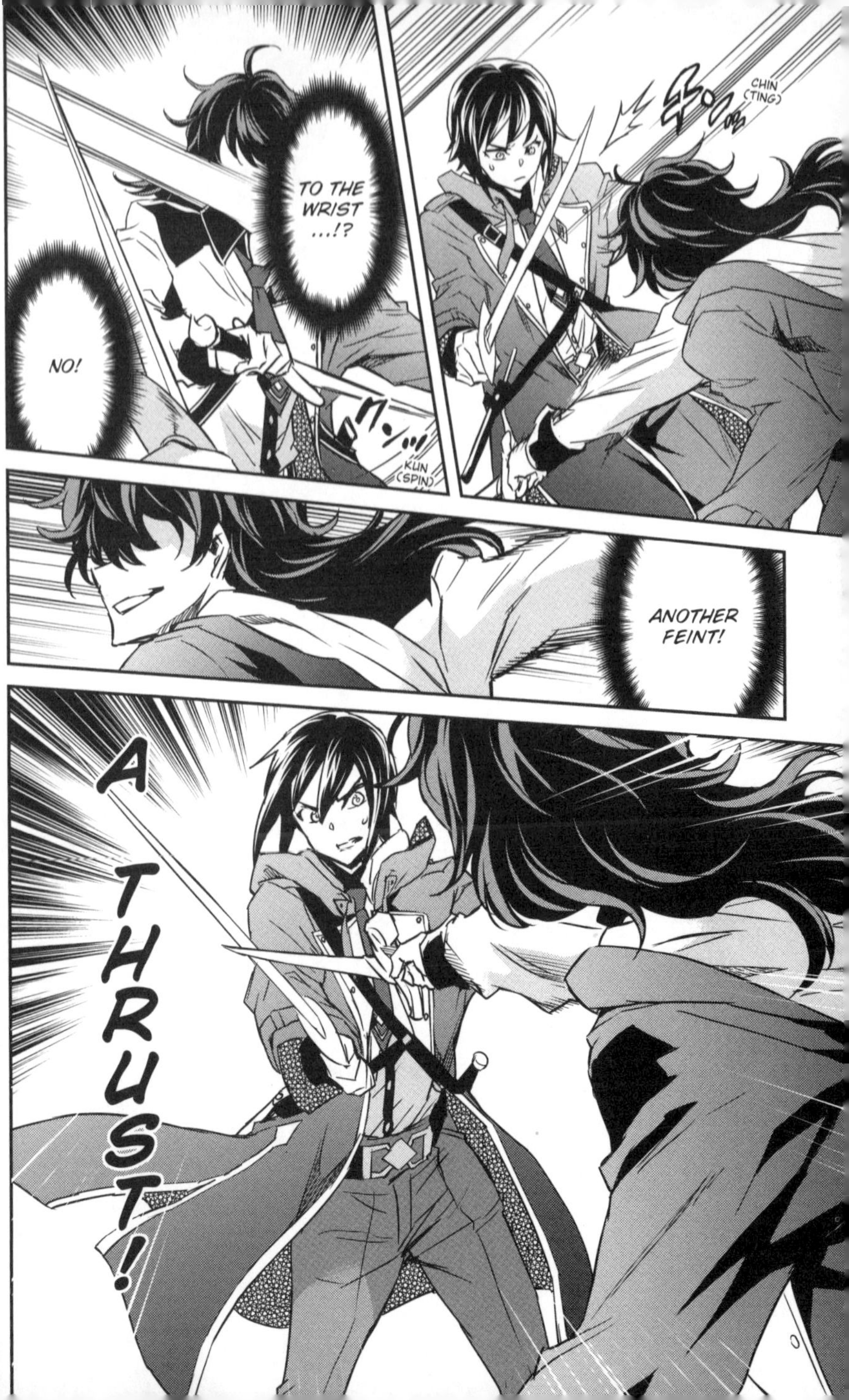
CHIN (TING)
TO THE WRIST ...!?
NO!
KUN (SPIN)
ANOTHER FEINT!
A THRUST!!

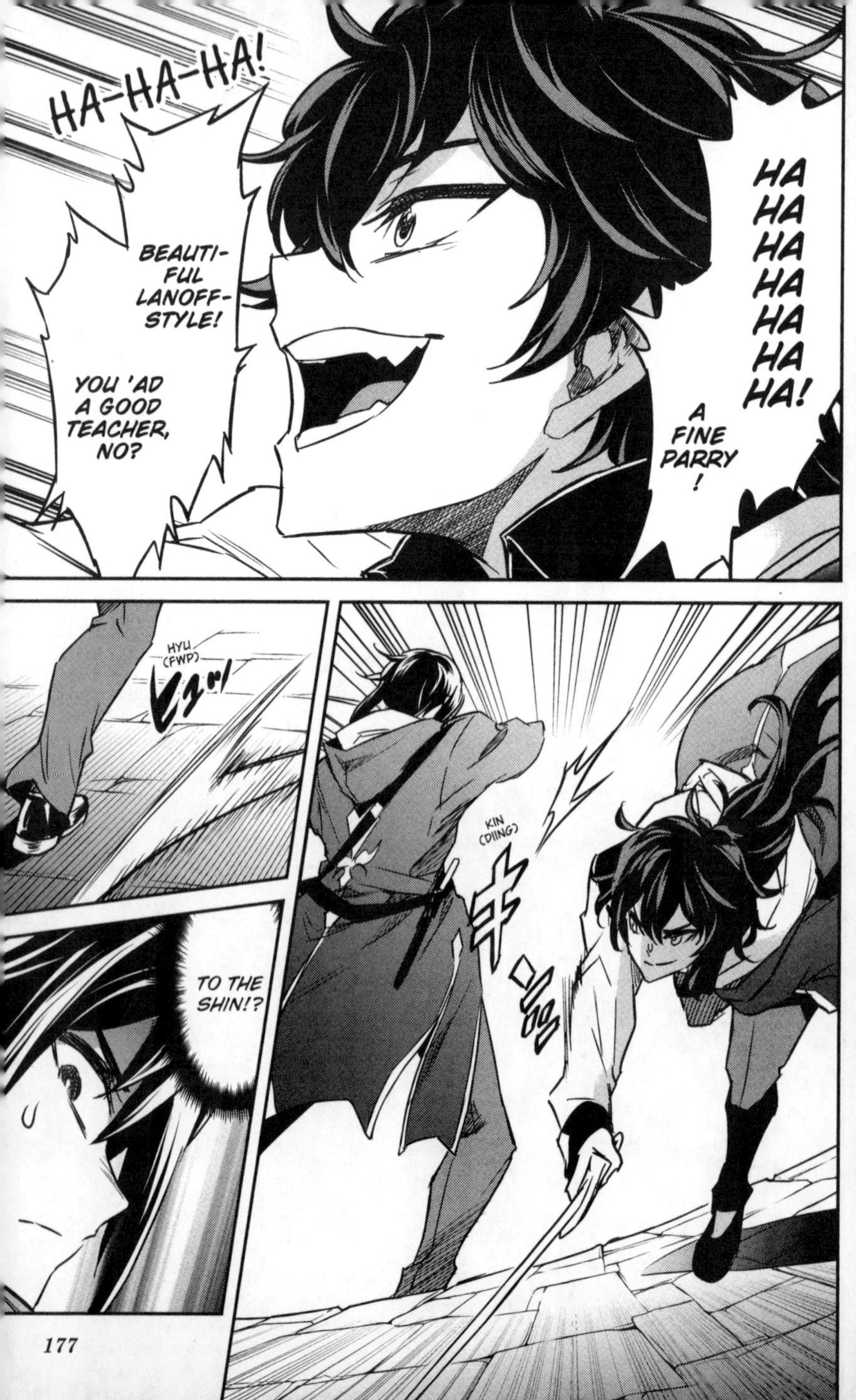
HA HA HA HA HA HA HA!
A FINE PARRY!
HA-HA-HA!
BEAUTIFUL LANOFF-STYLE!
YOU 'AD A GOOD TEACHER, NO?
KIN (DIING)
HYU (FWP)
TO THE SHIN!?

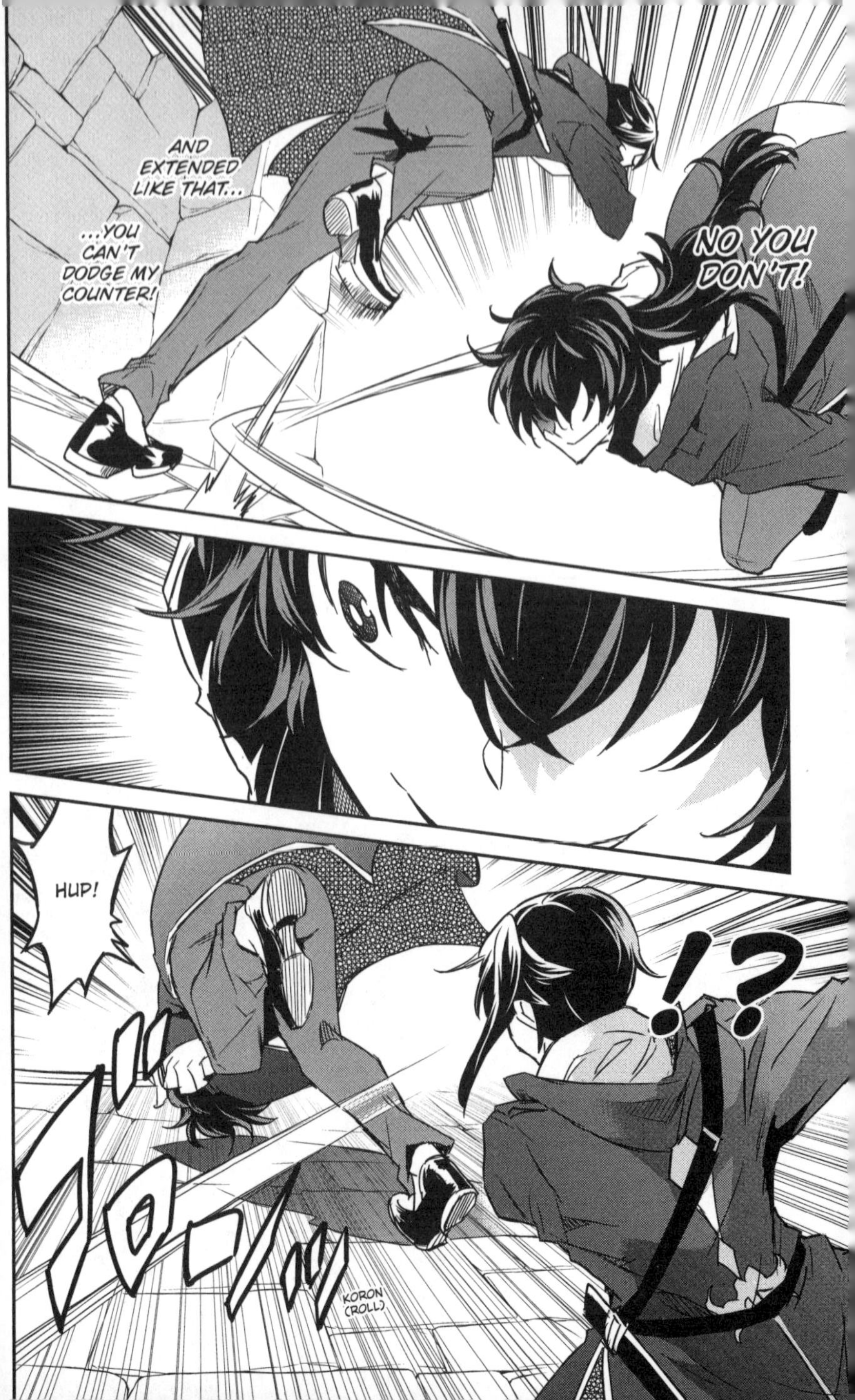
AND EXTENDED LIKE THAT...
...YOU CAN'T DODGE MY COUNTER!
NO YOU DON'T!
!?
HUP!
KORON (ROLL)

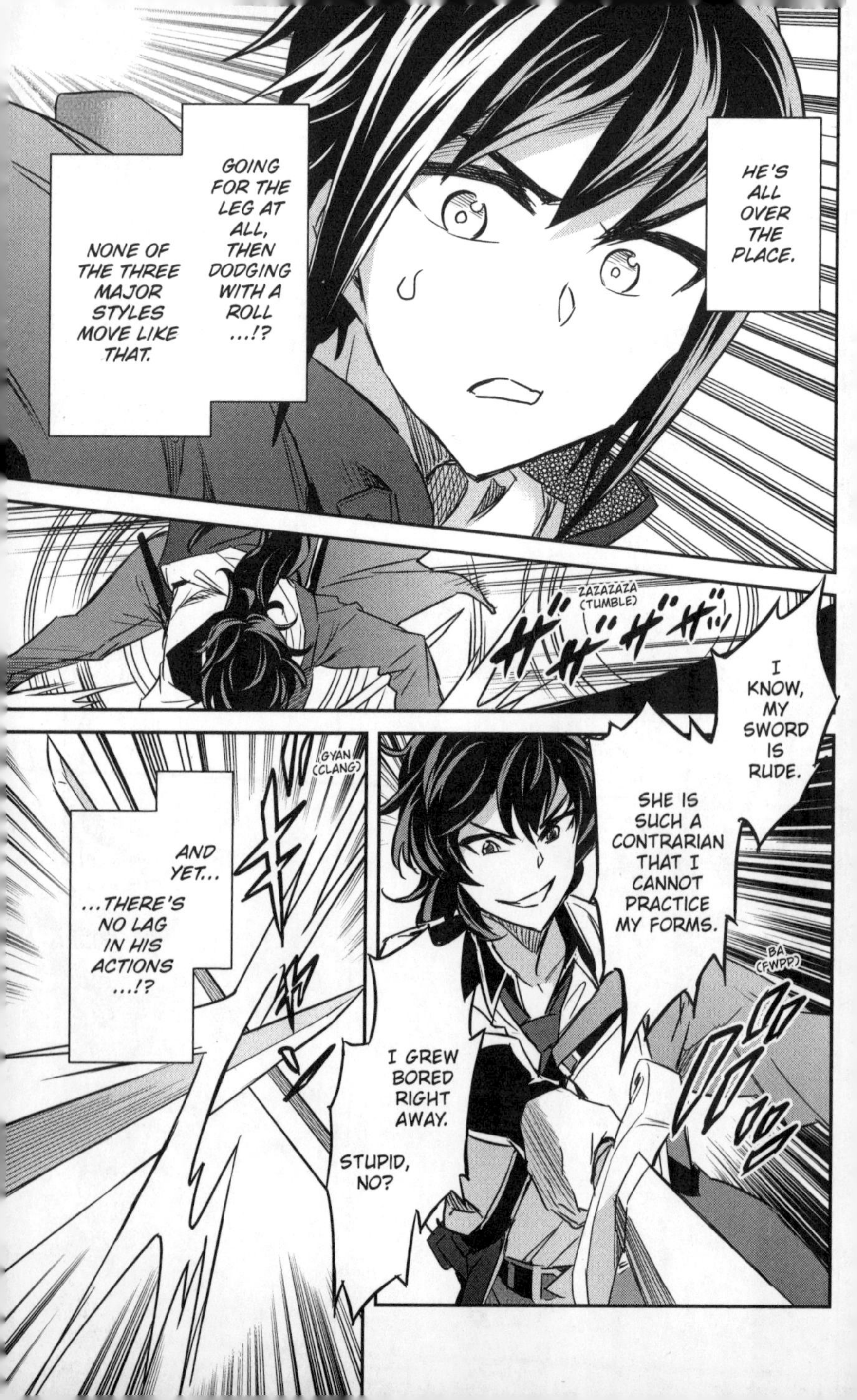
HE'S ALL OVER THE PLACE.
GOING FOR THE LEG AT ALL, THEN DODGING WITH A ROLL ...!?
NONE OF THE THREE MAJOR STYLES MOVE LIKE THAT.
ZAZAZAZA (TUMBLE)
I KNOW, MY SWORD IS RUDE.
SHE IS SUCH A CONTRARIAN THAT I CANNOT PRACTICE MY FORMS.
BA (FWPP)
I GREW BORED RIGHT AWAY.
STUPID, NO?
GYAN (CLANG)
AND YET...
...THERE'S NO LAG IN HIS ACTIONS ...!?

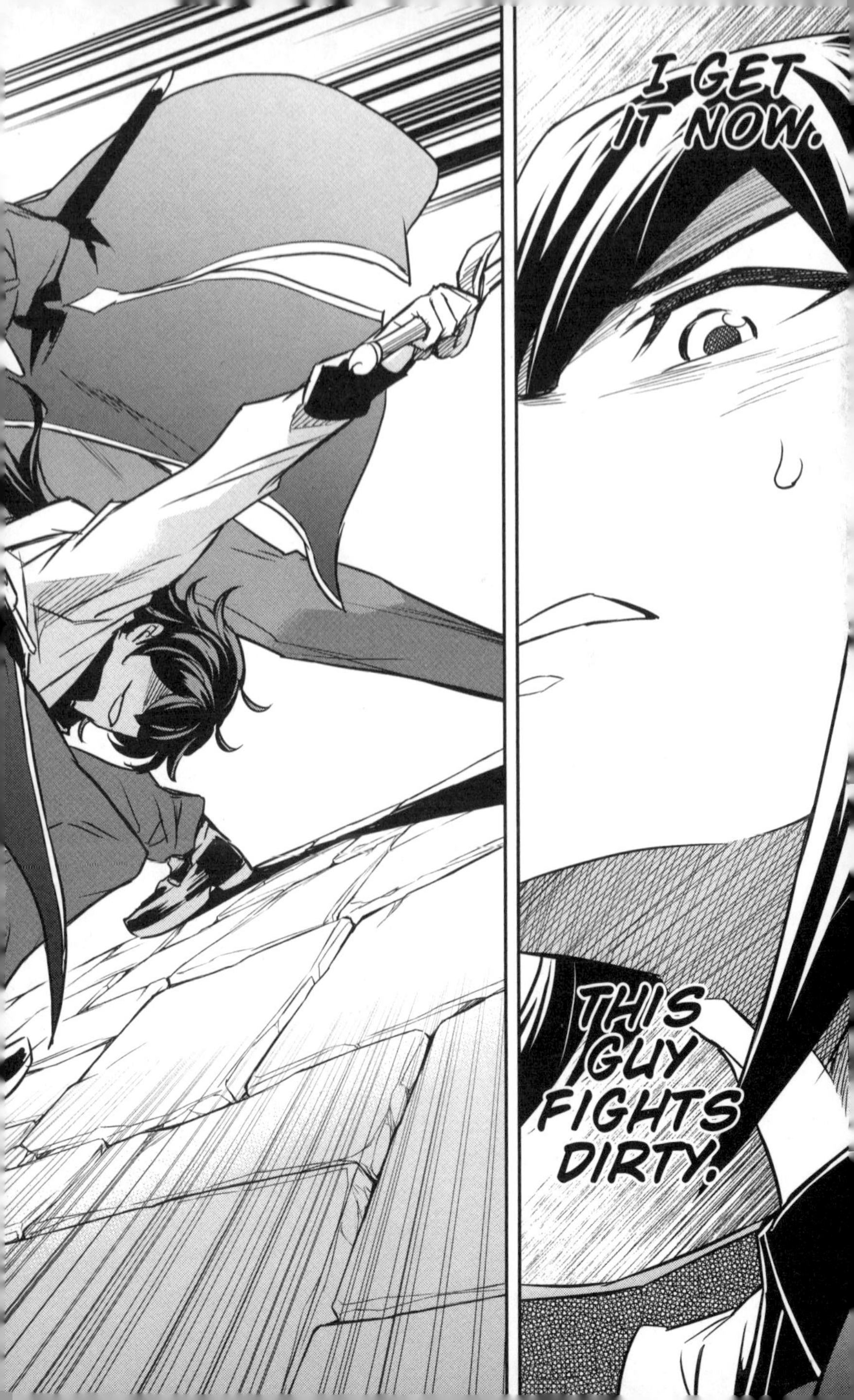
I GET IT NOW.
THIS GUY FIGHTS DIRTY.

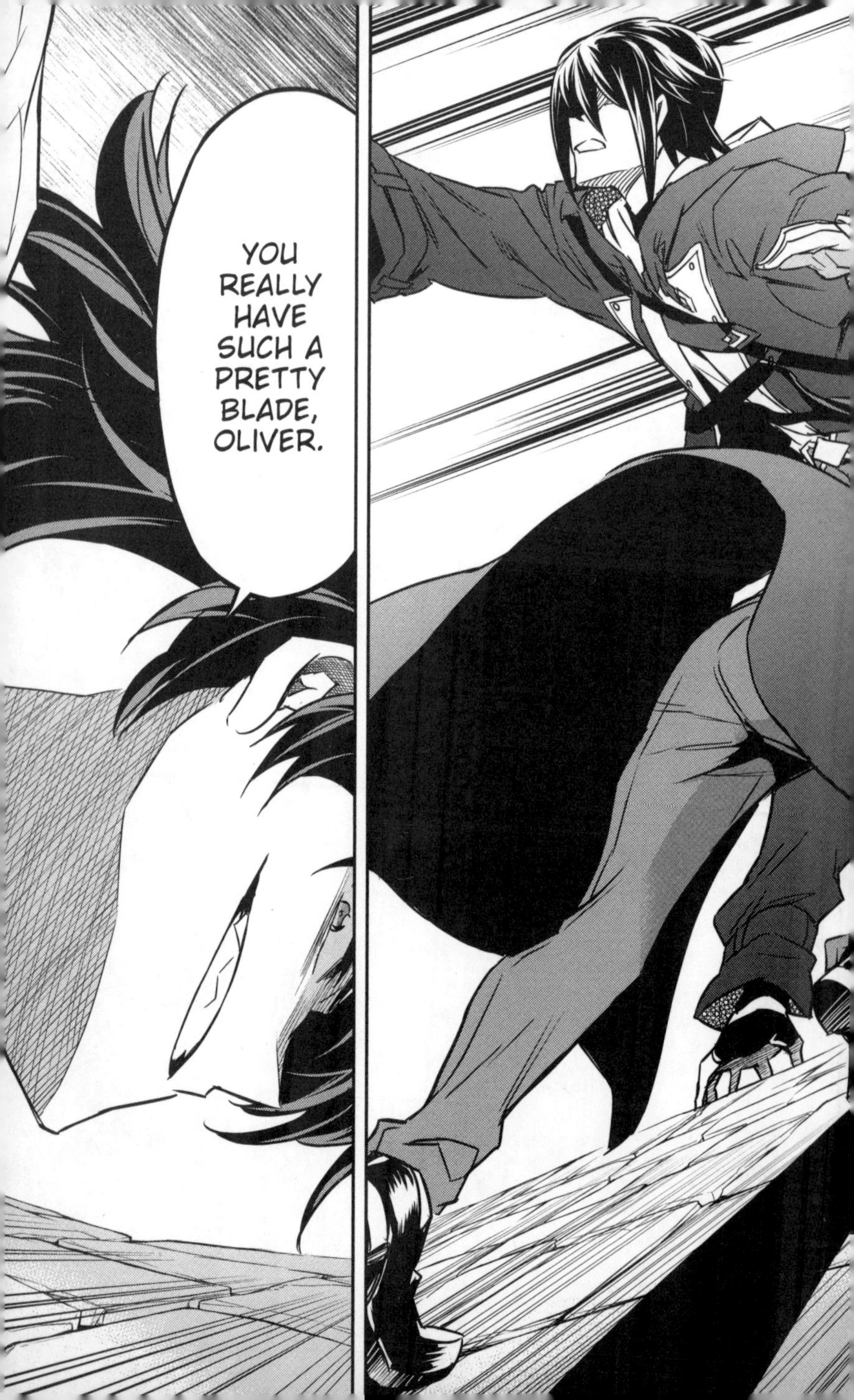
YOU REALLY HAVE SUCH A PRETTY BLADE, OLIVER.

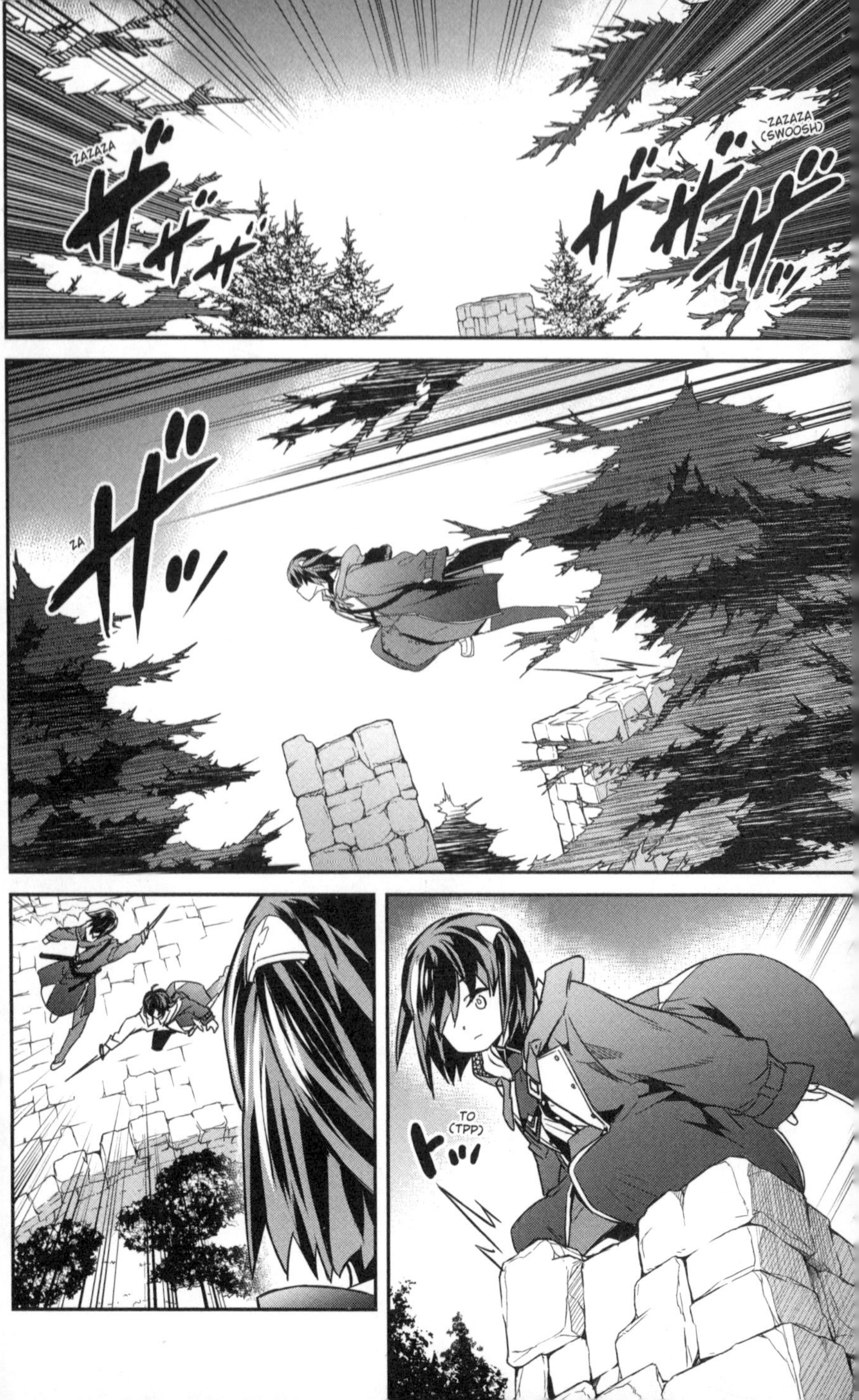
ZAZAZA (SWOOSH)
ZAZAZA
ZA
TO (TPP)

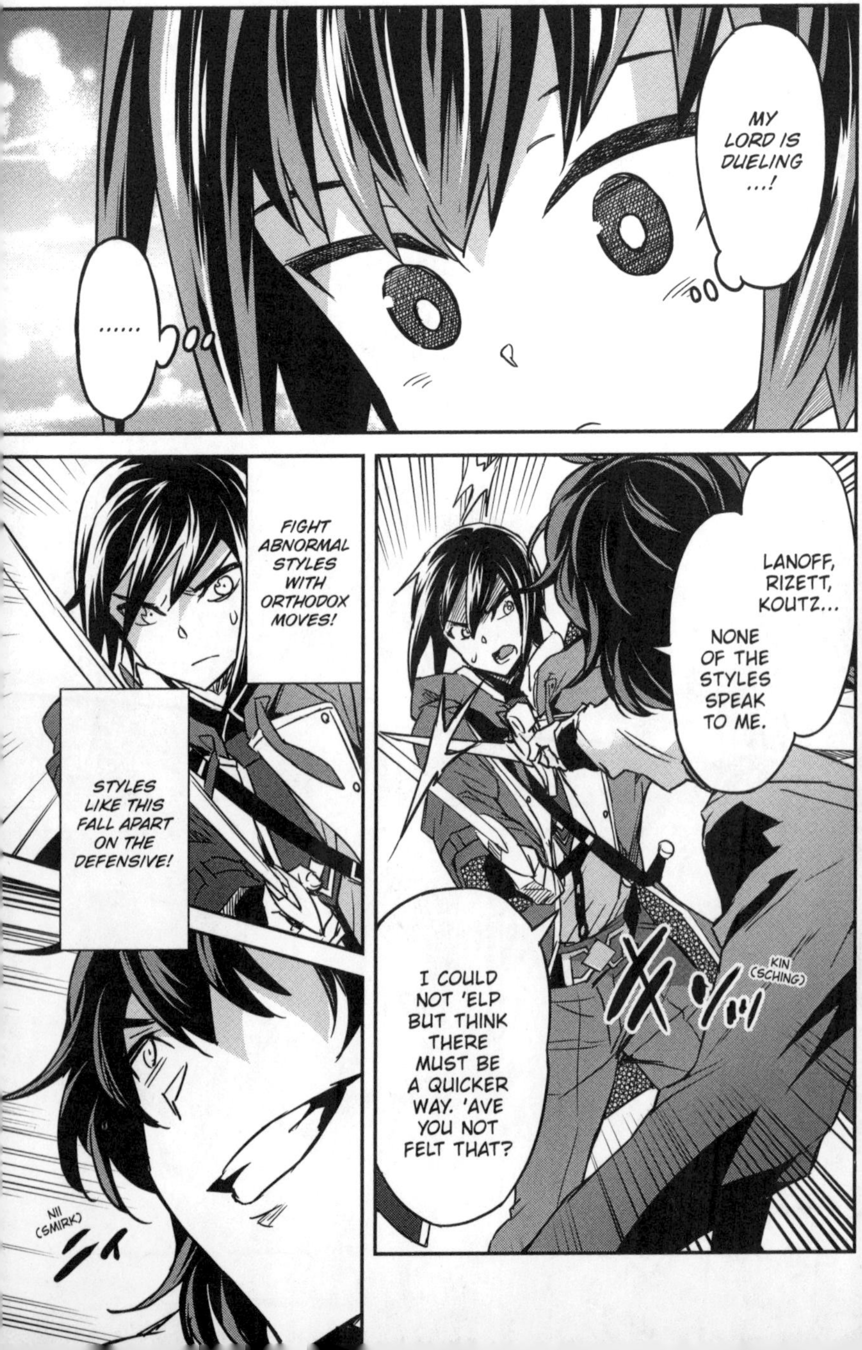
MY LORD IS DUELING ...!
......
LANOFF, RIZETT, KOUTZ...
NONE OF THE STYLES SPEAK TO ME.
KIN (SCHING)
I COULD NOT 'ELP BUT THINK THERE MUST BE A QUICKER WAY. 'AVE YOU NOT FELT THAT?
FIGHT ABNORMAL STYLES WITH ORTHODOX MOVES!
STYLES LIKE THIS FALL APART ON THE DEFENSIVE!
NII (SMIRK)

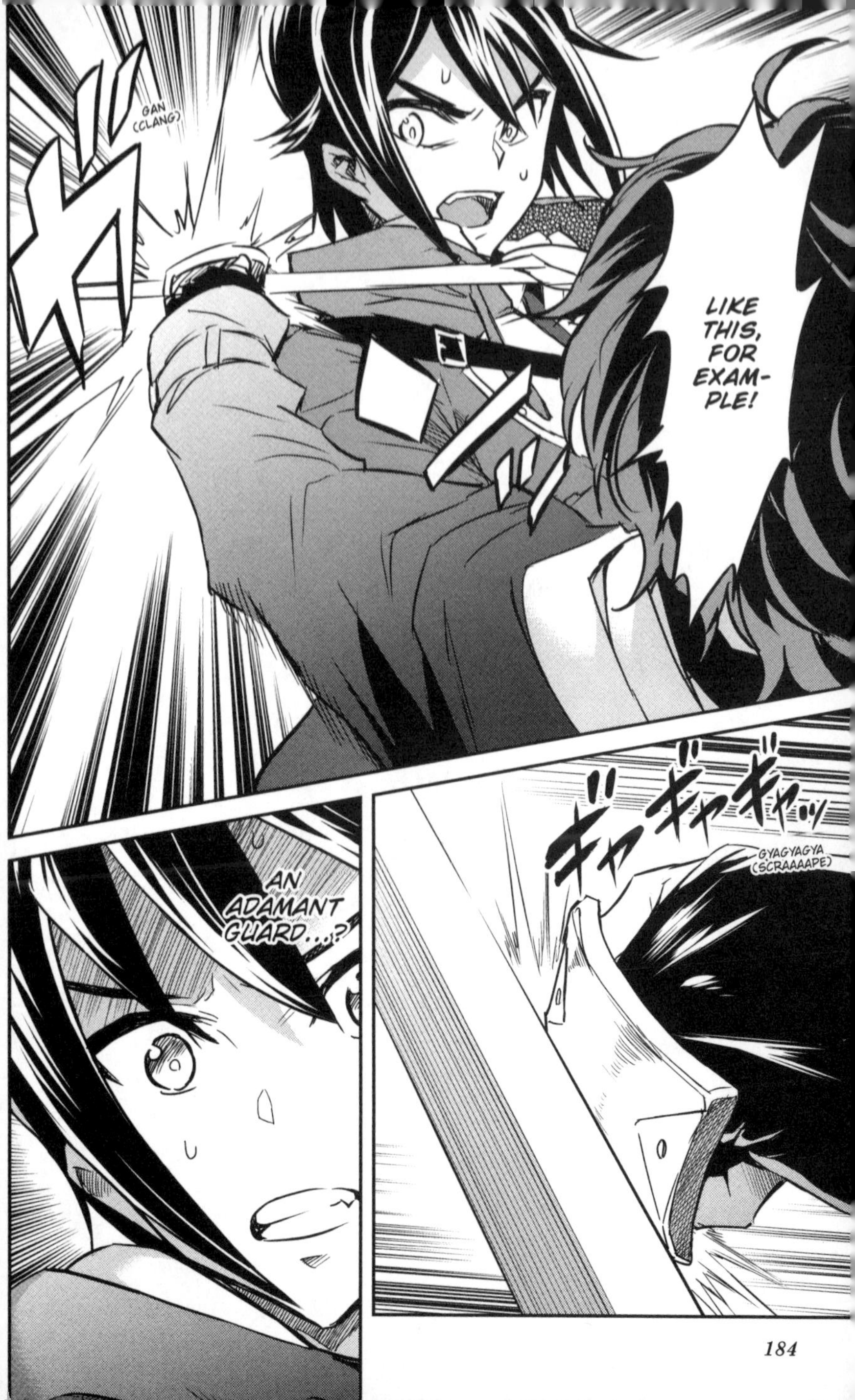
LIKE THIS, FOR EXAMPLE!
GAN (CLANG)
GYAGYAGYA (SCRAAAAPE)
AN ADAMANT GUARD...?

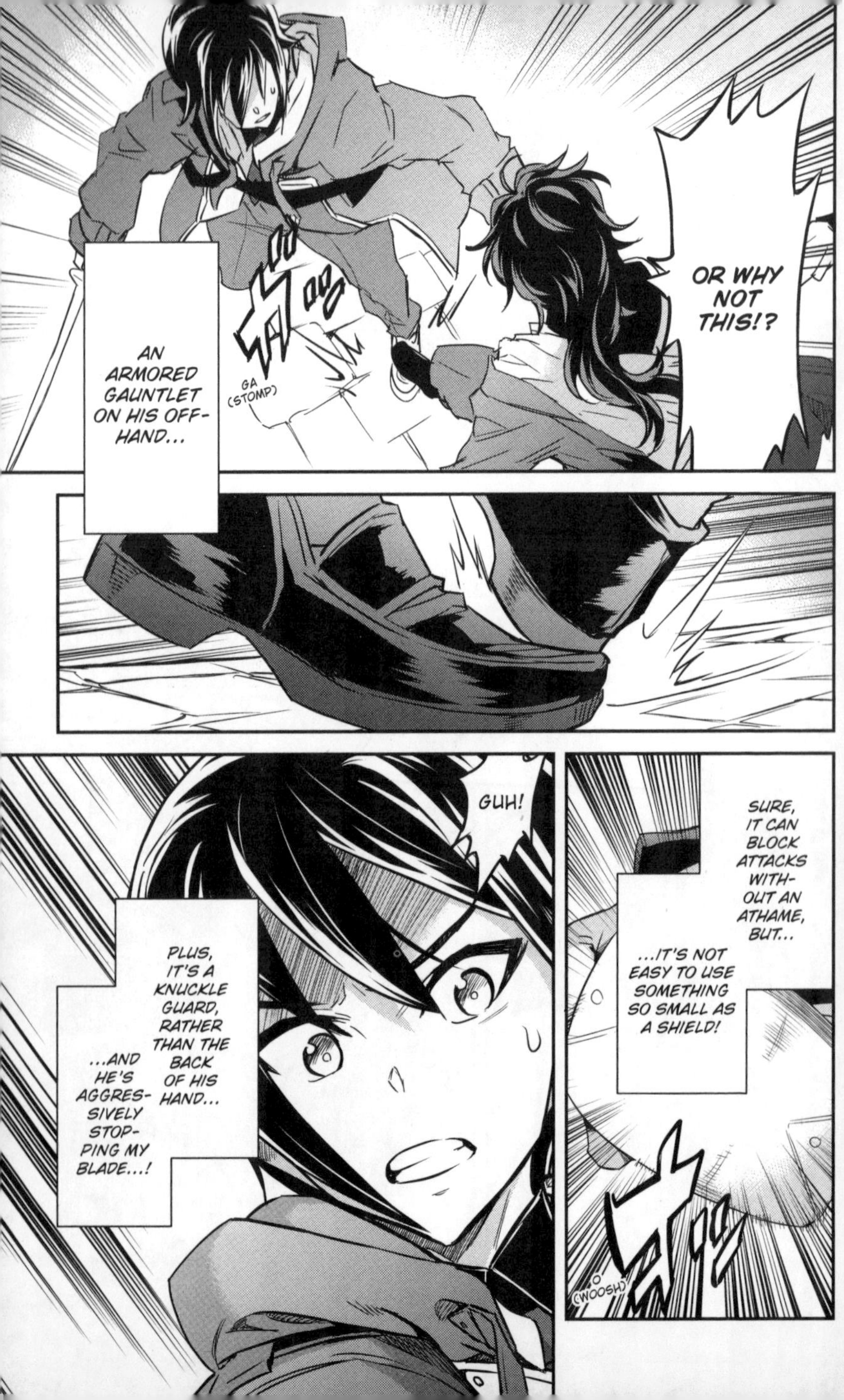
OR WHY NOT THIS!?
AN ARMORED GAUNTLET ON HIS OFF-HAND...
GA (STOMP)
SURE, IT CAN BLOCK ATTACKS WITH-OUT AN ATHAME, BUT...
...IT'S NOT EASY TO USE SOMETHING SO SMALL AS A SHIELD!
O (WOOSH)
GUH!
PLUS, IT'S A KNUCKLE GUARD, RATHER THAN THE BACK OF HIS HAND...
...AND HE'S AGGRES-SIVELY STOP-PING MY BLADE...!

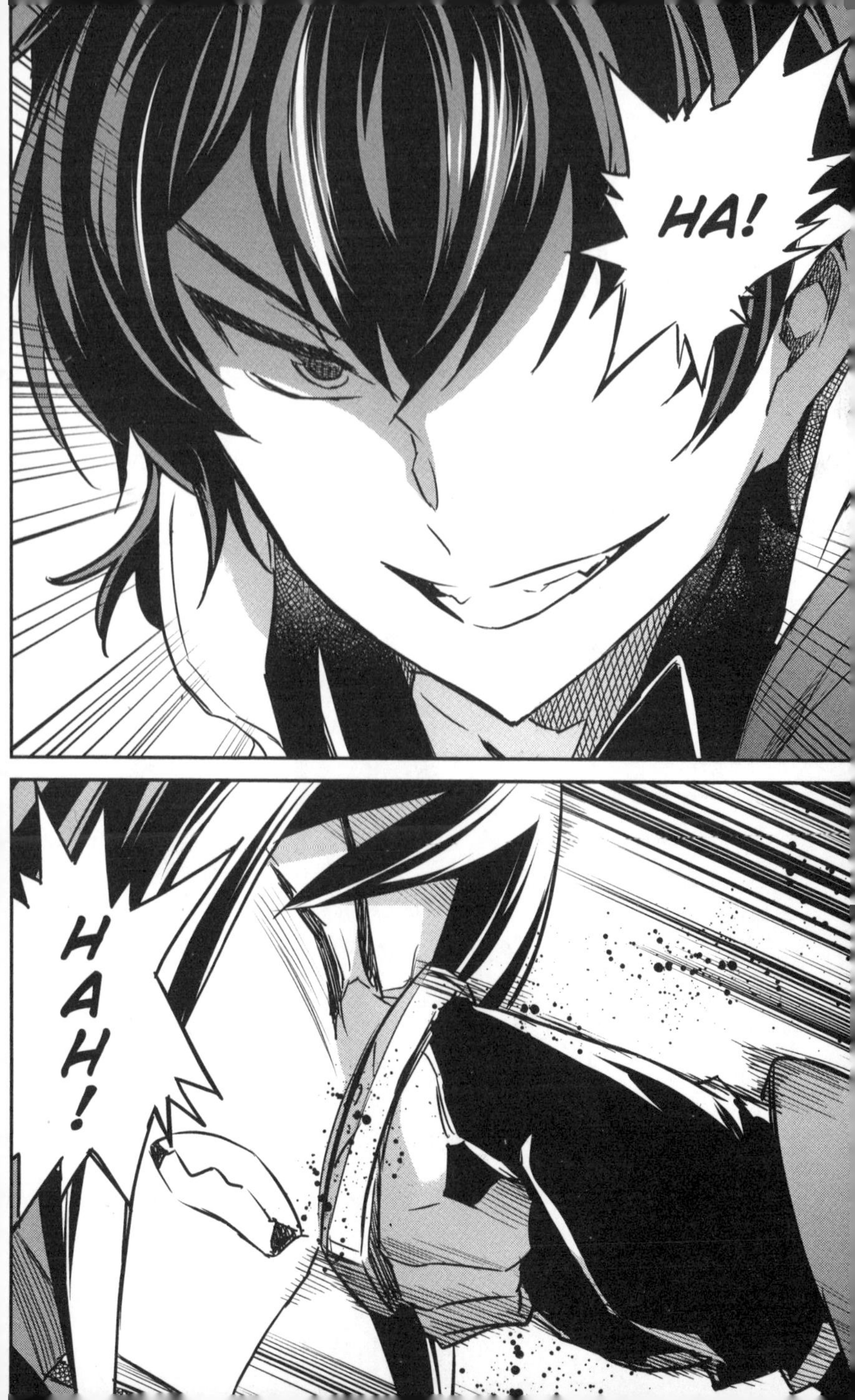
HA!
HAH!

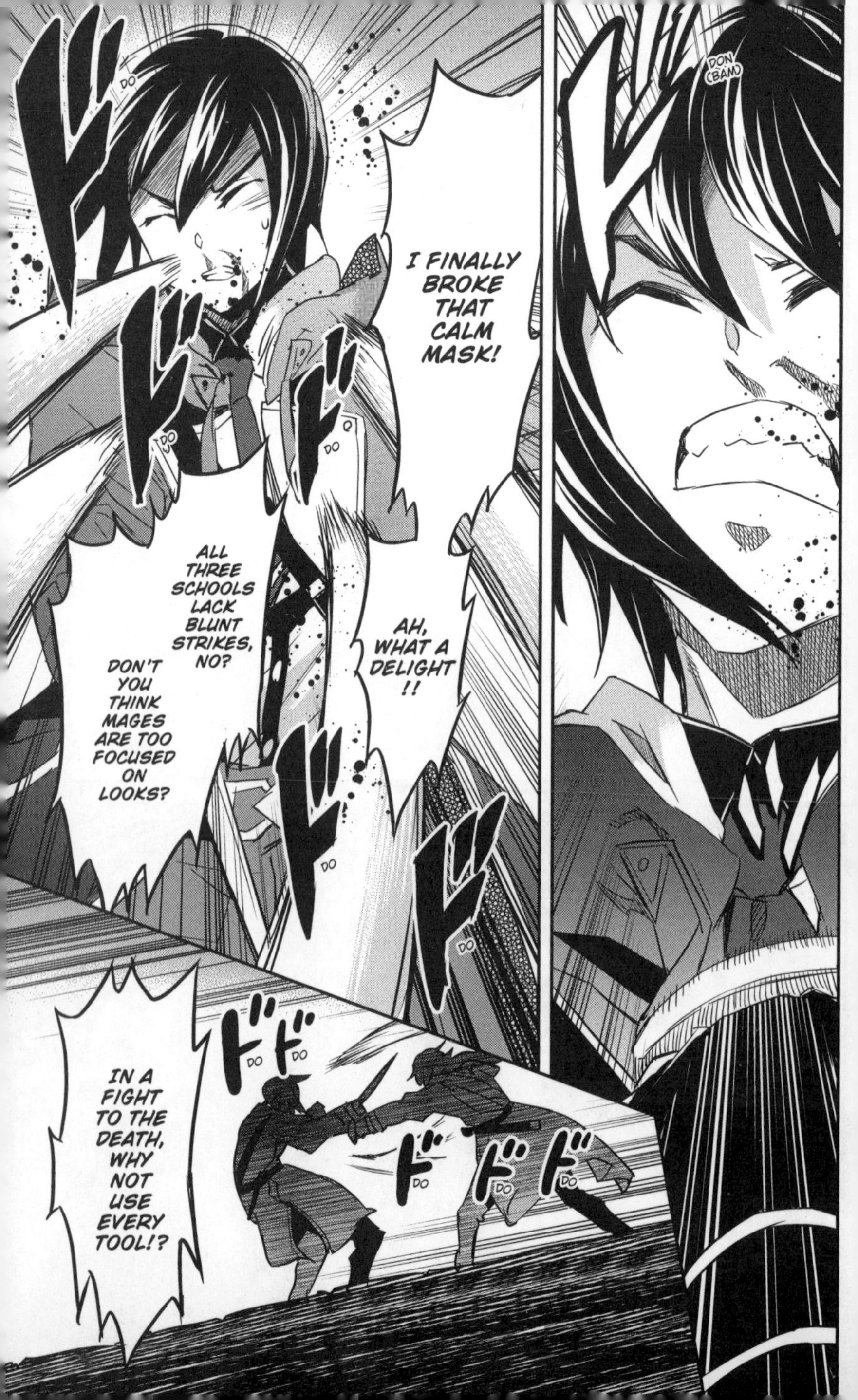
DON (BAM)
DO
I FINALLY BROKE THAT CALM MASK!
AH, WHAT A DELIGHT!!
ALL THREE SCHOOLS LACK BLUNT STRIKES, NO?
DON'T YOU THINK MAGES ARE TOO FOCUSED ON LOOKS?
DO
DO
DO
DO
DO DO
IN A FIGHT TO THE DEATH, WHY NOT USE EVERY TOOL!?
DO DO DO

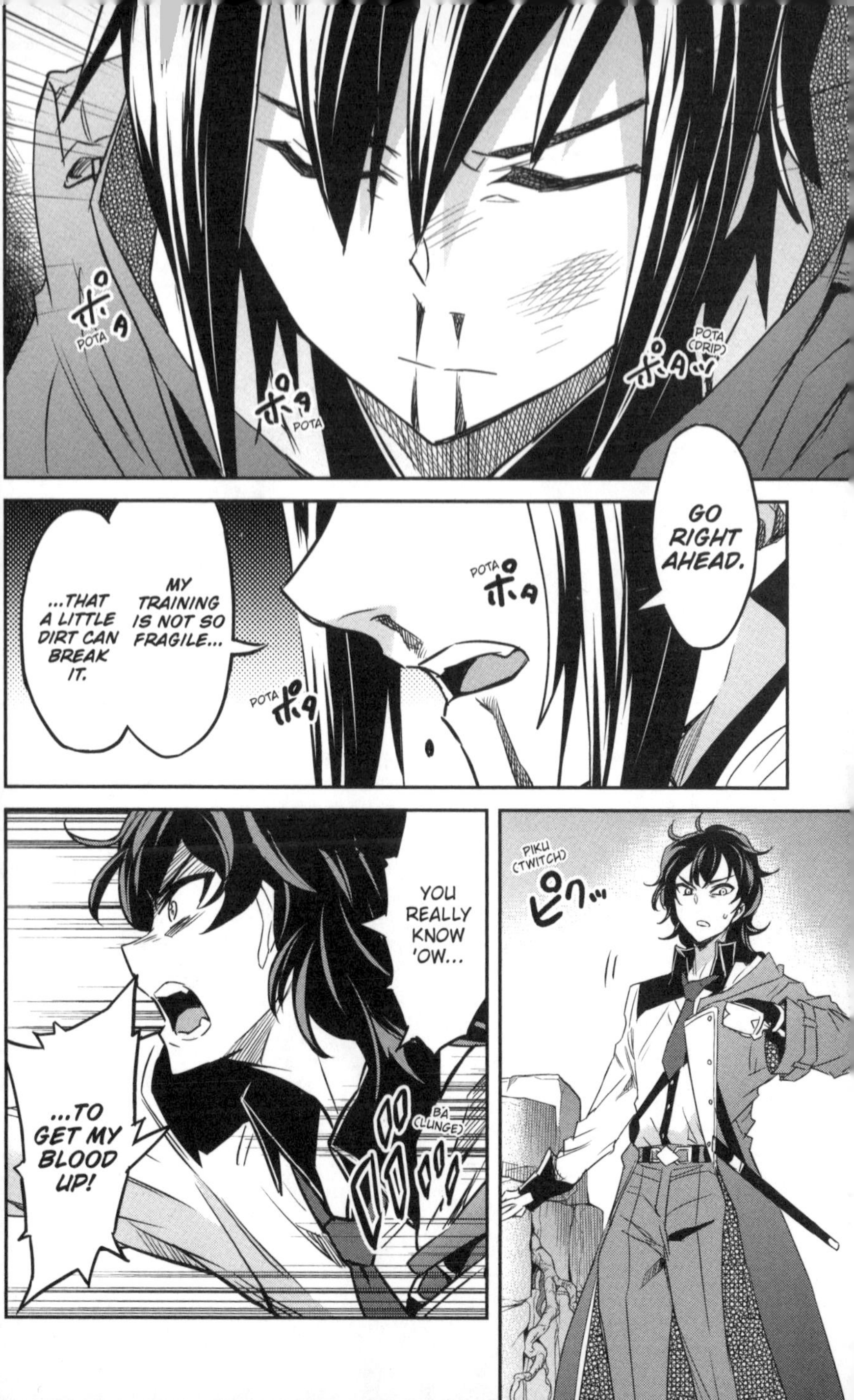

POTA (DRIP)
POTA
POTA
GO RIGHT AHEAD.
POTA
MY TRAINING IS NOT SO FRAGILE...
...THAT A LITTLE DIRT CAN BREAK IT.
POTA
PIKU (TWITCH)
YOU REALLY KNOW 'OW...
...TO GET MY BLOOD UP!
BA (LUNGE)

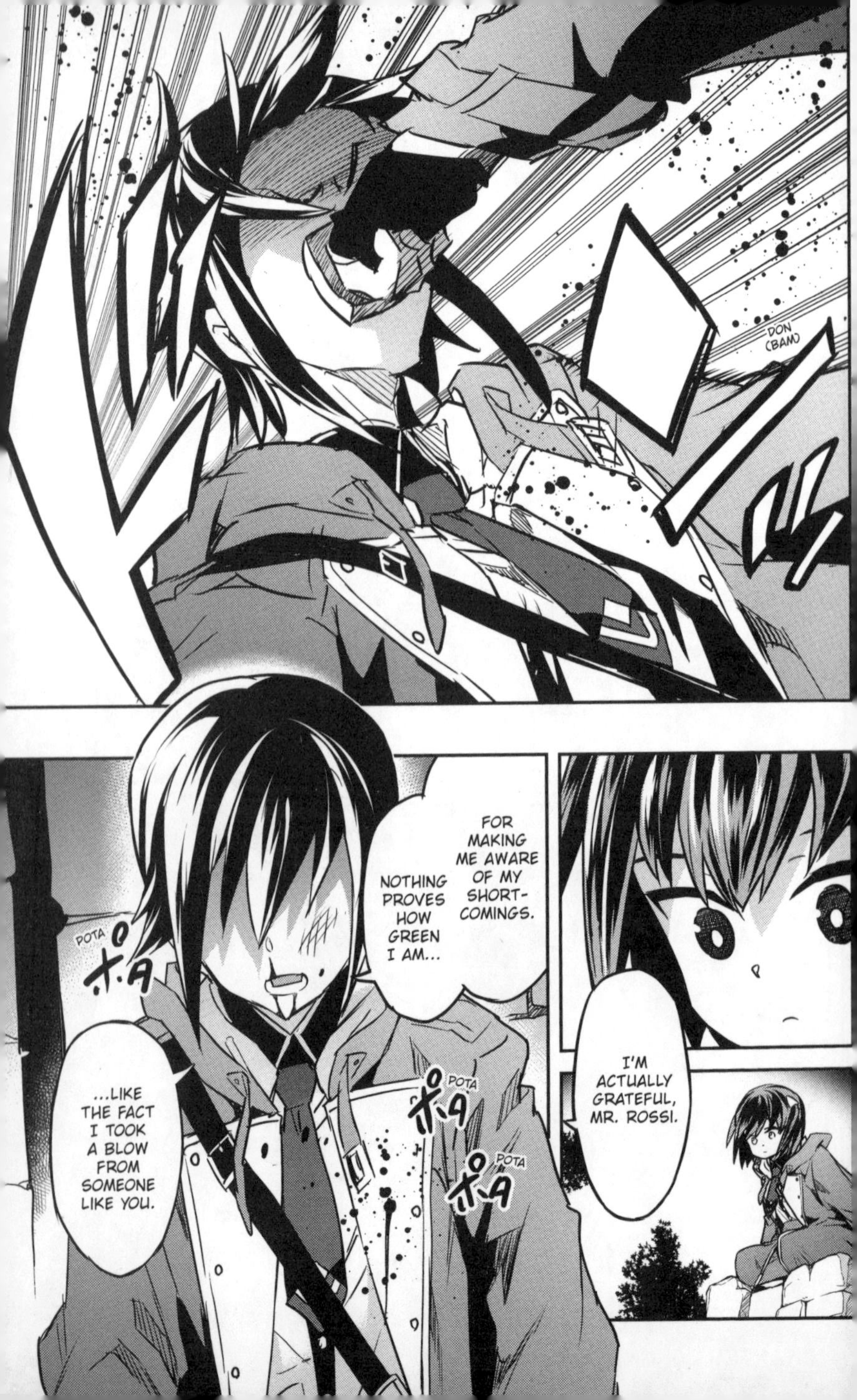
DON (BAM)
I'M ACTUALLY GRATEFUL, MR. ROSSI.
FOR MAKING ME AWARE OF MY SHORT-COMINGS.
NOTHING PROVES HOW GREEN I AM...
POTA
POTA
POTA
...LIKE THE FACT I TOOK A BLOW FROM SOMEONE LIKE YOU.

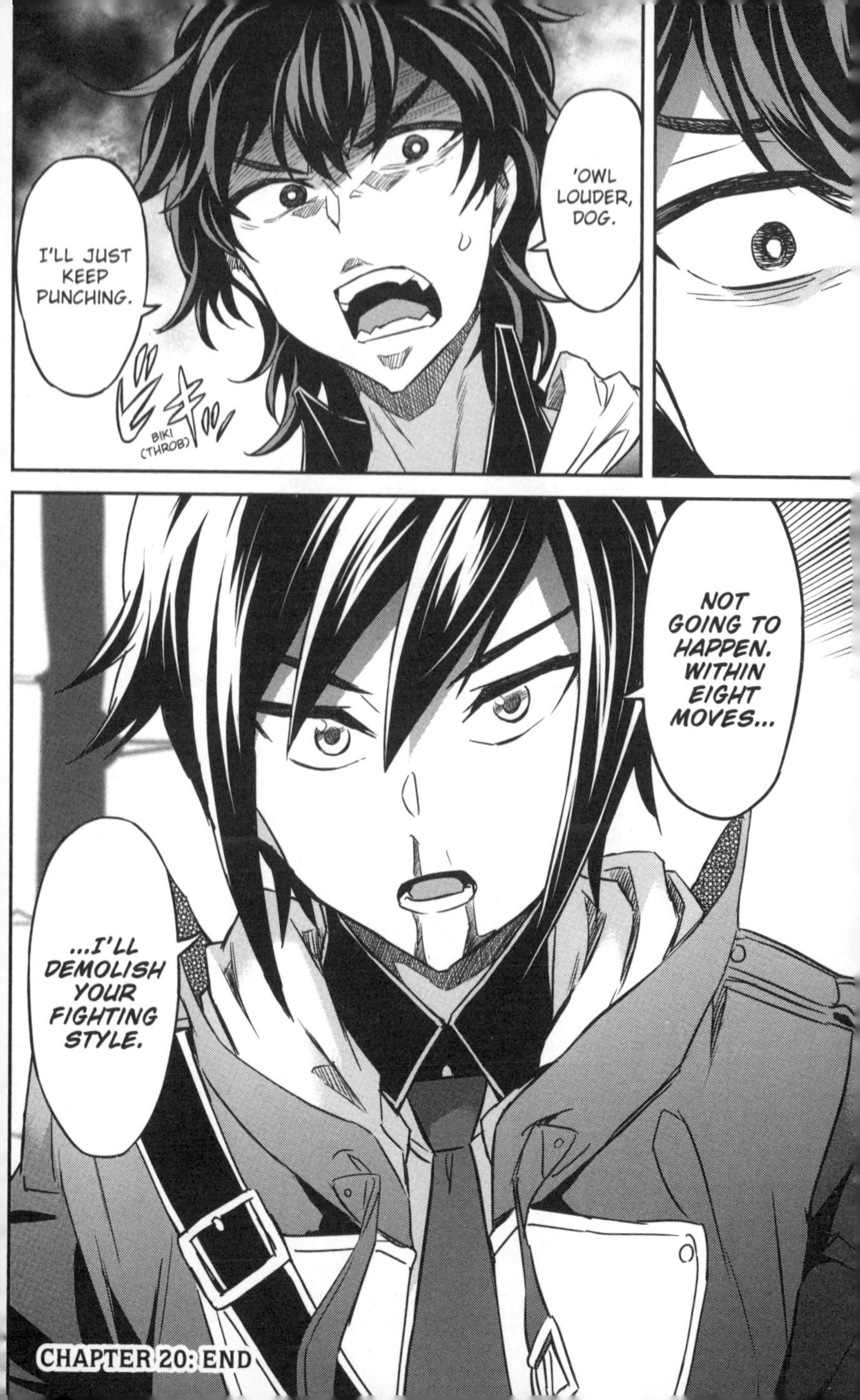
'OWL LOUDER, DOG.
I'LL JUST KEEP PUNCHING.
BIKI (THROB)
NOT GOING TO HAPPEN. WITHIN EIGHT MOVES...
...I'LL DEMOLISH YOUR FIGHTING STYLE.
CHAPTER 20: END

To Be Continued...

Early Character File 02

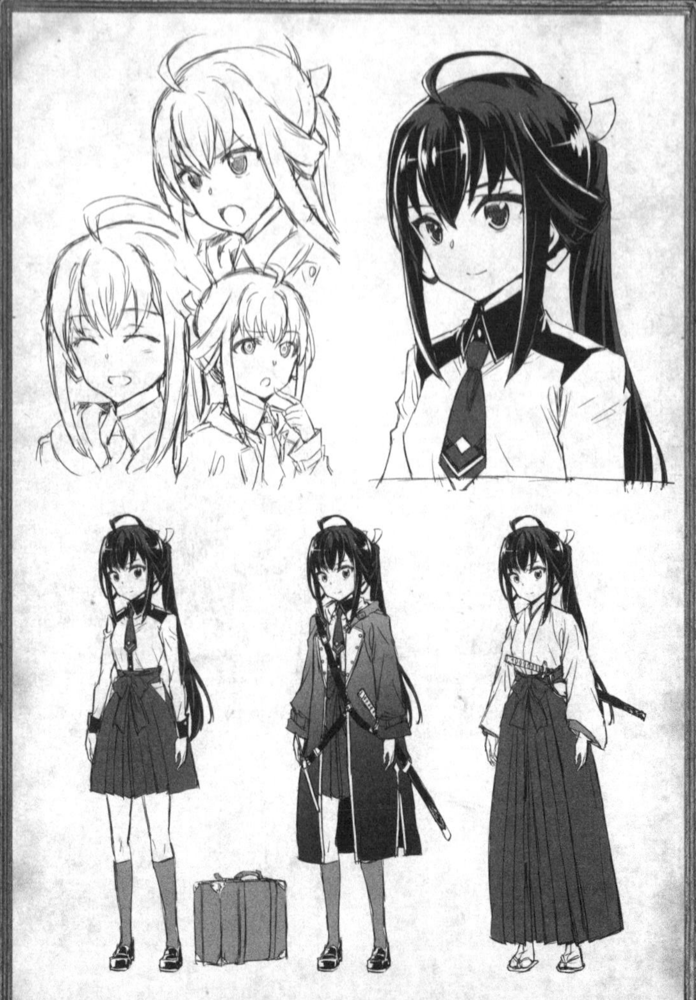

Early Character File 03

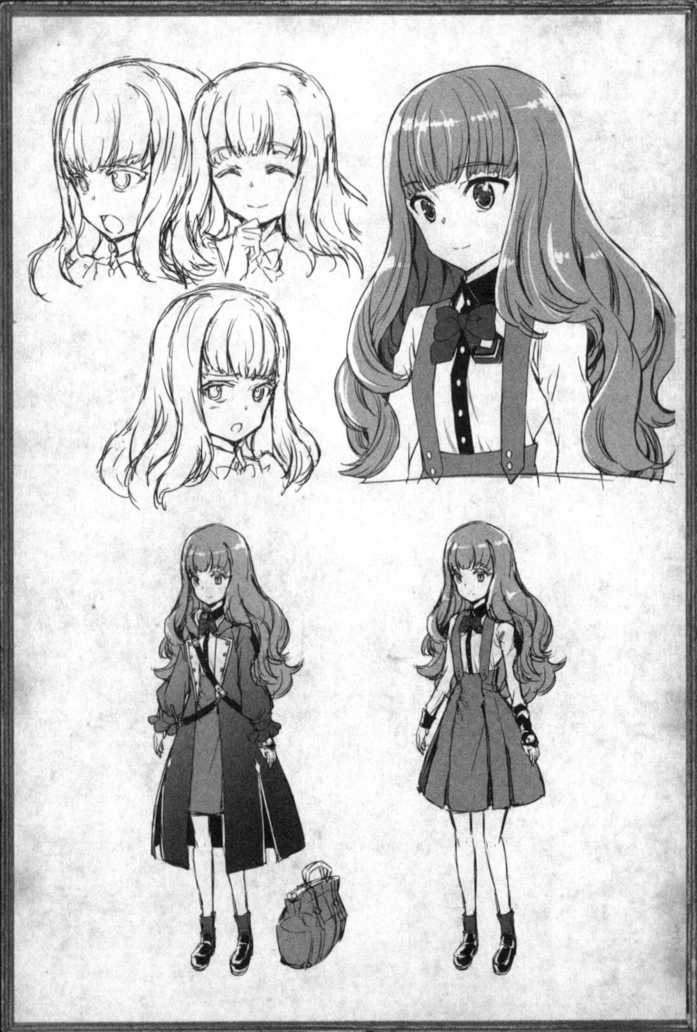

04

Early Character File

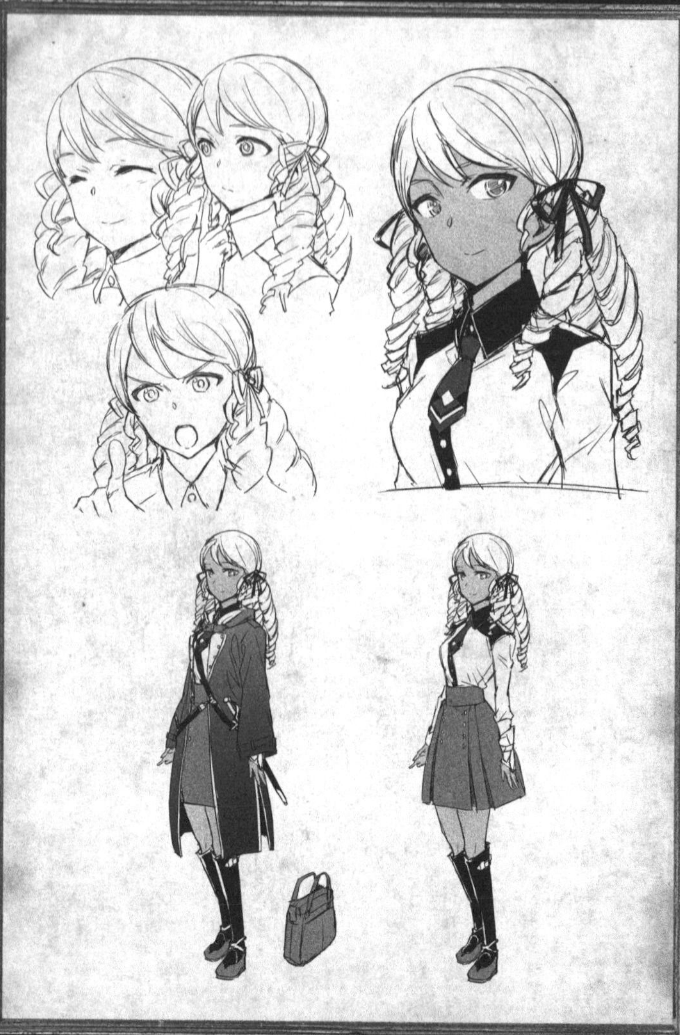

| Michela McFarlane |

Reign ᵒᶠ ᵗʰᵉ SEVEN SPELLBLADES

Reign of the SEVEN S

Sakae Esuno ORIGINAL STORY Bokuto |

TRANSLATION
Andrew Cunningham

LETTERING
Brandon Bovia

NANATSU NO MAKEN GA SHIHAISURU Vol.4
©Sakae Esuno 2021
©Bokuto Uno 2021
First published in Japan in 2021 by KADOKAWA CORPORATION, Tokyo. English translation rights arranged with KADOKAWA CORPORATION, Tokyo through TUTTLE-MORI AGENCY, INC., Tokyo.

English translation © 2022 by Yen Press, LLC

Yen Press
150 West 30th Street, 19th Floor
New York, NY 10001

Visit us at yenpress.com ◆ facebook.com/yenpress
twitter.com/yenpress ◆ yenpress.tumblr.com
instagram.com/yenpress

First Yen Press Edition: August 2022
Edited by Yen Press Editorial: Thomas McAlister
Designed by Yen Press Design: Jane Sohn, Andy Swist

Yen Press is an imprint of Yen Press, LLC.
The Yen Press name and logo are trademarks of Yen Press, LLC.

The publisher is not responsible for websites (or their content) that are not owned by the publisher.

Library of Congress Control Number: 2021943178

ISBNs: 978-1-9753-4276-0 (paperback)
978-1-9753-4277-7 (ebook)

1 3 5 7 9 10 8 6 4 2

LSC-C

Printed in the United States of America